FAIR
catch

LEIGHTON U BOOK THREE

CE RICCI

Fair Catch

Copyright © 2024 by CE Ricci

Published by Deserted Press

All rights reserved.

No part of this book may be reproduced in any form or by any electronic or mechanical means, including information storage and retrieval systems, without written permission from the author, except for the use of brief quotations in a book review.

This is a work of fiction. Names, characters, businesses, places, events, locales, and incidents are either the products of the author's imagination or used in a fictitious manner. Any resemblance to actual persons, living or dead, or actual events is purely coincidental.

The author acknowledges the trademark status and trademark owners of various brands, products, and/or restaurants referenced in this work of fiction. The publication/use of these trademarks is not authorized, associated with, or sponsored by the trademark owners.

Editing: Amanda Mili of Amandanomaly

Cover Design: Emily Wittig Designs

To anyone still trying to figure out who they are:

It's okay not to know just yet.

You've got your whole life to find the missing pieces.

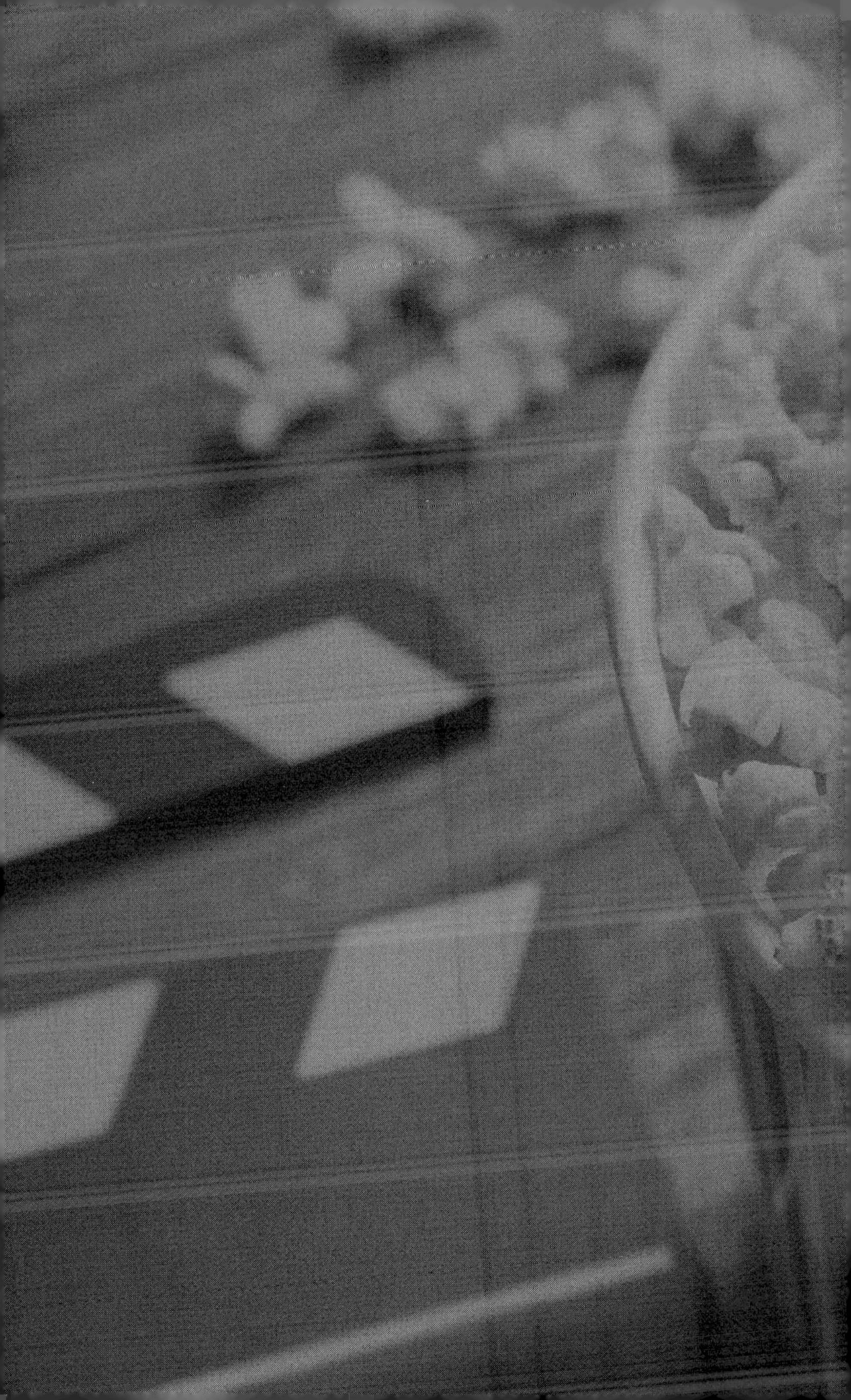

And to all the guys on Bumble in the PNW:
The obscenities in this book had to come from somewhere.
Y'all are the real MVPs.

50
40
30
20
10
100

"NOT UNTIL WE ARE LOST DO WE BEGIN TO UNDERSTAND OURSELVES."

— HENRY DAVID THOREAU

Theme Song

mother tongue—Bring Me The Horizon

Playlist

THATS WHAT I WANT—Lil Nas X
Hey Jealousy—Gin Blossoms
Moving Boxes—With Confidence
Just Friends—Take The Name
All Signs Point To Lauderdale—A Day To Remember
I Like Me Better—Lauv
All the Fucking Time—Loote
I Fall Apart—Post Malone
Through Hell—Melrose Avenue
Haunted—The Band CAMINO
SICK ABOUT U—TITUS
Cautious—Emarosa
Addicted—Loveless
sTraNgeRs—Bring Me The Horizon
Hammer—Point North
fuck, i'm lonely—Bilmuri, Dayseeker
THE DRAIN—Bad Omens, HEALTH, SWARM
One Last Time—Broadside
Juice—Dear Youth, Broadside, Oliver Baxxter
Doomed—Bring Me The Horizon
Cursed—Rain City Drive
So Poetic—Sundressed
WAYSIDE—Ekoh, Loveless
A Part of Me—Story Of The Year
IDWT$—Bad Omens
Here With Me—Halocene, Barbie Sailers
Promise Me—Dead by April
Pretty Handsome Awkward—The Used
Who's Going Home With You Tonight?—Trapt
Lucky Strike—Troy Sivan
Beautiful Way—You Me At Six
Break—I See Stars
I'll Run—The Cab
I Miss You—blink-182

Listen to the playlist on Spotify

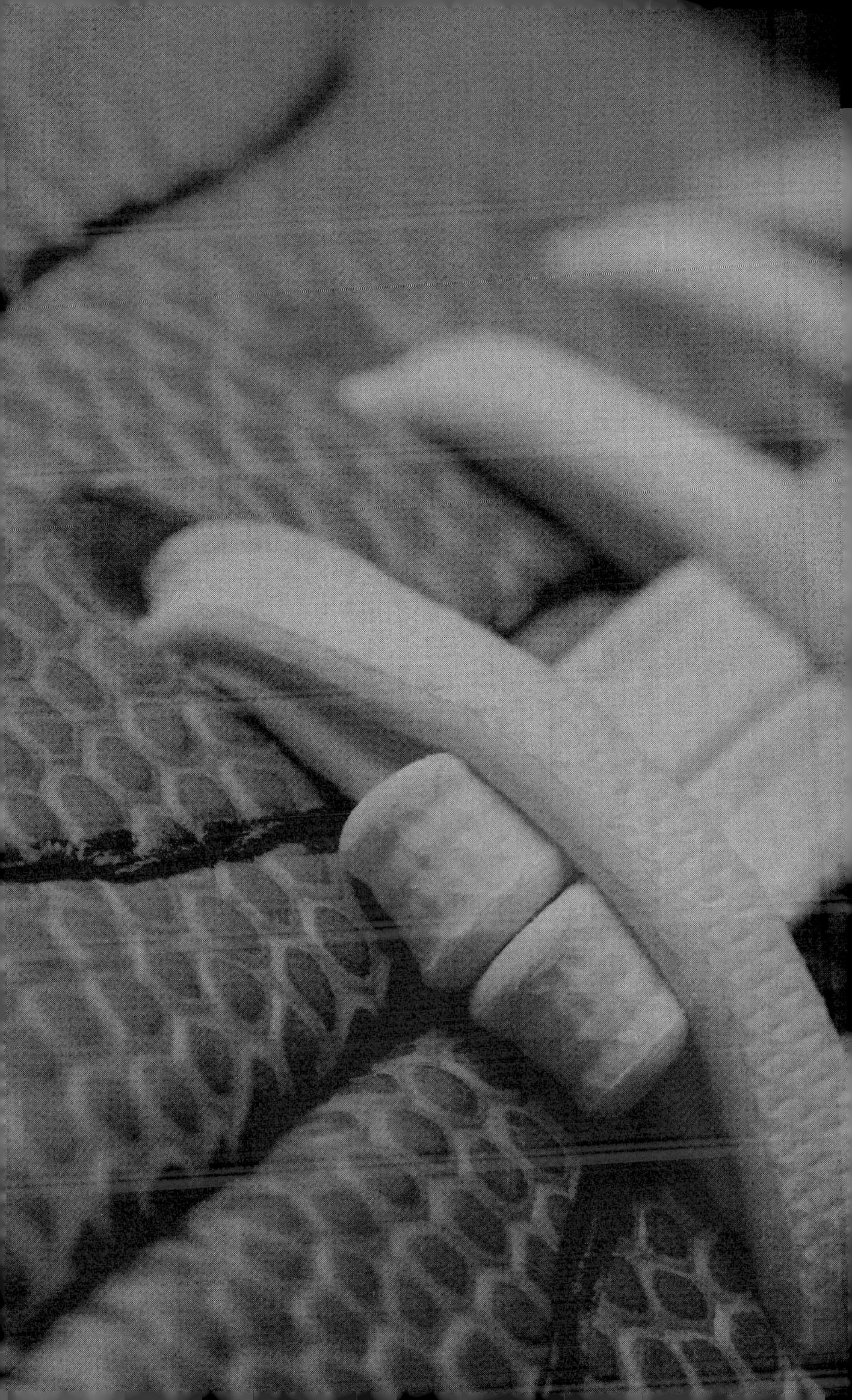

Disclaimer

As a dedicated sports enthusiast, I've done my best to portray all aspects of the NCAA and NFL seasonal schedule, rules, and regulations as accurately as possible. However, sometimes rules, when applied in a fictional setting, need to be bent to fit within the narrative, so some creative freedoms and liberties were taken for the plot purposes of this book.

Leighton University, along with any other university within this work and series, is completely made up, fabricated so as not to misrepresent the policies and values, curriculum, or facilities of real institutions. The views in this book in no way reflect the views and principles of the NCAA or NFL as it is a work of fiction.

Author's Note

Fair Catch is the third book in the Leighton U series, and while this is a series of standalones—where each book is a different couple—there are crossing timelines between some of the stories. So while it is not a necessity, it's highly recommended to read the series in publishing order.

This book includes demisexual representation, which is on the asexual spectrum. It's often described as someone requiring a deep emotional connection in order to feel sexual attraction. As demisexuality isn't one-size-fits-all, Hayes is representative of a singular lived experience of demisexuality. This does not invalidate any demisexual people who may experience attraction differently, and I hope through Hayes' explanation within the novel, it sheds more light on the other wide variety of demi lived experiences.

Please also note that there are brief, on-page **mentions** of domestic violence and child abuse in this work of fiction. However, these are very real issues. If you or a loved one are in need of help or support, please use the resources below:

United States: (800) 799-SAFE (7233)
United Kingdom: 0808 801 0327
Australia: 1800RESPECT (737 732)
Canada: Find the information for your territory on canada.ca

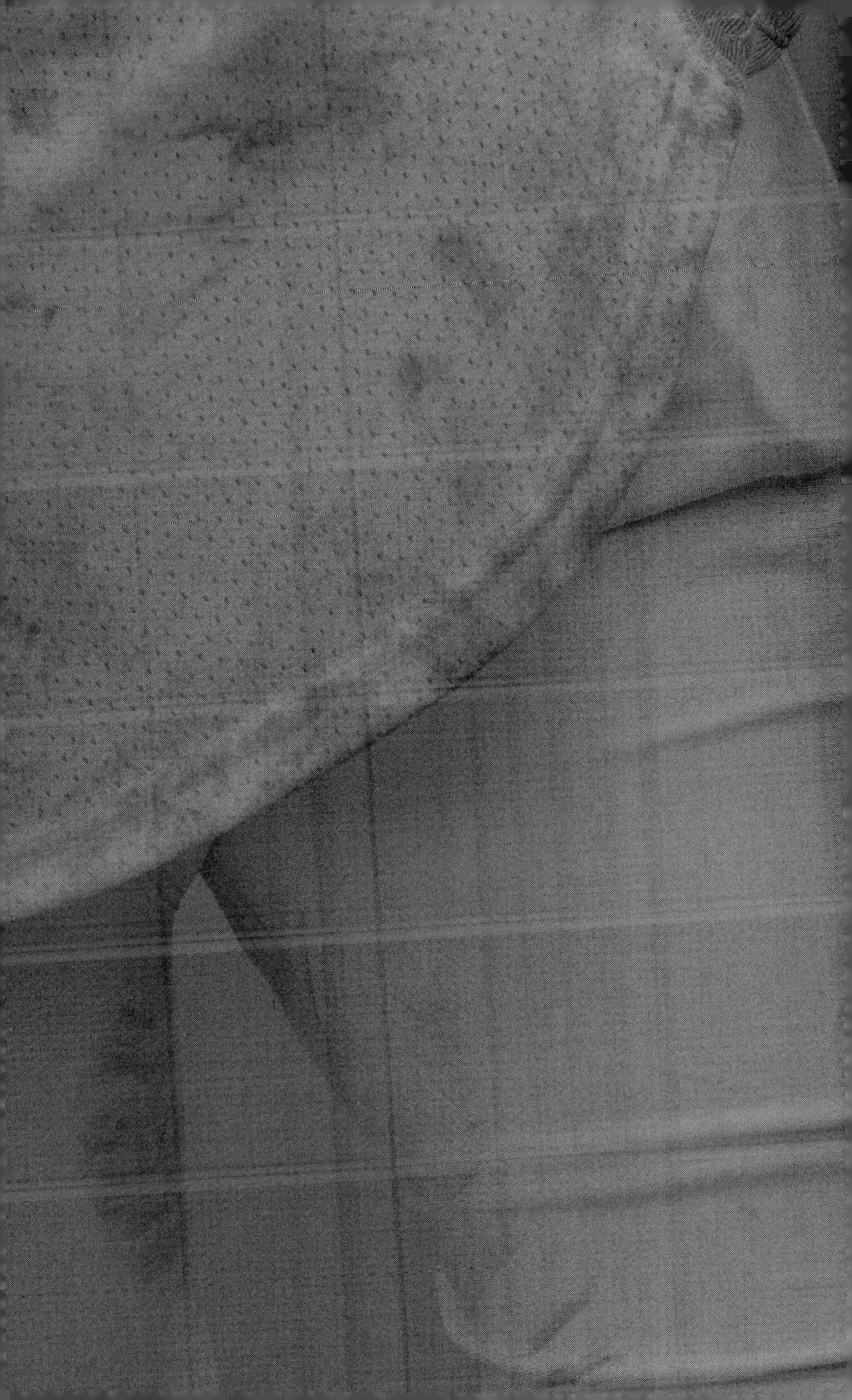

PROLOGUE

Kason

April—Junior Year

Today might be the most Monday of all Mondays to ever Monday. In the course of my morning, I've managed to crack my phone screen on the edge of the toilet before it promptly dropped *into* it, found out my essay for the elective history class I'm taking didn't save on my computer, and I caught my belt loop on the door handle *twice* today, the second time ripping it clean off.

And on top of all that, it's now downpouring outside, and I don't have a jacket or umbrella with me as I go to meet with this new roommate prospect.

"Well, that's just fucking great."

I should've asked Hayes if we could reschedule our meeting.

My mood is still in the dumps after the conversation I had with Phoenix last night—explaining my plan to move out when our lease ends in July being one of the many things we discussed. Add in the Monday from Hell, and I'm in no state to have a first meeting with the person I'll be living down the hall from next year.

Potentially, because it's not set in stone yet.

Throwing my car into park down the street from Page Turners, I steel myself to brave the rain and shove open my door. I make a beeline for the locally owned bookstore near the edge of campus, complete with what might be the world's best coffee shop tucked off to one side.

At least I know Hayes Lancaster has good taste in coffee if this is the location he chose to meet.

My clothes are half-soaked with rain by the time I push open the front door, and I'm equally annoyed, frustrated, and just meh. I let out a sigh and check my watch. I have five minutes until I'm due to meet Hayes, which is just enough time to grab a hot cup of coffee to warm up and—

"Kason, hey!" a soft, feminine voice calls from behind me, drawing my attention.

Turning, I find Ivy, the sweet little bookseller one of my friends is dating, and offer her a genuine smile. "Hey, Ives. I didn't realize you were working today."

"Feels like constantly this semester." Her head cants to one side before her eyes make an assessing sweep of my body. "Where are you off to in such a rush? And looking like a half-drowned rat?"

I could do without the rat comment, but if I know anything about Ivy, it's that she's brutally—albeit not very tactfully—honest. "I'm meeting a potential roommate for next year at the coffee shop."

She frowns and tucks a strand of hair behind her ear. "Things with Phoenix are really that bad, huh?"

Clearly she was filled in on the drama that's occurred in the past couple months.

Talking about everything that's transpired between my best friend and me is the last thing I want to do at this moment, and even if I did, I don't have the time. Which means she gets the condensed version of yesterday's heart-to-heart.

"We need a break from each other. Can't really do that when we're still living together."

Ivy offers me a sympathetic smile before gently resting her manicured hand on my arm. "Time and space can be good for a friendship. It's not a death sentence."

So everyone keeps saying, but I'm no closer to taking those words at face value than I am to becoming the next President of the United States.

"Look, Ives, I'd love to catch up with you, but I'm actually running late to meet him."

I'm technically not late *yet*, but I want to grab a drink before sitting down with him for this little *get to know you* session. Plus, with him being my only prospect as a roommate, I need to make a lasting good impression. Showing up late to meet him for the first time isn't going to do that.

"Oh, yeah! No worries at all." She's already taking a few steps away from me when she quickly adds, "I hope you like your new roommate!" And with that, she flits off in the other direction, disappearing within the rows of books in an instant.

I hope so too.

The thought isn't a new one; it's been in the back of my mind since answering the ad one of my teammates had sent me last week.

Hayes has been hard to get a read on through the emails and texts we've sent back and forth since I initially reached out, though I blame that to lack of emojis on his end. From the little I've gathered, his personality is very cut and dry; no nonsense or funny business. Besides that, the only real thing I really know about him is he spends a lot of his time studying as a double major, and his current roommate is Quinton de Haas.

Not sure how the hell that pairing happened, but at least this guy is aware of the comings and goings of a D-1 athlete. It'll make my schedule less of a shock to him than it would most other people.

I do my best to shove any worries from my mind though, entering the coffee shop with a cautiously optimistic outlook on this meeting. After all, we don't need to be best friends. We just need to tolerate cohabitation for the duration of senior year.

Taking a deep, calming breath, I scan the café area, trying to see if I can place any of the people here as Hayes Lancaster—my new roommate.

Potential.

I have to keep reminding myself of that. The lease isn't signed yet, and if the guy hates me on the spot, then there's a good chance I'll be living in the dorms my senior year of college, or risk being homeless.

With my discreet perusal, I find an attractive guy with dark hair currently paying for his drink, two girls in line behind him clearly giggling and checking him out, and other than that, there are only two other guys sitting at random tables working on their computers. None of them scream "nerdy double major who spends all his time studying," so there's a good chance I'm actually the first one here, and that Hayes isn't waiting on me to show up.

Relaxing slightly, I head to the small line formed by the counter and wait my turn to place an order.

The giggling girls in front of me watch as the dark-haired guy walks away from the counter, shoving his wallet in the back pocket of dark-wash jeans, and when I catch a glimpse of his profile, I understand why.

He's the definition of a Greek god.

That might be exaggerating a bit, but it's not far off.

He's tall—maybe a couple inches shorter than my six-foot-three—and lean beneath the jeans and a dark, well-fitting gray Henley. The shirt does everything for him, clinging to him like a second skin and showcasing arms and a chest that could rival that of *The David*. The slight waves of his nearly black hair and the sculpted lines of his jaw and nose make him something right out of my Achillean fantasies; a fact further proven when his eyes slide to me briefly as he passes by, revealing their staggering cobalt color.

Holy fuck.

His gaze leaves mine as quickly as it collided, and I clear my throat, suddenly overcome with nervous anticipation. No doubt the guy is straight, because my luck is never that good, but the anxiety causing my stomach to churn doesn't care. Making eye contact—however brief—with a hot guy does that, regardless of what his sexuality may be.

Thankfully the girls in front of me are done paying, allowing me to distract myself by placing an order with the barista: a large americano with two creams, one sugar.

After paying, I step to the side for the middle-aged woman behind me and continue scanning the patrons seated throughout the coffee shop.

Not one seems to fit the picture of Hayes I've built up in my head.

You should've stalked him on social media like Mal suggested, then you'd know who you were looking for.

My simple yet delicious drink is up before I can so much as blink, the dainty barista not even bothering to call out my name when she sees me loitering by the counter.

She sets another drink down beside it before calling out in a sugar-sweet voice, "Large iced matcha with oat milk for Hayes?"

My ears fixate on the name of the guy I'm here to meet, and I quickly glance to my left to see who comes up to the counter. After all, Hayes isn't a common name, and even if it was, I doubt there's more than one in this coffee shop.

Except no one in my line of sight seems to move.

Frowning, I grab my cup from the counter and turn to my right while attempting to fix the lid that's not pressed down completely. Of course, thanks to my attention being focused on my task, I fail to notice the person behind me reaching to grab their drink and run directly into them.

And to make matters worse, that lid I was trying to secure? It pops right off on impact, spilling over half the cup of scalding americano all over me and the person I just collided with.

"Fuck," a baritone voice hisses, and a second later, a green drink lands on the floor between us, flooding my Nikes and his VANS with the liquid.

Disbelief and absolute mortification wrack my body, and my jaw drops slightly as I stare at the carnage I just caused.

No, no, no.

Dragging my eyes up a pair of now-coffee-stained jeans and Henley, I find the Greek god I was checking out in line. The Adonis with two sapphires for eyes.

Right now, they're more like shards of ice as he glares at me.

"I am *so* sorry," I rush out, immediately bending to grab his fallen drink—the cup empty save for a few surviving ice cubes. "I didn't hear you come up behind me."

Sexy stranger's jaw tics, and he shakes his hand out, which is now covered in americano and green matcha.

"It's fine," he mutters, though from the bite in his voice, it most definitely *isn't* fine. "I was hoping to get second degree burns when I woke up this morning."

I wince, knowing he has every right to be annoyed, pissed, whatever it might be. Lord knows most people would be after having hot coffee spilled on them.

"Can I at least buy you a new drink?" I ask as he grabs for a few napkins and starts drying off his shirt.

Shaking his head, he mutters, "I'm good, thanks."

"Well, do you want help—"

"You've done enough," he says curtly, not bothering to look up from the task at hand. However, it quickly becomes clear he's gonna have one helluva time drying himself off with just napkins. A huff of frustration leaves him as he drops the wad of them in the trash can beside the counter. "Whatever, I'm going home after meeting with my new roommate anyway."

Just like that, the floor drops out from under me.

I was so embarrassed by the scene I just caused, I'd completely forgotten *who* ordered the damn iced matcha that was just dropped at our feet.

"Roommate?" I ask, my voice coming out an octave higher than normal.

His eyes flash up to mine. "Yeah."

Fuck my life so fucking hard right now.

"Hayes Lancaster?" I ask slowly, praying like hell the next word to pass his sinful lips is no; that he says his name is James or Brad or fucking Reginald. Literally *anything* other than one three-letter word.

But luck is not on my side and Jesus doesn't answer my pleas, because the guy frowns.

"Yes," he murmurs, and from the distrust etched into his features, he probably thinks I'm some kind of stalker. "How'd you know that?"

I hold out my hand—the one not holding my now half-empty americano—for him to shake. Rather than taking it, he just looks at it like I'm offering him a steaming pile of shit.

Yeah, today could not possibly get any worse.

Dropping my hand to my side, I offer him a pained smile and formally introduce myself.

"I'm Kason Fuller. Your new roommate."

ONE

Hayes

Four Months Later—August

The second my best friend appears on my phone via FaceTime, his dark eyebrows damn near shoot to his hairline.

"Whoa. Who pissed in your Cheerios this morning?"

I roll my eyes before aiming a glare his way through the screen. Leave it to Quinton to take one look at the irritation on my face and decide opening with a joke would be a good idea.

Too bad for him, I'm not amused.

"You did, jackass."

Blue eyes widen slightly, and if possible, his brows inch even further up his forehead. "And dare I ask how I managed to do that all the way from New Jersey?"

"Because rather than listening to my gut instinct, my brain decided it was time for an uncharacteristic lapse in judgment by listening to you about Kason Fuller becoming my roommate," I bite out.

A dark chuckle leaves him, and I'm annoyed further when I catch the amusement in his black-framed eyes. "Oh, c'mon. It can't be that bad after putting up with my ass for the past three years."

That might be true, but Q's also been my best friend for most of our lives. We know the ins and outs of each other, and while he might've been a bit unpredictable at times, there was still a decent amount of "knowns" with him. Consistencies I could count on.

This guy Kason, though? He's barely more than a stranger. An awkward as hell one based on the first impression he made a few months ago, yet somehow Quinton managed to dissuade my apprehension about taking the guy in as a roommate this year.

Even called it a favor, as if that would get me to cave.

Which it did.

"You forget about the part where he drenched me in coffee before we officially met?"

Quinton's lips twitch, attempting to hide a smile. "I remember that day vividly. But it was an accident. Just keep your coffee away from him whenever you're in the same room."

I roll my eyes. "You're not funny. He hasn't even made it here, and I'm already miserable."

"You're bound to be if you're going into it with that attitude."

I might kill him.

"Well, we can't all be as optimistically evolved as you've become between the bliss of coupledom and starting to live out your NHL dreams."

His dimples pop, grin growing to nearly face-splitting. If I wasn't so glad to see him finally finding the sense of happiness and belonging he's been craving for years, I'd probably be irritated. I can't be anything other than happy for him, though.

"Okay, but we aren't talking about me and my awesome life. We're talking about you and your sour puss mentality about getting a new roomie."

My nose wrinkles up. "Say the words sour puss again, and I'll personally fly to Jersey to kick your ass."

A bark of laughter leaves him, and he shakes his head. "Promises, promises, you little sour puss."

"I'm hanging up on you," I mutter dryly, which only makes him laugh harder.

"Don't be so dramatic. That's my job."

"Guess I'm filling the role while you're gone."

His grin sobers slightly. "It's all gonna be fine, man. You're getting worked up for nothing, and with football season right around the corner, I'm sure you'll barely see him."

There's truth in everything he's just said, and I'm both smart and self-aware enough to realize I might be *slightly* overreacting. It still doesn't change the amount of dread I feel at having to share a living space with a stranger until graduation.

"For both our sakes, I really hope you're right."

"Who knows, maybe he will turn you into a people person since I sure as hell couldn't."

I arch a brow. "Let's not get ahead of ourselves."

"Quinn, we gotta get going," I hear muffled on Quinton's end before his boyfriend, Oakley, appears on the screen. His eyes meet mine via the screen, and he gives me a slight nod. "Hey, Hayes."

"I'll be ready in a sec," Q says, glancing up at his boyfriend before his attention returns to me. "We've gotta get going, though, man. We're going to dinner tonight, and Oak's got a stick up his ass about being late."

"Don't you dare put this on me." Oakley glares down at Quinton before a slow smirk takes over his face. "And on the topic of asses, the faster yours gets moving, the sooner we get back here so I can shove *my stick*—"

"And I think we're done here," I interject quickly, realizing there's at least *one* thing I won't be missing about having Quinton for a roommate: the explicit, vivid details of his and Oakley's sex life.

"Oh, don't be a prude, H," Q chides while shoving Oakley in the stomach until he's off screen. "It's not like you haven't heard us have sex a hundred times by now."

I wrinkle my nose in both mock and actual disgust. "So not the fucking point, and you know it."

Oakley's deep laugh floods through the speaker before he reappears in view and kisses the side of Quinton's head. "Okay, we really do need to go, though. Especially if you're teaching me to ride after dinner."

"Two minutes. Go grab the car and I'll be right down."

I catch the faint twitch of Oakley's mouth before he nods in concession. Then again, ever since they officially got together, he hasn't been able to deny my best friend much of anything.

My relationship with Oakley, on the other hand? It's been tempestuous at best.

After all, I saw first hand the way his secrets and betrayal affected Quinton, who has been nothing short of a brother to me. So while Q might've forgiven Oakley's transgressions rather easily, there's still a lot of work to be done before I'm willing to forgive and forget—and a small portion of me thinks I'll remain reserved toward Oakley.

Apprehension Oakley is more than aware of, if the way his eyes warily shift back to me are any indication.

"I really do appreciate you doing this, Hayes," he utters softly.

I offer a tight smile and slight nod, and with that, he disappears from view again.

He smirks, clearly the only one amused by the slight amount of friction present between his best friend and boyfriend, before correcting, "We *both* appreciate you doing this, to be clear."

A long sigh leaves me, and I rake my fingers through my hair. "I know, Q."

I don't really know what happened last year between one of Oakley's old roommates and my soon-to-be one, only that they called it 'a favor for a friend of a friend' by asking me to take Kason in. And honestly, I don't really care to know the sordid details, either. The drama of college romance is so far outside my realm of reality, it's laughable.

All I want to get from college is a degree and then to get the fuck out.

So being dragged into someone else's drama? It's not exactly my idea of a good time.

Reading my expression the way only he can, Q's voice takes on a more serious tone. "It's gonna be fine, man. I promise. Kason's a decent guy." Then his demeanor lightens a bit, and he aims one of his shit-eating grins at me. "Just don't go turning him into your new bestie now that I'm gone."

I snort and shake my head. "As if you'd ever let that happen. Even from four states away."

Another laugh leaves him, and honestly, the sound is one I'm glad to be hearing from him. Despite how I might feel about what happened between him and Oakley, it's clear he's the happiest he's been in a long time.

"Does he know yet?" I ask, shifting the topic to something a little lighter, and a lot more exciting for the two of them.

"Louis is calling to tell him tonight when I take him to ride the bike. I got these for him too." Q produces a pair of hunter green, black, and white striped socks; the team colors for the New York Knights. There's a little

#33—Oakley's number—stitched in the sides and everything. "He's gonna shit a brick when he finds out."

He's so disgustingly in love, I could actually vomit.

Grinning from ear to ear, he tucks them out of view again. "I really do need to get moving, but don't be a stranger. Call me whenever."

A twinge of sadness rushes through me, but I shove it down as best I can.

"Same goes to you, Q. Seriously. I know you'll be busy, but…" I pause and shrug. "I dunno. It's not gonna be the same here without you."

His expression sobers instantly. "I know the feeling."

"Talk soon then," I tell him, going to end the call.

"Hey, H," Quinton says just before I hit the end button. When I arch a brow, a clear signal for him to continue, he adds. "Promise me you'll give him a chance. A real one."

Rolling my eyes, I utter the word *fine* before closing out of FaceTime and dropping back on my mattress, all the while hoping this doesn't end up being a complete disaster.

Of course, no more than ten minutes later, those prayers go completely unanswered when I hear knocking from the apartment's front door. Although, *knocking* is the nice way to put the repetitive, incessant pounding happening from down the hall.

"Jesus, I'll be right there!" I shout, dragging myself from my bed and toward the sound that doesn't even falter.

Annoyed, I yank the door open to reveal my new roommate, and Jesus Christ, I don't remember him being as tall as he is. The guy's got at least a couple inches on my six-one frame, nearly filling the doorframe in front of me.

He certainly wasn't as disheveled as he is currently the last time I saw him; his reddish brown hair a wind-whipped mess and emerald eyes a mix of anxiety and panic.

Actually, come to think of it, this isn't far off from the guy I met a couple months ago at the coffee shop. The version in front of me just looks the part this go 'round.

Frowning, I move out of the way for him. "Why'd you knock? You have a key."

Kason winces visibly as he steps past me with the precariously stacked boxes he's holding. "Yeah, but I have no idea where it is. I think I accidentally packed it in one of the boxes?" He says it more as a question than a statement, and it only serves to make me more irritated than I was on the phone with Quinton.

"You think," I repeat slowly.

"Yeah. I mean, I'm pretty sure it's in one of them. I thought I put it on the key ring with my car keys, but—" He makes his best attempt at a shrug, but the motion has the top box sliding entirely off the other two it was stacked on.

Of course, on its way to the floor, it happens to slam right into my knee.

"Goddamnit," I curse, immediately bouncing on my good leg from the throbbing pain in my kneecap. "What the hell was in there?"

It only takes a second for me to realize the impact must've caused the box to bust open, the contents spilling all over the entryway for me to see. Medals and small awards, some loose change, and a pile of papers cover the floor, and I am fucking *pissed*.

Kason might as well be a deer in headlights when his eyes lift from the mess to meet my death glare.

"Shit, I'm so sorry," he rushes out, quickly setting the other two boxes down before one of those falls next.

"Yeah," is all I say as I limp my way to the couch, careful not to step on all the shit now strewn about. Kason's already begun gathering all his belongings before I can drop onto the couch, kicking myself for not grabbing some pain meds first.

My annoyance builds as I listen to Kason picking up his crap, the awkward silence stifling.

"On the plus side," Kason says slowly, drawing my attention back to him. "I found the key. And an ice pack for your knee…minus it being warm. But at least it wasn't coffee?"

He lifts each of the items in question for me to see, and it takes every ounce of me not to bite his head off. Instead, I force a smile and wonder what kind of hell I've signed myself up for. Because if first—and second—impressions are correct, there's one thing I'm certain of.

This is gonna be a long fucking year.

TWO

Kason

"**H**e fucking hates me."

Mallory, one of Leighton's cheerleaders, glances up from where she's lounging across a blanket on the lawn outside of the practice facility. I wasn't expecting to run into her after my voluntary lifting session, but I could use her listening ear.

"Hello to you too, Kason," she says, closing the book she was reading. I scan the cover of it, noting it has a shirtless man with some seriously toned abs on the cover, before dropping down on the blanket beside her.

"Sorry, should I have asked if you were enjoying your smut instead?"

A sweet lilt of laughter hits me, and she smacks me playfully with her paperback. "Not sure that's any better of a greeting, so let's circle back to your first try. Who is *he* and why do you think he hates you?"

Rolling to my back, staring up at the bright blue sky, I mutter, "Hayes.

My new roommate." Turning my head, I add. "And I don't know for a fact that he hates me. It's just a vibe."

"A vibe," she repeats dryly, her brow lifting. "That's what we're basing this on?"

"Believe me, if you meet him, you'll understand. We're barely forty-eight hours into this living situation, and I feel like I'm constantly walking on a minefield because he's just so…" I wrack my brain for a kinder way to say *douchey* or *dickish* without sounding like one myself. "Standoffish?"

She lets out a soft, airy laugh—the kind that somehow eases some of the discourse rampaging my thoughts. "Well, I certainly doubt that means he *hates* you, Kason. You're the furthest thing from hateable."

Pretty sure she has to say that, being one of my closest childhood friends and all.

Rolling my eyes at her clear exaggeration, I murmur, "His vibe says he hates me."

"He doesn't even know you." She shifts to lay down beside me, propping herself up on one elbow. "And believe me, once he has the chance to, there's no way he doesn't like you just as much as everyone else does."

I let out a low hum, doing my best to not be a Debbie Downer about the whole situation. Which is difficult, considering I made an idiot out of myself within the first minute of arriving at the apartment a couple days ago.

"Unless he doesn't want to," I remind her, that unsettled feeling still sitting on my chest.

"Well, you could be right, but you'll never know if you don't try making nice with him first."

Scoffing, I ask, "Why do I have to be the one to be nice?"

Her brows draw together and she purses her lips in thought. "I suppose you don't *have to*, though that'd be my recommendation. Your other option is to make due 'til graduation by hiding out in your bedroom or the library."

Ah, fuck.

None of the above sound favorable, but I guess if I'm being forced to choose, I'll make my best efforts at being Roommate of the Year.

Mal must pick up on my frustration with the subject, making an effort to change it, "Enough about the new roomie. Tell me how you're doing."

I roll my head on the blanket, shifting my attention back to the sky and studying the passing clouds like they're the most interesting things in the world. Part of me would rather go back to talking about my living with Hayes than go here.

After all, it doesn't take a rocket scientist to know that she's talking about my severed friendship with Phoenix, which is still raw in many ways. Having to adapt to a new roommate after three years of living with him only serves as a reminder of his absence in my life as of late.

"I'm okay most of the time," I say truthfully, though the knot in my throat makes me feel anything but.

Mal's gaze burns a hole in my cheek as she hedges, "And the other times?"

Blowing out a breath, I murmur, "Those times, I feel really, *really* fucking lonely."

"I'll try not to take offense to that," she teases, and I can hear the smile in her voice before I turn and see it for myself. I attempt to amend my comment, but she lets out another soft laugh and shakes her head. "Don't get your boxers in a bunch, I'm just joking. I know you love my company when I bless you with it."

"Oh, do you?"

"Absolutely. Because I, for one, am a fucking delight."

Chuckling softly, I have to admit she's right, even just to myself.

If there's one thing I can be grateful about when it comes to my friendship with Phoenix crumbling, it's that it opened the door for me to rekindle friendships with other people, like Mal.

The dainty, brown-haired sprite came into my life back when I still lived in Alabama, her house right down the road from mine before Dad moved us to Nashville. She's one of the few people I kept up with even after moving, and finding out she got a cheer scholarship to Leighton was yet another highlight of leaving for college.

Between her and Phoenix, I was finally surrounded by *my* people.

The ones who love me for me. My chosen family.

Right up until it all went to shit last spring.

"Earth to Kason," Mal sing-songs and taps on my forehead. "Did you get lost in the clouds?"

"Nah, I was just thinking how much I wish you would've just let me room with you."

She rolls over toward me, drawing my attention to her. "As much as Ivy and I love you, I think pushing you outside of your comfort zone will end up being a good thing." A hint of a smile crosses her face. "Besides, would you really want to share a bathroom with *two* women?"

No, but...

"Still sounds better than where I ended up."

That earns me a scoff, which is probably the only unlady-like sound this southern belle is capable of making. "You say that now, but trust me, you wouldn't last two weeks in our place. I love that girl more than life, but damn if she doesn't take a million years to get ready in the morning."

"And yet you're still the happiest you've ever been, right?"

"Yeah, you're right about that." A little sigh slips from her, and when I glance over, I catch a tiny, blissful smile spreading across her face. "Then again, that's what love does to you."

Something I wouldn't know anything about, considering I've never felt it before—and not for a lack of trying.

I want what she has with Ivy. What Phoenix and Holden have. What fucking everyone seems to have except me. And I'm no closer to finding that than I am to knowing what I plan to do after college if the draft doesn't work out, which is a whole 'nother debacle I can't even think about right now.

If only chatting about these things at length with my therapist gave me some clue or direction or prospects. Unfortunately for me, that's not how it works.

Mal cuts through my thoughts, asking the one question I've been waiting for; the one I was hoping she wouldn't ask.

"How were things back home this summer?"

"I didn't go," I mutter slowly.

Mal narrows her gaze on me. "Then where were you?"

"Here in the city." Her shoving my shoulder at my elusive answer, I elaborate. "Phoe moved his things into the house with Holden after last semester ended. Which meant I had the old apartment to myself all summer until our lease was over. Happy, Miss Nosey?"

"Perfectly."

The girl was probing and invasive even when we were kids, and it's clear that some things don't change when I glance her way, catching the look in her eyes. One I've seen many times before. One that says there's more she wants to know, she's just not verbalizing it.

"What?" I ask, laughing with exasperation. "Speak, woman. I can't read your mind."

"Believe me, if men could read our minds, life would be a lot simpler," she mutters, raising her hands.

"Oh, my God, *Mal.*"

Her teeth worry her lower lip before she finally puts me out of my misery, only for me to wish she'd never asked in the first place.

"How was it, living there alone?"

I'd be a damn liar if I didn't say it was lonely as hell, living in a space that had years worth of memories and friendship embedded within the walls. There were a few times I'd even forget he wasn't there anymore, heading down the hall to see what he wanted to grab for dinner or catch a movie.

Just goes to show, I might've already forgiven him for the lies and the betrayal, but the reason we're on this little *break* is still entirely valid.

Even if I hate it.

"Being there alone was a better option than going home."

In fact, it was the only option.

Thanks to mine and Phoenix's blow out during his duel at St. Seb's last year, I'd ended up staying in Nashville with my father for spring break. And after pinning Dad's drunken ass to the kitchen floor when he came at me with a broken beer bottle, I made myself a promise to never set foot in that house again. I've fallen victim to his rage and cruelty too many times, and I'm not willing to put myself in that position anymore.

"Did you at least keep yourself busy?"

"Oh, yeah. I took advantage of a couple summer classes to lighten my course load this season."

She smiles. "Smart man. You'll be thanking yourself for it when you get extra sleep your teammates are all gonna be deprived of."

I nod in agreement, knowing I'll take more shut eye if I can. But the bigger thing I need to prioritize is training for the NFL Scouting Combine in March—pending I get an invite—and minimizing my distractions from school work seemed like the best way to make that happen.

We settle into a comfortable silence after that, relaxing on the blanket until Ivy shows up to steal her girlfriend away for dinner.

"You're welcome to join us, Kason," Ivy says, brushing a wispy piece of white-blonde hair back from her face.

I'm quick to wave her off and pull Mal to her feet. "Nah, I think I took enough of Mal's time for the day. She's all yours."

"You say that like I'm your property to just give away," my friend accuses playfully before snatching her things from the ground.

"I know, I know. Fuck the patriarchy," I say with a laugh. My tone sobers on a dime, though, and I rest my hand at her elbow. "Really, though. Thanks for being in my corner. I'm not sure what I'd do without you."

Mal gives me the faintest smile—one that says *always* without actually speaking the word—before she rolls her eyes. "Cry hopelessly in the corner, obviously."

"Obviously," I mock, though there's the tiniest dash of truth in her statement.

She's always been good at having hard conversations, even if I'm not. It's probably the only area of friendship in which she surpasses Phoenix; always managing to pull the feelings out of me.

Honestly, sometimes she does it better than my therapist—a testament that she'll make an amazing guidance counselor one day.

"I'll see you at practice on Monday, I'm sure," I tell her, already stepping toward the direction of home.

"Absolutely. And I'm looking forward to hearing about how you made nice with your new roomie when I do."

A sharp laugh leaves me, and I shake my head.

I have a feeling Hayes Lancaster doesn't make nice with anybody.

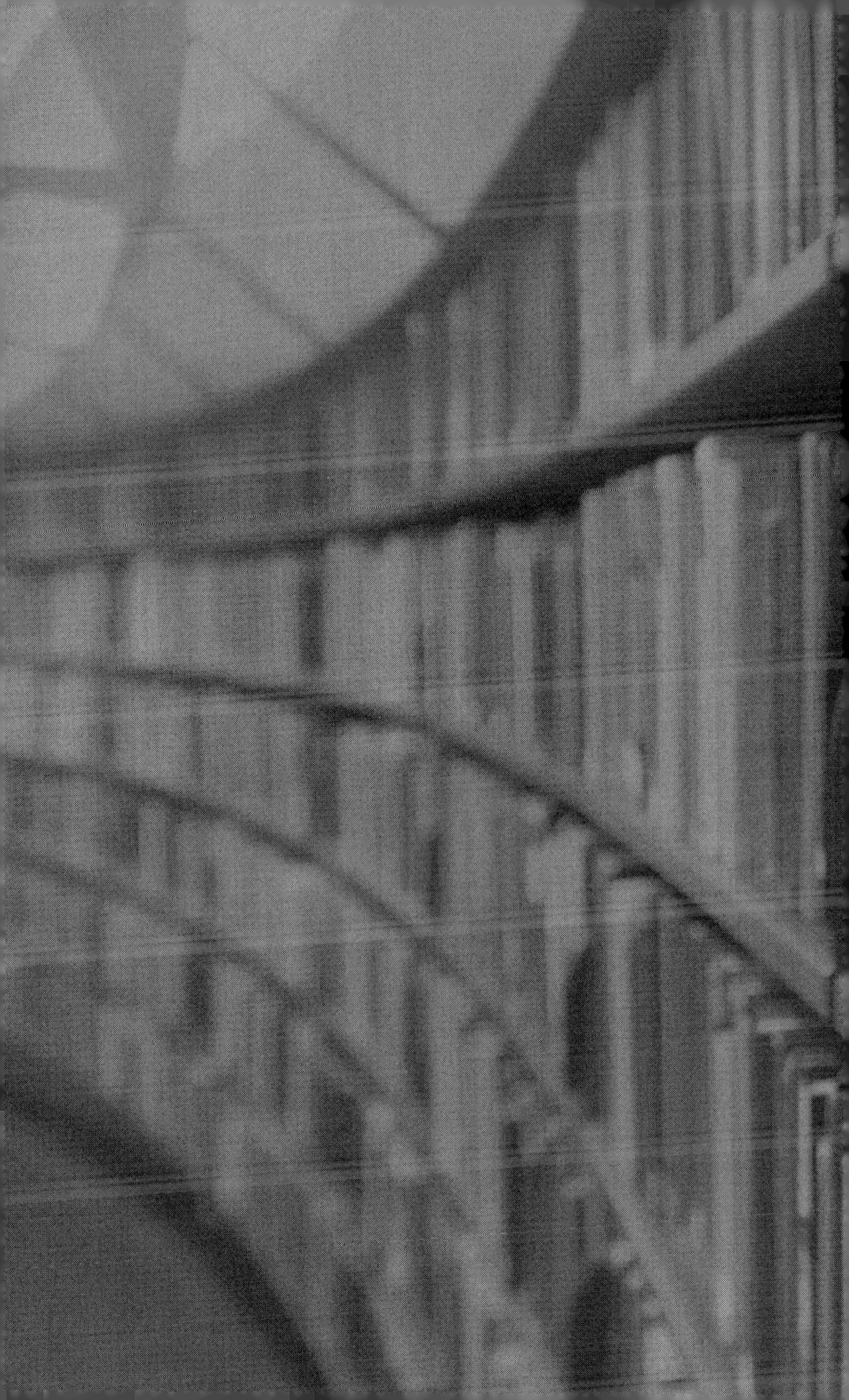

THREE

Hayes

The sound of an alarm blaring sends me bolting upright in my bed far sooner than my body expects. Disoriented and slightly panicked, I grab blindly for my phone to silence the damn thing, but no matter how many times I swipe at the screen, it doesn't stop.

Groaning, I peek my eyes open, only to realize, it's not *my* alarm.

I also realize from looking at the screen that it's only five in the morning.

Motherfucker.

Aggravated thanks to being woken up only three hours after going to bed, I rip the covers off my body and storm down the hall, the dim glow from the stove light guiding my way. The annoying beeping grows louder as I reach Kason's door, my assumption of the source correct.

"Kason, wake up," I yell through the door.

The only sound that comes from the other side is the alarm…and the muffled sound of his deep snoring.

Fucking wonderful.

Irritation at an all-time high, my hand pounds on his door hard enough, I'm surprised it doesn't splinter. It rattles in the frame, echoing through the apartment when I shout at him again.

"Kason! Turn off your fucking alarm!"

His snoring stops, but I still don't hear any footsteps or the alarm turn off.

And I've completely lost whatever patience I had this early in the morning, slamming my fist into the wood like a deranged lunatic. At this point, I'm ready to go Kool-Aid man on his ass and blast through the wall if I have to.

"*Kason!* I swear on all things holy, I will break down this door if you don't—"

A bleary-eyed, mostly naked Kason opens the door while I'm mid-swing, and I have to physically reel myself back so I don't deck him in the face with my fist.

Inadvertently, of course.

After all, if there's one thing Oakley Reed and I have in common, it's being a pacifist.

My eyes rake down his body instinctively, noting he's only in a pair of tight fitting boxer-briefs that do absolutely nothing to hide the rather impressive morning wood he's sporting. Which he's either oblivious to, or doesn't care about letting me get an eye full of, because he makes no move to make himself more decent.

"Jesus, Hayes," he mutters while rubbing his fist over his eyes. "Didn't need to try breaking my door down."

You've got to be kidding me.

"Apparently I did if I wanted you to turn off that goddamn alarm," I bite out. "Which is still going off, I might add."

Rather than waiting for him to do it—which could be never at this point—I slip into his bedroom and swipe away the notification on his phone, leaving us in wonderful, blissful silence.

"Sure, come on in," he says dryly, still standing at the door.

"The real question is why the fuck is it going off at five in the morning when classes don't start for another two weeks." And even if they had begun, the earliest classes start at eight. Meaning there's no reason on God's green Earth for it to be going off at this hour.

"Morning lifting starts today." Kason yawns as he walks over to his dresser and starts rummaging through the drawers.

Oh. Right.

I was used to Q's schedule of coming and going for the past few years, and I'm no stranger to early morning alarms for two-a-days, lifting, whatever it might be. But he was *never* setting alarms for five in the morning.

A very brief flash of guilt hits me as I ask, "What time does your coach have you guys in the gym?"

"Gotta be to the training facility by six-thirty."

My eyes bug out a little, that regretful feeling disappearing instantly. "Then why in the ever-loving fuck is your alarm going off at five? It takes ten minutes to get over there, max."

His silhouette moves from the dresser to his bed, where I can vaguely make out him shoving clothes into some sort of bag. "I have a hard time waking up early, so I set one every fifteen minutes. It helps me not oversleep."

Oh, hell no.

"Every. Fifteen. *Minutes?*" I repeat, gritting my teeth. "Please, tell me you're joking."

"It's either that or I risk missing practice."

I hear his footsteps move toward the closet. Moments later, he's shuffling around in the bottom of it, making a ton of racket as various items collide with the walls or floor while he searches in nearly complete darkness for who knows what.

And if my fuse wasn't already lit, it sure as fuck is now.

Let the record show, if this guy just doesn't come home for days on end at any point during our time living together, I will not be the one filing the missing person's report. I will be too busy relishing in the silence.

"Did I leave my shoes by the front door?" he asks, likely more to himself than me, because keeping up with where he leaves his shit wasn't part of our roommate agreement.

"Oh, for fuck's sake," I grumble, storming toward the door and flipping the switch. The room is flooded with light, blinding us both, but at this point, I'm already awake. Might as well make it official. "That help?"

"Shit, Hayes. A little warning?" Kason shields his eyes from the onslaught of brightness and starts blinking rapidly.

Once his eyes seem to adjust, he turns my way, and the semblance of a scowl that was on his face quickly shifts to something else. Almost sheepish as his jade-colored eyes lock onto me.

And he just stares.

"What?" I ask, unable to keep the bite of exasperation out of the word.

His attention moves to the floor, a hint of pink creeping up his neck. "I…Uh…You're basically naked."

Out of all the fucking things…

"Because I was *asleep* when your alarm went off, and I came down here to get you to turn it off," I snap, my tone full of ice and venom. "And my lack of clothing is really what you want to talk about right now? At five in the fucking morning?"

"I just wasn't expecting it," he mutters defensively, his gaze still cast downward. "You don't need to bite my head off for mentioning it."

I hold my arm out in his direction, where he is in the exact same state of undress. "You're the one who opened the door with a tent pitching your boxers, but you didn't hear me pointing that out."

He looks down, as if just realizing he is *also* mostly naked—minus the boner damn near poking out, thank God—and the pink on his neck crawls up to his cheeks and ears now too. I don't stick around to ease any embarrassment he might be feeling, though.

"Don't forget to lock the door after you leave," I mutter before heading back to my bedroom, letting the door slam closed behind me.

For the next twenty minutes while I lay in my bed, attempting to go back to sleep, it sounds like a herd of elephants barreling through the apartment. Faucets running and feet stomping around and cabinet doors slamming, all with little-to-no care about the noise level. I stare at the ceiling the entire time, counting backward from one hundred, then two hundred, then three-fifty just to keep me from going out there and getting into it with him. The last thing I need is one of our neighbors calling the cops on us for having a screaming match in the wee hours of the morning.

Thankfully, things start to quiet down after all that, and I hear barely a sound coming from the crack beneath my door.

Good. Maybe he's left early for lifting and I can grab a few more hours of sleep.

Nestling back into my pillow, I allow my eyes to fall closed and unconsciousness begin pulling me under again.

That's when the blender starts.

My eyes shoot open instantly, now glaring daggers at the door.

Homicide is illegal, and the only person who'd help me hide the body now lives in New Jersey.

It takes repeating that sentiment internally a few times before I settle for the next best thing: grumbling a few profanities under my breath, slamming my pillow over my head, and making a mental note to order something to soundproof my goddamn bedroom.

The next four days are more of the same—Kason screwing with my sleep schedule in the mornings—and I'm about to explode because of it. Not even the ear plugs I bought can drown it out, and if this is how it's gonna be throughout the year, or at least the entirety of football season, I might lose my mind.

My only saving grace is the few hours Kason isn't around the apartment because of lifting and practice, but unfortunately, those hours aren't as frequent as I'd hoped. But with classes starting just around the corner to keep both of us busy, I'm praying the two of us don't cross paths more than once or twice a day.

Tonight is actually the first night since he moved in that he isn't home immediately after practice, and it's given me exactly what I've been craving: some peace and fucking quiet.

Until he comes crashing through the front door around ten o'clock while I'm unwinding by doing some reading in my bedroom. I do my best to ignore the noise he makes for about ten minutes, but when my stomach starts growling and I realize I haven't eaten dinner yet, my hand is forced.

Sighing, I drop my textbook on the bed and grab the glass on my nightstand. I might as well make sure he didn't actually break anything while I grab my leftover chicken and mashed potatoes.

I find the kitchen dark at the end of the hall, save for the stove light we always keep on, and Kason rummaging through the cabinets like some kind of food gremlin.

"You could turn the light on, you know," I tell him as I open the fridge.

More dishes clatter at the sound of my voice, and Kason curses under his breath. "Jesus, you scared me." His head pops out from behind the cabinet door, and he meets my gaze in the dim light. "You're like a mouse. I didn't realize you were even home, you're so quiet."

As opposed to a giant neanderthal who couldn't be quiet if his life depended on it?

The lack of sleep has made me ornery to say the least, and I'm well aware of it. I'm also aware that we have the entire school year—which hasn't even *started* yet—to live together. Shoving down some of my irritation will probably be best for our cohabitation.

"I was getting in some reading. Doesn't require making a whole lot of noise." My attention moves to the fridge where my container of leftovers should be, only to find the spot empty. "Where's my chicken?"

Kason's face is guilty as hell the second my eyes slide back to him, and he holds up his hands. "I took it for lunch because I knew I wouldn't have time to get something between lifting and practice." His face screws up in grimace when I don't say anything, and he adds, "I texted you about it and you read it, so I figured it was fine."

Blinking, I pull out my phone and check my texts. Sure enough, there's one from him that I must've opened when I was half asleep, because it's marked read at barely after six o'clock.

Kason: I'm taking your leftovers for lunch. I'll get you back when I cook this weekend.

I could actually kill him.

First my sleep, now my food. What's next? Him using my fucking toothbrush?

"My old roommate and I didn't really have rules about leftovers, but if I grabbed his, I'd leave him my leftovers the next time I cooked. Or vice versa," he explains. Bumbling awkwardness radiates off him in waves more potent than that goddamn body spray or whatever the hell he wears, and he adds, "That's what I meant when I said I'd get you back."

"Right," I say through gritted teeth. "I guess I'll order Thai instead."

"Well, that's one thing you'll never have to worry about me eating," he says brightly, clearly an attempt to make a joke that doesn't come close to landing.

I do make a mental note about the Thai, though.

"You said you were reading for classes?" he asks, switching the subject as I close the fridge and fill my water instead. When I nod, he asks, "Isn't it a little early to start doing that?"

I give him a tight smile, wishing this stupid water dispenser would move a little faster. "Yup, kinda what *getting ahead* means."

Okay, so maybe I can't completely rein in the snark.

Deciding my glass is full enough, I move to go back to my room without any further conversation. Until Kason pipes up with an off-the-wall question.

"What are your majors again?"

I pause in the opening of the hall and look back at him. "Finance and business administration."

I don't ask him what his major is because, frankly, I don't care. Just like I don't care to continue this conversation he's attempting to have via a follow-up question.

"What kind of jobs are you planning to look for with those? Clearly something involving—"

"Look, we don't have to do this," I say, cutting him off.

He frowns, his brows crashing together. "Talk to each other?"

"Play this whole getting-to-know-you thing." I explain and motion between us with my free hand. "We're roommates, and that's cool or whatever. But we don't need to be friends. I have enough of those."

Scoffing, he mutters, "I find that hard to believe," just loud enough for me to hear it.

I'm fully aware he made the comment to piss me off, and I'm happy to let it hit the mark. After all, two can play at that game.

Stepping toward him, I paint a hostile smirk on my face. "Maybe you've heard of this thing called quality over quantity?"

"So that automatically means you're a dick to everyone else?"

"In case you didn't notice, I don't fucking like people. You're a human. That makes you people." Frustrated and now a bit hangry, I make my way back to my room, calling over my shoulder, "And do us both a favor and only eat your own fucking food from now on."

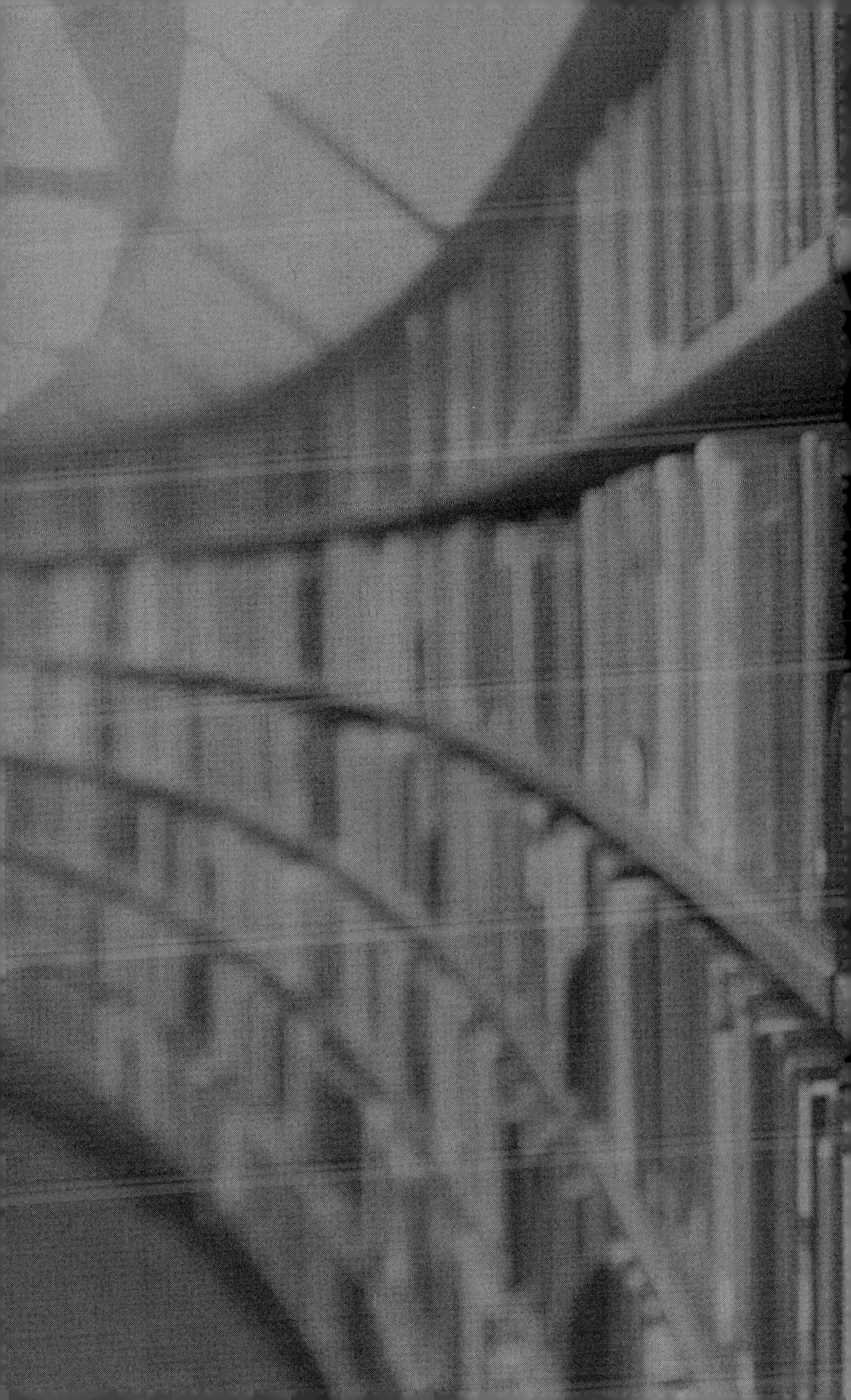

FOUR

Hayes

I'm mid-round in a game of *Apex*, doing my best not to die in a one versus three battle when a familiar voice fills my headset, startling the ever-loving shit outta me.

"Hayes! You got room for me?"

"Jesus Christ, Q," I hiss, jumping a little in my chair.

The sudden movement causes my mouse to shift, and subsequently, gives my position away to the team I'm trying to battle. Trying and *failing* now, because one of them manages to sneak behind me and take me out from behind with a pistol to the head, execution style.

Cursing under my breath, I exit the game and load back in the lobby.

"Were you hoping to give me a heart attack or just fuck with my game by coming in here like that?" I ask my best friend, not bothering to hide my annoyance.

Q scoffs, the sound filling my headset. "It's not like my name didn't pop up on your Discord, so don't give me that bullshit."

"Yeah, well, I just died because of you."

I can hear the smile in his voice when he says, "That just means I came in at the perfect time. Now answer the question."

Quinton de Haas, everyone. Always a jackass.

"I guess," I mutter while sending him a game invite from the lobby, which he quickly accepts. "Though, I'm surprised you even have a minute to get on here with me. You've been too busy with your boyfriend and your new friends in New York and—"

"Nuh, uh. I don't wanna hear it from you, college boy," he cuts in. "Some of us are working men. Now, are you gonna make me beg to be Lifeline?"

I silently switch to Bloodhound and roll my eyes at more than just his neediness to play as a certain character. Only Quinton would act as if getting to play the sport he loves can even be classified as work. And to do it with his boyfriend, no less.

"Yeah, yeah. I'm sure the life of a pro athlete is more work than I could ever imagine," I mutter dryly, not bothering to hide my sarcasm. "I don't know how you two do it."

"If you wanna be like that, I can go spend time with Oak instead. I'm sure he'd have no objections to me *getting off.*"

I groan at his innuendo, and though I might prefer Quinton in comparison to Kason, I most certainly don't miss *that* part of being his roommate. "Pretty sure I heard you two fucking this morning from all the way in Chicago."

My best friend gasps, and I can almost see him holding his hand against his chest mockingly. "Only in Chicago? Guess that means we weren't loud enough."

"You two are disgusting."

"And you're an insufferable smartass. We both make sacrifices in this friendship." He goes silent for a beat, and when he speaks again, it's drastically more sober. "But I am sorry for not being able to talk much lately. I know you've been going through the ringer since Kason moved in. Things have been kinda hectic around here, but that's not an excuse."

His tone change instantly has me on edge more than the match we just loaded into. "Everything okay? You and Oakley settling in?"

Because I swear to God, if anyone on the team or in the league is giving them a hard time, or Oakley has brought out his douchey side again, I will get in my car and drive to Jersey. No hesitation.

"I feel like I should be the one asking *you* that, considering the last time we spoke."

Surprisingly, I don't want to talk about the disaster that is my current living situation, so I reroute the conversation back toward him while the two of us gather weapons. "You're the one living the high life now as a full-fledged adult. I'm still just a college boy, remember?"

Quinton snorts. "I'd hardly call it the high life, and don't think I can't see right past that deflection. You forget I've known you for over half of your life?"

As if he'd ever let me forget.

"Fine, but you go first. How is living with Oakley?" I ask, genuinely curious about how their first year of cohabitation is going. "I'm sure not nearly as great as it was living with me, but hopefully it's at least subpar."

"Oakley puts out, so there's really no comparison."

Rolling my eyes, I mutter, "And the times when the two of you aren't boning?"

He chuckles at the same time he tosses a frag grenade into one of the buildings an enemy team just entered. "It's been good, honestly. There's been a few hiccups now that we're living together full time, figuring out a new routine and whatever else. Lord knows I will *never* be touching his laundry after the first time I attempted to wash a load of our clothes together. But everything else is pretty fucking perfect."

Hearing how happy he is and how easily—for the most part—he and Oakley have shifted into cohabitation makes me happy in turn, of course. But I'd be a liar if there wasn't a tiny little piece of me that hoped to hear he was having a hard time adjusting to this new living situation too.

"And what about hockey?"

"I really like the team. They've all been really accepting of us as rookies, and shockingly, of Oak and I as a couple."

"As any decent human being should be," I mutter, annoyed that acceptance of people being who they are could be shocking. But that's just the world we live in, and I'd be a shitty best friend if I said I wasn't worried about Q heading off to the world of professional sports. One where there are very few openly queer athletes—and none in hockey before the two of them got drafted.

Add on that he'd be doing it with his boyfriend on the same team? Let's just say, I was waiting for someone to make a sideways comment and for the old, hot-headed, fist-throwing Quinton to resurface.

I'm just happy to hear my worries were disproven.

"All right, enough delay. Tell me how things are going with Kason."

I groan, and not because of the fucker who just nailed me in the shoulder with a bow and arrow, of all things. Talking about my living situation makes me *think* about it, and I've taken to pretending that when I'm in my bedroom, there isn't a blundering buffoon just down the hall.

"His alarms are annoying, he has no respect for my sleep schedule when he's getting ready at the ass crack of dawn, and he eats my food."

"Sounds like he makes living with me and my overactive sex life a dream come true."

You could say that again.

"Believe me, I might've bitched about hearing you and Oakley fucking like rabbits at all hours, but it would be preferable over this." A little scoff leaves me before I add, "I had to buy soundproofing boards and shit for my room, Q."

"And write your name on all your food now too?"

He says it like a joke, but it's so not funny. "Thankfully the food thing has only happened the one time."

Quinton remains quiet as we zone in on a fight with another dude, him taking the high ground on top of a building and me rushing them from below. It's only a few minutes before the members of their team are dead, and we're looting the bodies.

"Have you talked to him about it?" he finally asks, swapping out frags for a sniper.

"No, but—"

Tsking his tongue, he playfully chides, "Use your words, H. You're a big boy."

For all the bullshitting and jabbing we do with each other, I know he has my back. If I needed advice about this—which I don't, because I know communication is key here—he'd give it in a heartbeat. Just like I know, if I decided I really did want to commit a felony, he'd be here to help me hide the body.

It's just that some of the things I need to communicate with Kason feel pretty obvious. Common courtesy, common sense, that kinda thing. Like not eating food that isn't yours and being quiet during the early hours of the morning.

But apparently not to Kason Fuller.

"You're such a dick sometimes," I mutter under my breath.

"Where do you think I get it from?"

"Funny, considering I was a nice, innocent angel of a human before I met you."

"Hmm, if that's true, then I guess you wouldn't dare fight fire with fire and be an absolute terror for Kason to live with," Q goads, and I can hear the smile in his voice.

"Don't fucking tempt me," I say slowly, enunciating every word.

The two of us fall into a relatively conversation-free battle for the rest of the game, only chatting coms for the match until we pull out a victory. The two of us are unstoppable in this game as a duo, even if he refuses to admit that I play better as Lifeline than he does.

"Maybe you should come out our way to visit during winter break," he offers while we load into a new match. "You could get away from your roomie from Hell, spend some time around people you actually like."

"So why would I come see you?"

"Like I said earlier, where do you think I get it from?" He laughs, the sound filling my headset. "But be real for a second. I hear Times Square is the place to be on New Year's Eve."

Uh, what?

"I hate people and you want me to ring in the new year surrounded by damn near a million of them in that tiny slice of Manhattan? Do you know me at all?"

"Touché, didn't think about that," he concedes before offering up an alternative. "But there's always Christmas. Ice skating at the Rockefeller, sleigh rides in Central Park. We've got home games bookending the holiday, so Oakley's family is planning to make the trip out for one of those too."

"You know my parents would likely disown me if I didn't show up for Christmas." I bite my tongue, realizing my slip-up before I could reel the words back in. "Shit, sorry."

"It's fine," he tells me, and it sounds like he really means it. Maybe those two assholes he calls parents cutting him loose was for the best after all. "Break's a month long, though. Surely you could slip away from Chicago for a long weekend or something."

"That could be possible."

"Just offering. Let me know."

"Careful, Q," I caution as we start gathering weapons again. "Keep talking like that and I'll think you actually miss me."

He laughs. "Oh, that was just a pity invite. I couldn't care less if you actually come."

"Dick," I mumble, swapping a pistol for an AR.

All Quinton does is laugh some more before wrapping around to the unresolved matter at hand. "So what are you gonna do? About Kason, I mean?"

Out of nowhere, a sniper knocks my ass to the ground, and I start crawling out of shot before he kills me completely, calling out, "Fuck, I'm down," to Q as I hide.

"'Kay, give me a sec."

Sitting back in my chair, I debate my options with Kason, realizing there's really only one. The last thing I need is to spend my senior year having some kind of ridiculous turf war with the roommate I'll all but forget about by this time next fall.

"We're gonna have to call a truce eventually. Which means I'll have to talk with him about it," I acknowledge, however begrudgingly it might be.

"I can hear the *but* at the end of that sentence."

"No *but*. Just stating a fact."

He scoffs. "You're a shit liar."

"And you're a shit Lifeline if you don't get it together and fucking revive me," I counter.

"Okay, okay. I got you."

True to his word, I'm revived a few moments later and ready to find the jackass that sniped me to near-death.

And like with my roommate, I'm planning to give him a taste of his own medicine.

FIVE
Kason

Early morning lifting sessions paired with finally getting back on the field for practice has been kicking my ass the past two weeks, and now that we are officially back in classes, I feel like death warmed over.

But it's our one day off a week, which means today, I have no intention of doing a goddamn thing besides veg out on the couch watching something mindless. The only task before that is taking a shower to wake my ass up.

Lathering shampoo in my hair, I allow my mind to start wandering wherever it wants to go, meandering through nothing in particular. Thoughts of practice, of some of the new plays, of what I could make for dinner tonight.

Food makes my mind shift back to the run-in with Hayes and his leftovers—which I still haven't gotten him back for, seeing as he's been such a douche ever since—and thinking about Hayes being a dick makes me think about all the bickering moments we've had over the past three weeks. One of which stands out most vividly in my mind: the morning he was in my bedroom wearing nothing but his underwear. Don't ask me how that thought process happens, but it does, and what's worse is my mind fixating on it.

I wasn't wrong when I'd thought Hayes could pass for a Greek god, and seeing him damn near naked was further proof of it.

He must hit the gym at least a couple times a week with how lean and toned his muscles are, like that of a swimmer or a track runner. Otherwise, he has to have one high metabolism to have a body like that with little to no effort.

I've done my best to ignore the attraction I feel for Hayes—a feat that's usually pretty easy, considering he's more prickly than a porcupine in a cactus patch. But then there are moments where I can't help but notice.

That morning was definitely one of them.

My dick feels heavy between my legs as I remember the lines between each of his abs on his stomach, the shape of his pecs where they meet his collar bone. The width of his shoulders and the curved muscles on his arms.

And God, those fucking eyes; two blue pools of animosity and disdain.

I'm aching for release in no time as I wrap my hand around my length. Giving a harsh squeeze to the tip, I do my best to push down the desire building in my lower stomach.

But I can't fight the way my brain remembers details of his body I'd only seen once. Can't keep my hand from reaching for the body wash. Can't stop myself from pouring it on my erection that could cut diamonds.

Can't hold back the harsh breath leaving me as I give in to the lust, stroking my length to thoughts of the one person I shouldn't.

My teeth sink into my lower lip, biting back a moan so Hayes doesn't hear me from down the hall. Things are tense enough between us, what with the alarms and the food and the completely opposite schedules. The last thing I want is to tack on another reason for him to hate me.

But as my fist moves faster over my cock, twisting around the head before dropping back to the base, I can't help the little noises that manage to slip free.

"Mmm, fuck," I groan, my head pressing into the cool tile of the shower wall.

My mind runs on a loop through images of Hayes' body like a flipbook, each delectable piece turning me on, building the need for release in my balls and curling at the base of my spine.

And God, those stunning, hate-filled eyes that—

The sound of a faucet running a little too close to be coming all the way from the kitchen has my hair standing on end, and not in the pending-orgasm way.

Dropping my cock like it's a live grenade, I grab the shower curtain and pull it back enough to see the rest of the bathroom, praying that my intuition is wrong. That I'm just hearing things, and I'm still alone.

But sure as shit, my worst fears are realized.

Because there's Hayes, dressed in a hoodie and jeans with his back to me.

Only five feet away…brushing his goddamn teeth.

"What the hell, Hayes?" I snap, squeezing the tip of my dick painfully hard in efforts to deflate it.

He glances up, meeting my gaze through the mirror that's begun to fog and arches his brow in one of those looks that says *what?*

I let out a mortified laugh, because what the hell else can I do besides laugh about the object of my desire being in the same room while I'm getting off to thoughts of him?

"I...Um," I stumble, attempting to wrangle my thoughts into a sentence. "Did you somehow fail to notice the shower was running when you walked in here?"

Hayes turns around, staring right at me now, and his gaze is so much more potent than it was reflecting through the mirror. All the heat and need that was coursing through my veins earlier increases exponentially now that he's right before my eyes, damn near close enough to touch. It has my blood boiling, and I struggle to keep my hand from shifting back down to stroke myself with him right there, only the curtain maintaining my decency.

Then he shrugs, all nonchalant, and shakes his head to answer my question.

That's all it takes for the lust and desire to wash down the drain, like it was doused with a bucket of cold water.

Clearing my throat, I ask, "If you knew, then you wanna explain why you're still in here?"

"Can't be late. You were taking too long." He takes a second to turn, spitting in the sink before tacking on, "And you're the one who left the door unlocked while you're in the shower."

Sure, because that just makes it an open invitation.

"Well, you could *knock* at the very least," I point out the obvious, not bothering to hide my annoyance.

"You said it yourself, I'm like a mouse." He shoves his toothbrush back in his mouth and continues around it. "I figured I'd be in and out before you even knew I was in here."

I'm not sure if that would be preferable at this point. Especially if I'd managed to come while he was in here...

God, no.

I shove those thoughts away as best I can and mutter, "Well, clearly not."

All I get is another shrug and a semi-garbled, "My bad."

I gape at him, floored by his audacity. And also shamelessly fixated on his movements.

Watching him brush his teeth shouldn't be something I find sexy, but as it disappears between his lips, all I can think about is replacing it with my—

"Dude, seriously," I say, nearly pleading now as I pinch the head of my dick hard enough I think it might pop off entirely. "Can you at least take it out to the kitchen sink?"

His brow arches as if to ask *why?*

I can feel color creep into my cheeks, knowing full well it has nothing to do with the heat of the water. "I'm kinda in the middle of something here."

He holds my gaze, those cobalt eyes staring straight into my soul, simultaneously turning me on and pissing me off. The combination is confusing enough without my cock twitching when Hayes smirks around his toothbrush.

"Please," I add, because I'm not above begging for some privacy right now.

Raising his hands in defeat, he grabs the mouthwash and salutes as he exits the room, the door clicking loudly behind him.

Releasing a long, deep breath, I release my death grip on the shower curtain and sink back against the wall tile. Then I turn the knob to the coldest I can stand, hoping it does enough to cool my temper as much as it does my libido.

Unfortunately, the little incident in the shower is branded in my mind like a bad tattoo, and it ruins my mood for the day, and even into the next. Mal must notice too, because after practice on Monday, she's waiting outside the team locker room, arms crossed and a no-bullshit look on her face.

"Hey there, grouchy pants. You look like you're about to march to the gallows," she says, pushing off the wall when she sees me.

"Grouchy pants? The gallows?" I echo, my lips lifting at the corner. "That's really what you decided to go with?"

"I wanted to see if you still knew how to smile." She points to my face. "And you clearly can, seeing as it worked. Now you'll be good company when you walk me out to my car."

"Brat," I murmur with a laugh.

As we fall into step beside one another, heading for our vehicles in the parking lot, she knocks her shoulder into mine. Or, at least, she attempts to. Considering I have about a foot on her, she only manages to hit my elbow.

"Ah yes, but I'm *your* brat."

"Last time I checked, Ivy was the one who's chosen to claim you, not me."

"Yes, well, that's just because I'm not interested in anything that has an extra appendage swinging between its legs," she chirps brightly. "But speaking of dicks, how are things with the new roomie?"

The mere *mention* of Hayes brings my mood back down into the dumps, and more than anything, I wish he didn't have this effect on me. That I didn't care if he's a dick or doesn't like me. But I can't just pretend it doesn't bother me.

Sighing, I mutter, "The whole situation has me in a funk."

"The way your face just fell at the mention of him kinda said that for you." Mal offers me an encouraging smile. "You wanna tell me what's going on?"

Jesus, where to even start?

"We just aren't compatible as roommates. Or even as people."

It's the most basic overview of the situation, but that damn near sums it up.

A pensive look crosses her features. "Have you *tried* to be?"

"Of course I've tried!" Not trying goes entirely against my personality. "He's got me all in my head, thinking I'm the world's worst roommate, when I'm not doing a damn thing differently than when Phoenix and I lived together."

As we reach her car, she turns and leans back against the driver's door. She's got her no-bullshit face back on as she studies me, arms crossed in front of her again. "And how did things work with Phoenix?"

They were easy as hell, for one.

"We were in sync about everything. There wasn't much, if any, bickering or fighting, unless it was about whose turn it was to use the TV in the living room, because he fucking hates horror movies and only ever wanted to watch *Friends* reruns."

Come to think of it, that's one thing I don't miss, but I'd deal with it—even trade my NFL prospects—to go back to living with him. In a heartbeat.

"And sure, we basically lived together for years back in high school, so that had to help some. We already knew how each other operated, we understood each other's schedules, habits, everything."

She nods a couple times before saying, "That makes sense, seeing as he's your best friend, right?"

"Yeah," I say slowly, knowing damn well she's about to slam some sort of philosophical crap in my face, and in turn, make me feel like an idiot. And in true Mal fashion, she whacks me upside the head with it in a single question.

"So, since Hayes used to room with *his* best friend, don't you think it's possible he's used to a different kind of roommate too?"

Well, shit. I'd never really thought about it like that.

"You have a valid point," I grumble, hating myself for having to say it aloud.

Mal, on the other hand, seems to be enjoying it, lifting her hand to her ear and playfully saying, "I'm sorry? What was that? I couldn't hear you."

"I'm not saying it again," I tell her, vehemently shaking my head. "No chance in hell."

She lets out a soft *hmph*. "Like I said. Grouchy pants."

"Yeah, well, you'd be a grouchy pants too if you had to deal with Hayes Lancaster as a roommate," I retort with a shake of my head, unable to stop my mind from slipping back to yesterday morning in the bathroom.

Her eyes narrow on me in that knowing, analytical way when she's trying to read between the lines. "There's something you aren't telling me."

"What makes you say that?"

"Boy, I swear, you forget I know you better than just about anyone." She arches a brow, daring me to disagree, before motioning toward me with one manicured hand. "Now spill."

Absolutely no part of me wants to divulge what happened yesterday morning. If anything, I wish I could wipe the mortifying incident from my memory altogether. But just like Mal said, she and I have known each other forever, so I'm more than aware this is not something she'll drop.

"He walked in the bathroom while I was in the shower," I mutter, kicking a rock near my foot as I try to tamp down the embarrassment threatening to spread a pink tint over my cheeks.

I glance up at her in time to see her frown. "Well, why didn't you lock the door?"

"That's your first reaction? To blame me for not locking the door?"

"It's the most obvious question!" she rebuts, her hands lifting in the air.

"I was still half asleep. And truth be told, I assumed hearing a shower running would prevent someone from walking in to begin with." I pause, knowing the next thing she'd say before she even has a chance. "And yes, I know what they say about assuming."

"Well, the curtain was closed, right?"

"Yes."

She frowns. "Then what's the harm—"

"It's called privacy!" I blurt, tossing my arms out. "And walking in the bathroom while I'm in the shower is a complete invasion of it."

"You're telling me in all the years you and Phoenix were roommates, or even before, he didn't walk in the bathroom while you were taking a shower?"

Goddamnit.

"I mean…" I trail off, not wanting to admit she's right. Again.

"Then what's the problem with Hayes doing it?"

Biting the inside of my cheek, I mutter, "It's not that it was Hayes who did it instead of Phoenix. It's that, when it happened, I was…*occupied.*"

The last word comes out in a pained whisper, and I'm praying like hell she doesn't ask me to elaborate any further. But while it takes a second for her to pick up what I'm putting down, she eventually does. The audible gasp she lets out before she claps her hand over her mouth is something right out of a sitcom.

"You're joking," she whispers.

I shake my head. "God, I wish."

The last thing I expect is her to start giggling hysterically. "Oh, my word. The amount of second-hand embarrassment I'm feeling for you right now is…" She lets out a breath, shaking her head. "Wow. Yeah, I can see why you'd be a little peeved about it."

A little is a complete understatement.

"I know we're both dudes and it shouldn't matter."

"But you're gay, and your roomie is a hottie?" she supplies off-handedly.

I blink at her, wondering how the—

"How do you know what Hayes looks like?"

She lets out a little scoff. "You think I didn't immediately go find him on social media after you told me about meeting with him back in April?"

It's not like I didn't have the exact same idea myself, but I didn't actually follow through with it.

"You internet stalked my roommate?"

"Oh, please, Kase. I moonlight as an FBI agent when it comes to people my friends are involved with. It took me all of five minutes on Quinton's Insta to find this sexy roomie of yours." A devious little smirk tugs at her mouth. "And honey, he might not be your usual type, but he's still fine."

"Just because he's good looking doesn't mean—"

"I'm gonna stop you right there," she says, holding up her hand. "It doesn't take a rocket scientist to know you were shucking the corn to thoughts of a certain blue-eyed dreamboat who looks like a less buff version of Clark Kent."

My brows crash together as I frown. "Hayes doesn't wear glasses. Are you sure you weren't looking at Quinton?"

"I'm not an idiot, Kason," she chides with a roll of her eyes. "And if you keep insulting me like that, I'm gonna leave you to your own devices to figure out this debacle with your sexy roommate."

I wince. "Please stop calling him that."

"Ignoring the facts doesn't make them any less true," she sing-songs as she pushes off her car and steps toward me. "But since you seem hell-bent to die on the hill of denial, I'll let it slide and just tell you what you're gonna do."

Now it's my turn to roll my eyes. "Okay, Obi-Wan. What am I gonna do?"

That hellish smirk from earlier returns, growing into a full-blown grin now. And from the look of it, I'm not sure I'm gonna like the answer.

Scratch that: Knowing Mal's theatrics, I definitely won't like the answer.

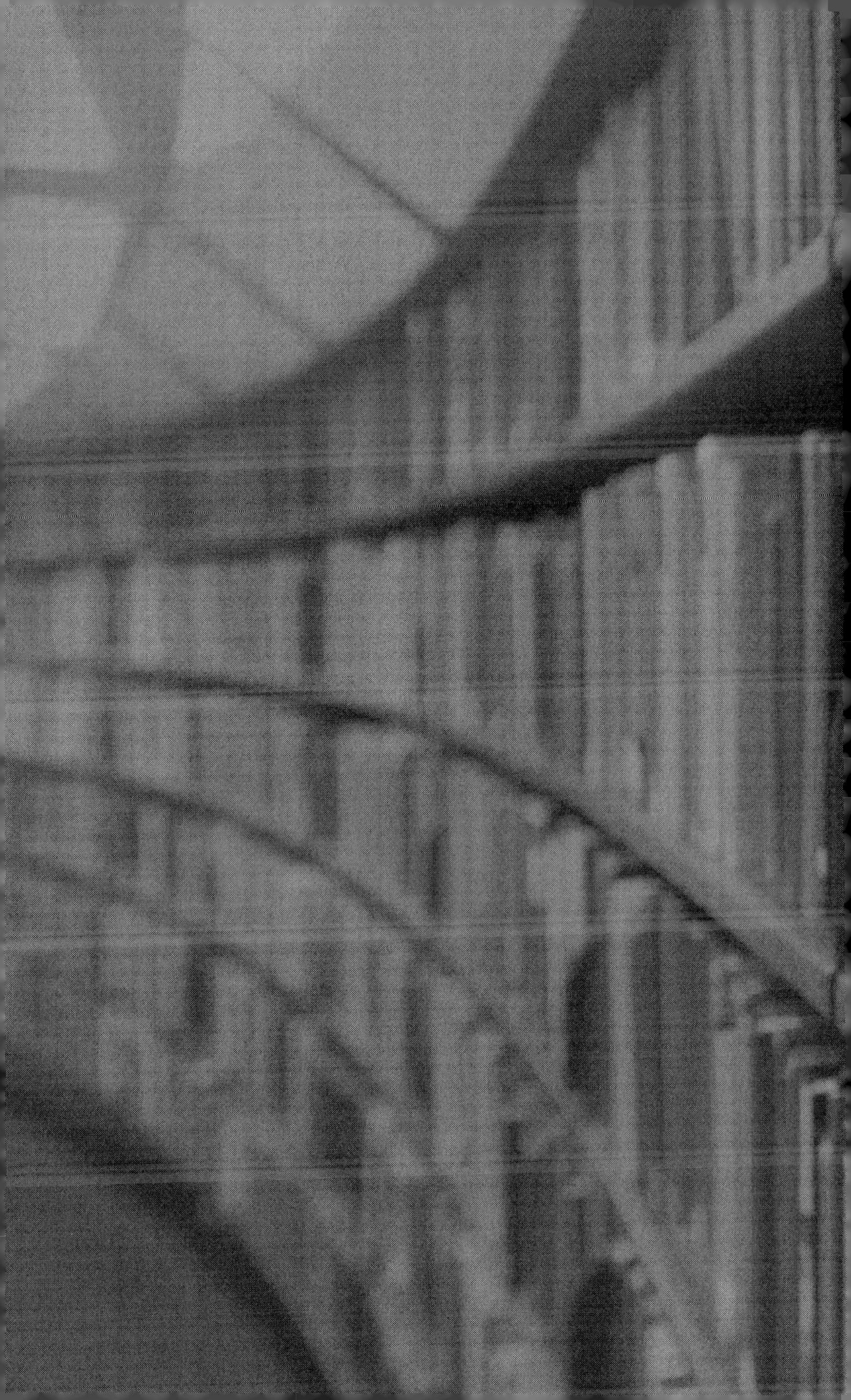

SIX

Hayes

The front door opens when I'm in the middle of cooking dinner on Monday night, and I don't have to turn around to know it's Kason getting home from practice. One, because I've come to know his schedule since he's moved in, and two, because he makes more noise than a monkey playing the cymbals when he gets home. Kicking off his shoes, dropping his key to the counter, stomping through the house, all while grunting like a freaking gorilla or something.

Then again, men are supposedly descended from apes. Kason just must be a little less evolved than the rest of us.

Do not lose it. Do not. Lose. It.

"You got a minute?"

"Plenty, actually. If I live to be eighty, I have about," I pause briefly, doing the math in my head. "Twenty-eight point five million left, give or take."

"Did you just make that calculation in your head?"

It's on the tip of my tongue to ask him why he can't, but then again, he is a football player. He's likely taken one-too-many hits to the head to even count past fifty.

Instead, I just mutter, "What is it you need?"

"A house meeting."

That piques my interest, however slightly. Rolling my tongue over my lower lip, I debate continuing with my smartass remarks or not, before going for aloof.

"Considering I can't leave the stove unattended, I guess I'm at your mercy," I reply dryly.

I hear him moving around behind me, then the audible scrape of the bar stool on the laminate that immediately grates on my fucking nerves. Jaw clenching, I continue stirring the homemade sauce I'm using for my spaghetti. Hell, maybe if I ignore him long enough, he'll just go away.

Unfortunately, it only takes about thirty seconds before he breaks the silence.

"Can you at least turn around, so I'm not talking to your back?"

Rolling my eyes, I turn to face him and plaster on my *I'm trying not to kill you* smile.

"You were saying?"

Kason's gaze locks with mine briefly before he finally speaks, breaking the silence. "I think it's time we make some rules. To make this whole living situation go a little bit smoother from here on out."

"Do you, now?" I cross my arms, leaning back against the granite countertop as I take measure of his fucking audacity. "You've been here less than a month, and you wanna start deciding how things work around here? Or did you forget I was the one who invited you to live here in the first place?"

"That doesn't change the fact that I still deserve respect and privacy."

Ah, yes.

Now I have a sneaking suspicion that I know exactly what he wants to address at this little *house meeting,* seeing as he's made himself scarce around the apartment since our little rendezvous in the bathroom yesterday.

"Maybe you do," I agree, tainting my tone with venom. "Just like I deserve some peace and fucking quiet, but it seems like we're both gonna have to live in disappointment."

Some mix of a scoff and laugh leaves him. "You walked in on me in the *shower* without so much as a word."

My sneer is involuntary, as is the taunt that falls from my tongue. "Is that really the issue here, or is that your self-love session was interrupted by my presence?"

His cheeks heat, embarrassment rushing to the surface after confirmation I knew what he was doing behind that curtain. Which, of course, he denies.

"I wasn't—"

"I'm not stupid, Kason. I know what someone looks like when they get caught jerkin' it," I snap. "We're both human beings with biological urges. It's really not that big of a deal."

Something about his expression has me thinking it's a lot bigger of a deal than I'm making it out to be, only for it to be confirmed when he mutters, "I doubt you'd be the one saying that if the roles were reversed."

"You think I haven't been caught with my dick in my hand before? Because you'd be sadly mistaken," I admit, shrugging with indifference. "Shit happens. I needed to get in there so I wouldn't be late leaving the house. In the past, Quinton and I had an understanding—"

"Except, I'm not Quinton!" he shouts, cutting me off. He shoves the barstool back, a death grip on the counter while he rises to his full height. "I don't *care* what kind of understanding you two had or how things worked when he was your roommate, because he's not anymore. I am. And I don't want you coming into the goddamn bathroom when I'm taking a shower."

My eyes flick up and down his body, a snarl on my lips as my voice comes out as a deadly whisper.

"You're right. You're nothing like Quinton."

Tension lines his jaw as he stares at me with pink tinting his neck and cheeks, fury blazing like a wildfire in those green eyes. I've hit a nerve. I'm not sure how, nor why, but it's obvious. His body language is easier to read than a goddamn picture book.

"If he's someone who could actually call you a friend, I'm pretty fucking glad about that."

With those parting words, Kason shoves away from the counter and storms down the hall toward his room. A few seconds later, the door slams so hard, it rattles the windows, the walls, the television mounted all the way in the living room.

While his mild insult rolls off my back easily enough, it still takes every ounce of my willpower not to call after him and ask if we're making these house meetings a weekly thing. That would be more dickish than necessary—a line which I'm positive I've already jumped clear over.

I know some ground rules for the apartment isn't the worst idea I've ever heard, and I did have every intention of speaking to him about how we can make this cohabitation a bit more tolerable…after I had my fun first.

But tossing jabs shouldn't be enough to get him that pissed. After all, he seems to be a relatively cool-headed guy—at least from the encounters where I try to dig under his skin, only for it to fail.

Which means tonight, I struck some sort of unknown trigger in him. And it doesn't feel nearly as good as I'd hoped it would.

All I really feel is guilt.

Ah, shit.

Blowing out a long, tempered breath, I finish making my dinner, only to eat in silence at the counter. I don't hear a single peep from down the hall the entire time, nor while I'm cleaning up the kitchen and putting away my leftovers.

As I'm stashing it on the top shelf of the fridge, I'm struck with an idea, and quickly grab a pad of sticky notes. Scrawling a message on one, I slap it on the lid of the spaghetti.

Not sure if you can have this (athlete's diet and all), but it's yours if you want it.
No, it's not poisoned.
-Hayes

It's not exactly an apology, but it's a start.

Despite my measly attempt at making nice—and Kason did at least take the food—the rest of the week goes by without the two of us speaking to one another.

Four whole days, and it's the most painfully awkward four days of my life.

We've gone from heated interactions and biting each other's head off to walking on eggshells any time the two of us are home at the same time, let alone in the same room. At this point, I'm making it my mission to escape as often as possible. To the campus library or the gym or literally anywhere to keep myself away from the apartment whenever there's the slightest chance Kason might be there.

It's only thanks to his athletic calendar posted on the fridge that I have a general idea of when he's lifting, practicing, or has a game, otherwise I'd be gone except to sleep.

The thought alone is as insane as it is ridiculous.

It's been less than a month of living together in total, and the guy has basically chased me out of my own home. Classes have barely started, and at this rate, I'm praying for the year to already be over now more than ever.

I'm aware that avoidance at all costs isn't tenable in the long term, which is why I know the two of us really need to come to some sort of compromise—sooner rather than later. And that realization only makes me feel like even more of a dick than I did at the beginning of the week, when he was offering just that.

He has an away game tomorrow evening—again, thank you calendar—so I'm surprised to find the television on and him posted up on the couch in the dark when I arrive home from the library, another excessively long study session under my belt. Long enough to have the first month of reading done for every single class.

All six of them.

I have every intention of sneaking in as quietly and unnoticed as possible; harnessing those mouse-like powers he claims me to have and slipping into the safety of my bedroom. But then I notice the movie playing on the flatscreen happens to be my favorite, and I'm halted in my tracks.

The words fall from my lips without permission, startling both Kason and myself.

"*Oculus?*"

His eyes slide over to me, and even in the dim glow from the screen, I see the apprehension in his expression. "Yeah, why?"

I'm certain he's expecting me to admonish him for his taste in films or to turn it down so I can't hear it from my room. His face says it all.

"No reason," I tell him, rolling back on my heels. "It's a good movie, that's all."

He blinks in surprise. "You know it? It's one of my favorites."

Well, damn. And here I thought we'd never agree on anything.

"Same," I say slowly, not trusting the alternate reality we've just fallen into. That's the only explanation for the bit of personal information I willingly let slip free. "I used to watch it once a week as a kid. It gave me nightmares from hell for years, but it didn't matter. I had to keep watching."

"A trainwreck you can't look away from, yeah," he says, a little hint of a chuckle in his voice. "I definitely get what you mean."

I definitely get what you mean?

My hackles rise on instinct, suspicion and distrust immediately rearing their heads as I stare at him across the room. Because just earlier this week, we were in a screaming match.

Now, we're—

"Do you wanna watch it with me?" he asks, cutting through my thoughts. His tone has the same tentativeness one might use approaching a trapped, rabid animal. "I'm only ten minutes in, so I don't mind starting it over."

My eyes shift from him to the screen, indecision warring within me.

This is pretty much the only decent interaction we've had in nearly a month. Extending it into an entire movie's length would be asking for shit to hit the fan. For one of us to piss the other off so badly that this movie is completely ruined for the rest of our lives, especially considering the last conversation we had.

Yet, for some unknown reason, the lure of my favorite film has me slowly dropping my bookbag to the floor and nodding.

"Uh...yeah. Sure. As long as you don't mind."

Kason shakes his head and scoots over to one end of the couch while I round the other, dropping on the cushion. With a few clicks of the remote, he's restarted the movie from the opening credits, and I'm filled with the tiniest thrill.

I love horror movies. I'll watch them alone whenever I can, but it's always more fun to do it with other people around. Watch their reactions, guess if they'll jump or hide behind their hands, that kinda thing.

It's actually one of the few instances where I'd prefer to not be by myself.

We settle in to watch *Oculus*, and as the familiar terror Tim and Kaylie go through—all due to a haunted antique mirror—plays across the screen, I find myself slowly relaxing more and more. The silence between us is surprisingly comfortable, the only sound coming from the television and him opening a package of candy that I'm damn near positive isn't on whatever plan the team dietitian gives them.

He catches me looking at him one of the times while he's popping a few round candies in his mouth before holding out the package toward me.

"Want some?"

At first I think they're Skittles, but the faint scent of peanut butter hits me, and I realize they're either peanut butter M&Ms, or—

"Reese's Pieces?" I ask. When he nods, I hold out my hand for him to dump. "Yeah, sure."

I pop a few in my mouth, the delicious mix of chocolate and peanut butter coating my tastebuds. Kason does the same, the two of us silently munching on the bite-size candies.

"These are twenty times better than the actual cups," Kason says, breaking the silence as he refills my palm. "Especially when you toss them in popcorn."

I stare at him, mouth opened. "Are you messing with me right now? Or somehow get in contact with Quinton?"

He frowns. "No. Why?"

We hold each other's gaze for a moment, me measuring his authenticity, and him, my sanity, while his brows crash together in confusion.

Shoving down my paranoia, I murmur, "I just thought I was the only person who did that."

"Like you invented it?" Kason snorts. "I know you're wicked fucking intelligent and whatever, but c'mon. I'm pretty sure you can buy it premixed now."

"One, I never said *invent,* and two, I did it way before they ever decided to premix the bag. It doesn't taste the same that way." I roll my head back and forth, trying to figure out the best way to explain myself. "All I meant was that I've never met anyone else who likes it. Q always thought I was insane when I'd mix the bags if we went to the movies. Made me get my own bucket of popcorn and everything."

"Well, now you *have* met someone who does it too." He pops a couple more of the chocolate-coated peanut-butter candies in his mouth. "The only reason I didn't was because we don't have any popcorn."

"Damn shame," I utter, and I find myself meaning it. After all, it's one of my go-to movie snacks for occasions such as this. "But the kind from the theater is always better."

"Oh, absolutely, There's no contest."

My thoughts exactly.

The weirdness of this little bonding moment sits in the back of my mind as silence settles over us once again, Kaylie's unfortunate encounter with a lightbulb on the screen taking our attention from each other. It's the best kind of mindlessness, watching something I've seen countless times, to the point where I could quote the entire thing. Which, come to think of it, is sort of strange to do with a horror movie.

But I love the predictability of it, and oddly, the comfort.

Maybe because I already know how it ends.

Before I know it, the credits are rolling, and Kason pauses the movie and looks at me cautiously.

"You wanna watch another?"

More than one movie might be pushing it, even if we did have whatever little *moment* with the popcorn and candy convo. An hour and a half is probably a safe limit to keep us at for the time being.

"I'm actually gonna turn in. But, uh, thanks for letting me watch with you."

I go to rise from the couch, stifled by the awkwardness of turning him down, but Kason grabs my wrist before I so much as stand.

"Can I..." He blows out a breath, clearly uncomfortable with whatever he's about to say as he releases my wrist like it's a hot potato. "Look, Hayes, the last thing I wanna do is rock the boat here. And I know I'm not what you asked for when it comes to a roommate. Believe me, you're the furthest thing from what I'm used to living with too."

I raise a brow and lean back against the sofa, wondering where the hell he's going with this. "I'm assuming this is leading somewhere better than where it currently is?"

He winces before shifting to face me better, pulling one leg up on the cushion between us. Gesturing from me to him, he says, "This is all new to both of us, and if we're gonna make this work..." He trails off with a sigh, as if he can't bring himself to say the words.

So I do it for him.

"We have to get along. Before we go insane," I mutter, my eyes sliding to the television screen briefly. The second they move back to him, I see his silent nod of agreement.

"I'm not trying to be intrusive, insensitive, a pain in the ass, or anything else. I've only ever lived with the same person since freshman year, and you're…" He lets out an awkward laugh, and I catch him shaking his head in the light from the television. "You're basically a stranger."

"Yeah. Same here," I murmur, sort of hating myself for agreeing with him. Or maybe hating myself for letting things get this uncomfortable between us before finally talking about it.

"A lot of what Quinton and I had were…unspoken rules," I offer, choosing my words as carefully and tactfully as I can. "Things like not eating each other's food without having permission. Quiet hours between eleven pm and six am where any loud appliances weren't to be used." I shoot him a little half-smile. "Those are things I thought would be pretty standard, but I can see that your past rooming situation might've had seemingly obvious things about them that I don't see that way too."

Kason's eyes narrow on me, processing my point of view while he cocks his head to the side. I expect him to tell me what he's been used to in the past, but instead, he surprises me by uttering, "You know, that is the closest thing I've heard to an apology from you since we've met."

My lips quirk slightly, but I school my features before he can notice. "It's just facts. We're used to different things, and we need to come up with some middle ground before we drive each other crazy."

Nodding a couple times, he offers, "So let's call a fair catch."

My brows crash together as I frown. "A *what?*"

"Fair catch," Kason repeats, as if I'll understand it any better the second time. "It's a football term. Basically means that the player receiving a kick calls for no interference from the opposing team."

"So you don't want me to interfere with you while you live here," I surmise.

"No, no. When they call for a fair catch on the field, it means the other team can't hit them when they're—"

I hold up a hand between us, stopping him in his tracks. "I know you pissed me off a few times since moving in, but I don't believe in solving issues with violence. I'm a pacifist."

"Oh, my God," he grumbles, giving me an exasperated laugh. "I wasn't gonna hit you, I'm trying—"

"To call a truce. I know."

He looks at me, that emerald stare searching my face while he processes what I said. Then they widen dramatically, and his jaw drops open ever so slightly.

"Are you cracking a joke right now?" When I can't hide my smirk, he points at my face and starts laughing. "Holy shit, and here I thought you didn't have a sense of humor at all."

"Yeah, well," I murmur, lifting my shoulder in a shrug. "Now, you know."

"Okay, noted. But the first rule of this truce? Stop interrupting me every time I try to talk."

I nod a couple of times, as if I'm mulling it over, before letting out a long, dramatic sigh. "I hate to say this, Kase, but I think you've hit my hard limit."

I catch Kason rolling his eyes in the faint glow from the television, clearly starting to get a hang for my brand of dry humor and sarcasm. "Let me guess, you wanna enact a safe word when I touch on those?"

"Oh, kinky Kason," I muse, full-on smiling now as I waggle my eyebrows suggestively. "That's a side of you I wasn't expecting to know about."

A tinge of pink crawls up his neck, spreading onto his face that's visible even in the dim light, and I have to admit, embarrassed Kason is kind of adorable. In a dopey puppy dog kind of way.

"Is there anything else?" I ask, choosing to take a small amount of pity on the guy by changing the subject.

"If the bathroom is occupied, the other needs to wait their turn. Even if the door is unlocked," he says pointedly.

"Or you could just lock the door," I supply. "Then this entire rule would be moot."

"You have a smartass comment for everything, don't you?"

"An unfortunate habit I picked up from Quinton over the years. But yes, I can agree to your bathroom terms." I take a deep breath, the next words spilling free without my permission. "And…I apologize if I made you uncomfortable the other morning."

"You *do* know how to apologize," he murmurs, brows lifting in surprise.

"Now who's being the smartass?"

Smiling, he nods. "Is there anything you'd like to add to this agreement?"

Not needing him to ask twice, I immediately blurb, "For the love of all things holy, can you pre-blend your stupid protein shakes the night before? Soundproofing only does so much to hide that god-awful sound at six in the morning."

"You actually sound-proofed your room?"

"There's one thing I don't joke about, and it's sleep." Crossing my arms over my chest, I mutter, "That's definitely one area where you and Q do have a little bit in common."

This time, he can't stop the smile from spreading across his face as he laughs. "Okay, no blenders before eight o'clock. Got it. Anything else?"

I let out a low hum, the stolen food thing coming to mind. But more than anything, I find myself intrigued by his idea now that the annoyance has passed. "We can try this weird leftover thing you used to do. Just make sure I actually respond to you before you go taking it. I might be a delight to be around most of the time, but the exception is when I'm hangry."

"I'm not touching that comment with a ten-foot pole." He laughs, and I honestly think this is the most I've ever heard it.

It's kinda nice.

"Thanks for the spaghetti, by the way. The homemade sauce was…" Shaking his head, he sighs. "I might dream about that for the rest of my life."

"I can't take credit, it's my great aunt's recipe."

"You tell her she can adopt me into the family any day, 'cause I love to cook."

The information is surprising, to say the least, but I put that in my back pocket in hopes this leftover swapping ends up with me getting the better end of the deal.

"Anything else?" he asks, clearly all ears as to how he can do his part in making this cohabitation a bit easier on both of us.

As much as I'd love to ask for him to spend less time at the apartment so *I* can have some alone time, this is his home too, and I can't bring myself to bring it up.

So instead, I just shake my head, muttering, "I think we've officially come to an agreement."

SEVEN

Kason

There's nothing like kicking off the season with a win on the road, and like the rest of the team, I'm on a complete high as we load the bus back from Milwaukee late that same night. Most of the guys are rowdy and restless to hit the road for the short ride home, apparently some are planning to go to the Kappa Sig party over on Greek Row.

I'm scrolling through my phone in a window seat near the back of the bus, idly waiting for everyone to finish loading up when a shadow appears over me.

"You care if I sit here for the ride back?"

Lifting my gaze, I find it's one person I certainly wasn't expecting to ask me that.

Holden Sykes.

After a few dumbfounded seconds of staring, I managed a flustered,

"Uh, yeah. That's fine."

Holden doesn't seem put out by my luke-warm welcome and shoves his bag into the upper cubby before sliding into the empty seat beside me.

Besides chatting about football, the two of us haven't talked much after what happened last year. There's no bad blood on my end—after all, with the bit of stalking I did on his and Phoenix's social media this summer, I truly believe they belong together. And while creeping on them is probably something I shouldn't do, I'm kinda glad I did. I've never seen Phoe as happy as he does in the photos they posted right before Holden had to report for training camp with the rest of the team.

I'm about to open my mouth and make an attempt at small talk, but I'm interrupted by Noah, one of our cornerbacks, when he barrels down the aisle and stops at the seat in front of us. "You two going out tonight to celebrate?"

"The Kappa Sig house, right?" I ask.

"Absolutely," Noah confirms, nodding enthusiastically. "First victory party of the season, and we can't do it without our two captains."

Despite things being a little less awkward around the apartment with Hayes, I'm still tempted to hit the party with the team; something wildly out of character for me. The only real downside would be going alone. I'm not nearly enough of a social butterfly for that.

There's a good chance I could get Mal and Ivy to hit the party with me too, except Ivy usually works at Page Turners on Sunday mornings.

Weighing my options, I go for as non-committal as possible.

"I'll think about it."

Noah snorts and shakes his head. "That's a no if I've ever heard one." He turns his attention to Holden and nods. "What about you, Sykes? Ready to celebrate kicking off our season with a dub?"

Holden shrugs. "Maybe. Haven't decided yet."

That is not the answer Noah wanted or expected before he frowns. "Man, you get tied down and it's like you never leave the house. What happened to the life-of-the-party guy you've been the past three years?"

"I grew up. Fell in love. Realized there's more to life than getting blackout wasted and having meaningless hookups." Holden leans back in the seat beside me, a little smirk forming when he looks at Noah. "Maybe you should try it sometime. Lord knows you and Luca bicker enough to be a married couple as it is. Maybe it's about time he makes an honest man outta you."

Noah all but blanches at the insinuation before his nose wrinkles up. "That'll be a hard pass for me."

Ah, and here I almost forgot about Noah's slightly homophobic tendencies.

With those parting words of disgust, Noah heads back up the aisle to his seat. Holden and I share a look as he goes, the two of us chuckling under our breath.

"Me thinks thou doth protest too much," Holden murmurs, and the two of us start laughing some more.

"And he'll continue to until his dying day."

He chuckles some more and shakes his head. "Probably will from his grave too."

It's moments like this where I'm reminded *why* everything went down last year. Holden is a lot of fun to be around, always making jokes to lighten the mood. It's one of the things that attracted me to him in the first place—drawing from his personality, not his looks.

I'm just glad things aren't weird after the drama between me, him, and Phoe, especially when it comes to football and the team. I've actively forced myself to leave all that shit on the sidelines the moment I step onto the field, and from what I can tell, he's been doing the same.

"You killed it tonight, you know." His words break through my thoughts, and when I glance his way, those whiskey brown depths are both honest and familiar.

"Thanks, Hold."

His expression remains earnest. "No, seriously. I can't remember the last time I've seen you dialed in like that."

A hint of a smile curls the corner of my mouth before admitting what I'd just been thinking. "I'd be lying if I said I wasn't worried about how things would be this season after last spring."

He waves me off. "Nah, nothing to worry about. No hard feelings, no bad vibes. We're the same friends we were before."

Hearing that is all I need to let the history between us wash away, giving us a blank slate as friends. One we quickly make use of, spending the rest of the bus ride back to campus chatting about his summer, including tales of his stay at Phoenix's family condo and his trip back to Cali to visit his grandma. And it's good. Normal, even, and by the time we pull up outside the training facility, I feel like we've completely put the bridge of awkwardness we'd been teetering on in the rear view.

But that's before I climb off the bus, only to find Phoenix leaning against Holden's Jeep in the parking lot.

It's a knife to the gut, slicing clean through me, but not in the way I expected. Because as I stand at the bottom of the stairs, my eyes fixated on one of the few people in this world I trust more than anything, all I feel is longing.

For Phoenix. For our friendship.

For the guy who has always been my number one.

Someone stops beside me, and this time when I glance over, I'm not surprised to find it's Holden. There's a big, dopey smile on his face as he looks over to where Phoenix is waiting for him, watching the two of us.

"He'd kill me for telling you this, but he misses you," Holden murmurs suddenly, his attention shifting to me now.

Tension coils inside me as I try to keep my emotions reined in. Because the fact of the matter is, I miss Phoenix the way I'd be missing an amputated limb, and that's ninety percent of the problem.

He's been my crutch for longer than I care to admit, and I'm ready to stand on my own. Even if doing so is painful as hell.

"I miss him too," I whisper, unable to stop my voice from cracking on the last word.

Holden gives me a tight smile, clearly wanting to say more. He must think better of it, though, because he simply shoulders his bag, tells me to have a good night, and heads over to where Phoenix is waiting.

I watch as they greet each other, unable to look away. The smile on my best friend's face—the happiness radiating from it, even at this distance—is the same I'd seen in those photos this summer. And it's everything I could ever wish for him to have.

I just wish like fucking hell that I could share it with him.

Holden rounds the Jeep, jumping into the passenger seat as Phoenix moves to get behind the wheel. But just before Phoenix climbs in, his gaze collides with mine, and he gives me a half-smile and a simple wave.

That's what all these years of friendship have been reduced to.

A smile and wave.

My hand lifts of its own volition, and I'm left frozen in place, staring as the doors close and they drive off into the night…and feeling more alone than I have in a long time.

I'm on autopilot by the time I get back to the apartment, moving without a single coherent thought. There could've been an elephant playing *Hot Cross Buns* on the trombone in the living room and I wouldn't have noticed, which makes perfect sense why I blow past Hayes quietly lounging on the couch.

"Kason?"

I halt halfway across the living room, still in a bit of a daze when I meet his eyes. "Hey, sorry. I didn't see you when I came in."

The analytical look in Hayes' stare intensifies as he continues looking at me, and like so many times before, I feel completely transparent. A piece of glass that's capable of shattering at the wrong touch.

"You good?" he asks slowly, brows crashing together at the center. "Did the game go okay?"

"Uh, yeah. It was fine. We won," I tell him absently.

"That's what matters, right?"

I nod and force a smile. "I guess so."

My answer has his frown deepening. "Then why do you look like someone kicked your puppy?"

Sadness shifts into frustration, and I lift my arms. "Do you even care?" It comes out with more bite than it should've, and guilt for it hits me immediately.

We've had shaky moments since calling our "fair catch," but for the most part, we've kept true to the truce and the rules we set together. And it's paid off, minimizing the blow ups and frustrations on both our parts.

Which is why Hayes is clearly taken aback, sitting up straight on the couch.

"Look, normally I would have a completely different reaction to your snappiness," he starts, clearly choosing his words carefully. "But if we're gonna make an attempt at being friendly, there's this thing that has to happen."

"Not biting each other's heads off?" I supply, my lips curling up a little. "Probably a good idea. Sorry."

"That, yes." A returning grin pulls at the corner of his mouth. "But I was actually meaning the part where we talk to each other about the things bothering us."

Oh.

An ear to listen wasn't what I was expecting Hayes to say. Quite frankly, it's the exact opposite of what I'd have thought, figuring he'd make a smartass comment about keeping our feelings to ourselves or saving the mental breakdowns for the confines of my bedroom.

So hearing his offer to unload has me spilling my guts before I can think twice.

"I saw Phoenix tonight, after getting back from the game. It was the first time since he moved out of our apartment after last semester ended, and I wasn't expecting it."

"And Phoenix is…an ex?" Hayes supplies, doing his best to fill in the blanks.

And that's when I realize this guy barely knows a damn thing about me, and I can't help but laugh.

"Oh, God no." I shake my head, the mere thought strange and uncomfortable. "My old roommate. And my ex-best friend. Or still my best friend that I'm currently on a break from? I'm not really sure which, at the moment."

A couple expressions cross Hayes' face—everything from confused to amused—before he lets out a sharp laugh. "That doesn't sound messy one bit."

I blow out a dramatic breath. "Believe it or not, it's actually one of the more simple things in my life."

The two of us just kinda stare at each other for a second, neither of us knowing what to do or say after that. I'm about to just call it a night, head to the privacy of my room and sulk alone, but there's part of me telling me to join him on the couch. Maybe even take him up on his offer to get this shit off my chest, with someone other than Mal or my therapist.

I'm about to ask Hayes if he's being genuine in his offer, but my "Are you—" comes out at the same time he starts with, "Would it—", our words overlapping each other.

Both of us laugh awkwardly before Hayes motions toward me. "You go first."

Again, that transparent feeling comes over me as I look at him, and I force myself to push the words out before I can second guess them.

"Look, are you serious about this whole 'talking it out' thing? Because if you have better things to do—"

"Yes. Now, shut up and sit down," Hayes says, cutting me off.

"Remember that thing about you not interrupting me being part of our fair catch agreement?"

"Remember the part where I told you that was a hard limit?" he volleys right back before pointing at the cushion beside him. "Now, sit."

Well, shit. Okay, then.

Doing as he says, I kick off my shoes and drop down on the couch, only to be even more confused when Hayes gets *up* from it. He must read it in my expression too, because he lets out a little laugh that has butterflies swarming in my stomach while he holds his hands up in surrender.

"Relax, okay? I just think this is a conversation that requires something a little more than water."

He heads to the fridge before producing two glass bottles of beer, twisting the tops off before bringing them back to the couch with him.

Frowning, I take the bottle he offers me, looking at it questioningly. "When did we get beer?"

"I bought it this afternoon." He motions toward me with his own beer, "It's not poisoned, so you're safe to drink it."

I immediately take a nice, long swig of the cold beverage, the flavor flooding my tastebuds. He was right—this conversation will be a lot easier with some liquid courage.

"I didn't take you for the beer type."

"Well, there's a lot you don't know about me," Hayes mutters, taking a drink from his own bottle. "I'm full of surprises."

Hayes and I are definitely not in a good enough place for me to be eyeing the way his Adam's apple bobs when he swallows, or how nice his lips look wrapped around that bottle, but I can't stop myself from watching anyway. Just like I can't prevent what the sight does to my stomach, knotting and coiling it so tightly, I might damn near explode.

I've been trying my best to tamp down whatever attraction I've been feeling for him, but unfortunately, ever since I've been seeing the nicer side of him, it's only managed to grow. Unbearably.

Clearing my throat and reminding myself that Hayes is most likely *straight,* I try to find a place to start with this whole Phoenix thing.

"It's a big campus, but it's not that big, so it wasn't like I thought I'd go the rest of college without seeing him. Especially when we share some areas of the training facility with the baseball team. I just wasn't expecting him to be there picking up Holden after the game."

"And Holden is?" he asks, trying to fill in some of the pieces.

"Our quarterback, and his boyfriend."

I do my best to gauge his reaction to this information, get a read on how he feels about *non-traditional lifestyles,* as some would say. But his expression remains entirely impassive as he prompts me to continue.

"So you saw him when he was picking up his boyfriend, and now you feel some type of way about it because…" He pauses, allowing me to fill in the gaps.

"He waved at me from across the parking lot, and it felt like I was waving back at a stranger instead of my best friend."

It sounds stupid when I say it aloud, and I know that. If anything, I'm making this sound more and more like a break-up—and God knows the ache in my chest makes it feel like one.

But maybe that's because it basically is.

The ending of any relationship is a break-up, and I'm starting to realize that just because there were no romantic feelings between us doesn't make it any less painful or heartbreaking to lose him.

And the worst part of it all is *he* is always the person I'd talk to about this kinda stuff.

Now, I can't.

Something in my expression must give off that thought, or Hayes must have some kind of second sense, because he prompts me yet again to continue.

"Now's the part where you tell me what happened between the two of you. If you want to."

I scoff and take another drink, because if I'm in for a penny with all the drama I'm dumping on him, I might as well be in for a pound. "Do you want the long or the short version?"

"Whichever you're willing to tell me," he says, falling back into a more comfortable position against the cushions. "I'm here for the long haul now."

My tongue rolls along the inside of my cheek as I lift my gaze to meet his, only to find him already studying me intently. Eyes roving my face as he waits, I do my best to piece together the best place to start this saga.

After a moment, I start with my version of the story.

"The short is that he lied to me. A lot, and about things that it should have been easy for him to tell me if we're truly as close as I thought we were."

Hayes nods. "And the long?"

"Makes it so much more complicated." Rolling my tongue along my cheek, I mentally recount the fights with Phoenix at the end of last semester. "Our friendship spans over a decade, and in my mind, we could tell each other whatever, whenever. Which is why finding out about this lie was so fucking devastating, and I was pissed on top of it. But it wasn't until I took a step back to realize it wasn't *what* he was lying about, but the fact that he felt he needed to in the first place that upset me the most."

He hums briefly, his cobalt stare meeting mine. "It's one of *those* situations."

It is indeed.

Sighing, I nod and continue. "The worst part is, as much as I still wanna be pissed about it, I also understand why he did it. There were things he was afraid to tell me, decisions he made that he'd felt were embarrassing and shameful. Those are powerful emotions, you know? Sometimes enough to wanna hide them from the people you're closest to."

"The ones who you only want to see the best in you," Hayes confirms, his attention still focused on me. "And while that's understandable, the rationale behind it doesn't make it right for him to lie."

I tip my beer toward him in acknowledgment. "No, it doesn't. It just makes it a lot fucking harder to hate him for it."

Hayes is a logical person, at least from what I've gathered. With how cut and dry he is—and how easily he will put me in my place—I know he'd be the first one to tell me I'm overreacting or don't have a leg to stand on.

The two of us fall into a comfortable silence, watching but not watching the movie flashing on the screen while we finish our beers. I'd figured the conversation is as finished as our beers, but I'm surprised when Hayes grabs my empty from me and fetches two more.

"So this lie," he starts, while handing me a second beer. "It was obviously big enough to put a massive strain on your relationship."

"Yeah, it did, but it's more than that now, because I've already forgiven him for it."

He frowns as he drops back down beside me. "So if that's the case, I guess I'm just confused why you still aren't talking?"

"And here comes the complicated part," I tell him, a sardonic laugh falling from my lips. "When this all happened last year, it also uncovered some issues in our friendship that both of us had become pretty blind too. Or maybe we weren't blind to it, but we were too afraid of what fixing it would mean going forward."

Part of me still is, though I choose to leave that part out when I continue.

"We'd been friends for so long, he felt more like a brother. But in turn, we'd grown very codependent on each other—to the point of it being toxic to both of us. He'd always been the protector, always putting my happiness before his own, but it turned him into my crutch which led to me eventually feeling like he was being overbearing." A long, relenting sigh leaves me. "And the lie just ended up being a by-product of him finally choosing to put himself first."

"You were feeding each other until it became a cycle you couldn't break out of, no matter how stuck you both felt," Hayes murmurs, clearly filling in the blanks. "Which is why you're now spending some time apart."

All I can do is nod before taking another drink from my beer, the heavy, somber feeling not getting any lighter, even with sharing some of its weight. Even if it makes me sound more like a neurotic mess than he already thinks I am.

"I know you didn't sign up to play therapist when I moved in, but I appreciate you listening."

"No, I didn't," he confirms, nodding his head a couple times. "But if we're gonna make this situation work through the end of the year, then knowing stuff like this about you is helpful."

I frown, unsure I heard him right. "Really?"

"Absolutely. That way I don't do or say something that'll trigger you or set you back on the progress you're trying to make. I'm not that much of an asshole."

Rising off the couch, his second empty in hand, he heads to the kitchen and tosses it in our recycling. He glances over at me afterward, catching me gawking at him like he's a fucking Jonas Brother or something.

"What?" he asks, halting in his tracks.

Shaking my head, I say, "Nothing, I'm just surprised."

The wink he gives me before heading down the hall has my stomach flip-flopping like a pair of sandals, but the way my full name sounds falling off his lips when he calls back to me is nearly enough to melt me into a pile of goo.

"Like I said before, Kason Fuller. I'm full of surprises."

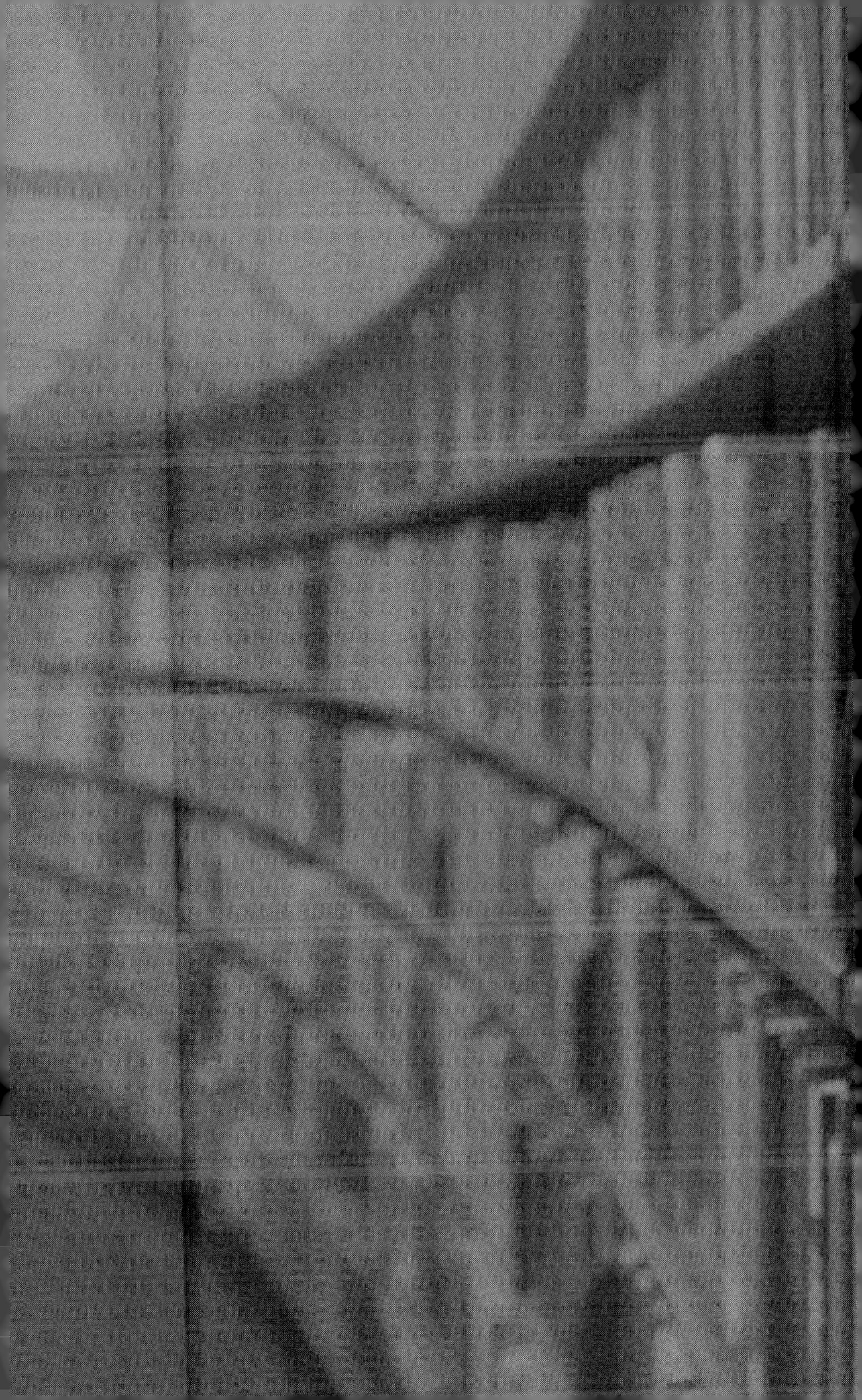

EIGHT

Hayes

September

The past couple weeks have been both interesting and unexpected when it comes to Kason, and I'm not entirely sure if I like it more or less than when we were at each other's throats. Nothing has really changed, yet if feels like since he gave me a little more insight into who he is—plus why he's living with me and his rocky relationship with Phoenix—I've started to be a little more tolerant. At least in the moments of silence when we're watching horror movies, which has become a pretty regular thing, tonight included.

"What're we watching tonight?" I ask, strolling down the hall into the kitchen, catching Kason already lounging on the couch with the television on. My stomach growls on cue as I open the fridge, and I add, "And more importantly, what do you wanna eat, because I'm hungry enough to gnaw my own leg off."

"Cannibalism is frowned upon in this household unless it's on the television screen, Hazey."

Hazey?

Despite my irritation level with him reducing quite a bit, there are still plenty of moments where his neanderthal side annoys me, and this is the perfect example. Because clearly he's gotten a little too big for his britches when it comes to our little *fair catch,* especially if he thinks a nickname like that is on the table.

"Call me that again and we can find out if murder is also."

He snorts. "I'd like to see you try."

I hate that he knows the threat is an empty one, so I choose to ignore it.

"Is there anything you're not allowed to have when you're in season? Like excessive…carbs, or whatever?" I keep searching the fridge and freezer without waiting for an answer, coming up with a few options. "We could do garlic chicken and broccoli, always a classic. Otherwise we've got plenty of eggs, and I found some hash browns in the freezer, so we could make some kinda breakfast casserole that'd be good for breakfast this week too." Still nothing from Kason, and I close the fridge. "Or we can just say screw it and order Thai."

I'm almost positive that will get him to acknowledge me, remembering his distaste for my favorite food, but when he remains silent even with that looming threat, I get a bit concerned.

"Earth to Kason? Care to come back to reality for a minute so I don't starve?"

Still nothing.

Did he just pass out while sitting upright?

Crossing to the living room and glancing over the back of the couch, I find Kason very much awake, busy scrolling on his phone, and more importantly, not paying attention to a thing I'm saying.

Typical.

Shoving down my growing annoyance, I lean over the back of the couch to look at his phone screen, his scent—all oak and smoke—wafting over me in plumes as I do. I'd figured he'd be on some sort of social media, but instead I find him scrolling through the details of a Toppr profile.

"Really? This is why I was standing in the kitchen, talking to myself like an imbecile?"

Kason all but throws his phone across the room at the sound of my voice directly behind him, it dropping out of his palm and clattering to the floor next to the couch.

I can't help the laughter that slips free, my head dropping down on the back of the couch cushion as I try and fail to rein myself back in.

"You know, it's really hard to believe you play football with how fucking clumsy you can be sometimes."

"You scaring the shit out of me isn't the same thing as catching a ball that I know is coming," he mutters indignantly while grabbing his phone from the floor, aiming a glare at me when he rises back up. "There's a big difference, actually."

"Yeah. Sure," I say, the words coming out dripping in sarcasm. "And here I thought it was just me making you nervous and jumpy while you're swiping on some shitty dating app."

He coughs and blinks a couple times, his neck and cheeks taking on a pink tint to match the red hands I just caught him with.

"Actually…now that you mention it. I'm, uh…" he trails off and lets out an awkward cough, clearly unable to hide his discomfort. "This might be a good time for me to tell you…I'm gay."

"Okay," I say slowly, frowning at him. "And you're bringing this up, why?"

He winces, full of awkwardness and unease, and a good part of me is wishing I would've just ignored what he was doing and made the dinner choice on my own. Especially if we're about to have another heart-to-heart or whatever.

Blowing out a breath, he continues, "I just wanted to make sure you're…okay with that, I guess?"

I arch a brow. "Because my opinion on your sexuality matters to you?"

"It's more that I want to know it's not gonna be a problem for you or that you won't be uncomfortable?"

I can't help the dry laugh that comes out, mixing with a scoff.

"If you were worried that could be an issue, don't you think you should've mentioned that the day we met at the coffee shop? Or when you reached out to me in the first place?" I counter.

"Yeah, probably, but—"

"Let me stop you there," I cut in, holding up my hand. "I don't give a shit who you sleep with as long as you aren't interrupting *my* sleep when you're getting laid. Lord knows you already do enough of that as it is."

He looks utterly shocked, like he was expecting me to be some homophobic douchebag instead. "You really don't care?"

I blink, not sure if I'm offended that he'd assume I would have any issue with something no one has any control over.

"Considering my best friend is bi and I'm also a member of the alphabet mafia, I'd be one helluva hypocrite if I had any issue with you being into dudes, Kason."

Frowning, he repeats, "'Alphabet mafia?'"

"The queer community."

Kason looks completely rattled, staring at me with wide eyes. "Really? Why didn't you say anything? What are you?"

The questions come out in rapid-fire succession, and each one of them makes me roll my eyes.

"Not that it's any of your business, ace spectrum. Demi, if you want to be specific." Leaving it at that, I motion behind me with my thumb. "Now are you gonna answer me about food or go back to swiping on that dude who looks like he's taken one too many hits off a joint."

He ignores my comment about food entirely when he finally speaks, only to come up with, "He did not look like that," as his best defense.

"Oh, he definitely did." I point to the phone in his hand. "Pull it back up and I'll show you."

"Oh, my God," he mutters under his breath. "You're insane."

But he must be curious, because he unlocks the screen and reopens the app he was just scrolling through. The same guy's photo pops up that he was looking at prior to his impromptu game of hot potato, and the two of us stare at the screen while he slowly scrolls through the six images on his profile.

"That one," I say, pointing to the photo I was talking about. "I dare you to say I'm wrong while looking at that picture."

Kason mumbles something under his breath rather begrudgingly, thumb hovering over the screen.

"Kason, don't be so stubborn that you swipe yes on that dude just to prove a point," I chide, reaching for his phone to swipe for him.

"Ugh. Fine, you win," he concedes before swiping left.

My chest swells while humming, a little too pleased with myself. "Like I said. Higher than a fuckin' kite."

At first I think he's planning to swipe out of the app after he gets rid of that stoner bozo. Then I catch Kason's thumb teetering toward the right on the next guy—who looks like he barely has two brain cells to rub together with a bio to match—like he's planning to swipe yes on him, and I can't stop myself from speaking up.

"Seriously?"

The judgment in my tone must be what finally pulls his attention away from the screen, and he meets my disapproving gaze. "What now?"

I arch a brow and nod at his phone. "You're actually contemplating swiping yes on" —I lean in more so I can read off his screen verbatim— "Zak, who 'is not gender fluid, but is definitely tryna put fluid in every gender'?" Doing my best to keep my laugh in check, because it is kinda funny, I ask, "So what I mean is, 'seriously, Kase, that sounds like someone you want?'"

Kason's ears tint the slightest shade of pink at my assessment, and he silently swipes left to reveal the next guy rather than rebut my point. Unfortunately for him, from this guy's bio alone—*Poly, partnered, and kink positive, so I'm just looking to tie you up, not tie you down*—he's not much better.

"Next," I tell him before reaching down and swiping left for him.

Next is Ben. *If our conversations don't bang, neither are we.*

I swipe for him again. "Nada."

Kris is promising for all of point five seconds, till I see his answer to *what is one way your friends describe you?* is *Dongzilla*.

"Nope," I say, popping the P.

Then there's Patrick. *I have hand tattoos, so you know I like making bad decisions.*

Glancing at Kason, I murmur, "If you're into that, I guess."

He hesitates before ultimately swiping left, and honestly, this is starting to feel like a gameshow.

Next to the screen, we're welcoming Logan, who states: *I have arthritis in my neck and back, but my bussy and my crack are just fine.*

I grimace before muttering, "Jesus Christ, guys are fucking idiots."

"Further proof that sexuality is *so* not a choice," Kason adds.

Another left swipe on Logan reveals Nicholas. *Pro: I drive a big truck. Con: It's compensation.*

"Absolutely not," I tell him, shaking my head, because there's no fucking way in hell I'm being woken up by some giant diesel engine roaring outside the apartment.

A disgruntled sigh leaves Kason, and he aims a glare at me. "Am I the one on this app or are you?"

My rebuttal is on the tip of my tongue, but he has a fair enough point. Still, I feel like the pickings are slim as hell, and from the few he was even entertaining, he needs all the help he can get when it comes to choosing someone even remotely worth the time.

"Online dating is…" He trails off, shaking his head. "Well, clearly, it's shit."

"I don't even use them and I could've told you that," I counter before jumping over the back of the couch and plopping down beside him. "Apps aren't gonna get you much more than a one night stand these days."

A sour look crosses his expression, nose scrunched up in distaste. "Explains why making it three messages without receiving a dick pic is a damn miracle."

"*That's* because guys our age have a tendency to think with the head in their pants instead of the one housing their actual brain." I pause, swiping my tongue across my lip before adding, "And to be frank, you don't seem like the kinda dude who just wants to get dicked down. Or vice versa."

Nodding a couple times, he mumbles, "It'd be nice to have a real relationship before I play hide the salami for the first time."

Despite the semi-serious topic, I can't help the laughter that slips out.

Clamping my hand over my mouth, I mutter, "You did not just allude to sex as *hide the salami*," from behind it.

Kason's eyes are wide as he watches me try to contain my chuckles. "I did, actually. And in the same sentence I told you I'm also a virgin."

I'd been so focused on the euphemism, I completely missed that important detail, and it only has me cracking up harder. I'm talking keeled-over, breathless laughter. The kind that eventually goes entirely silent because noise becomes physically impossible to make.

Thankfully, Kason joins in, deep chuckles coming from him too, and it only keeps me going longer.

I manage to compose myself after a couple minutes—way longer than it takes Kason—and when I clear the tears from my eyes and sigh, I find him staring at me.

"I'm still shocked you know how to laugh," he says eventually, shaking his head. "I don't think I've seen you smile before, let alone laugh. You damn robot."

Snorting, I roll my eyes. "Just because I don't like people doesn't make me a robot."

"Regardless, it's nice to hear it."

We stare at each other briefly, comfortable silence surrounding us like we're sharing some sort of bonding moment, and I'm not really sure how I feel about it.

It's just weird.

Everything about this situation is, and it's mostly because I'm torn between holding onto my dislike for him and my growing fondness. But regardless of which direction I go, there's a big part of me that would love more time here by myself, getting to study in the peace and comfort of my own room instead of one at the library. So if getting him on dates will get him out of the apartment, I'm all for it. The poor fool just needs a little help picking someone that'll stick around for more than a night."

An idea goes off in my head, lighting up like a lightbulb, and I motion toward his phone.

"Well, now that I know the stakes are even higher, since you're swiping that V-card, I think we can do better than the garbage that's been coming up on your screen."

Kason arches a brow and drops his cell to the cushion. "So it's *we* now?"

Shrugging, I try to brush off the mild slip-up. "What can I say, you got me invested in this little endeavor of yours to get laid before graduation. Sue me for not wanting you to come home depressed or dissatisfied after sleeping with one of these lint-lickers."

"Lint-lickers," Kason echoes, arching a brow. "Can't say I've heard that one before."

"You haven't seen that commercial?" When he shakes his head, I let out another laugh. "Then you must've grown up under a rock."

"Something like that," Kason murmurs, and from the slump of his shoulders and beaten down look on his face, I can tell there's more on his mind than just the shitty pickings on the app.

Not wanting to pass up the opportunity—or let him wallow in defeat—I motion to his phone resting face-down on the couch.

"How 'bout I swipe for you. Narrow down to guys that would even be worth your time. The ones looking for a relationship, not a quick lay."

He frowns. "Sounds good in theory, but what makes you think we have the same type?"

"Well, I don't really have a type, so that wouldn't be an issue," I maintain, doing my best to make my case. "And besides, I wouldn't be looking at whether they're attractive to *me*, just what they have to say about themselves. How they come across through the screen. After that, it'd be up to you to decide if you're attracted to them enough to give it a shot."

He doesn't look convinced in the slightest, and I put on my best salesman smile.

"What else do you have to lose?" I pause, before adding wittingly, "Besides the unsolicited dick pics?"

He remains quiet, his fingers picking at the edge of his phone case while my offer digests. Honestly, I don't really blame him for not jumping at it either. God knows I wouldn't give anyone this kind of power over my dating life, my best friend included.

And Kason and I? We're barely even friends. Why would he trust me with something like this, given our less-than-stellar track record?

Taking his continued silence as a rejection, I rise and start for my bedroom, only for his voice to stop me in my tracks seconds later.

"Fine. We'll try it your way."

Fuck yes.

Excitement taking over, I plop down on the couch again, planting my ass right beside his. Ready to set to work immediately, I hold out a waiting palm for his phone.

"All right, Fuller. Hand it over and go make us something to eat."

NINE

Hayes

I'm in the middle of a practice quiz for one of my finance classes when there's a knock on my bedroom door, pulling me out of the groove I've found when Kason's voice calls from the other side of the door.

"Hayes? You decent enough for me to come in there?"

What the fuck?

Frowning, I shout back, "Uh, yeah?"

I hear the door open behind me, and I turn to find Kason stepping into my room. Nervous energy radiates off him when he enters, and his eyes are cast downward as he takes a seat on the edge of my bed like he owns the damn place.

"Make yourself at home," I murmur, motioning toward the bed he's already sitting on. "Can I get you a snack? Or maybe a beverage to quench your thirst?"

My sarcasm pulls his attention up to my face. "Would you rather me just stand there awkwardly like a fucking dumbass?"

It's on the tip of my tongue to tell him it's no better than sitting there awkwardly like a dumbass, but I manage to catch myself. Barely. But I'm intelligent enough to know that my constant digs and comments aren't very in line with our truce, and I'm definitely not gonna be the first one to go back on my word by pushing too hard.

See? *Progress.*

"Touchè," I concede instead, leaning back in my desk chair. "What's up?"

Kason taps his thighs with his fingertips before rubbing his hands down them, his anxiety filling the room so thickly, I might choke on it.

"Spit it out, dude. Before you spontaneously disintegrate on my comforter."

He lets out an awkward laugh before looking up at the ceiling, almost in prayer, before he finally vomits out, "So this guy I've been chatting with for the last couple days wants to meet up at the Kappa Sig house tonight and I'm really fucking nervous."

My immediate thought? *Hell, yes.*

Kason going out means I'll have the house to myself, and that's exactly what my hope was by helping him narrow down some decent options for dates. I'm just glad to see it's finally working.

I lean back in my desk chair, doing my damnedest to not look like I'm jumping for joy on the inside.

"So, naturally," I muse, cocking my head, "you're coming to me for talking points? Make sure you don't bore the guy to sleep within the first ten minutes?"

Okay, so maybe my dickish comments are slow to disappear entirely, but I'm still choosing to think of it as progress. And regardless, Kason isn't even paying attention to my digs, because he's too busy turning more pink than a sunburnt piglet.

"Not exactly," he says slowly, now running his fingers haphazardly through his ruddy hair. When his emerald eyes lift to mine again, there's a silent plea in them.

For help he doesn't think I'll give him.

"You want me to come with you." It doesn't come out as a question, because it's not. It's written all over the embarrassment in his face.

"Only if you want to." He shakes his head, anxiety taking the place of embarrassment. "I just don't know how to do this. I really don't have the best track record either, considering the last time I went to a party to meet a guy, Phoenix was with me, and the two of them ended up falling in love instead."

Damn.

I had my suspicions that the breakdown of the relationship with his best friend involved another guy, even if he never confirmed the theory until right now.

"So you're looking for a wingman who isn't gonna be Mr. Steal Yo' Guy."

He winces at my ill-mannered joke, and I'm immediately hit with guilt.

So much for not pushing too hard.

Kason might be a lot of very annoying things, but at the end of the day, he's a decent guy. It's not his fault for trusting the wrong people not to hurt him, and it's not fair for me to throw that in his face.

"In not so many words, yeah," he says slowly. "But if it's gonna make you uncomfortable, you don't have to. I know people aren't your thing, and obviously there will be a lot of them at a party."

That's very true on all accounts, and if I'm being completely honest, the idea of going to a frat party makes my fucking skin crawl. But damn, if the guilt for making his face fall like that isn't enough for me to have the most uncharacteristic statement fall from my lips without warning.

"I'll go with you."

Kason is equally shocked, blinking a few times before he manages to find his voice. "Hayes, you don't have to. Seriously."

Shoving away the temptation to take the out he's offering, I double down and shake my head. "I know, but I'll go. On one condition."

"Why do I have a feeling I won't like what it is?"

"I was just gonna ask for an IOU of my choosing. Nothing too crazy."

He gapes at me. "Anything of your choosing? That could lead to *plenty* of crazy places, you psycho."

I wave him off, choosing to ignore his name-calling. "I wouldn't ask for anything I wouldn't do in return. It's probably gonna be me asking you to do my laundry for a month or something."

"*Probably* is the operative word there," Kason counters before he drops his head to his hands, a rigid set to his shoulders. "This is gonna be hanging over my head like a guillotine ready to drop until you finally use it. But I'm desperate right now, so I guess you have a deal."

Smirking, I rise from my chair and move to my closet. Kason's head lifts when he hears my footfalls, and I catch his frown out of the corner of my eye.

"What're you doing?"

"Changing."

Glancing his way, I find him watching me with curious eyes. "To go to a party? Why?"

I motion down my body at the sweats and ratty old Nirvana tee I'm wearing. "Unless you want this date of yours to think you room with a slob, I probably should look halfway presentable."

His attention drags down my body slowly before he nods and gets off my bed. He heads toward the door while I strip my tee off my head and grab a clean shirt from my closet.

"I'll have you know, not even Quinton dragged me to a freaking party while we were roommates. So you better damn well know how one-in-a-million this occasion is," I tell him as I drag the light blue henley over my head.

When I turn back around, I expect to find Kason nearly out the door. But instead, he's barely two feet from where he was on the bed.

I also catch his eyes quickly darting to the floor while his cheeks turn that rosie color from earlier. Only, this time, it's not the same kind of blush from embarrassment. It's more the kind from being caught red-handed doing something he knows he shouldn't.

The same kind he had when I caught him on the dating app.

The guilty kind.

Oh, this is gonna be too much fun.

"Were you just checking me out?" I ask while I cross my arms in front of me, making sure to flex my biceps that my henley already clings to like glue. "God, Kase, you're about to go on a date. The last thing you should be doing is eyeing up your roommate like he's some kind of sex kitten."

Kason gawks at me, his mouth dropping open as he stumbles over his own tongue for a response. A plethora of half-choked words leave him, all garbled in a way that doesn't make sense, and I can't keep a straight face any longer.

I burst out laughing, shaking my head as I hold up a hand. "I'm just fucking with you, dude. Calm down, you look like you're gonna piss yourself."

Correction: Now he looks so relieved, it's possible he already did.

"That wasn't funny," he mutters, his face still fifty shades of red.

"I thought it was hilarious," I tell him with a shrug before dropping my sweats to the ground, revealing my dark gray briefs. He blushes again instantly, this time choosing to turn away from me entirely.

Another laugh leaves me as I pull on a pair of dark jeans, fastening the buckle at my waist. "You really are a nervous little virgin, aren't you? Can't even look at a half-naked guy without blushing like a schoolgirl."

"I'm already regretting my decision to ask you to go," he mumbles more to himself, his head tipped back to stare at the ceiling. "It's not too late for you to just stay here, is it?"

"Sorry to disappoint, but it sure is." I cross the room, grab my belt off my dresser, and slide it in place. "You just invited me to my very first college party, and I'm not passing up the opportunity to pop that cherry."

That statement snags his attention. "Seriously? So you haven't been to a college party at all?"

He sounds shocked by this revelation, and I'm not entirely sure why.

"Nope. You seem to forget that I really don't like people. People are at parties. Therefore, I don't go to them."

"Yet, you're going tonight," he says, and I don't miss the accusing tone in his statement.

I do my best to rationalize my decision to accompany Kason when I'd never do it for Quinton in the past. But then again, Q is larger than life and he fit in perfectly fine at parties while he was in college. Whereas Kason is just *so* awkward—bless the bumbling fool. Knowing him, he'll probably embarrass himself by spraying the guy he's meeting with the keg tap or something equally as ridiculous.

Going to this party as a sort-of chaperone is basically community service.

Looking out for the unsuspecting party-goers.

And yeah, there's the whole guilt factor that's also a driving force.

Rather than giving him any insight, I step up behind him to murmur in his ear. "It really just comes down to free entertainment. No need to read more into it than that."

He turns toward me, a glare on his face that's only inches away now. "It's okay to admit you'd miss having me here, Hazey. The world wouldn't end if you did."

"Call me that again, and I'll make damn sure to embarrass the fuck out of you in front of this guy." I smile, knowing it's gotta look equally threatening and innocent. "Maybe tell him all about the jock rash cream I found in the bathroom cabinet last week."

Frowning, he murmurs, "That's not even true."

"But he doesn't know that," I sing-song before slapping him on the ass and heading for the door. "Now, let's get it in gear. We've got a party to get to."

"Stop looking so nervous."

Kason glances over at me with a glare that's far too stressed to be intimidating. In fact, it's just fucking pitiful, which checks out considering in the ten minutes we've been here, the guy hasn't stopped looking like he wants to throw up.

"I can't help it," he laments, throwing his head back against the wall we've been leaning against. "I'm not very good at this."

"You'll be fine. Just be yourself," I tell him in the best attempt at reassurance I can muster, when in reality, I have no fucking clue if that's true.

Seems like a good enough suggestion, though.

There's a brief pause before he says, "You don't even like my normal self. Why the hell would you give me that advice?"

He'd be surprised to know that his slightly neurotic, himbo ass has started to grow on me. A miniscule amount, but it's growth regardless, and that's a lot coming from me.

"That's only sometimes true," I argue, knowing it's still more often than not. "But the good thing is, I'm not the one you're trying to impress here. So just relax."

Kason doesn't relax, though. In fact, if I was hoping to assuage his nerves, I think I failed. Miserably, because I don't think I made a dent in them. If anything, he looks *less* relaxed now than he did two minutes ago before I said anything.

God, where the hell is this guy?

"Is he here yet?" I ask, checking my watch to see it's almost eight-thirty. "In the car, you'd said he was meeting you at eight?"

"He is." Kason checks his phone again. "He hasn't texted back since I agreed to coming, though."

An uneasy feeling hits me.

In my experience, if someone is gonna be over half an hour late for a date, one of two things happen. The first is that they text *before* that much time to say they're running behind, or maybe to reschedule entirely.

The second, and likely the case here, is being stood up.

Shit.

Knowing he's gonna need some alcohol to soothe this kind of blow to the ego, I meet his anxious gaze and I nod toward the back door. "I'm gonna get you a beer so you can stop looking like a creep just standing in the corner watching all these people dry-humping each other like horny teenagers."

"A lot of them *are* horny teenagers."

"I rest my case," I mutter, painting on a smile. "I'll be right back. Keep an eye out for your guy."

I'm quick to leave him, heading toward the keg set up in an area off to the side of the kitchen. Grabbing a Solo cup from the stack, I fill it to the brim with the liquid, doing my best not to give him too much foam.

A sneaky glance back to where I left my roommate reveals him texting on his phone, a deep crease in his forehead.

Yeah, this isn't gonna end well.

Steeling myself to deliver the news, I make my way back to him, beer in hand. Worst comes to worst, I could always ply him with alcohol until he blacks out. After all, if he's so drunk to not remember being stood up, does that mean it actually happened?

Oh, the philosophical musings of a college student.

A tight smile on my lips, I hold out the drink between his phone and his face, blocking his view of the screen.

"Here you go. Bottoms up," I tell him, waiting for him to grab the cup.

He does a second later, pocketing his phone and taking a long, *long* drink that could probably be considered more of a chug.

"Easy there, tiger. You're gonna get acid reflux by drinking that shitty beer too fast," I tell him, nose wrinkling up. "And no one likes the beer burps, especially when they're making out."

"Funny," Kason mutters before taking another drink.

It's clear without asking, he's coming to the same conclusion I have, and he's licking the wounds with the drink I've provided.

Still, I choose to play dumb, cocking my head and nodding toward him. "What's that sour look for?"

Kason shakes his head. "I don't think he's coming."

There's one of two ways I could play this: I could lean into my MO and be a complete dick about it…or I could try to make him feel better about the dickweed who decided Kason wasn't worth the time.

Surprisingly, I go for the latter.

"Tell you what," I hedge as nonchalantly as I can manage. "Why don't we say screw waiting for this guy and go do something instead?"

"Nah, we can just go back to the apartment," he says with a shrug. "I've already taken enough of your time tonight for no reason."

There's no way in hell I'm letting anyone who gets stood up go back home and wallow in misery and loneliness. I might be a dick, but I'm not fucking heartless.

"Not happening. You've already drug me out of the house and away from my studies with the promise of being entertained." I hold out my arms, motioning toward him. "You've yet to entertain me. So we're going elsewhere and making it happen."

"Seriously, who are you and what have you done with my jackass roommate that brought me here half an hour ago?" He pauses, frowning before he adds, "Plus, didn't you say you had an exam tomorrow?"

I did say that earlier this week, though I'm surprised he remembered. More importantly, I'm surprised he'd actually care. "It's not until the afternoon, it'll be fine." When his expression doesn't change, I quickly add, "Unless you don't wanna—"

"No, getting out sounds good," he cuts in quickly, holding up his hand to stop me from changing my mind. "What're you thinking?"

I wrack my brain for a place that'll still be open this time of night and hopefully damn near empty. Somewhere off the beaten path, where not a lot of people go. Somewhere it's impossible to think about all the heavy shit.

And just like that, it clicks.

"I know just the place."

Grabbing his wrist, I weave us through the throng of people, heading for the front door. Fresh air hits us as we step out into the autumn night, a brisk breeze sending a chill down my spine as we reach my car.

"This feels like kidnapping," Kason murmurs as he opens the passenger door and climbs inside.

I shoot him a glare after settling in the driver's seat. "I'm not even going to dignify that with a response."

After that, it's a quick twenty-minute drive from campus to the area of town Pixel Palace—the last standing nickel arcade in Chicago—is located. Kason messes with his phone most of the way, and when I'm not fiddling with the radio to find a decent station, I discreetly check his screen to find him looking at the loser's profile who never decided to show.

It's on the tip of my tongue to tell Kason to block the guy and try to salvage the night, but what's the saying? Not my monkey, not my circus? Regardless, it's not my place to tell him how to handle the situation. I'm too busy trying to make it better.

When I pull up outside the old school arcade and throw the car in park, Kason finally looks somewhere other than his lap. He stares out the window for a second, not saying anything, before he turns to me with eyes the size of saucers.

"Is that what I think it is?" he asks, the excitement in his tone like that of a child on Christmas morning.

Motioning out the window, I ask, "You mean how I'm saving the night from being a total bust? Yes, it absolutely is."

We're out of the vehicle and heading inside a few seconds later, Kason now vibrating with glee beside me. It's a far cry from the emotions he was giving off a minute ago in the car, and I have the sneaking suspicion that Mr. No Show is nowhere on his mind now.

"Well, I'll be fucking damned," he murmurs once we're inside, standing beneath a sign stating every game costs five cents, leading to a room filled with endless colorful machines all at our disposal.

"How did I not know this place existed?" Kason looks at me, now buzzing with anticipation as he heads to one of the exchange machines. "I thought nickel arcades went extinct before we were born."

I bite my tongue on correcting him that businesses don't go *extinct*, and I also keep quiet about this particular one being purchased by my father when I was in grade school.

As a birthday present.

Kason knowing the wealth of my family hasn't been high on my priority list. Not because I don't trust him with that information—after all, his best friend's dad owns one of the biggest non-country record labels on this side of the Mississippi.

It's just that the amount of wealth my family has also comes with drawbacks. People wanting a chunk of it being one, of course, which I've learned first hand. But it's the way it seems to alienate me from the rest of the world, creating a deep-seeded sense of distrust, that I hate the most.

The only trouble is, keeping this close to the chest also means omitting details that can sometimes help shape the truth, and I'm getting fucking tired of doing that.

"Earth to Hayes? Did you stroke out from all the pretty lights and machines?"

Shit.

Shaking my head, I try to roll back to the question he asked. "Sorry, what'd you say?"

Thankfully Kason doesn't seem perturbed when he asks me again how he didn't know Pixel Palace existed, instead being too busy loading up his pockets with what must be twenty bucks worth of nickels.

"Because it's one of Chicago's best kept secrets, obviously," I tell him, and it's not *exactly* a lie. Just a small withholding of all the information.

Arching a brow, he asks, "Then how do *you* know about it?"

"Quinton and I would come here a lot as kids. The first time, our father's had brought us. They'd come here a lot when they were younger, and it was something sort of passed down to the two of us." Glancing around, I'm brought back to some of the moments I've spent here as a kid, and I can't help reminiscing. "We grew up with plenty of money, so it's not like we couldn't go to the fancier arcades with the 3D rides and go-karts and whatever else, but this place had been shared through our families for a long time. Back when nickels held more value than they do now."

A small smile pulls his lips up. "It's cool that you kept coming back instead of going to the big mega arcades. Help keep a small business afloat, you know?"

Fuck. This is it. Now or never.

"My dad actually bought it when I was in elementary school. It was going out of business because of all the big, fancy places, and he couldn't let it happen." Dropping my gaze to the floor, I add, "And while it was technically my birthday present, I think it was just as much for him too."

"Your dad bought you an entire arcade for your birthday?" Kason repeats, and when I finally grow a set to look him in the eyes, I find them widened in shock.

I hesitate for only a moment before murmuring, "He sure did."

"And it's still in your family even now that you're an adult."

Gnawing on my lower lip, I nod in confirmation.

Somehow, he keeps slicing off little pieces of me without even trying. Parts I usually do my best to keep hidden, I find myself freely giving him, and I don't entirely know why.

But I still feel far more self-conscious than I have in a very long time as he gapes at me, and I don't fucking like it. Maybe because I'm waiting for him to judge me or crack some kind of joke about me giving him his money back for all the nickels he just exchanged.

Instead, he shakes his head and lets out a little laugh.

"Wow. I didn't take you for the sentimental type." His eyes narrow on me in mock suspicion. "What other secrets are you keeping from me, Bruce Wayne?"

Relaxing, I let out a little laugh. "If I'm anyone, it's Tony Stark. Minus the playboy status."

He's quiet for a minute before nodding in agreement. "That does fit better, yeah. I think the real question isn't which rich super hero you are, but how many people have you brought here to cheer up after they've been stood up on a date?"

Snorting softly, I shake my head. "You'd be the first person I've brought since I was a kid, actually. Besides Quinton, I mean." When I glance over at him, I find him staring at me in awe or something. It's unsettling, and I try to brush it off. "Just don't go telling other people about it, okay? It's called a local's only spot for a reason, and I'd like to keep it that way."

"As if I'd risk you banning me from the establishment if I were to spill the beans? Nuh, uh. My lips are sealed." He even does the stupid thing where he pretends to lock his lips and throw away the key.

Unfortunately, the motion draws my attention to his mouth, where it remains for a few moments. Not long enough to be creepy, but long enough to take in the subtle bow of the upper and fullness of the lower.

Realizing how weird it is to notice that kinda thing, I lift my gaze back up, only to find his cheeks tinted pink.

Shit, he must've caught me staring.

I clear my throat and motion around the arcade. "So where do you wanna start?"

A hellish grin takes over his face. "You mean what game am I gonna be railing your ass in?"

"Poor choice of words there, Kase," I tell him, holding out my arms to the nearly abandoned arcade. "We both know I'm the one who'll be doing all the railing. Especially when it comes to any game here."

Kason's face becomes a deeper shade of pink than before, and it makes me smirk. Despite us making nice as of late, I really enjoy getting under his skin in other ways. As it turns out, getting Kason to blush is a lot more fun than throwing sarcastic digs ever was.

"Skeeball is my game," he tells me, an air of confidence in his voice. "There's no way in hell you're beating me."

It takes all my willpower to keep from laughing as I gesture in the direction of the machines in question. After all, I'm pretty sure I'm still the one with the reigning high score on every single skeeball machine here.

Leading the way, I call over my shoulder, "If you say so. Just know that I'm pretty good about getting it in the hole."

He breaks out in a coughing fit that sounds like he's been smoking eight packs a day since he was ten, and it goes on for so long, I'm starting to get concerned.

"Are you done choking on air?" I ask when he's finally managed to stop.

A sour look is aimed in my direction. "Depends, are you done being a complete perv on purpose?"

"If it helps me win? Absolutely not."

"You're ruthless," he says, laughing now, but pink still clings to his face and neck.

"I prefer the term…*competitive*." I stop us in front of the skeeball machines and motion for him to insert the nickels. "But regardless, it's time for you to put up or shut up."

"You forget I'm a college athlete? Competitiveness is literally ingrained in my DNA."

"Care to make a bet on that?"

His attention flicks to me as the balls start rolling down the track for us to throw. "What do you have in mind?"

Like taking candy from a baby.

"Five games. If I go undefeated, you cook for a week. You win a single one of the five…" I trail off, thinking of a good alternative. "I dunno? Then I have to come to one of your games this season."

"You'd do that?"

I shrug, not wanting to make a production out of the offered terms.

"I mean, I'm not exactly a fanatic for any sport, but I've gone to plenty of Q's hockey games. I'm sure I'll pick up on football just as quickly." Pausing, I add, "Not that I have any intention of losing to you in skeeball."

He ignores my skeeball comment, instead focusing on the fact that I'd dare to compare hockey and football.

"Football is a lot harder to understand than hockey. There are *way* more rules, and—"

Rolling my eyes, I mutter, "Yeah, yeah. I'm sure a baseball player would say the same thing. Now, are you gonna keep arguing with me to stall, or are you gonna put your money where your mouth is?"

I can tell he's trying to keep from circling back to the hockey and football debate—which he thankfully doesn't.

"Terms accepted. May the odds be ever in your favor, Hazey."

"Don't worry, they are." I smirk, grabbing my first ball. Not even that stupid nickname is gonna get in my head when it comes to this. "Let's see what you got, Fuller."

TEN

Kason

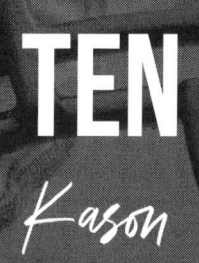

True to his word, Hayes annihilates my ass at skeeball the first few games. Somehow, I manage to sneak one win in against his four, which is all I need to win the bet, though that single win is the biggest fluke ever.

The entire time he's in such close proximity to me while we battle it out, I can barely focus on the task at hand. My eyes are too busy fixating on the way his arms flex beneath his shirt, or the taut muscles of his back every time he grabs a new ball.

With a view like that, I don't think anyone can blame me for taking a seat on the struggle bus.

He uses it to his advantage too, whooping my ass on the air hockey table, in foosball, and on some of the arcade games later on. I guess when he said he was competitive, he failed to mention he was also the world's biggest try-hard. But despite losing every single game but one, today has been the most fun I've had in a long time.

To my surprise, our evening doesn't end at the arcade, either. Hayes takes me to this hole-in-the-wall pizza parlor a few blocks away from Pixel Palace, claiming that the winner—him, obviously—was buying us a late, *late* dinner.

There's only one other table with patrons by the time our food comes out, and I get my first slice of actual heaven.

"Oh, my God," I mumble between bites of cheesy, gooey bliss. "This *so* isn't approved by the team dietitian, but I don't have it in me to care right now."

"Everyone swears by Giordano's, and don't get me wrong, it's good. But I prefer this place."

"Another locals only place, huh?"

"Always." He takes a massive bite of pizza, damn near swallowing it whole, before saying, "The less people around, the better."

"Of course. How could I ever forget your aversion to people?"

A laugh leaves him, and he shakes his head. "Glad to see you're finally picking up on it. I was starting to think I'd have to make it a little more obvious for you."

Hayes is quick-witted as hell, and his sarcastic humor is actually a lot of fun. It reminds me a lot of Phoenix, in a weird way, though Hayes is far, *far* drier. And funnier—not that I'd ever tell Phoe that.

"Can I ask you something that's gonna come off as semi-judgmental?" Hayes asks, cutting through my internal ramblings.

"At this point, I know you judge me for breathing, so do your worst."

He smirks. "Why do I never see you doing classwork?"

"I get it all done during my free time during the day. Usually I spend a couple hours studying between my classes making sure it's complete before even going to practice."

"You get it all done between classes? How many credits are you taking?"

"Full time for an athlete is six credits during the season, so that's what most of the team does in the fall, me included."

A snort comes from him, and he shakes his head. "That explains so fucking much."

"And this is where the judgmental part comes in," I surmise, though I'm not offended. I take what I can handle in season, just like everyone else on the team.

But his question does make me curious…

"Wait, how many do you take?"

Licking his lips, he replies, "Eighteen."

I almost choke on my slice of pizza. "Jesus fucking Christ, Hayes. Isn't full time normally twelve?"

He shrugs, the picture of nonchalant before saying, "I was taking twenty-one every semester until this year."

My jaw hits the floor, absolutely gobsmacked by the number that just left his mouth.

"Why the fuck would you do that to yourself? How do you even have time to sleep?"

"What else would I be doing in college besides going to class and doing course work?"

"Having fun, going to parties, hanging out with your friends," I offer, ticking the items off on my fingers.

"One, who said I don't find my course work fun. Two, as we've seen, parties are the exact opposite of fun. And three, the only friend I have lives four states away. Can't exactly call him up for a rousing night of Scrabble," he rebuts, countering all my points with ease.

"Scrabble?" I echo, arching a brow. "That's the game you'd choose? Really?"

"No, we play *Apex*. Scrabble just sounded more nerdy." His eyes flash up to mine, the cobalt color now shining with amusement. "You know, to fit with this little persona you've built of me in your head?"

"Clearly it's somewhat accurate, considering your course load," I say, holding up a slice toward him in cheers. "But hey, they do say the world is run by nerds."

His lips twitch a little. "That, they do."

The two of us take to eating in silence, finishing off over half the pizza before getting the remaining boxed up to take home for leftovers Hayes so graciously is allowing me to claim.

I guess he really meant it when he agreed to making us work as roommates.

But when the waiter drops off the check with our box and Hayes produces his wallet to pay, I frown. "You didn't need to get it."

"I said I was since I won the games and I'm the one who brought you out," he argues, handing the waiter his card. "Besides, I don't think it's fair to make the one who got stood up pay on a roomie-date."

Because, despite my immediate judgments of him, Hayes Lancaster is actually a good dude.

"Thank you for this," I tell him, my tone instantly sobered in gratitude. "Seriously. You didn't have to."

I get another shrug. "Don't mention it. All things considered, it was kinda fun." He smirks before adding, "Even if that *one* win you managed to take means I now have to attend a Leighton football game."

"A deal is a deal. Your ticket will be left at will call for the game this weekend," I muse, smirking at the thought of Hayes up in the stands without a clue to what's happening down on the field. "And that's what you get for underestimating your opponent."

He rolls his eyes, unamused. "Well, I expect the same show on Saturday, or I'm leaving a terrible review with the school paper. Maybe even pay them to slap it on the front page." Holding his hands up between us, he makes a show of reading the fiction article. "'Leighton's Star Tight End Fizzles Out.'"

I snort. "No pressure or anything, right?"

"It's my one and only football experience. All I'm saying is you better make it worthwhile." There's another damn shrug before his arms cross over his chest. "If anything, in return for taking me to the world's worst first college party."

Mention of the party has my smile faltering slightly. The dryness of his humor has gotten a lot easier to read as of late, so I know he didn't mean anything malicious by the comment. But regardless, I find myself leaning away from him against the booth's backrest while a bit of guilt laps at me like waves on the shore.

"I'm sorry if I made you feel like you had to come with me tonight." The words come out low, a bit like they're being dragged over gravel. "But I really hope you know I had a good time regardless. So again, thank you."

He arches a brow across from me and leans forward, crossing his arms on the table in front of him. "Tell me, Kase. Do I seem like the kind of person who can just be guilted into doing something I don't wanna do?"

"No, not at all." The answer comes out immediately. If I know anything about Hayes Lancaster, it's that he's stubborn as a mule and doesn't give on much. But I've also started to realize, on the rare occurrences that he does, it's something that shouldn't be taken lightly.

This is one of those instances.

"Then what makes you think you had any control over my choices tonight?"

"It's not that so much as knowing you only did it for me, and I…" I trail off, not knowing how to put what I'm thinking into words. Not just because I feel stupid saying it, but because Hayes makes me nervous as hell.

We're still on rocky terms at best, and half the time, I don't know if I'll get someone who takes me seriously or the slightly dickish side who loves to be a smartass. From the look on his face, the slightest amount of concern creasing his forehead, I'm hoping it's the former.

"Spit it out, Kase," he says slowly, eyes locked with mine.

Gnawing at my inner cheek, I finally sigh and manage to vomit out the thoughts plaguing me. "I don't want to just replace him with you. Phoenix, I mean. I don't want to use you as a crutch or whatever the same way I did with him, and with you helping me tonight, it kinda feels like I was."

Hayes leans back, mirroring my position across from me. "First of all, I wouldn't let you if you tried. Like I said, I don't do things I don't wanna do, so if I didn't want to go with you tonight, I would've stayed home. No amount of begging, pleading, or guilt-tripping on your end would've changed my mind."

"Then what made you say yes?"

He glances away for the briefest second. It's only when his eyes return to mine, bluer than the ocean, that he admits, "Because, despite our rocky start, you're kinda growing on me." Frowning, he adds, "Like a fungus or something."

I can't help the sardonic laugh that slips from me. "Thanks, I think?"

Hayes raises his beer toward me in acknowledgment. "It's the closest thing you're gonna get to a compliment, so you might as well take it as one." He takes a drink from the bottle, and I do my best not to watch the way his throat works to swallow.

Unfortunately, my eyes are glued to it.

Looking away, I clear my throat and attempt to get my head on straight. After the guy caught me checking him out half-naked earlier, the last thing I need is for him to discover me staring again.

"Truthfully, you don't give yourself enough credit," Hayes murmurs, pulling my attention back to him.

On some level, I know he's right.

If this had been last year—before I've put so much work in with my therapist to break out of the toxic cycle Phoenix and I found ourselves in—I wouldn't have offered Hayes an out. And yeah, I probably would've begged him to come with me.

I'm not perfect by any means, and I still have a lot of growing left to do, but I think it took this experience with Hayes to realize just how far I've come.

"That really was a compliment," I tell him, a little smirk forming on my lips. "I hope you know that."

"Yeah, well..." He trails off, simply shrugging before taking another drink of his beer.

We continue nursing our beers, allowing the peaceful silence to linger between us.

I glance his way every once in a while, mentally working up the courage to finally open my mouth and ask him some personal questions without feeling like I'm pushing for too much. Him taking the time to go to the party, and now this, is more than is required of a roommate, and I really don't want him to think I'm the type to take a mile when he gives an inch.

But fuck, I really would like to get to know more about him at the same time.

"Can I ask you something in return?" I hedge once I finally grow a set.

"Technically, you already did."

Shaking my head, I let out a wry chuckle. "I can't stand you."

"Feeling's mutual," he says, laughing as he plays with the label on his beer bottle. "But go ahead, let's hear it."

I have no idea how to go about this, so rather than trying, I just let the question blurt from me.

"You said you were demisexual, right?" When he nods in agreement, I force myself to ask, "How did you figure that out?"

He frowns, brows colliding in the center. "Honestly, I hadn't really thought about that. I knew I wasn't like other guys my age pretty early on. I mean, they were all out having sex way, *way* before any kids probably should be when I had no real interest in it at all for the longest time. Hell, until I was a junior in high school, I was convinced I was actually asexual. But then I met Camille."

"I'm assuming she was your first," I supply, an unwelcome feeling hitting my stomach at the thought.

"Yeah, but it took a damn long time for us to get there." He glances out the window, the tiniest smile hinting at reminiscence. "Even when we started dating, I never had the literal desire to fuck her. It took a lot for me to get to the point where I even saw her in a sexual way, and it's been the same for anyone I've dated. My sex drive doesn't shift into gear until that connection forms, but once I get there, I'm pretty insatiable."

Maybe this line of questioning *wasn't* the safest topic of discussion, because now I'm sitting here thinking about horny, sex-crazed Hayes, and it's causing my stomach to do all kinds of flips and tricks like it's a goddamn trampoline park.

Shoving those thoughts as far down as I can, I do my best to focus on the information he's giving me that's *actually* important.

I take a long drink of my beer, trying to reroute my brain. "So the demi part sort of came in when you and whoever you're with made a deeper emotional connection, right? Because that's when you started being…sexually attracted."

"That's the basis of it. But it's not like I want to fuck anyone who I have a good emotional connection with. I mean, look at Quinton," he offers in example. "He's my favorite person in the world, knows me better than any other soul on the planet, but there's absolutely no lust or desire there, even if I can admit he's an attractive guy."

I frown. "But you just said he's attractive."

Hayes takes another drink before nodding. "I did, and I stand by that. But there's a difference between someone being attractive and being attract*ed* to them."

I was following pretty easily before, but now, he's officially lost me.

"Explain, please."

His eyes study me briefly, those sapphire irises still seeing through me the way they always seem to. "Thinking someone is attractive isn't the same thing as feeling attraction *for* them. You can look at women like Scarlett Johansson or Taylor Swift and think they're pretty, beautiful, aesthetically pleasing, right?" When I nod, he continues. "See, but admitting that doesn't mean you want to sleep with them. We're too quick to lump aesthetic and sexual attraction together and call it a day, but someone who is demi is far more likely to see the difference between the two."

Nodding, I concede to his point. "Okay, carry on."

After the assurance that I'm following his logic, he continues, "Some demi people don't see aesthetic attraction at all, some see it sometimes for some people—which is where most non-demi people fall too—and some see it for everyone they encounter. The difference is that non-demi people can think someone is hot or sexy and immediately jump into bed with them without knowing a thing about them. Sexual attraction is the direct influence of aesthetic attraction. Whereas someone who is demi doesn't necessarily need aesthetic attraction, because it has no influence on sexual attraction for us. Emotional connection does instead, and while demi is far from one-size-fits-all, that's the common denominator. Does that make sense?"

"I think so," I murmur, though my brain feels like it's on fire a little bit. "Basically, emotions are a prerequisite for sex."

He laughs. "In layman's terms, yes. But why all the demi questions? Are you thinking you might be too?"

My immediate gut reaction is no, and I shake my head. "I feel sexual attraction, for sure. I think I just want it to mean something, you know?"

"So you just *want* the emotional connection before sex, but you don't *need* it," he supplies, to which I nod. "Seems fair to me."

"Exactly. And, I mean, there are plenty of guys I would've had sex with not long after meeting them, that I'd thought about in that way. Like when I saw you in the coffee shop the day we first met, fucking you was something that crossed my mind, but I had no intention of acting on it because, again, I wanted it to mean something."

The comment slips out before I have a chance to really think about what was said, but when I see Hayes pause with his beer halfway to his mouth and I do a little rewind to five seconds ago, my stomach drops straight to my ass.

Oh, fuckity fuck fuck. I did not *just say that.*

"I...uh," I stammer, looking for a way out of this nightmare I just landed in. "Obviously that...I don't...it was...not anymore. B-before, I mean."

I'm all sorts of embarrassed, mortified, and flushed, and all I can do is hope that whatever rambling just left my mouth did something to help the situation.

From the way Hayes is looking at me, as intensely and intently as ever, I realize it most definitely didn't. What's worse is this little revelation might've made this entire night—and all the progress we've made as roommates—a moot point, and he could very well go straight back to loathing me because of it.

But a slow smirk pulls at his lips as he raises the beer the rest of the way to his mouth and finishes it off. Then he proceeds to floor me further by opening his mouth and saying the filthiest, most seductive thing I've ever heard.

"And who says you'd be the one doing the fucking, there, Kase?"

I damn near choke on my spit at the comment, and I know for a fact my face has instantly turned cherry fucking red. Every brain cell I have left is telling me to abort or combust from embarrassment on the spot, and I quickly make an attempt to turn the conversation back to him, hoping like hell he won't heckle me too much about my blunder.

"How is it for you?" I ask, still coughing a little from the choking. "Attraction, I mean."

The glimmer in his eyes is more than enough to know he's debating on letting me successfully change the topic, and honestly, I think I'm due to live in embarrassment for the rest of the night.

But he surprises me for the hundredth time tonight by simply answering my question instead.

"I'm somewhat in the middle. I can look at some people and find them aesthetically attractive, and some people I don't. Again, like Quinton. But regardless of that, there's nothing sexual about it for me," he affirms, circling back to his statement earlier. "Now, that's not to say that I couldn't form some kind of emotional connection with someone I didn't find aesthetically attractive at first. It can grow as you become emotionally connected. That's actually what happened with the last guy I was seeing. In the beginning, there wasn't a whole lot that drew me to him regarding his appearance, but then we really got close and both those types of attraction sorta smacked me upside the head."

I'm well aware I should be focusing on the things he's currently teaching me, but my brain screeched to a fucking halt when he said *the last guy I was seeing*.

Because…*guy*.

"I didn't realize you've been with guys too," I say, my stomach twisting a little with a whole new kind of nervousness. Especially after that *fucking comment* that is now making me wish someone would just take me out back and put me outta my misery.

"Like how I casually slipped that in there for your dirty little fantasies?" he asks with a wry smirk. "Demi has no influence over the gender you're attracted to, only *how* attraction forms. You can be bi, gay, trans, hetero, pan, whatever it may be, and still be demi."

"Right," I whisper.

Truthfully, I'm still stuck on the *guy* comment, much to his obliviousness, because he keeps on chattering away.

"Realizing I could be attracted to guys was a shock for me, and I really wasn't expecting it. Just goes to show that there's no timeline for discovering this kinda thing. Some people go through their entire lives without understanding themselves to the fullest. Hell, if Camille and I hadn't broken up, it's likely a part of myself I never would've realized either."

Nodding while my heart rate finally slows down, I offer, "If Phoenix and I didn't have our blow up last year, there's a damn good chance I wouldn't be learning all this right now. Regardless of if it applies to me or not."

"Nope, you'd still be living in your old apartment with your bestie and completely missing out on the world's greatest roommate," he teases, smirking again. "And sexiest, apparently."

I will myself not to blush as I mutter, "Someone thinks pretty highly of themselves."

"I mean, I did take you out for a night of fun to cheer you up. And it was to two of my favorite, most secret spots," he points out, a winning grin on his face. "That's gotta earn me some brownie points in the roomie category."

"After the stunt you pulled in the bathroom, anything is an improvement."

"Funny, considering you're the one who was doing all the pulling that morning."

It comes out so casually, I almost miss it.

Almost.

Sighing, I grumble, "You're never gonna let me forget about that, are you?"

He shrugs off-handedly, deciding that's a good enough answer as any before nodding to my phone. "Now, pull up that app and let's get to swiping. We're not gonna let one ghostly asshole ruin the whole bunch."

All I can do is stare at him while I pull out my phone and hand it over, wondering when the enigma that is Hayes Lancaster will stop surprising me, because that's all he's seemed to do tonight.

At every fucking turn.

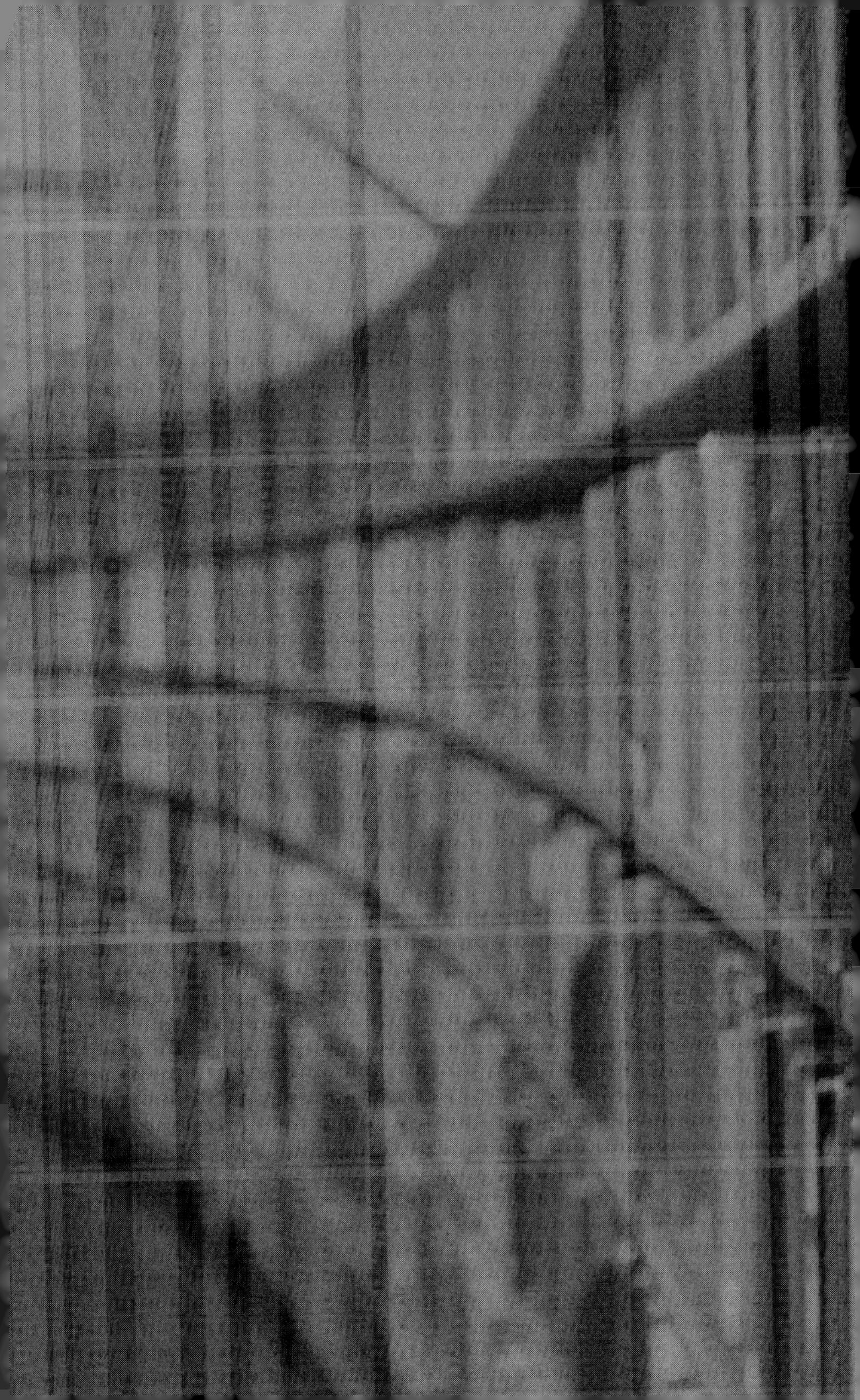

ELEVEN

Hayes

It's an hour 'til game time, and I'm standing outside Leighton's football stadium, dressed in the only LU Athletics shirt I own, with no idea what to do or where to go.

With all the hockey games I've attended to watch Quinton, I should have some clue where to find will call, but as I stand outside the massive stadium, I feel like a fish out of water.

Asking one of the thousands of passersby is out of the question—God knows I'm already damn near my limit of peopling today—so I grab my phone to send an SOS to the only person who might be available to help.

Me: Do you know where will call is at the football stadium?

It takes only a minute for my best friend to reply, thank fuck.

Q: My guess is the main ticket window. Why are you at the football stadium?

Slightly helpful, but still too vague.

Me: Okay, but where is the ticket window?

Q: By the main entrance. Why are you at the football stadium?

Well, shit.

Me: There is more than one entrance? The hockey arena only has one. Why is it so fucking big?

Q: Yes, there is more than one. It's so big because the football teams need to compensate for playing a less physically demanding sport. And FOR FUCK'S SAKE. WILL YOU TELL ME WHY YOU ARE AT THE FOOTBALL STADIUM?

Frowning, I type out my response.

Me: To watch the game? I thought that'd be obvious.

Q: You mean to support your new roomie? Glad to see you took my advice.

Me: And just like that, I'm blocking you for the rest of the day.

Q: Bet. Have fun watching the inferior contact sport.

Rolling my eyes at my dramatic best friend, I shove my phone in my pocket and glance around my surroundings again. There are people *everywhere,* completely decked out in Leighton colors and moving around me like a swarm of hornets in various directions. Some bump into me accidentally, mumbling their *sorrys* and *excuse mes* before continuing on their way like nothing happened.

Frustration coils in my chest as regret starts to sink in.

What the fuck have I gotten myself into?

But if there's one thing I'm not, it's a liar. So despite still having no idea where the main entrance is—if that's even where will call is located—I square my shoulders and pick a direction. After all, the damn thing is a circle. I have to find what I'm looking for eventually.

Right?

As it turns out, finding the will call ticketing counter was the easy part of this little adventure; it's getting to my seat that's an entirely different story. After what feels like an eternity of weaving my way through the billions of people in the stadium's concourse, I finally find the section labeled on my ticket, then the row.

Of course, we're already partly into the first period—no, *quarter*—so most of the seats in my row are already full. Excusing myself as I make my way down the row, situated damn near the center of the field, I come up to a brown-haired guy wearing a number eight jersey. He's too engrossed in whatever he's doing on his phone to notice me standing there.

"Excuse me," I tell him, a little annoyed by his obliviousness.

Then again, I've been irritated since setting foot within a quarter mile of this stadium, so it really isn't taking much at this point.

He glances up, his deep brown eyes meeting mine. "Oh, sorry. Need to get through?"

Nodding, I note the number on the vacant seat to his other side. "I think I'm the seat next to you. C12?"

"Oh, cool." He stands so I can squeeze past him before the two of us drop down into our seats.

Once settled in beside him, my eyes scan the field and sidelines in search of Kason. He said he's number eighty-seven, but I don't find him in my silent search. And all the while I'm looking, I can feel the guy's blatant stare on the side of my face. Almost like a white hot brand.

I do my best to ignore it, not wanting to chit-chat my way through my first football game. No amount of reading I did on it over the past week prepared me for actually sitting here trying to make sense of what's happening down on the field.

Are we on offense or defense right now?

"I haven't seen you at a game before," my seat neighbor finally says, breaking the silence.

Great, a regular footballer.

"First time," is all I say in response.

"You must be a freshman then," he supplies, clearly wanting to be a regular chatty Cathy.

Slightly perturbed by the assumption, I correct him. "I'm a senior, actually. Just haven't made it out to a game before now."

I shift my attention to him in time to catch his nod as he studies me. There's something in his gaze that is a bit unsettling, like he's making a mental assessment. It's only for the briefest moment before he arches a brow. "Not a football guy?"

I'm not a sports guy, if we're being honest. But what I lack in knowledge about athletics I tend to make up for in moral support for the people I actually give a fuck about—which Kason has apparently become—and that's gotta count for something.

"I don't know the next thing about football. Other than the Google research I did before coming today."

His lips pull up. "Yeah, I get that. I mean, I've watched enough football to know what's happening, but I'm more of a baseball guy myself."

"Hockey for me," I reply before tossing my head back and forth a bit, rethinking my statement. "I mean, if I had to pick one."

The guy laughs, his eyes crinkling at the corners. "Well, you're best friends with Quinton de Haas. I shouldn't be surprised that's where your loyalties lie."

My brows crash together instantly, and I get that weird feeling I always get when someone knows who I am when I don't know them—thanks, trauma.

"How do you know Quinton and I are friends?"

That earns me another grin, which only serves to confuse me more. "I think that's my cue to introduce myself." He holds out his hand between us. "I'm Phoenix."

"Hayes," I say slowly as I take his palm in mine. "But I guess you already knew that."

"Yeah, but it's nice to officially meet you." He releases me first because I'm still too stunned to do much more than stare at him. "And I guess I should take this opportunity to say thank you for taking Kason in as your roommate this year."

Just like that, the pieces collide at hyperspeed.

"Wait, you're Kason's best friend, Phoenix. The friend of a friend Quinton mentioned when he pitched me the roommate idea."

"Ahh," he says, letting out an awkward sort of laugh and wincing at my assessment—one more pained than uncomfortable. "Yeah, that's me. Though I don't know if the best friend part still rings true, but I was at one point."

A stagnant silence fills the air, neither of us really sure what to say next. How do you follow up a comment like that? I'm not a people person on my best days, and if it were anyone else, I'd let the conversation die there. Be done with it, ignore him for the rest of the game unless he talked to me first.

But he's someone important to Kason.

Someone who has lived with him, knows him like the back of his hand, who clearly cares about him. Making some semblance of an effort is the least I can do.

"Was he as much of a pain in the ass to live with when you two were roommates?" I ask, looking for a safe, mutual topic.

Phoenix aims a knowing smile my way. "Has he woken you up with the blender yet?"

"Oh, my God, yes." I laugh—a real, genuine laugh—and shake my head. "I think I was ready to toss that thing at the wall the first time it happened. And by the third, I ordered soundproofing for my entire bedroom."

"Do yourself a favor and get some earplugs too. Double up on the noise canceling."

"Already ahead of you," I tell him. "We made a *no blenders during quiet hours* rule."

Phoenix's body shakes beside mine as he chuckles. "Even better."

A grin tugs at my lips, and I decide in that moment that Phoenix isn't half bad. Which, for me, is a fucking miracle.

"Do you know where Kason is?" I ask, glancing from him to the field and back again.

Phoenix extends his arm and leans toward me so I can follow it to where he's pointing. "He's right there at tight end. Looks like he's off the O-line for this play."

I read enough via Google to know that O-line means the offensive line, and that tight ends are more of a flex player. They can block with the line, or go out for a pass like a receiver.

Now that I've found him, I fixate on his form whenever he's on the field, and stay that way through the first quarter and partly into the second. Which is why, when he goes out for a pass from the quarterback around halfway through the quarter, I witness a hit unlike any I've seen yet.

Because all the others before this, the player gets up, and everyone goes about their business until the next play starts.

Kason isn't getting up.

I'm on my feet in an instant, a bolt of adrenaline coursing through my veins as I stare down at the field, waiting for everyone to clear out of the way and see him rise to his feet. Except, when the players from both teams move, Kason is still lying flat on his back.

"Get up, Kase," I mutter, more to myself than anything, because it's not like he can hear my plea from all the way up here. A plea that goes unanswered. Instead, two medical personnel and, I'm assuming, their coach, head onto the field.

"You're a jumpy one. I'm sure you've seen Quinton take hits just as hard." Phoenix notes, though I don't miss the tiny hint of worry in his voice too.

"He was the one doing the hitting most of the time," I say absently, my eyes still locked on the field. "And I've never seen him down like this."

For about two minutes, a medical team is on the field assessing him, and I don't think a single person in the stadium makes a sound. I don't dare fucking breathe, and neither does Phoenix beside me, until we catch Kason shift into a sitting position.

The crowd starts cheering when two of Kason's teammates lift him to his feet and assist him in hobbling toward the sidelines. Phoenix starts clapping beside me too, drawing my attention away from the field for the briefest moment.

"He's up. You can sit down now," Phoenix says, meeting my gaze.

Oh. Right.

Taking his suggestion to heart, I drop back into my seat. Adrenaline and worry keeps my body on high alert as I focus back on the field, where Kason is now being helped onto an ATV looking thing behind the sidelines. After he's loaded up, he's quickly ushered toward one of the tunnels that I assume leads to the locker room.

But the game isn't over?

"What's going on? Where is he going?"

When I look at Phoenix, I find his attention fixed on Kason being carted away, a frown drawing his brows down. "The trainer is probably checking him out to make sure nothing is seriously wrong. It's pretty standard." He looks at me and gives a tentative smile, one that's likely meant to be reassuring. "If he's good to go, he'll be back out in a little bit."

"And if he's not?"

"Well—"

"He told me he wants to get drafted. That won't happen if he tore or broke something." I say this as if Phoenix isn't completely aware of his best friend's intention to go pro, but I can't stop myself. Just like I can't seem to rein in the worry that's still wreaking havoc on my nervous system.

"As athletes, we try not to think that way," Phoenix murmurs slowly. "We cross that bridge if we come to it."

"Shit. Okay, sorry," I mumble, and I do my best to think good, happy thoughts, which is not an easy feat considering the circumstances. When Kason doesn't make an appearance before both teams clear the field for halftime, I'm convinced he's on his way to the damn hospital.

"You're worried about him."

"And you aren't?" The question comes out defensive as hell, as do the next words that spill from my lips without merit. "Ex-best friend or not, you should still care—"

"No, of course I am. I just mean…you're *really* worried."

I don't know why. It's not *my* future on the chopping block here, and a month ago, I couldn't have cared less about anything having to do with Kason Fuller.

Yet, somewhere in all the roomie dates to the arcade or binge watching horror movies into the early hours of the morning or helping him charm his way into the hearts of the queer male population, I started to care for him.

Become protective of him too, it seems.

"He told you." It doesn't come out as a question. It's more of an awed statement, and I'm not entirely sure why.

"Bits and pieces," I confirm, nodding. "But I'm sure there's a lot more to it than what I've heard."

"I never wanted to hurt him." Tension lines his jaw, and he works to swallow. "I'll still always want what's best for him, and he'll always be one of my favorite people, even if we never get back to how things were before."

"Friends fight, even the best of them. My best friend and I get on each other's nerves constantly, it's just par for the course," I reason, my eyes locked on his profile. "Plus, I know he misses you. A lot."

If there's something I can be sure of, it's that.

Phoenix nods a few times, and it's obvious from the way his teeth sink into his cheek, he wants to ask for more information, but won't let himself.

Kason does end up coming out for the second half of the game with the rest of the team, but he's used sparingly on the field.

With my nerves somewhat extinguished, I'm able to focus on the game as a whole, asking questions to Phoenix as it continues. I'll be the first to admit, while I'm not a people person, having someone beside me explain what is happening is a fuckton easier than just reading about it on the internet.

By the time the game ends and the fans start shuffling out of their seats toward the exits, I realize Phoenix and I might've been talking the entire time. Mostly about the game, but a few times, we were just talking. Learning things about each other.

Weird.

Phoenix and I rise to our feet, waiting our turn to reach the aisle, and I take the opportunity to thank him for giving me a more thorough rundown of football.

"Don't mention it, man," Phoenix says, waving me off. "Are you gonna be coming to all the games from now on?"

I hadn't really thought about it, to be honest. But considering I'd go to Quinton's games whenever I had the time…

"Probably not every game, but when I can, I will. Why? Are you planning to be at all of them?"

Phoenix nods as we make our way up the stairs and into the main concourse. "The home ones, yeah. And probably a few of the closer away games." Pausing, he adds, "You're always welcome to ride with me if you decide to go."

The likelihood of me taking him up on that is low, but I thank him for the offer anyway.

"I'm going this way," he tells me, pointing in the direction further down the concourse once we reach the entrance I came through. "I'm gonna wait outside the locker room for Holden."

"Oh, cool. Well, thanks again."

Phoenix gives me a bit of a bro-nod. "No problem. Hopefully I see you around again."

Not one to drag out goodbyes—despite being a midwesterner—I leave him where he stands and head for the exit. I don't make it more than three steps, though, before I hear my name called from behind me.

"Hayes." Turning back toward Phoenix, I arch a questioning brow. He smirks and says two words that have absolutely no meaning to me. "Blue Gatorade."

I frown. "What about it?"

"It's Kason's favorite. I used to bring him one before every game, hand it to him over the wall. And if I couldn't go, I'd leave him one in the fridge at the apartment." There's a sadness woven into his tone when he adds, "It was sort of a tradition."

I wouldn't need to read minds to know exactly what Phoenix is thinking.

Or more, what he's *requesting*.

So I nod, and make a mental note to start buying blue Gatorades on my way home from class Friday nights.

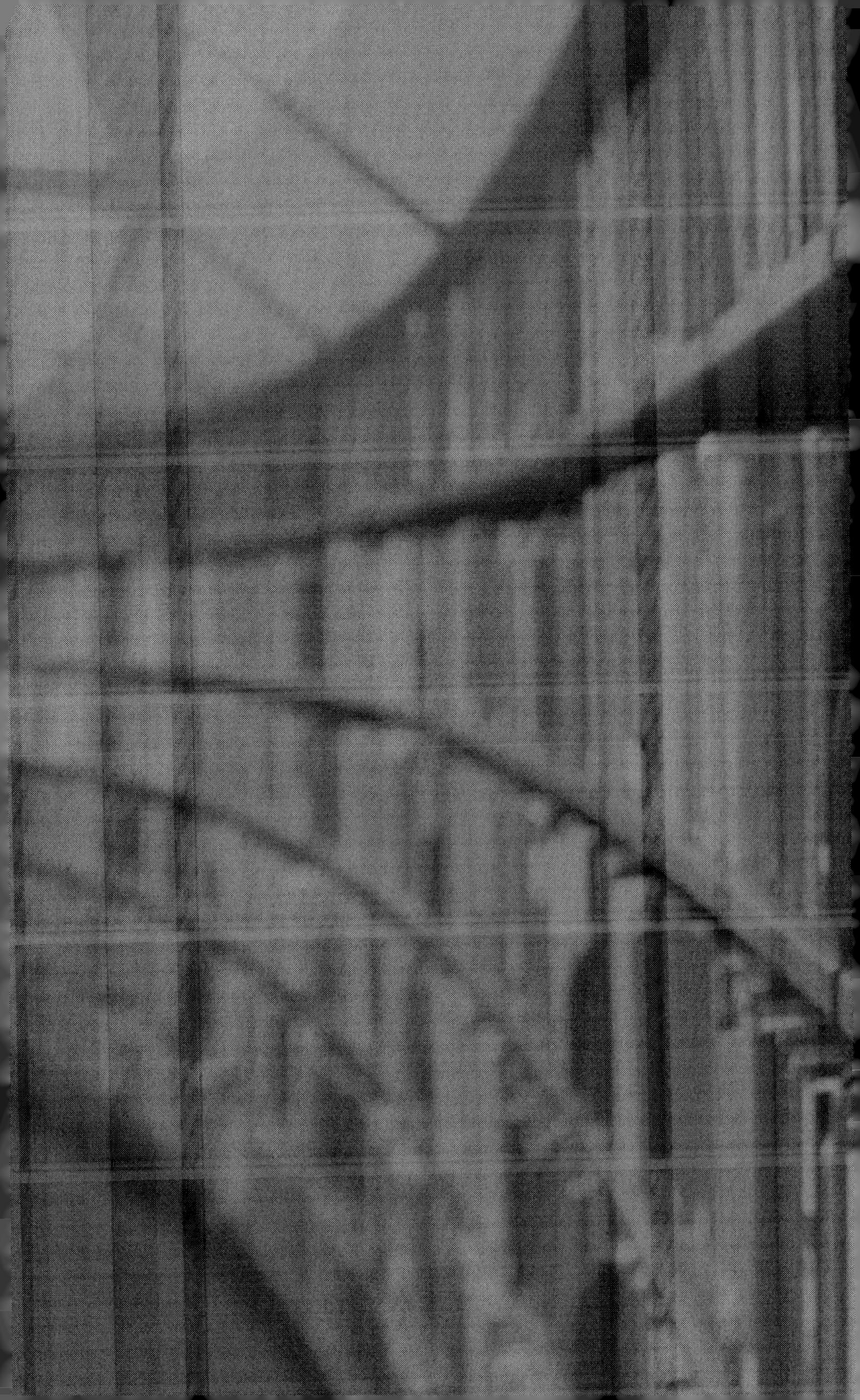

TWELVE

Hayes

The front door opens a little more than an hour after I get home from the game, and I glance up from my place on the couch to find Kason hobbling his way into the apartment. He doesn't notice me lounging on the couch right away despite having an episode of *American Horror Story* on the television.

It's not until I pause the show and drop the remote to the coffee table that he jerks in surprise, dropping his keys on the floor.

"Fuck, you really gotta stop acting like a mouse."

I blink at him. "The TV was on. I thought it would've been a dead giveaway."

His gaze shoots to where the television is mounted while picking up his keys, and he frowns. "Oh, shit. I guess you're right."

He looks all out of sorts as he limps his way to the kitchen, dropping his wallet and keys on the granite countertop. And while he's doing his best to look like he isn't in pain, the contorted features on his face give him away.

"You okay?" I ask, rising up from the couch and closing the distance between us. "I saw that hit you took, and then the medical team drove you back to the locker room."

"The trainer wanted to check me out," he says, confirming what Phoenix had told me during the game. "No big deal."

Noticing how he doesn't answer the actual question and considering he's clearly limping, I'd hardly say it's not a big deal.

"What did he say was wrong?"

He tries his best to play it off with a shrug. "It's just a minor sprain. A few days' rest and I'll be good as new."

I don't know if I want to slap him or laugh at how he's attempting to play this off. "Sprains are worse than breaks. Any athlete should know that, especially at the collegiate level."

"And I do," Kason says, arching a brow. "The question is, why do you?"

"You forget I've been best friends with a hockey player for most of my life?" I point out, crossing my arms over my chest. "I've seen my fair share of sports injuries."

"Then you should also know that with a little rest, ice, and ibuprofen, I'll be good to go by practice on Monday."

He says it so matter-of-factly, I think he actually believes it. Or maybe this jock has taken one too many hits to the head, but either way, I'm not about to argue with him when it comes to what he's putting his body through.

And yet…

"Okay, well walking around the apartment isn't what I'd call resting or icing, so go sit on the couch."

"Can I at least grab some stuff before getting comfortable?" he asks with a laugh.

"No, I'll get it." Not waiting for a response or argument, I usher him toward the couch until he drops down onto one of the cushions. I grab a couple of the throw pillows my mother insisted we have and stuff one under Kasons's ankle and hand the other to him for his back.

His eyes stay locked on me as he gingerly takes it from me, not looking away as he tucks it behind him. I feel him watching me as I head back to the kitchen, and I glance back to meet his gaze.

"What? Why're you staring?"

He shrugs. "You being nice is still kinda weird."

"Yeah, well, don't get used to me being *this* nice. This is me helping the needy, seeing as you're basically a cripple."

"Guess I spoke too soon," he mutters, chuckling from his spot on the couch.

"My point exactly." I say absently before adding, "You said ibuprofen, right?"

"Yeah, but I'm good there. I already took some meds in the locker room."

So just a drink and an ice pack, then. Got it.

Grabbing one of the many ice packs we have in the freezer and a bottle of water from in the fridge and head back to hand them off to him.

"Thanks," he says, sitting up to situate the ice over his ankle.

"No problem."

He settles in rather quickly, yet I remain standing over him like a damn nursemaid, and I don't know why. Quinton came home with injuries far worse than this during his college career, and besides making sure I didn't need to check on him for concussions, I never went out of my way to take care of him.

I definitely didn't wait on him hand and foot the way I am with Kason right now.

"I could've gotten this all by myself, you know. Set myself up in my room instead of taking the living room from you."

"It's fine, I don't mind," I tell him, and I'm surprised to find...it's the truth. I don't mind helping him. Or giving up the living room for the night.

What the hell is going on?

Clearing my throat, I nod toward the hall. "I'll be in my room, but text me if you need anything, okay?"

I don't wait for a response and head for my room, but I don't even make it to the hallway before he calls out to me.

"Wait, Hayes?"

Halting in place, I glance his way and raise a questioning brow. I'm expecting him to say he needs something else before I settle in for the night, from the way those big, green eyes look at me in a way I can only describe as a lost puppy dog.

But then he throws me off when he nods toward the television. "You wanna watch a movie?"

I don't know why I'm not expecting the question; we've been hanging out like this for the past few weeks now, but especially after the whole date debacle. Then again, I figured he'd want to decompress after ending up being carted off the field earlier, and the types of movies we watch aren't exactly the kind someone would use to unwind.

"I could be convinced," I hear myself saying. "Depends on the movie, though."

Kason purses his lips in thought before offering, "*The Conjuring?*"

"Only if you're down to do the rest of the series over the weekend."

He smirks, his brow arching. "Careful there, Lancaster. I might think you like me or something if you're asking to spend the whole weekend in my presence."

"Oh, shut up and make some room."

With a laugh, he scoots forward as best he can to make room for me on one end of the couch while I grab a few packets of Reese's Pieces from the pantry.

I toss one in his lap before dropping down in the empty spot behind him, glancing at him before saying, "We need to add popcorn to the grocery list."

He doesn't respond, instead smirking while he rips open the package in his lap.

Snagging the remote from the table in front of us, I start looking for *The Conjuring* on one of the many streaming services we have. Kason's silent beside me, but something about him is off just from the rigid set of his back and awkward way his torso is contorted.

"You okay?"

Shaking his head, he mumbles, "Do you care if I…" He pauses and makes a weird motion with his hands near my shoulder. "There's really no good way for me to keep my ankle propped up for long periods of time unless I lean back."

Oh.

Oh.

Clearing my throat, I mutter, "Uh, yeah. That's fine."

He adjusts his pillow, propping it up against my forearm and hip before settling in against my shoulder, his muscular upper back pressing against the length of my upper arm.

"Okay?"

"Yeah. I'm good," I reply, though it's not entirely true.

My arm is already tingling a bit, a tell-tale sign of it starting to go numb, and I know there's no way I'll last the whole movie like this. Still, I keep quiet and with my free hand, I continue searching for *The Conjuring*. We settle into comfortable silence once I hit play—despite the discomfort of our positioning—and the opening credits appear on the screen.

I do my best to ignore the discomfort and tingling radiating from my deltoid all the way down to my fingertips, but it's fucking hard when I'm hyperaware of every cell of my body that's touching his. It makes me realize Kason and I haven't had much physical contact before this. Come to think of it, I'm pretty sure it's the *only* physical contact besides maybe a brush here or there.

But this is damn near close to…cuddling.

"You're like leaning against a brick wall," Kason mutters, shifting so his shoulder blades are bracketing my arm.

I frown, glancing at the back of his head before asking, "Sturdy and supportive?"

"No. Fucking uncomfortable." He moves again but is clearly still unhappy with the result before he sits up and turns to look at me. "Would you rather have my foot in your lap instead?"

I'm so *not* a feet person, and I immediately reject that idea as quickly as he asks, muttering, "Absolutely not."

Sighing, he shakes his head. "Well, then you need to relax, because there's not a chance in hell either of us will make it through a movie like this."

"I can't help it that my arm's asleep already from your massive body cutting off its blood supply," I grumble. Lifting my arm to rest on the back of the couch, I grab the extra pillow and prop it up against my ribs. "Try it now."

He hesitates for the briefest moment, and I'm almost expecting him to change his mind. But then he's turning around and positioning himself in the opening between my torso and arm, surprising the both of us when he fits in the space perfectly.

Only now, we *really* might as well be cuddling.

But despite the closeness, eventually, my body relaxes back into the couch cushions, and Kason is able to lean against me in a way that's comfortable to us both. As weird as it might be—the two of us sitting like this—I'd be a liar if I said it wasn't sort of nice too.

I'm chalking that up to being touch-starved, though.

We watch the movie in easy silence after that, the only sound coming from the television and the soft munching of Reese's Pieces. Neither of us even make a single movement until the part of the movie with the goddamn creepy lady sitting on top of the wardrobe.

That's when Kason damn near jumps out of his skin, and I start cackling like a damn harpy.

"Don't laugh at me," he gripes, shoving his shoulder into mine as he gets comfortable again.

"Oh, c'mon," I grouse, giving him a playful nudge back. "You had to know it was coming. You said you've seen this before."

"Still doesn't mean I won't get freaked out!"

I chuckle some more, my body shaking against his until I manage to calm down, and once again, we're blanketed in peaceful silence.

That is, until an unexpected compliment slips from me before I can reel it back in.

"You played great today, you know."

It must surprise Kason too, because he shifts to glance up at me over his shoulder. "How would you know? You know absolutely nothing about football."

"That's not true. I did a little bit of research before I went." I nod my head back and forth against the couch cushion. "And I might've made a new friend at the game who helped me understand it a little better."

"You, making friends? I highly doubt that."

Rolling my eyes, I mutter, "There's no need to be an ass, you know. It's not the best way to keep this little *fair catch* in place."

That makes him laugh.

"I wouldn't dare. Being an ass is your job."

Damn. Kason Fuller is getting sassy with me? Living with me must really be starting to rub off on him.

"I'm a ray of fucking sunshine," I remind him. "And my new friend would probably agree with me on that point."

He scoffs, his head rolling against my shoulder as he murmurs a dubious, "Right. I'm sure."

He's clearly not taking the bait, and honestly, I'm a bit perturbed by it. In fact, I'm kind of annoyed that he didn't mention seeing me at the game in general—even if it was a deal I agreed to—and the slightly petty part of me decides to dangle the carrot a little more.

"You might know him actually." I pause, letting his mind run for a second before continuing. "Says he plays on the baseball team—which is yet another sport I know nothing about. But I guess if I'm already learning football, I might as well get that one under my belt this spring."

Kason remains quiet for a bit, and his silence sets me on edge more than this horror movie ever could.

"You do know who I'm talking about, right?"

"Phoenix," is all he whispers, the name coming out shredded and raw.

I nod, despite him not being able to see it. "Kinda surprised you didn't notice me sitting right next to him."

"I've been trying to stay zoned into the game with all these NFL scouts starting to come around." There's another pause, and I can tell Kason wants to fish for information. Too bad for him, I'm not willing to spill tea without being asked to pour it first.

Eventually, he caves, murmuring, "What'd he say to you?"

"Not a whole lot. Like I said, he mostly taught me about football. Which is a lot harder to understand than hockey." I give him another little nudge with my shoulder. "Don't ever let Q know I said that, or it will be the end of my life."

"Trust me, the last thing I'd ever want is to come between best friends." The somberness in his tone almost has me regretting the mention of Phoenix, but he does his best to brush it off by clearing his throat and changing topics. "Did you have a good time at least? I know it wasn't hockey, but…"

"Yeah, I had fun. Besides watching you get carted off the field."

"I'm not always that dramatic, I promise." I watch as he fiddles with the hem of his shirt, completely oblivious to the movie now when he adds, "I can prove it if you decide to come to another game."

"You just want your own little cheering squad made up of me and Phoenix."

Kason's low chuckle reverberates against my arm, and it does something weird to my stomach. Makes it flip-flop like a damn fish out of water.

"Yeah, that's it. Couldn't possibly be that I just want my friend to come watch me play?"

"Friend?" I echo, looking down at him. "Is that what I am now?"

"Would you rather me call you my matchmaker?" His forest gaze lifts, meeting mine. "Which, by the way, I have a couple dates lined up this week, thanks to you."

Fingers crossed they actually show up this go around.

"Maybe if you actually make a decent match with one of these ding-bats."

"First they're lint-lickers, now they're ding-bats?" Kason laughs. "If I didn't know any better, I'd say you were jealous, Hazey."

"Call me that again, and I'll kick your bad ankle," I mutter, but the threat comes out lacking the bite it would normally have. My mind is too stuck on his obscene jealousy comment.

But there's absolutely no way.

Just the thought is crazy, considering I'm still trying to help him actually get out there—and more importantly—out of the house. The first failed attempt was just a one-off. A fluke.

Shoving thoughts of Kason and dating far, *far* away, I circle back to our previous conversation.

"He's nice. Phoenix, I mean," I find myself admitting. I know it's none of my concern, and definitely not my place to get involved, but apparently, that's not enough to stop me, because my mouth keeps going. "He misses you. The same way I know you miss him."

A long sigh leaves Kason, and he shakes his head. "I don't want to miss him. Missing him feels too…needy. *Codependent,* or whatever."

"Missing someone is normal. I miss Quinton sometimes too."

"I guess," he whispers, playing with his shirt hem again. "As much as I know we both need this, I also wish it never got to this. That he could've just talked to me about how he was feeling before it got this bad."

Understandable, but…

"Would you have heard him, if he had?"

"That's something I've talked about with my therapist too." Kason sighs, his head leaning back against my shoulder. "And just like her, I know you're right."

The mention of a therapist takes me a bit by surprise; I wouldn't have taken Kason for the type to put much stock into talking through his feelings with a stranger. Oddly enough, it makes me respect him. Having some way to cope with the pressure and stress of being a college student *and* athlete would be the best way to maintain his mental health.

Adding in this riff between him and his best friend—even if it's for the best—I'm sure has only made things harder in that regard too.

"I don't think you've told me how the two of you met."

He hums in a way that sounds almost pained. Maybe even bittersweet, and it makes me regret saying anything at all. And that's before he tacks on a sighed, "That's a saga in itself."

I can feel him shutting down on the topic, and that's perfectly fine. Prying things out of people that they have a hard time talking about isn't exactly my style, and it's clear this topic is still a touchy one, even after he spilled quite a few details to me a few weeks back. So I'm not asking for anything else. If he wants to tell me, then he'll be the one to bridge that gap.

And if he chooses not to, then we'll just sit back, enjoy the rest of our movie, and—

"It was actually because of my father," Kason murmurs, derailing my train of thought. "The reason I met Phoenix, I mean."

There's a strange sort of fluttering in my chest from him shoving down whatever discomfort he was feeling about this topic, choosing to confide in me instead. Although it makes no sense, it seems I wasn't cognizant of my hope that he'd share this with me.

Treat me like an actual friend.

It takes him a second to continue, but when he does, my focus is his and his alone; movie be damned.

"He moved my mom and I to Nashville for a new job. He'd gone to work drunk or reeking of alcohol one too many times at the place he was working down in 'Bama. Promises were made to convince my mom that carting us up to Tennessee was the right move: that things would change, that *he'd* change and be a better father, husband, provider, you name it. And for a little while, he was." I watch silently as his fingers pick at his shirt in what's clearly a nervous tic while he continues. "Since I was still just a kid, I'd been naive enough to believe he could actually follow through on all these promises he'd made the two of us in the long term. But it didn't take more than a couple months for him to slip right back into his old habits."

My stomach churns. I certainly didn't picture any of this playing a factor in his friendship with Phoenix, but it must, if this is how he's choosing to tell the story. Part of me wants to know—is curious to learn more about Kason's upbringing and how he became the person he is today. But the sense of foreboding weighing on my chest tells me I'm not gonna like the answer.

Fortunately—or maybe unfortunately—Kason, once again, saves me from asking by freely divulging more of his past.

"You see, when my dad would drink, it wasn't just one or two and he'd call it a night. It'd be six, seven, eight. Sometimes an even dozen, depending on the day, and as our time in Nashville progressed, it was more often than not. That much alcohol in him, and it didn't take much to light his fuse—which was short on the rare occasions he was sober. And when Dad would get angry? Well, he needed somewhere to put it.

"In the beginning, it was just my mom he'd hit. Usually once, and it would be enough to temper whatever fit of rage he'd spiraled into. Then I think he started to like it. Get off on it, maybe. So he'd do it some more. Slap, hit, punch. Kick."

He pauses to clear his throat, then takes a long, deep breath, like he's steeling himself for the words that come next. Words that I know are about to leave his lips, yet I'm not prepared for when they finally do.

"The first time he hit me, I was twelve. It was because I broke a plate doing the dishes after dinner. He smacked me square across the face… and my mother didn't say a thing. I think she knew if she did, he'd turn his anger on her, and why would she want that, right?" His voice cracks just the tiniest bit on the last few words, and he clears his throat again. "When I came home from school the next day, my mother was gone. No call, no text, no note. Just disappeared into the ether, like a phantom, leaving her only son to take her place."

My eyes sink closed, my jaw ticking to keep my emotions in check. Because right now, I want nothing more than to throttle the woman who gave birth to him for leaving him in the hands of a monster.

Who the fuck does something like that?

"During this whole time, school was the only escape I had. But after that night, I didn't even have that anymore. I was still the shy, scrawny new kid, and now whose mom just walked out on his family. I was already an easy target for the bullies, both mentally and physically, and boy were they quick to take advantage of it; her bailing just kicked it up a notch. Didn't help that I wouldn't put up much of a fight. One of the only people who was nice to me was Phoenix.

"We'd met maybe a month before my mother left. Partnered on a school project and overnight, he became my best friend, my favorite part of the day, my only refuge from the hell I endured at home. And like I told you before, he was my protector. He'd been fighting anyone who looked at me sideways since the first day of school, but even with him having my back, it wasn't enough to help what happened at home. And Phoenix is smart, so it didn't take much for him to realize what was happening, even if we didn't talk about it. He noticed the bruises or cuts I'd come to school with and put two and two together. That's when he started inviting me around his family more. Sleepovers, weekend trips; you name it, I was invited. Like if he couldn't stop the things happening at home, he'd do his damnedest to keep me away from there as much as possible."

A raw, grated sort of laugh leaves him, and he shakes his head, the back of it rolling against my shoulder. "That's what I mean when I say he became a crutch; it was easy to accept the support, 'cause I'd never had someone do anything like that before. And it wasn't long before his whole family became mine. My chosen family, anyway. With them, it was the first time I'd ever truly felt wanted or loved or like I was worth something. Like I was safe."

The calloused, unfeeling heart in my chest cracks a little at that.

Maybe because this tale he's told me sounds eerily similar to one I've lived myself. With Quinton. The way my family took kindly to him being around all the time as kids, and would welcome him with open arms whenever they could.

And take out the alcohol and the physical violence, and Kason's parents aren't all that different from the ones Q has.

Abusive…and absent.

Two options where I'm not sure which is worse.

Wetting my lips, I murmur the only thing I can think to say. "Because you were finally being treated the way you deserved all along."

THIRTEEN

Hayes

October

I'm primed with anticipation as I shove my key into the lock of the apartment door, goodies loaded up in my bookbag, and one thing on my mind.

The Midnight Meat Train.

With October being the best time for horror movies, Kason and I made plans to binge a different, obscure horror flick—every night this month—that neither of us have watched; a feat that's proven to be difficult in itself because of how many we've collectively seen. But tonight is night five of the month-long marathon, and more importantly, *my* turn to pick.

Kason's face when he sees the title of what I've chosen is gonna be fucking priceless.

I cut my study group in the library early this evening to stop by the store to grab some snacks—Reese's Pieces and popcorn being the must haves we've long since run out of—and the movie is ready for streaming.

Everything is set to go…except Kason.

"Kase!" I call, dropping my bag on the kitchen counter and heading toward his room. "You ready for—"

I halt in my tracks when I notice Kason isn't in his room. He's styling his hair in the bathroom mirror, wearing a dark purple dress shirt, jeans, and dress shoes.

The fuck?

"Why the hell are you dressed like that?"

His green gaze collides with mine through the mirror, and he frowns at me. "I've got a date."

I blink, confused. "Since when?"

"I told you about it like four days ago, and that we'd do a two-for-one tomorrow." He sighs and drops his hands, clearly done trying to fix his hair that looks to already be perfectly in place to my eyes.

I wrack my brain, trying to think of when the hell this came up in conversation, only to come up short. In fact, after the last couple dates he went on that went horribly wrong—one catfish, the other a complete creepy clinger—he has barely made any mention of going out again, despite the few prospects I'd approved recently.

Surely him setting up an actual date with one of them would've come up between then and now.

"Are you sure you did?"

Nodding, he says, "Granted, you were in the middle of doing some reading for class—"

"So I definitely didn't hear you," I cut in, cursing myself internally. "Well, hell, I was really looking forward to making you watch my movie pick tonight. I even got a little recording camera set up in the living room so I could catch you jumping in my lap. Y'know, since you seem hell-bent on claiming it never happened last week during *Sinister*."

"Because it didn't, and I know you think you're funny, but trust me, you're not."

"You're right, I'm *hilarious*."

His eye roll makes it very apparent that he disagrees with me on that matter, and while that would normally brush off my back, I find myself irritated. Or maybe I'm just irritated that he won't be here tonight when we made these plans for our horror-thon.

I do my best to shove the annoyance down, though, and lean against the door jamb. "So which guy is it?"

"His name is Madden. He plays baseball for Blackmore University."

I frown, cocking my head to the side. "Isn't that our rival school on the other side of the city?"

"It is, but he was on your list of approved guys that I matched with. Though with only two guys left after you were done with them, I guess I can hardly call it a list."

After the last few horrible dates he's gone on, I've gotten a lot more picky about who I say yes to. Listening to him complain about how shitty they were afterward was the furthest thing from entertaining; I just felt bad for him wasting his time on fuck-knuckles that I'd approved in the first place.

"Two is better than none," I point out.

"You say that, but you're not the one who's actually going out with the slim pickings you're giving me. Which haven't been all that great so far, by the way."

Quit reminding me. I already feel bad enough.

"No, but should he be the *right* guy, I'll have to meet him eventually.

This way, he has gone through a thorough vetting process to get my stamp of approval."

That earns me another eyeroll. "Yeah, whatever. Can you let me finish up here in peace?"

Raising my hands in surrender, I leave him for the living room couch and scroll for something to watch on my evening alone. Again.

It's weird, considering the entire point of him going out on dates is so I *could* get some alone time at the apartment. But I dunno…it's like the more time I actually spend trying to actively tolerate the guy—either working on homework, hitting the nickel arcade for some friendly competition, or watching whatever horror movie we decide on—the more I seem to not mind him being around.

Or maybe even *like* having him here. It's fucking weird.

"Do I look okay?" Kason's disembodied voice asks from behind me as my thumb hovers over *A Nightmare on Elm Street,* feeling a classic tonight if we aren't gonna be doing our marathon.

Turning, my eyes scan up and down his body, taking in a better look than I got in the bathroom. He managed to rein in his dark auburn hair, sweeping it back off his forehead, the part sitting more to the left. He's in a deep plum dress shirt, which I found to be an odd choice at first when I saw him in the bathroom, but now looking at him, it actually manages to bring out the green in his eyes. Not to mention, the thing looks like it might've been tailored just for him, clinging to the lines of his chest and arms like saran wrap.

He spins in front of me, and it seems like the dark wash jeans he's wearing *also* might be made just for him with the way they mold around his thighs and ass.

My stomach swirls a little, and I quickly chalk it up to checking out

Kason the way his date likely will. And from what I can tell—and after scoping for untucked shirt tails or hairs out of place—he's more than first-date ready.

Clearing my throat, I offer him a little smirk. "You don't clean up half bad. Certainly good enough for *Madden*."

The emphasis on his date's name was unnecessary, but it's fun garnering a reaction; which I get when Kason rolls his eyes yet again.

"Thanks," he mutters dryly.

Taking a long, deep breath, he grabs his keys from the kitchen counter. And despite his attempt to calm himself, it doesn't take a high IQ to realize he's an anxious mess.

"I guess I better get going," he says after he straightens to his full height, now fiddling with the buttons on his shirt cuff.

There's not much I can do to alleviate his worries, but I do my damndest anyway.

"Look, I don't wanna make you nervous" —*more than you already are*— "but if you feel uncomfortable or like the date is going south or, God forbid, it's another catfish, I've got your back. Shoot me a text, and I'll call you with some kind of fake emergency, get you outta there. Then we can order in Thai and binge some old-school scary movies."

Kason's nose wrinkles up. "You know I'd rather eat a head of lettuce whole than Thai food."

"Well, then I guess you better hope your date isn't a total disaster." My attention lingers on him, noting the nerves still radiating off him in palpable waves. "Okay, you have to actually *leave* the apartment to go on this date. The anticipation is what's making it worse."

"You're right." He blows out a breath. "I'll let you know if I need anything, but hopefully it'll be fine."

"Take another deep breath and knock 'em dead. Or break a leg. Or whatever the hell the saying is for moments like this."

Kason cocks his head at me, brows crashing together at the center with both confusion and amusement. "Pretty sure both of those are for actors when they go on stage, not for when someone goes on a date."

"True. But I mean, that's basically what you're doing." I point out. "You're heading to this restaurant and *acting* like you're not a complete bumbling fool when it comes to dating."

A sharp laugh comes from him, though I can tell the joke didn't quite hit the way I'd wanted it to.

"You're on a roll with those zingers tonight, Hazey. Truly."

"Always here to service you, roomie."

"You're ridiculous. And a pervert."

I hold up my hands, feigning innocence. "It's not my fault Quinton liked to rub off on me."

The smallest smirk pulls at his lips, and I know I've cracked through at least some of the anxiety—which was the main goal of tossing the playful euphemisms that never fail to get him blushing the most perfect shade of pink.

Just like he is right now.

But embarrassment doesn't stop him from lifting a challenging brow. "Keep it up, and I'll make sure to plug the blender in right next to your door on Monday morning."

"Those are fighting words," I remind him.

"Exactly," he says, pulling the door open. "Enjoy your date with Freddy while I have one with an actual human being."

I've gotten so used to bumbling, easily flustered Kason, sometimes I forget this version exists too. The feisty one that fires back shots. It's the side of him I wish I could see more of lately.

Flipping him the bird, I shout, "Get lost, and remember I'm the best emergency contact you have!"

His response never comes—just the signature sound of the front door clicking shut—and I know he's off to meet Madden at the restaurant I'd recommended to him. And while I want this date to go well for Kason, something isn't sitting right.

Part of me is tempted to call him back here and convince him to cancel. To spend the night here watching old horror flicks with me, keep with the same nightly pattern we've fallen into since he called for a truce.

I don't give into the temptation, though.

Kason wants this. *Needs* this, even.

The last thing I'm gonna do is stand in his way.

Kason's been gone for almost forty-five minutes, and I've yet to hear from him.

Each date he's gone on thus far, I've always heard from him within twenty-minutes, tops. Granted, it was because things were going terribly, but still. I would assume he'd do the same thing even if the date was going well too.

I check my phone again—for what might be the fifteenth time in five minutes—only to find it still void of notifications. And though I shouldn't, I find the matter rather unsettling.

What the hell is going on?

Even my attempts at filling my night with Freddy Krueger aren't able to get my mind off it, and eventually, I give in and text him for some reassurance.

Me: You good?

I stare at the message, practically willing those three little bubbles to pop up on the screen, followed by a request to come save him from what has to be the world's most boring date. But as a minute passes, then a few more, only for Kason to not respond, another pang of anxiety hits me in the gut.

What if something is going wrong and he can't message me back?

Me: Please tell me he didn't kidnap you.

Five minutes later, still nothing.

Me: Earth to Kason. Send proof of life or I'm sending the police for a wellness check.

No response, and now we're at over an hour without hearing a thing.

Fucking hell.

Anxiously, I tap my phone on my knee and try to convince myself to let it go. That everything is likely fine, and he's just busy having a good time on his date. Hell, maybe even a great time, schmoozing it up with *Madden the baseball player*.

More importantly, I should be enjoying this time I get to myself. It's what I wanted all along, and was always the plan to make this truce work even better than it already is.

So why can't I let this go?

Maybe it's because, despite the walls I've attempted to maintain, Kason has sort of become a friend to me. And friends look out for each other in situations like this.

Sending texts for updates should be pretty standard stuff. I mean, it's not like I'm storming the restaurant to find him. Except, once that idea manages to worm its way into my thoughts, there's no erasing it. But I mean…if we are friends, it shouldn't be that big of a deal to make sure, even if it's just from a safe distance.

Right?

Well, that's what I keep telling myself as I'm walking into the restaurant he and Madden are at for their date.

I spot them near the back corner of the dining room, tucked in a corner booth. From the looks of it, they're in the middle of eating their main course, and everything is going just fine.

They're chatting and laughing, seemingly getting along, and Kason… is *smiling*.

One of the happiest, most genuine smiles I've seen him have.

See? Nothing to worry about.

Which is why I should turn around. Walk out and go home before Kason spots me and wonders what the hell I'm doing here. I'm just about to do it too—return to my own date with Freddy Krueger and wait to hear about his evening when he gets home.

But then *Madden* reaches across the table, resting his hand on top of Kason's while they laugh about something I can't hear from this distance.

And rather than seeing red, the most vibrant shade of green floods my vision.

Just like that, somehow I end up at the edge of their table, staring down at my roommate until he meets my gaze, doing a double take before his brows crash together in confusion.

"Hayes?"

"Hey, Kase!" I say, sliding into the booth beside him. My eyes quickly flash over to Kason's date. Up close, it's a bit easier to recognize him—though his looks were one of the last things I was concerned about when it came to who Kason should be chatting with on these apps.

And my first impression is…holy fuck, he has a lot of ink.

There's no way all of it is visible right now. Bits of tattoo peek out from the long sleeves of his dress shirt, covering both of his hands as well as creeping up past the collar on his neck.

I think I can even see some through the shortly shaved dark hair on the sides of his head, but in this lighting, I can't tell for sure.

All I know is, from looks alone, I'm shocked I approved this guy. Then again, photos were the last things I was focused on when I was sorting through to find the cream of the crop for Kason.

Sticking my hand out across the table, I offer an introduction to the guy. "Hey, man. I'm Hayes."

The guy's brow lifts over hazel eyes as he takes my hand in his firm grip. "Madden."

I aim my winningest smile his way when I release his hand, uttering a clipped *nice to meet you* his way before focusing back on Kason.

His eyes are already locked on me, widening imperceptibly as he cants his head to the side. "Uh, hi. What are you doing here?"

The question comes out as confused as it does irritated, but it's the latter that doesn't sit well with me. Neither does the very subtle glare that's telling me to get lost.

"Walked over to that Thai place I love, but I locked myself out of the apartment," I lie while plastering on a smile. "You care if I borrow your key?"

I'm perfectly aware Kason sees right through my bullshit, but thankfully, he doesn't call me out on it in front of his date. Instead, he pulls out his keys, slips the one to our apartment off the ring, and presses it in my waiting palm.

My skin is on fire where his brushes mine, and I quickly swallow down the knot in my throat that's appeared out of nowhere.

What is going on with me right now?

"Cool. Thanks. Gonna hit the road, but, uh, I'll leave the door unlocked for you." Slipping the key in my jacket, I look across the table. "Sorry for the interruption. It was nice to meet you, Madden."

He smiles—a perfect, dazzling white smile—and gives me a nod. "You too, Hayes."

Embarrassment spreads through me like a wildfire, licking at every exposed cell and nerve in my body as I rise from where I'd been sitting beside Kason. I can still feel the heat of his body radiating toward mine as I cross the restaurant.

Needing a second to compose myself, I push open the door to the restroom, located right beside the exit. Thankfully a quick sweep beneath the stalls confirms I'm alone, and I take a moment to finally breathe and regroup.

Resting my hands against the cool stone vanity, I stare at myself in the mirror, hardly recognizing myself.

"What the hell are you doing?" I ask the fool staring back.

And more importantly, why the hell are you jealous?

Because this isn't me. Feelings and emotions and dating aren't a priority right now. Getting through this year, making it to graduation, holding that diploma; those are the things that—

The door to the bathroom is shoved open so hard, it slams against the wall behind it, causing me to damn near jump out of my skin.

But nothing scares me more than the outrage on Kason's face as his eyes meet mine in the mirror.

"What the actual fuck, Hayes?" Kason snaps, locking the door behind him.

I compose myself as best I can before turning to face him. "What?"

"Don't just *what* me?" He takes a step forward, then another. "Why are you going all kamikaze on my date? And don't fucking say because you lost your keys, because we both know that's a bold-faced lie."

I'm struck silent as I stare at him.

At the broadness of his shoulders, the taper of his waist.

At the strong line of his jaw as tension ripples through it. The flare of anger in his vibrant, clover eyes. The freckles dotting his nose, spreading over his cheekbones. The piece of hair that's dropped onto his forehead.

At all the things I never noticed before, yet are in vivid technicolor now.

"Are you gonna answer me, or just stand there like—"

He doesn't get to finish his thought before my lips land on his.

The first brush is electric, sending bolts of lightning down my spine and through my extremities, and I'm instantly hooked. My hand wraps around the back of his neck, the other anchoring on his hip, and I haul his body against mine.

Every inch of my body presses into his, and I just...kiss him.

And it feels *good*.

Like something just clicks in place.

My fingers slide through his hair, curling around the back of his head as my tongue trails along the seam of his lips. Kason lets out a soft moan, barely more than a sigh, and his lips part before he's kissing me back.

And the second my tongue brushes his, I'm done for.

Drowning in his oaky scent, in the bite of pain from his stubble, the way his hips arch toward mine. Consumed by the strong fingers digging into my waist, holding me tight against his body.

Completely lost in him.

"Fuck, Hayes," Kason mutters into my mouth before sealing his lips to mine again.

He walks us backward until I'm trapped between the counter and his body with no means of escaping. Escape is the furthest thing from my mind, though. The only thing my brain can focus on is every delicious connection our bodies are making.

I feel him *everywhere* as we devour each other—which is the only way

I can describe what's happening, because there's nothing soft, gentle, or sweet about this.

It's all the frustration, irritation, and annoyance I'd felt when he first moved in.

It's all the pain and loneliness he's expressed to me.

It's all the tiny, seemingly insignificant moments we've shared up 'til now.

It's everything we are.

Taking charge, I flip our positions, kicking his feet apart and pinning *him* against the sink. I roll and grind my hips into him while flicking my tongue against his, our bodies moving in perfect synchronicity.

My cock strains against my zipper, begging be released from its confines, and—

Holy shit, I'm hard.

The realization has me breaking away far sooner than I'd intended, the desire flowing within me far more than I'd realized, and I press my hands to his chest to keep him from diving in for more.

And seeing his kiss-swollen lips, flushed cheeks, and wide, green eyes brimming with equal parts confusion and lust makes me want things I haven't wanted in a long time.

Both of us are panting, attempting to catch our breath as we stare at each other.

Neither of us move, neither of us do more than breathe.

My gaze shifts, flashing to the mirror behind him, and I'm shocked to find my reflection in a similar state to his, and it's a bucket of cold water.

What is happening?

Wordlessly, I take a step back; away from him and the relentless urge to haul his mouth back to mine, consequences be damned. And mark my words, there's likely to be a fuckton of them. To the point where I might've just fucked everything up all over again.

An eternity passes before Kason lets out a sigh of…exasperation? Confusion? Uncertainty? I can't be sure.

"What—" He pauses. Shakes his head. Clears his throat. "Hayes…"

Fuck, fuck, fuck.

Fear of misreading the situation has me taking another step back, then another. I keep moving toward the door and away from the embarrassment that's sure to come from this massive fucking mistake I've just made.

"I—I'll see you at home," I pant, hand on the door handle.

Then I yank the damn thing open and bolt like my life depends on it.

FOURTEEN

Kason

I'm left staring after Hayes long after the restroom door swings closed, attempting to process what kind of mental breakdown caused the scene he just made in the restaurant, let alone here in the bathroom. Yet, try as I might, there's no explanation for his interruption, and definitely not for the way he just kissed me like a man starved of oxygen.

What the hell is going on?

I don't have time to figure it out, though, because despite being hard, confused, and a little bit irritated, I still have to go back out there and finish the rest of this date with Madden.

Fuck, *Madden*.

He's probably wondering where the hell I've run off to, or worse, left while I was in here thinking I was ducking out on our date.

Equally flustered and furious, I glance in the mirror to fix the hair Hayes must've mussed up with his fingers, then do my best to hide the tent in my pants before heading back to my dinner companion. If he's still there.

Luck is on my side, at least, because my date smiles when I arrive at the table looking none the wiser. If he notices anything is off with me the rest of our meal, I'm glad he doesn't comment on it. I'm mortified enough from Hayes' rude interruption, and I don't want to make matters worse by—as Hayes so aptly put it—acting like a bumbling fool.

And there he is again, worming right into the front of my mind when he shouldn't be.

Goddamnit.

It doesn't help that whenever there's the briefest silence between Madden and I, my brain immediately zones back in on that kiss, on Hayes' tall, lean body pushing me into the bathroom sink, the ridge of his cock pressing into mine.

It's fucking torture, and every time it happens, it only makes me more irritated.

So irritated, that by the time the date is over—ending with my telling Madden we'd be better off as friends, thanks to the confusion I have over Hayes—I'm fucking pissed.

Seething, actually, when I shove open the front door of the apartment.

The living room is dark when I get inside, the only light coming from down the hall beneath Hayes' door. I let the front door slam closed behind me, not a care in the world about the noise I make, and storm toward the source. Without knocking, I shove that open too and march across the room to where he's sitting, headset on, at his desk playing a game on his PC.

His back is to me, so he doesn't notice my presence until I grab his headphones and yank them off his head, dropping them to the desk with a clatter.

"What—"

Hayes wheels around, those cobalt eyes wide when he spots me glaring down at him, and I don't give him the chance to speak before I hiss out a harsh, "What the fuck, Hayes? What was that at the restaurant?"

He stares at me like a deer in headlights, lips slightly parted, and the way my eyes latch onto them only serves to piss me off more. Not to mention, confuse the hell outta me.

"God fucking damnit, will you just answer the question?"

The bite in my tone must snap him out of it, because he turns back to his desk and speaks into his mic.

"Q, I gotta go," he says before muting it and closing out the game he'd been in the middle of. Guilt and shame cross his features the second he turns back around, meeting my gaze for the briefest moment before he looks down at his hands. "Look, Kase, I'm sorry. I wasn't think—"

"Nuh, uh. That's not cutting it," I snarl before he dares finishing whatever bullshit apology was about to leave those sinful, perfect lips. "You don't get to crash my date, kiss the fucking daylights out of me in the bathroom while I'm still *on* said date, then run outta there like your ass was on fire and think a simple apology is enough of an explanation."

His teeth worry his lower lips, and *my God,* I wish he'd stop drawing my attention back to them. Because I don't know what to think or what to feel about whatever is going on inside his head.

And from his anguished expression, I don't think Hayes has any more of a clue than I do.

"You're right." The statement comes out gritty and raw, and his gaze lifts to mine briefly, then drops back to the floor. "I wish I had more I could say than that, but I don't know why it happened, Kase. I didn't plan to, I just…couldn't not."

Couldn't not? What the hell does that even mean?

Fuck, until recently, I would've said he doesn't even like me as a human being, let alone enough to interrupt my date and kiss me.

I let out an unnerved breath and shake my head, as if that'll help me make any sense of this.

Spoiler alert: It doesn't.

"But...we're just *friends*. You've never looked at me like that, you're not attracted to me—"

"Apparently, I am now." His head drops to his hands, clearly as frustrated by this turn of events as I am. "I mean, my dick doesn't exactly lie about this kinda thing, and I know for a fact you had to feel exactly what I mean."

I did. God, I fucking did.

The press of it against my thigh as his mouth devoured mine has permanently fixed itself in the front of my mind since it happened.

But it still doesn't explain the when or the how or the *why*.

The conversation we had less than a month ago about demisexuality—and how he sees and feels attraction—comes back to me, but as much as I wrack my mind through all the interactions we've shared, I can't find any specific time or moment where things could've shifted for him.

"When did this happen?" I ask, my voice coming out rough and grated.

He lets out an agonized, "I don't know," and runs his fingers through his dark, wavy hair.

"Why didn't you say anything?"

"Because I didn't know! I don't exactly make the rules for this, Kase. It just happened." There's a flare of fury and a heat in his eyes as they finally lift to meet my gaze, two vibrant blue flames. "I thought we were becoming friends, that's the bond we were making. I don't know what triggered it, I don't know why now or why you or anything other than that since you've moved in, I've created a different emotional connection with you. One that's deep enough for this attraction to appear." He pauses, head falling into his waiting palms again before adding a disgruntled, "And apparently, my dick really fucking likes it when I'm kissing you."

There's a beat of silence that lingers between us as we both process that final sentiment. It's not funny; no part of this entire scenario is funny. Yet as I stare at my roommate who I've been doing my best not to fantasize about for *months* now—the one I'd accepted that there's no way anything would ever happen with—I can't help the laugh that bursts free.

And it's not just a single chuckle, either. It's an uncontrollable fit of laughter that has me gasping for air and covering my mouth because of how inappropriately timed it is.

Hayes looks less than amused as he rises from his chair. "Oh, fuck you, Kason. This isn't funny, and I'm not gonna sit here and listen to you laugh at me all goddamn night."

Shoving past me, he storms out of his room and down the hall. I follow him, still trying to contain my amusement, which earns me a glare as we enter the living room.

"I'm not laughing at you, I swear," I say between chuckles that slowly begin to fade.

His expression is dubious at best, and he crosses his arms. "Then what would you just call what you're doing?"

My laughter finally subsides into a long sigh. "Honestly? Confusion. Or maybe irony?" My fingers rake through my hair absently, searching for some explanation for how I'm feeling. The problem is, I really don't know what that is.

"It's just...fuck, Hayes. You're the one who pushed me into dating.

Who *really* set me up on this stupid app. Who took it upon yourself to vet these guys for me until the so-called *right one* came along, and when I finally find a guy I even enjoy being on a date with, you go and do this."

"I know," he mutters, eyes falling to the floor again. "Believe me, I don't understand what is happening inside my head any more than you do."

Silence falls over us, lingering in the air like smog over the city. It slowly becomes more suffocating, and while I don't know what to say to him at this moment, I know if one of us doesn't break it soon…

I don't know.

I don't know fucking anything right now other than Hayes kissed me back at that restaurant, and I really want him to do it again.

Unfortunately, Hayes currently looks like he'd rather jump out a ten-story window than even look at me, so I have the feeling a repeat is the last thing on his mind.

"Look, we can forget about it if that's what you want. It's not gonna hurt my feelings or whatever. And if you're not comfortable living here anymore because of this…" He trails off, gaze lifting to the ceiling like the answers he needs are etched in the drywall there. "I dunno. I guess we'll figure something out if that's the case."

My brows collide, wondering why the hell he'd ever think I'd want to move out or forget about what happened.

And that's when I realize he must think this is one-sided.

That I'm not feeling what he's feeling.

God, could this be any more ironic?

Here I was, working my ass off to ignore his pervy jokes and how dangerously attracted to him I was so we could be friends. Hell, I did my best to play off my horrifying slip-up a few weeks ago by lying straight to his face, telling him any attraction I felt was gone now.

And yet the entire time I was shoving these feelings down, our building friendship was making his own attraction grow for me.

"Can you say something, please?" he asks, eyes taking on a softness I've yet to see from him.

"I—" I clear my throat and take a step forward before starting over. "I'd like to know what you wanna do. Do you want me to move out? To forget it ever happened?"

Each question falls from my lips as I take another step, leaving only a couple feet between us. My approach pulls his attention back to me, his gaze boring into mine with the same heat I'd seen back at the restaurant. The same desire licking at me like an open flame before he slammed his mouth to mine.

But there's more lingering in those irises, and I wouldn't have to know Hayes Lancaster one bit to realize he's also shutting down. Closing off before he opens up enough to get hurt. It's obvious from the bite in his tone when he speaks.

"I don't think that's really up to me here, considering I'm the one who mauled you without prompting."

Oh, you beautiful fucking fool.

"Then let me return the favor," I murmur before cupping the back of his neck and reeling his mouth to mine.

While Hayes might not've expected me to kiss him, he recovers a helluva lot quicker than I did earlier. It's maybe half a second before his lips start moving beneath mine, his hands slipping up my chest before gripping the collar of my shirt.

My free hand grabs his hip, anchoring his body so tightly against mine, a piece of paper wouldn't fit between us, and I lose myself in the way he's kissing me. With the same hunger and ferocity as at the restaurant.

This time, though, there's no reason for it to end.

Well, other than oxygen, and it's the only reason I'm the first one to break away.

"There. We're even."

"Not even fucking close," he growls before dragging my mouth back to his.

My fingers grip at the collar of his shirt, holding on for dear fucking life as he kisses me fiercely and without a second thought.

His tongue spears between my lips, finding mine and coaxing it to life, and it's like every atom in my body has been tossed into an inferno. But I'm more than happy to bask in the flames, because this is exactly what I've wanted.

What I've been waiting for.

What I've been missing until this very moment.

Hayes breaks away first, ripping his mouth from mine and panting against my mouth.

"I know what I want. I want you to delete that app and never see any of those fuckers again," he utters, the words coming out like a harsh command. "Not a single one of them is good enough for you, Kase."

I smile, fingers gripping his waist. "And you think you are?"

"I wanna try to be." His forehead collides with mine. "For you, I wanna try. And that alone is…"

"Insane?"

He nods, nose brushing mine when he does. "Yeah. Absolutely insane."

Then he's kissing me again. Hungrily. Punishingly.

Achingly.

A tinge of desire has sparks flying and butterflies swarming in my stomach, and rather than being terrified of them, I allow them to embolden me. Wrapping my arm around Hayes' lower back, I haul him against me and walk him back toward the couch. But like at the restaurant, he quickly takes control from me, swapping our positions.

The backs of my knees collide with the seat cushion, almost causing me to stumble, while his mouth moves. First from my lips to my jaw, then my throat, as he peppers hot, wet kisses over my skin. His hands move too, mapping over my body, tracing the lines and planes of my muscles before shoving me down onto the couch, my ass landing on the leather cushions.

I stare up at him, taking in his heaving chest and straining dick behind the gray sweats he's wearing, tenting them at the front. His hand squeezes the bulge, adjusting himself, and a shot of adrenaline immediately spikes through me at the sight of him touching his cock, even through his pants.

Part of me wants him to take them off, so I can see him completely.

But the other part of me...

"Just so we're clear, I don't think I'm ready—"

"I know. Relax," he whispers before leaning down and brushing a kiss along my jaw. "I don't even plan on rounding first base. So you're just gonna have to settle for a good, old-fashioned makeout session."

When he pulls back, the heat in his sapphire eyes could melt the Arctic tundra as he crawls into my lap, thighs straddling mine. My cock aches behind my zipper, and despite my protests about wanting to get naked right away, there's a big part of me pleading for Hayes to strip me bare and have his way with me anyway.

Especially when his ass starts grinding down on my dick with every slow, seductive movement of his hips.

"Oh, shit," I mutter, my head falling back against the couch. "That feels so fucking good."

Hayes' low hum has my stomach knotting some more as he leans forward, claiming my mouth again with fervent lips and a sinfully wicked tongue.

His erection presses into my stomach at this new angle, trapped between us. The friction of his ass rolling over my length sends another sharp bolt of lust to my lower stomach, causing it to twitch beneath him. Paired with his tongue flicking against mine, teasing me, it's the most pleasurable form of torture.

"Think you can come like this?" he rasps after breaking the kiss again.

I nod, rocking my hips up into his while his teeth scrape down my neck. Goosebumps break out over my skin, and my hands tighten at his waist, holding him firmly against me while our bodies move together.

His lips pull up in a devious smirk before he murmurs a rough *good*, then dives back in.

We're all hips and tongues and hands, kissing and grinding and groping each other like a couple of horny teens desperate to get off before someone catches us. His teeth scrape over my skin, his fingers seeking as much as they can find too, and I'm doing my best not to blow my load a mere two minutes in.

"You can touch me. I want you to."

His words come out hot and strained against my throat, and I'm so caught up in the feel of his mouth on my skin, I almost miss it entirely.

My hands get the memo, though, because they skate beneath his shirt to find the skin of his back and ribs blistering with heat beneath my touch. His shirt bunches up against my wrists as I trace over his obliques, and more than anything, I want it gone.

I want the sight that greeted me that day he came pounding on my door, a lit fuse under his ass.

Gripping the hem in my fist, I murmur, "Can I—"

He doesn't even answer—let alone allow me to finish the question—

before grabbing the hem himself and ripping it over his head. I don't know where it goes after that, only that it disappears from view, leaving me with the sight I'd just been praying for.

And my fucking God, Hayes without a shirt is something straight out of my fantasies.

He's lean with muscle mass in all the right places—his shoulders, biceps, and chest—almost like the body of a swimmer, complete with flat stomach and a tapered waist that disappears beneath the sweats resting on his hips.

I already want to see more.

Hayes remains still as my gaze rakes over him, committing this sight to memory, and it's not until it finally lifts to meet his wild, cobalt eyes that he dares to move.

Wetting his lips, he grabs the collar of my dress shirt, waiting for permission to proceed.

I nod, my heartrate kicking up a notch as I watch him work open the buttons down my torso. He's quick with it, reaching the last one in no time before shoving the sides open, revealing my bare chest and stomach.

It's his turn to map every inch of my skin now, but Hayes doesn't use his eyes. His hands, lips, tongue, and teeth get in on the action too while he explores my body. Fingers tease my nipples while his mouth moves over the thin, sensitive skin of my collarbone, his tongue dipping into the hollow space while he continues rocking in my lap.

I feel him *everywhere*.

Emboldened by lust and need, my hands move around his back, tracing the tight lines and muscles on either side of his spine that lead all the way down to his waistband. I don't stop when I hit the fabric, though, allowing my fingertips to dip below the elastic and slowly move toward his crease.

Teeth scrape over my throat now, and I can tell he's smiling against my skin when he murmurs, "That's not yours," in a rough, graveled tone.

"Then show me what is," I pant, feeling more alive and reckless than ever before as my fingers circle around to the front of his pants, right above his cock. "Let me see you."

He leans back, one hand anchored on my shoulder for balance, and I find his pupils are blown with desire as his lips tug up at the corners.

"Go ahead, then. Seems like you've got that handled."

I'm not sure if he's testing me, pushing my limits, or what. All I know is that want and need is my driving force, and they aren't allowing me to second-guess my actions right now; they're forcing me to take the fucking reins.

My fingers slip further under the waistband, sneaking beneath his briefs too, and I start to shove them over the sculpted globes of his ass. He doesn't even let me push them down past it though, only enough for his length to be freed, the base of his cock holding down the elastic waistband.

And holy fucking *shit*.

That thing they say about the tall, skinny ones? Absolutely true.

My heart pounds against my ribs as he wraps his long fingers around his shaft, giving it a long, leisurely stroke. He stares down at me while he does it, an air of confidence about him that only adds to his sex appeal, and I don't miss the hint of challenge in his deep blue irises.

"Well, baby? You got what you wanted. Now, are you planning to stare or play with it?"

If I thought Hayes was filthy when he was joking around, it's got nothing on when he's serious.

My dick twitches beneath him, loving the idea of touching him myself, yet I'm too mesmerized by his hand instead.

"I think I'd rather you show me what you like," I say slowly, my gaze flicking between his cock and his eyes. "Teach me how to touch you."

He doesn't need to be told twice, dragging his palm up and down his shaft, collecting the precum seeping from the tip and spreading it back down his length. I remain fixated on his movements, analyzing and memorizing them should I get the opportunity to try them out myself.

"You're gonna return the favor for this," he murmurs, a delicious grin on his face while he watches me watch him. "I've decided that's what my IOU is."

Fucking sold.

The idea of him watching me get off is as alluring as it is frightening, but I'm down regardless. Whatever he wants, he can fucking have it.

"Later," I mutter in agreement, my breathing coming out in sharp pants. "We'll go for round two."

My fingers dig into his hips again, doing my best to keep up with the pace he's setting. Every grind of his ass on my aching length brings me closer and closer to the edge, even with the friction of my underwear being less than ideal.

And watching him touch himself while it happens?

Fuck.

It's too much, but not nearly enough.

"I wanna come on you," he tells me, the fingers of his free hand leaving my shoulder and skating over my skin between the openings of my shirt. "Right here."

Yes.

Yes, yes, fuck yes.

All I can do is nod a thousand times, one for each *yes* running through my mind at the idea of Hayes marking me like that. It was something I didn't think I'd want until now, being faced with the option.

But more than anything, I just wanna watch him.

Take in his every movement and feature, file it away for safekeeping. Just in case.

"Shit, baby," Hayes hisses, his hand moving his shaft at hyperspeed now. "If you keep looking at me like that…" Shaking his head, a harsh laugh leaving him. "God, I'm not gonna last."

The only thing I can think is *good* as I grab the back of his neck and drag his lips back to mine, kissing him like he's the very essence my body needs to survive.

Our bodies continue rocking and moving together while our tongues tangle, climbing toward release, using each other to get there. My grip on his ass and hips has to be near-painful now, but Hayes doesn't seem to mind. He leans into it, giving it back to me in turn as the blunt ends of his fingers cling to my shoulder like an anchor.

"I…I—" I pant, unable to form coherent words as Hayes' teeth sink into the taut muscle between my neck and shoulder, and the bite of pain has my own orgasm slamming into me out of nowhere. Cum jets out of my dick, filling my underwear and spreading around inside them as his ass continues bearing down on me as best it can.

Hayes finishes moments later, his tongue lapping at the teeth marks in my shoulder while his cum spills onto my chest and stomach. It pools on my heated skin, dripping down my torso while he works himself through his orgasm with rushed, stuttered movements.

My head collides with the back of the couch, lost in oblivion as I attempt to calm my erratic heartbeat. I pull him with me, his naked chest sticking to mine thanks to the cum.

But I don't care.

"So, I might've stolen second. Unintentionally," he muses, still slightly out of breath before pressing his lips to mine.

He could've stolen third too, and I don't think I would've minded. Everything about what just happened was addictive and amazing and fucking…

Perfect.

He breaks the kiss, dropping his head to my shoulder and kissing the area he'd sank his teeth into, soothing the brutalized skin.

"That was…" I trail off, unable to put how I'm feeling into words. "Who needs sex? We could do that for the next six months and I'd be perfectly okay with it."

Hayes laughs into the crook of my neck, all deep and raspy. "Trust me, once you start hitting doubles and triples, you'll be singing a different tune."

I have no doubt, and more importantly, I can't freaking wait. But I don't fail to notice he's missing one very, *very* important base.

"No home runs? Or is it just lack of baseball knowledge that's making you leave those out?"

Hayes pulls back, surprise drawing his brows up. "When the time comes."

"And when do you think that's gonna be?" I hedge, both terrified and thrilled by whatever his answer will be.

A small smile pulls the corner of his mouth up in what might be the sexiest smirk of them all—or maybe it's because *I'm* the reason for those sinful lips being red and swollen.

"Let's take it slow. Just at first. There's no rush, you know?"

I know I can do slow. I've done slow my whole life.

Except after this? Learning the way Hayes is capable of making my body fucking sing beneath his touch? Knowing how it feels to fall apart at his hands?

I don't think I *want* to go slow.

Hesitating, I ask, "Are we going slow for like a demi reason, or…"

I earn another laugh with that, and it does something stupid to my stomach, sending the butterflies in a lurch all over again.

"No, but I think you should pace yourself." Another one of those silly, sinful smirks takes over his face. "After all, they don't have home runs in football."

FIFTEEN

Hayes

After detangling ourselves from each other, we clean up separately; Kason heading for the shower thanks to being covered in both our cum, and I take to the kitchen and use some damp paper towels to wipe my chest and stomach clean.

My mind races while I absently clean myself, then the living room, running in a thousand different directions.

It's almost as if my entire body is buzzing like a crack addict on a high, and it's hard to believe I forgot how this kind of want and desire feels. Sometimes it makes me wonder how the hell I can go so long without it, because once attraction finally smacks me in the face, so does my sex drive, and my libido wants to make up for all the lost time.

And when that happens—Exhibit A being today with Kason—I start questioning if I'm even demi at all. I can't wrap my head around it, despite being the one living it, and likely the reason I didn't connect the dots for years.

But regardless of how confusing it is, no part of me regrets what just happened. Not at the restaurant, not on the couch, none of it. Yet, as I slip back into my discarded shirt and grab a seat at the kitchen counter, I can't help but wonder where we go from here.

There's no fucking way we can go back to platonic roommates or semi-kinda-friends like we were a mere twenty-four hours ago. After making out and dry humping until we both came, we're in one of those *bells that can't be unwrung* situations.

The faint sound of the running shower ceases, and my stomach tightens and coils into knots at the thought of seeing him. Which is *wild*. Insane, even, because there's never been a moment in time since we've met where Kason Fuller has made me nervous.

Irritated? Annoyed? Pissed off? Absolutely.

This is as new as it is unexpected, much like my attraction for him.

It hit me out of nowhere like a ton of bricks, and I know for certain, I haven't had this kind of bone-breaking desire for someone in a long fucking time. Or *any* desire since things ended with my ex over two years ago.

And even then, it wasn't this potent.

"Hey," a low, deep voice says, immediately pulling my thoughts back to the present.

My attention immediately flashes to the source, finding Kason standing in the mouth of the hallway, his auburn hair appearing more brown now that it's wet and pushed back off his forehead. He's redressed in sweats but still shirtless, his skin glowing red from the heat of his shower rather than blushing embarrassment like it normally is.

I catch sight of a slight bruise just above his collarbone where I'd bitten him, and I smirk at the hickey. It wasn't my intention to mark him;

I'd just gotten caught up in the heat of the moment. But now that it's there, branded on his skin, I'm not exactly mad about it either.

Nor am I all that upset about him smirking while I check him out. In fact, he leans against the counter and patiently waits—a lot longer than it should take—for me to finally meet his gaze.

"Done admiring your handiwork?" he muses, emerald eyes glittering with amusement.

Oopsie.

"I guess I didn't realize how much pressure I was using." My brows clash together while I cock my head, studying the mark some more. "I think I can definitely make it darker next time."

He lets out a wry laugh. "Yeah, I don't think so. You're lucky I don't pin you down and give you one to match."

"Threats are only effective if you actually follow through on them, you know."

"Noted," he murmurs, eyes heating as his gaze scrapes down my neck. "But as it stands, I'm definitely gonna get some questions when I'm dressing for practice tomorrow. Any ideas on how the hell I should answer them?"

"It could definitely be a bruise from your shoulderpads," I attempt to reason, my lips quivering while I try my best not to smile. "That's the perfect placement for them, right?"

Kason's brow arches, not buying my charade one iota. "A bruise that just appeared out of nowhere? I don't think so."

"Most of them have been concussed so many times, I'm sure they'll just fill in the blanks with whatever makes the most sense. Like shoulder pads."

"Definitely not how it's gonna go down, but I like your commitment to the bit." He takes a step toward me, then another, before leaning on the counter across from me. "Some of the guys might buy it, but I can name a few who'll be grilling me alive when they see it. Holden being one of them. So how would you explain what happened then?"

There's a challenge in his stare as he asks it, but it's not the kind that is meant to be intimidating. It's quite the opposite; more playful and lighthearted than anything. He's having fun with this, trying to get me to crack or squirm or bend beneath his perusal.

And what's more interesting is the amount of fun I'm having tossing it right back in his face.

I lean back in my chair, crossing my arms over my chest. "Is this you trying to get an apology outta me? Because I'm pretty sure I've proven just how hard those are to come by."

There's a brief pause before he murmurs, "I'm well versed in just how hard you come, yes."

Holy fucking shit.

I'm not sure what I was expecting him to say, but it certainly wasn't that. Or anything of that nature. Apparently, Kason has a deviant little pervy side hidden beneath all that bumbling buffoonery, and all that was needed to unlock it was a single, mutual orgasm.

And for once, I'm left speechless.

Kason takes my momentary silence to round the island, closing the space separating us until he's directly next to me. He brackets his arms on either side of me—one resting on the stone countertop, the other on the back of my chair—and it makes it impossible for me to ignore his overwhelming presence.

His bare chest brushes against my shoulder as he leans forward to whisper in my ear. "Are you even sorry?"

"Not in the slightest."

"Good." A hellish grin crosses his face when I look up at him. "I'm not either."

I hold his gaze, taking in his proximity while I search his deep, forest irises for any idea as to how he's feeling about all this. About the things I said in the heat of the moment. About how he pictures this going forward.

And I find myself equally terrified and thrilled by what that might be.

There's a beat where the two of us just look at each other, and I feel like I'm staring straight into his soul. Seeing everything I was too blind or stupid or stubborn to see before, all lingering right below the surface.

"If everything on the couch didn't make it entirely obvious," he starts, the hand on the counter reaching up to slide through my hair. "I like you, Hayes. Despite my better judgment, and no matter how much I tried not to."

I know the feeling, because I was the one sitting home alone trying to convince myself that crashing his date was out of anything other than jealousy.

"I like you too," I find myself whispering.

"Yeah, I got that. The way you kissed the daylights out of me kinda gave it away." He grins, all stupidly boyish and unfortunately adorable. "And while I don't want to put any pressure on you, I'd also be lying if I said I wasn't hoping we could repeat it a lot more often."

"I think I could be convinced."

"Challenge accepted," he whispers.

What the hell is happening?

It's like my entire world has been inverted, making no sense. Because this is *Kason*. The guy I was trying to run out of this apartment barely more than a month ago. Shit, a month ago, I was hyper focused on getting through the rest of the year without murdering the guy and passing my classes. That was all. Classes, homework, fighting the urge to commit homicide, sleep, repeat. And now I'm—

Fucked.

I'm so fucking fucked.

Oblivious to my internal ramblings, Kason dips his head and takes hold of my attention, trapping it with his imploring gaze.

"I've gotta get to bed," he murmurs while skating his fingers over my back. Even through the thin cotton of my tee, the heat of his skin trailing over mine causes goosebumps to erupt in their wake.

Making an attempt at playing off the reaction, I smirk up at him and ask, "All that work on the couch made you that tired, huh?"

"Not even close. If you want to tire me out, you're gonna have to work a lot harder than that."

"I'm looking forward to it," I utter, dragging my gaze over his face.

His lips twitch into the most sinful smirk he's ever aimed at me, and the flecks of brown near the edge of his pupil shimmer with amusement.

"We've got two-a-days all week. But I wanna talk about all this in the morning, if that's okay?"

I'm all for talking this out, making sure we're on the same page so things don't get awkward or uncomfortable around here. But there's just one little problem with his plan.

"You're cute if you think I'm waking up at the ass crack of dawn for anything."

"I'd argue that I'm cute regardless of what I think, but fair enough."

That he is, but there's no chance in Hell of me admitting it to his face. Not anytime soon, at least. I've already shown him a damn good portion of my hand; he can work for the rest of the cards.

But that doesn't mean I can't give him a tiny peek.

"You're all right to look at, I guess," I concede, dragging my gaze down his torso and back up for good measure.

It's weird, all the things I'd noticed before when it came to his appearance but never thought of as attractive until now. It's almost as if they'd started to unlock overtime, as we'd gotten to know each other.

Like his cologne or bodywash or whatever the hell it is that makes him smell so fucking good that I can discern from here, even over the cleaning supplies. It used to be annoying, giving me headaches if I smelled it for too long. Now, I could douse my entire body in it, and it wouldn't be enough.

The freckles dotting the bridge of his nose and cheekbones, spilling over both of his shoulders. The flecks of brown in his green eyes that only come out when the light hits them just right, like they are right now.

The pale scar that peeks out above his left eyebrow, only visible at the closest distance.

"You know you're staring, right?" he asks, a shy little smirk forming.

Damn. That's sexy too.

Shaking my head, I murmur, "Just taking in all the things I didn't seem to appreciate before."

"Like how much you enjoy having me around?"

I roll my eyes. "Let's not get ahead of ourselves there, Kase."

"You don't have to admit it, I already know I'm right. It's just too bad you didn't figure it out sooner instead of trying to get me out of the house at every turn." He must notice the way my eyes widen, because he smirks and nods. "Yeah, I saw right through that offer you made about helping me with the dating app."

I'm baffled. Absolutely mind-boggled that he outplayed me.

"Then why did you let me do it?"

"How else was I gonna make you so jealous you'd come storming in and ruin my date?"

Rolling my eyes and rising from my seat, I mutter, "And on that note, I'm leaving."

I move to push by him, heading for my room, but his hand reaches out, snagging my wrist before I can make it out of arm's reach. He holds me captive, our gazes colliding as he reels me in, not letting go until I'm in his arms, his mouth only inches away.

The overwhelming urge to plant mine against his is fucking intoxicating, and from the way I catch him staring at my mouth, he must be thinking the same thing.

"I thought you said you're going to bed?" I whisper, hating how soft and off-balance the question comes out.

"I am. But you forgot something."

Leaning in, his mouth lands on mine, kissing me far gentler than any time before this. It's slow, sweet, and corny as hell, but damnit, it makes my stomach flutter with a swarm of stupid butterflies that have appeared out of thin air.

The chemistry between us is as electric as it is sudden; a lightning strike I never expected to hit. Yet, now that it's here, I can't ignore it, and I most certainly can't will it away.

Truth be told, I don't want to.

My entire body is vibrating all over again when his tongue sweeps across mine, just the lightest of caresses while his hand changes the angle of our kiss. The command in it has those butterflies fluttering their wings even harder, making me damn near nauseous with want.

Kason breaks away first, breathing heavily and pressing his forehead to mine. "I'll see you tomorrow after practice, then? And we'll talk?"

I nod, my nose brushing his with the movement before I move to step back.

But once again, I don't get far, and he pulls me in for another kiss. I have to force myself to pull away after a few seconds, or it's possible a round two really will happen before either of us make it to our rooms.

Pressing my hand to his chest, I manage to actually put some distance between us again.

"You're not gonna get any sleep if we keep that up."

"It's not my fault I wanna keep kissing you."

"Well, if you can't figure out a way to control your urges, you'll be a zombie at practice because you were too busy spending the night making out with me in the kitchen."

He pauses for all of two seconds, barely thinking through his answer before whispering, "So fucking worth it."

And then his lips are on mine, claiming them all over again.

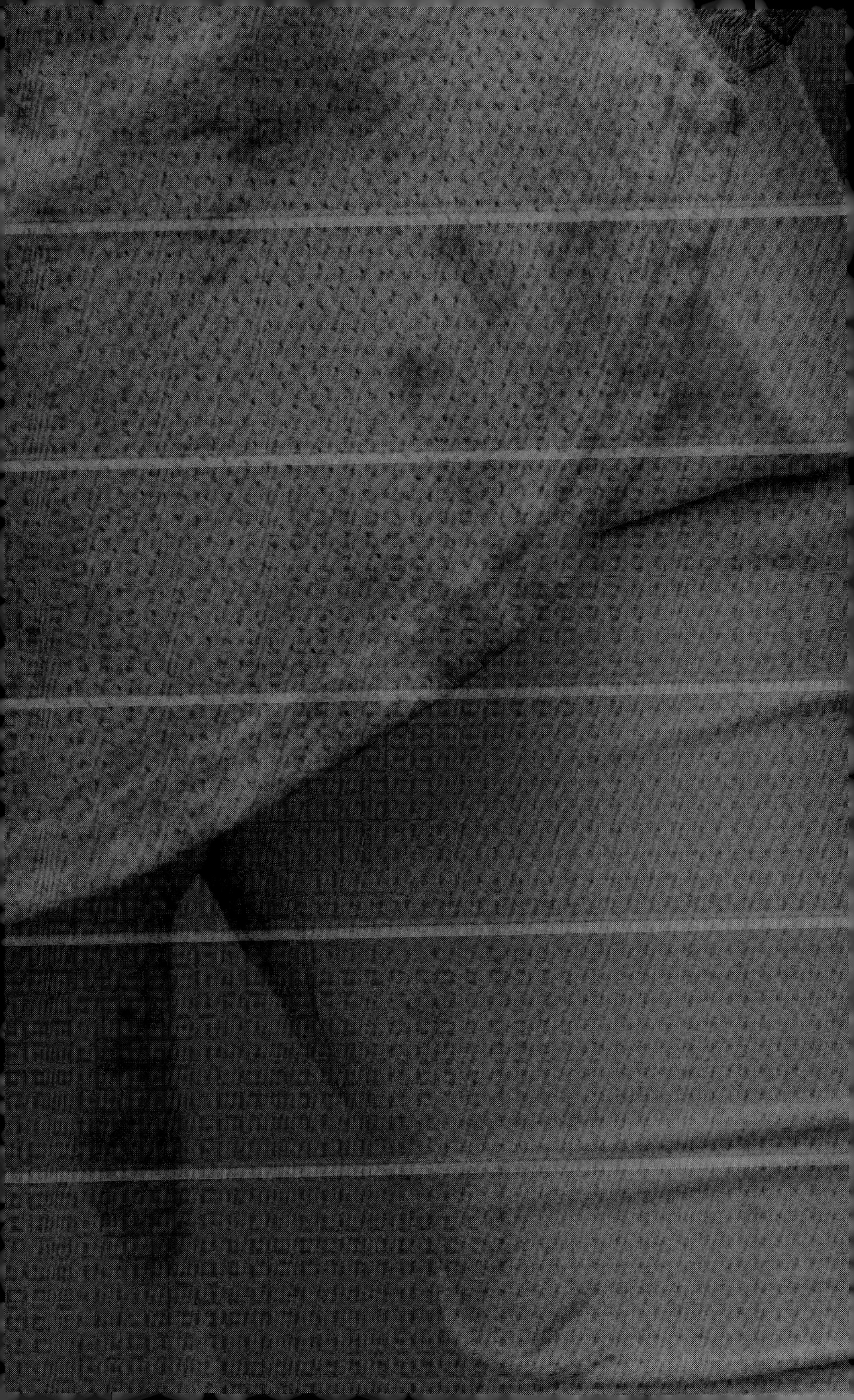

SIXTEEN

Kason

I'm out of practice an hour later than normal thanks to Coach deciding we needed to watch film after we'd showered, and while I usually don't care about that kinda thing, it had to be *today* when he decided to do this.

The one day I'm actually itching to get home.

But today only gets weirder when I do finally get home, only to find Hayes not in his room gaming or watching a movie on the couch. Instead, he's in the middle of scrubbing down the microwave like it personally offended him.

What the hell?

I open my mouth to greet him, considering he's making so much noise that he obviously didn't hear me come in, but I think better of it when I catch the muscles in his back and shoulders flexing beneath his form-fitting shirt while he works.

Those same muscles that my hands mapped and traced last night have been on my mind all day, spinning on repeat like a broken record, along with every roll of his hips, bite of his teeth, and taunting kiss he'd peppered over my skin. It's a wonder I even made it through practice, let alone my classes with all the daydreaming I did.

And now that I have the subject of those fantasies in front of me, it's taking all my willpower not to cross the room and plant one on him, talking or consequences be damned. After all, that seems to be a theme with us. Might as well keep with the MO.

But gauging where both our heads are at now, in the light of day, is the more responsible thing to do, so I keep my libido reined in and stick to innocent, shameless ogling instead.

It's not until he's completely finished cleaning the damn thing that he finally turns around, jumping when he notices me standing in the entryway. He even does the thing where his hand lands on his chest, and I pretend it's from seeing me there, not because I just scared the ever-loving shit out of him.

"Jesus Christ, how long have you been home?" he snaps, tossing the cleaning supplies back under the kitchen sink.

"Long enough to wonder if that microwave would end up pregnant with how hard you were going at it." I drop my duffle on one of the bar stools at the counter and motion toward the now-spotless microwave. "I never took you for a stress cleaner."

He frowns, crossing his arms over his chest, and once again, it draws my notice to his toned muscles—this time, of his biceps.

Get a fucking grip, Fuller.

"How do you know I wasn't just cleaning because it needed to be done?" he counters, cocking his head.

Well, that's because if the roles were reversed, I'd be doing the exact same thing.

Otherwise I'd be going damn near insane waiting on him to get back from the library or class or wherever else, brimming with nervous energy. And no matter how much Hayes wishes he could hide that he's feeling it, I can see it in his eyes as he looks at me. They aren't their usual sharp, crisp cobalt. There's a softness around the edges that's usually not there.

"We're a lot more alike than you'd care to admit, Hayes," I murmur, leaning forward on the counter. "So while I'm doing my best to play it cool, in reality, I've spent the entire day thinking about last night. About what it means for us going forward. And I have the feeling you're in a pretty similar place."

"You're not wrong, even if it might kill me to admit it."

I offer him the same out he offered me yesterday after I'd returned from my date—which, fuck, already feels like a lifetime ago. It's an out I'm praying to any god who will listen that he doesn't use it, but I'm prepared regardless.

"So should we talk about it, get it all out in the open? Or would you rather pretend it never happened and go back to being roommates?"

"I don't want to pretend that it didn't happen," he murmurs, his eyes locked on the granite counter. "But I also worry I might've set a precedent last night that I can't keep up."

My brows collide in a frown. "What do you mean?"

Hayes' teeth roll over his lower lip before he finally lifts his gaze to mine, and I think this is the most docile I've ever seen him. Gone is the dry-humored, snarky dick filled with banter that would make most people start swinging.

The guy in front of me is nothing if not completely vulnerable.

"This might've come out of nowhere for both of us, and last night might've been very lust driven, but I need to be clear with you. I'm not built for casual sex. I know I said a repeat was on the table, but there are stipulations when it comes to that. Like exclusivity, or nothing at all." His hands lift in a helpless sort of shrug. "I just can't do it any other way."

I blink at him, wondering where things got lost in translation. Because the way he's making it sound, it's almost like he expects me to fight for some casual, meaningless fling. Like he hasn't watched me crash and burn on multiple dates with these random internet guys trying to find the very opposite.

The thought has me stumbling for a second, and it's like a lightbulb switches on.

"Exclusivity," I repeat, echoing his sentiment. "So when you said you wanted me to delete the app, that wasn't just the heat of the moment talking."

He's silent for a moment before he mutters, "No. I meant it."

Well, fuck. That's an easy fix.

I study him for a moment before pulling out my phone, dropping it on the counter between us, and with a few quick swipes, the app is both deleted and uninstalled.

"There. Done," I tell him, shoving the phone over for him to see.

He blinks, shaking his head. "That wasn't me giving you some kind of ultimatum or—"

"Look, at the risk of looking like a complete fucking idiot in front of you for what might be the millionth time…there's no one else I'm even remotely interested in. So whatever this thing is between us, I wanna see where it can go. If that's what you want too."

Hayes just stares at me, unmoving, and it's almost as if he's shuttered all his emotions.

The silence is deafening, and the longer we stand here and look at each other, the more anxious it makes me.

Taking a tentative step around the counter, then another, I slowly close the space between us. He watches me the whole way, those royal blue eyes fixated on my face never wavering.

There's never been a moment I've wished I could read someone's mind more.

"Please, say something."

His lips part for a second before a tiny smile creeps up at the edges. "I think I'm just in shock that I won't have to battle with all those dudebro dickweeds on that stupid app."

What?

"You just said you don't do anything other than exclusivity," I point out, unable to hide my confusion.

He scoffs, brows arching. "That doesn't mean I would go down without a fight. Have you met me?"

I can't help it; I start laughing. Because I most definitely have, and at this moment, I don't think I could be more grateful.

"Trust me," I assure him, my hand locking around the back of his neck. "There's no competition."

I close the distance between us, my mouth landing on his in a kiss that's meant to be sweet and gentle, like the start of something new. And while it may begin that way, Hayes quickly takes it to a whole new level when his tongue skates over my lower lip.

Fuck, that's so hot.

All the sweet and gentle is gone after that, replaced with hunger and need as we devour each other. His fingers slide into my hair as I back him into the counter, my hips pinning him to the granite as our mouths explore some more. My cock aches, desperate for more friction from where it's trapped against his thigh, and the second I feel his coming to life too, I break away.

Panting against his lips, I murmur, "I meant what I said last night. I don't want to pressure you or make you think the only thing I want from you is sex, but—"

His fingers tighten in my hair and he shakes his head. "Bedroom. Now."

Thank fucking God.

"Mine or yours?"

"Does it fucking matter?" he mutters before grabbing my wrist and hauling me toward his room. I go willingly, my heart hammering in my chest harder than it was an hour ago at practice.

Anticipation has my entire being vibrating with need as Hayes closes us in his bedroom, and it only builds more when he grabs my shirt and yanks it over my head without any preamble. His is gone seconds later too, along with his jeans, leaving him only in a pair of tight, emerald briefs while I slowly strip down to match him.

I take the opportunity to map his near-naked form, unable to stop myself.

"God, how do you look this good when you're not an athlete?" I mumble, my fingers greedily tracing the valleys between his abs and the defined ridges of his pecs.

The question being more of a rhetorical one than anything, Hayes answers it anyway, grinning as he pushes me toward the bed.

"Normal people go to the gym too, you know. Even the nerdy ones."

"So that's where you were all those hours you were avoiding me," I muse, dragging him to the mattress with me. He lands over top of me with a thud "And here I thought you would be holing up in the library reading Tort Law just to pass the time."

He shakes his head, brushing a kiss over my jaw. "Nope, but I did memorize the first three hundred digits of pi."

"Tell me you're joking."

"Not at all," he mutters, pressing a kiss to my mouth again. "It's called balance."

This guy. I swear, he's planning to surprise me at every turn.

There's little talking after that, his tongue diving between my lips and stealing my ability to think, let alone speak. My hands skate over the smooth expanses of his back and shoulders while he rolls his hips down into mine. Our bodies move in sync with each other, grinding and groping with fevered enthusiasm while our mouths fuse down to the cellular level.

And fuck, I might come in my underwear for the second night in a row at this point.

Hayes has other plans, though, because he breaks the kiss, licking and nipping at my jaw and throat before he whispers against my skin.

"How far do you want this to go?"

I hadn't really thought about it, only that I'm desperate to get my hands and mouth on him again. I know I'm not ready for actual sex, but I'm not against anything else.

"I...don't know," I say slowly, realizing that's probably not the answer he's looking for.

His mouth continues trailing over my neck, working down to my collarbone as he ruts against me, the friction from our dicks rubbing through our underwear making it hard to focus on his questions.

"Well, would you rather give or receive?"

I shake my head, hands clinging to his shoulder. "I don't know."

His mouth is at my nipple now, tongue licking around the tight bud before taking it between his teeth.

"How do you like to be touched?" he murmurs once he releases it, only to move to the other.

Fuck.

"I don't know that either."

He stops suddenly and leans back, looking down at me. Letting out a frustrated laugh, he rakes his fingers through his dark hair. "What the hell *do* you know, Kase? I gotta know where to start."

"That I have no idea what I'm doing, so why don't you stop asking me questions and just fucking *teach* me?"

The words leave my mouth with exasperation, full of so much flustered emotion, it leaves Hayes momentarily speechless. Stunned into silence as he stares at me beneath him, naked save for my briefs.

But then he starts laughing, and I'm instantly mortified.

I feel the heat creeping up my neck and chest, embarrassment visibly tinting my skin like it always seems to when it comes to Hayes. Only, instead of choosing to smirk and ignore it the way he normally does, he just keeps laughing.

"If this is payback, it really isn't fucking funny." I look away, unable to meet his gaze. "At least you weren't almost fucking naked when I did it."

It isn't enough to stop him from laughing, though, and now I understand why he bolted when the roles were reversed. Because that's exactly what I plan to do now, slipping out from beneath him and heading to the door.

"Hey. Kase, stop. I know it's not funny."

My hand is on the handle when he grabs my other wrist to keep me from leaving. Spinning to face him, I find a smile still on his face, his chest rumbling with soft chuckles.

"And yet, you're laughing," I grumble miserably, my head dropping back against the door behind me.

"Because I'm…" he trails off, clearly in search of the words to not make this any worse. And I'm even more stunned the moment it leaves his mouth. "I'm nervous."

I arch a disbelieving brow. "*You're* the one who's nervous? At least you've fucking had sex before."

"Yeah, sure, but this isn't exactly territory I've explored either, you know. You've waited this long to have all your firsts with someone, and I don't…" He cuts himself short, but I can read the unspoken worry in his expression, and do my best to fill in the blanks for myself.

Don't want to make it bad for you.

Don't trust myself with something as important to you as this.

Don't want you to regret it.

I'd be willing to bet my life one—hell, maybe all—of those thoughts are racing through his head right now.

Stepping in closer to him, I snake my fingers through the hair at the base of his skull and shake my head. "You won't, Hayes. I swear it."

The certainty in my voice causes him to waver, but not enough. The worry, the fear, the anxiety is all still right there, ready to boil over.

"You said you want this to mean something."

I nod, searching his eyes. "And with you, it will."

I'm not sure if it's the conviction in the words, or something else, but the doubt in his gaze morphs from pensive to smoldering, ratcheting the temperature in his bedroom up a few degrees. The sexual tension is damn near stifling as it blankets us, and it only gets more potent when he uses the hold he still has on my wrist to pull me deeper into his room again.

Only when we're stopped at the edge of his bed does he release me.

Then he wordlessly drops his underwear to the floor, giving me my first view of him completely naked.

And my God, if I thought the sight of him on my lap last night, stroking himself until he came, was something out of my dirtiest dreams, I was fucking mistaken.

This is a whole new level of fantasy my imagination could never even conjure.

"What are you doing?" I ask, my words coming out strained and breathless.

I force my gaze away from the thick length of his cock and up to his eyes to find him watching me, a little smirk on his lips.

"Teaching you," he whispers, the statement coming out raspy. "So, take off your boxers."

SEVENTEEN

Kason

My stomach knots and coils in anticipation, the words *teaching you* sounding far filthier coming from his lips than they have any right to. It has my dick twitching with desire, my balls drawing up with want as I follow his command and shove my underwear to the floor.

His gaze scrapes down my naked body, nostrils flaring when it reaches my waist, and if I thought I was vibrating with anticipation before, then I'm ready to explode with it now.

And that's before he makes a command that has my legs buckling beneath me.

"Now, get on your knees."

Doing as he says, I slowly drop to the ground in front of him until I'm face to face with his erection. My hand twitches with the instinct to reach out and wrap my palm around it, and the pull is so strong, I can't fight it.

Curling my fingers at the base, I give him a long, slow stroke, then another, testing the waters.

"That's good, but that's not where I want it." The words come out in a low, seductive timbre, and I glance up to find him smirking at me. "Use your mouth."

Licking my lips, I lean in and wrap them around the head of his cock, keeping my eyes locked with Hayes' cobalt stare the entire time. Tentatively, I swirl my tongue around the tip, licking like he's a lollipop before hollowing my checks to suck.

The technique must work, because I feel his dick twitch in my mouth before a salty bead of precum hits my tastebuds.

It's unfamiliar, but not at all unwelcome.

Feeling emboldened by his obvious arousal, I open my mouth wide, allowing more of his length to slide over my tongue, but I don't get more than a couple inches before my gag reflex kicks in, forcing me to pull off him.

"Don't worry about taking it all, deep throating can be saved for another day. Just let your instincts guide you. Breathe through your nose," he murmurs, his hand caressing my jaw. "And watch your teeth, okay?"

Nodding, I dive in for more, repeating what I did at first before taking him in a little further, finding that focusing on my breathing helps. Then I go a little further after that, his cock sliding over my tongue, the warmth of his skin sending a sharp bite of lust to my stomach.

Hayes smirks as he watches me, his fingers cradling the back of my head with a strong, firm grip. He doesn't use his hold to guide me, though, but more for support. For connection while I begin bobbing up and down on his length in long, slow movements.

"You're doing great, baby. Just like that," he rasps, his fingers tightening in my hair fractionally.

My own cock throbs between my legs at his approval, quivering with need. He must notice too, because a grin stretches across his face.

"You like it when I praise you? Does it turn you on?"

I can't respond—his cock keeping my mouth rather occupied—but I hum around his shaft in affirmation, and the vibration has him sucking in a sharp breath.

"Fuck, that feels so good. Fucking perfect." His nostrils flare again, and he tilts his head. "Can you go deeper?"

I have no idea, considering the way I gagged on him the second I went too far, but we're about to find out if it gets him to keep praising me the way he is now.

Breathing through my nose, I allow his dick to slide in further. Not all the way by any means, but deeper than last time, and it's enough to clearly make a difference from the way his grip on my hair becomes downright painful.

My free hand automatically raises up, tapping on his wrist.

"Sorry," he rasps, loosening a bit. "Can you keep going?"

At this point, I'm ready to go for it all again, so when I gag a little this time, I fight the urge to bitch out and pull away entirely.

Please, for the love of fucking God, do not let me puke on this man's dick, because I will never hear the end of it.

But where I stop must be perfect, because Hayes' dick twitches and pulses between my lips some more. His hand at the base of my skull holds me on his length. Not pushing or thrusting, just keeping me steady while my cheeks hollow around him and I swirl my tongue.

"Stay right there, baby. That's it," he whispers, watching me with lust-filled eyes. "Now, try to swallow."

I do as he says, my throat constricting on his length, and another low groan leaves him.

"Fuck. Perfect, Kase. You're doing great." The words are strained and breathless when he releases my head, allowing me to back off his length again. "Keep going, baby. Do what it takes to make me come down your throat."

God, he's one of those *talk you through it* guys, and I'm in fucking heaven over it.

With the freedom to continue without his guidance, I start rolling my tongue around the head before sucking him in deeper. Not nearly deep enough to swallow around any part of him, but I use my hand to stroke near the base where my mouth doesn't reach.

He doesn't seem to mind it, though, his eyes closing and head falling back between his shoulder blades. His fingers return to my head, weaving through the hair at the top, and I can tell it's more for his sake than mine now. To steady himself as he mindlessly rolls his hips ever so slightly into my mouth. Begins to lose himself in my touch.

More precum spills onto my tongue, filling my mouth with the salty flavor as I move over his length, and from the way it quivers and twitches, he must be getting close.

"Fuck, baby. You're a fucking natural. Absolutely perfect," he mutters, the praises falling off his lips in rapid succession and going straight to my dick.

It's long since been leaking between my legs, and as much as I want to reach down and stroke myself, I don't want to lose focus on Hayes either. I want to be wholly, completely lucid as I watch him fall apart again, not drunk on my own pleasure.

More than anything, I wanna taste him.

Humming around his shaft at the thought, I move as quickly as I dare, stoking the flames of lust inside him until his fingers tighten in my hair all over again, attempting to hold onto his control. But it's slipping; I can tell from the way his hips are moving of their own accord now, going a little deeper than before. Seeking more of what my mouth is giving him.

"Shit, shit, *shit,* baby. I...I—"

His words die on his tongue and he rips me off his cock before yanking me back to my feet, the harshness and brutality in his touch turning me on even more than I already was.

"Bed," he rasps.

I'm on my back before I realize what's happening, Hayes' body blanketing mine as his mouth steals a searing kiss. Our hips roll against each other, hands traveling each other's bodies frantically, touching as much bare skin as we can find.

The only time he breaks away from me is to produce a bottle of lube seemingly out of nowhere, popping the cap and squirting some into his palm. My eyes take him in, panting harshly while he spreads it down his length, and for the briefest fucking second, I wonder—

"No home runs," he reminds me, as if reading my mind.

A little smirk crosses his face when his body covers mine again, leaning up on one elbow while still stroking his dick with the other. It's only when he wraps his palm around my aching length too that I realize what's about to happen.

The feel of his dick rubbing and bumping against mine as he strokes us together has my stomach tightening with a need I've never felt before. My toes curl against the mattress as I fuck up into his fist, my teeth sinking into my inner cheek to keep from moaning like a goddamn fool.

"Don't be shy. Let it out," Hayes murmurs, his head dipping to pepper kisses over my neck and jaw. "I wanna know how good I'm making you feel."

Jesus.

There's something about the way he whispers these things in my ear that just make it impossible to resist. I can't stop myself from being pulled under the intoxication of his praises or his commands, and though I know it could makes things really fucking messy, I don't really want to either.

I draw in a gasp when his crown rubs against mine in a way that gives me a spine-tingling shiver, and I find him leaning back to smirk at me.

"You like that, don't you? Playing with the tip?" he asks, angling his hips to make our heads bump together again. When it elicits the same reaction, he grins some more. "I love how responsive you are, baby. This is gonna be so much fun."

There's not a doubt in my mind, especially when his fist rolls over our crowns, spreading both our precum down our shafts, mixing with the lube. He does it again, circling the heads before pressing the nerve below it, and my eyes damn near roll back in my head.

"Oh, fuck, Hayes," I pant, my dick aching now; throbbing with the need to find release. Eyes falling closed, I lose myself in his touch, my fingers clamping around his shoulder. "Kiss me. Please."

His mouth is on mine seconds later, swallowing down my moans, drinking them like a man dying of thirst. Pleasure builds at the base of my spine, curling there as he sinks his teeth into my lower lip, tugging on the flesh and then soothing it with his tongue while his fist shuttles furiously over our dicks.

It's all too much. His tongue against mine, his fingers wrapped around us, the press of his bodyweight over me, and I find myself falling off the cliff before I even know it's happening.

Cum spills from my cock, coating my stomach and his hand with release. It doesn't so much as faze him, though, and he spreads it down our lengths and continues stroking us to high heaven.

"Fuck, fuck, fuck," he hisses, chasing his own orgasm as my just starts to subside. And then it hits him like a freight train, his own cum joining mine on my chest and stomach.

He's panting and breathless as he drops down, his forehead resting in the crook of my neck. The two of us are quiet for a moment, settling into the orgasm high while we wait for our rampant heart rates to subside.

"You're a really quick study," he murmurs against my throat before letting out a soft chuckle.

I pull away to look at him as best I can, which is pretty impossible when he's lying on top of me like he's as light as a feather instead of a six-foot-plus dude.

"I don't know if I should be offended that you sound surprised or glad you were impressed."

He laughs again, his breath soft and warm against my skin. "The second. Definitely the second."

Part of me still isn't convinced, but I decide to let it slide.

"Speaking of second…what base was that, exactly?"

He snorts and pulls back, his eyes finding mine. "Let's call it somewhere between second and third. I'm not giving you a triple until you've tasted my cum."

I grin, not at all put off by that idea. "At this rate, we'll be hitting home runs in no time."

"Let's walk before we run, okay?" he counters, chuckling softly. "I haven't even introduced you to your prostate yet, so we've got quite a few lessons to go."

"Oh, more lessons, you say? Better be careful, Lancaster, or I might think you like me."

"Keep being a smartass and maybe I'll have to change my mind."

"Better a smartass than a dumbass," I counter.

He rolls his eyes and makes a move to get up, but I wrap my arms around the small of his back to keep him from escaping.

"Fine, fine, you win. Don't go," I plead with a laugh, and I have to admit, I could get used to this. The fun, playful side of Hayes I haven't seen a whole lot of.

"Can I just say, this is one class I can definitely get behind," I tell him before adding, "Pun intended."

It's his turn to laugh, amusement and something a little filthier lighting up his eyes.

"You remember that when I decide to give you homework."

EIGHTEEN

Kason

"Knock, knock. Anyone in there?" someone says beside me, knocking on the helmet I'm wearing as I stretch on the sidelines.

Blinking a couple times, I glance over to find Holden beside me, grinning from beneath his own helmet. He's bouncing with energy like a literal golden retriever, and it's a wonder how anyone doesn't think he's cracked out when he sets foot on the field.

"Do you think I'm just some airheaded himbo or something?" I ask. "I have a brain in here, you know."

"Considering I said your name twice and you didn't answer…" He trails off, still smirking. "Just wanna make sure you're not so deep in mushy la la land that you won't be able to kick some ass today."

He has a point; my head is most definitely in a thousand other places, and each one of them involves Hayes instead of football. And honestly?

I'm not all that mad about it.

We've fallen into a bit of a routine as of late, and it's both comfortable and exciting all at the same time. Sometimes it'll be dates out to Pixel Palace, others it will be movie nights on the couch with the kitchen counter covered in dishes from cooking together or the occasional take-out containers. The nights we stay in are my favorite, usually ending with the two of us at least semi-naked on whatever horizontal surface we can both fit on.

Still, I know I've become a bit of a bad influence when it comes to how much time we're spending *not* doing the one thing we're in college to do: complete coursework to earn our degree.

Part of me feels guilty for it, but I'm growing more and more addicted to the attention Hayes is willingly giving me now. So much so, apparently I'm daydreaming about it on the field when I should be in game mode.

Whoops.

"And there you go again."

I frown. "What?"

"Stop thinking about your roommate's dick, and start thinking about the game. Otherwise I'm gonna make sure he stops putting out."

"How do you even know about—"

"You're really asking that right now?" Holden interrupts, his gaze flicking from my eyes to the stands behind me. "I think you're smart enough to figure it out."

Turning to follow his gaze, I find Phoenix sitting in his usual spot near the fifty-yard line, eyes cast down on his cell.

I should've assumed Phoenix would've put two and two together by now when it comes to me and Hayes. After all, Hayes has been at every home game since the one where they first met, and no roommate is *that* good of a roommate if there isn't something else going on.

Though, I would've thought he'd assume we became friends, not something more.

"Dude. Do you go deaf when your eyes are working overtime?"

Shaking my head, I turn back to Holden to find him smirking. "I'm good, I promise. You don't need to worry about me."

"Mhmm," he murmurs, the dubious look on his face letting me know he's less than convinced. "You know scouts are gonna be here today. I'm gonna do my best to make you look good out there, but you gotta be in the zone."

"I got it, Hold. I will be."

His hands raise in surrender and he takes a step back. "Okay, okay. That's all I needed to hear. I just think you've got one thing to take care of first." His eyes shift over my shoulder again before he motions with his chin to the stands behind me.

Glancing over, I find Hayes has arrived, and he's now standing at the edge of the stands a few rows in front of Phoenix. He's wearing one of the biggest smiles on his face that never fails to make my stomach do all kinds of cartwheels, but that's not the only thing causing my insides to get all bent out of shape.

It's him…wearing my jersey.

The sight does something stupid to my chest, causing it to squeeze just a little bit tighter, as I run toward him. That's before I see the heart-stopping grin on his face.

I glance at Holden, who is clearly trying not to smile, before heading over to where he's waiting. The only thing separating me from Hayes is an eight-foot wall, and more than anything, I wish I could scale it and kiss him for luck—PDA be damned.

Instead, I settle for smiling back as I look up at him.

"Hey, I didn't realize you were here already."

He nods. "Just got here. It didn't take me nearly as long to find my way now that I know where I'm going." He's still grinning down at me when he adds, "Plus, I wanted to be early to give you this."

He produces a bottle of blue Gatorade from behind him and it makes my stomach drop.

It doesn't take a genius to realize Phoenix must've told him about our old tradition the first time he came to our game. He's left a few in the fridge the past couple weeks and I've always made sure to put one back after taking it, but when there wasn't one waiting for me this morning, I must've thought it was a fluke.

Him handing me one now proves it wasn't.

And it also proves he cares enough to pick up where Phoenix sort of…left off.

A mix of bittersweet emotions clogs my throat as I take the sports drink from him. "Thanks."

"Don't mention it." He looks up to the field, jutting his chin toward where some of my teammates are already warming up. "And kick some ass down there today."

"I'll do my best."

Another smile sends my heartrate into overdrive. "I know you will."

I'm full of butterflies and stupid, silly emotions that have no business taking up my mental space—at least, not right now. But there's something about Hayes that reduces my brain capacity to nothing.

"I've gotta get going before I get reamed a new asshole," I tell him, my lips tugging up at the corner.

"No worries, I'll see you at home."

"Will you wait for me after the game outside the locker room?" I ask hesitantly, not wanting to push for too much. "Phoenix can help you get there. If you want to go."

Hayes glances back over to where my best friend is watching us, the biggest grin on his face, before meeting my gaze again. "I think I can be convinced."

That damn answer again. I swear, he gets off on being as elusive as he can. But if he wants to play hard to get, fine. Then I'll just have to be convincing.

"I'll make it worth your time once we get home," I say as quietly as I can, but not bothering to hide the suggestive wink I give him.

There's a devious sparkle in his eyes now, and he nods.

"I'm holding you to it."

The game ends in a win for Leighton over our rivals at Blackmore University, and as expected, the entire team is on a high as we leave the field. After Coach gives us his typical post-game run-down—and the threat to behave ourselves if we go out to celebrate—plans and parties become the only chatter I hear spreading through the locker room.

I'm quick to shower off the sweat and grime, ready to get the hell out of here and back home with my guy, especially knowing he's waiting for me just outside these four walls.

God, it's still so weird to think those two words in reference to Hayes. Almost like it's too good to be true, and that the other shoe is gonna drop, sending us right back to barely tolerating each other's existence.

Pulling my bag out to start redressing, I feel a presence at my back. A quick glance over my shoulder reveals it's Holden still wrapped in his towel, blond hair dripping wet from his shower.

"Killa K came out to play this evening," he says when he notices me looking at him.

"You're the one who was throwing like a pro today. I think I should be saying that to you."

He waves me off with a laugh. "Nah, I'm just doing my job. You, on the other hand? You're putting up numbers those NFL scouts won't be able to ignore."

That's the hope. With this season being my last opportunity to impress the scouts, I know I need to make a lasting impression if I want to get an invite to the combine in March—which is the first real step for me to getting drafted at the end of April.

"Here's to hoping," I reply while slipping into my pants. "Lord knows you don't need any help in that department, though."

Holden shrugs as he pulls his shirt over his head. "I don't think I'm gonna declare, actually."

I blink at him like he just told me a pod of whales just made a moon landing. "You're joking." When he shakes his head, I tack on, "Why the hell not?"

"It's not set in stone or anything, but it's something Nix and I are still talking about," he tells me while he finishes redressing in his street clothes.

It's hard to believe Holden would give up a shot at the NFL for anything, Phoe included. I can't imagine giving up something I'd worked tirelessly for; something I've dreamed of for as long as I can remember.

But, then again, I guess that's what happens when you find the person who you plan to spend forever with.

"You ready to head out?" he asks once his shirt is on and I've fastened my belt into place.

Nodding, I grab my bag and shoulder it before heading to the door, Holden right on my tail as we exit the locker room.

Hayes is waiting with Phoenix, like he said he'd be, and I stop short to observe the two of them from afar. Phoenix is leaning against the wall, body casually posed with his arms crossed as he listens to whatever Hayes is talking to him about. He's smiling and nodding, clearly invested in whatever conversation the two of them are having.

The sight has my heart squeezing in my chest.

"Nix likes him," Holden utters beside me.

I glance at him, my brows furrowing. "He said that?"

Holden shakes his head before motioning toward the two of them with his chin. "He doesn't have to; I can read it all over his face."

My attention moves back to Phoe and Hayes. It's a tough pill to swallow, knowing my best friend for a good chunk of my life is so easily winning over the guy it took over a month to even tolerate me. And the taste only gets worse realizing that while the two of them are forming this…friendship, the one I have with Phoe is still very much on the outs.

"You're good for him," I find myself saying before looking at Holden.

"Is it being cocky if I say *I know*?" he muses, a shit-eating grin on his lips.

That has me laughing, and I shake my head. "A little bit, but at least you're honest."

At the sound of my laughter, Phoenix is the first to notice us, nodding in our direction before he says something to Hayes. They exchange a few more words and a quick wave before Phoe heads toward Holden and me.

With a *see you later* to Holden, I move toward my guy. Somewhere in the middle, Phoenix and my paths intersect, and he offers me a gentle smile and a *good game, Kase*.

And as much as it might sting to still only have these small, meaningless interactions with my best friend, I can't even focus on it right now. I'm too caught up in the way Hayes is smiling at me as I approach him.

Or how good that number eighty-seven jersey looks on him.

Those two things combined, though? It takes every fiber of my self control not to kiss him at the sight. Pin him against the wall and devour him like the glutton I've become for him. And then I realize, there's nothing stopping me.

Well, other than the people waiting around who'd get an eyeful of two horny college guys going at each other like rabbits in heat.

A simple kiss wouldn't hurt, though.

"Hey," Hayes says, still grinning.

"Hey yourself," I murmur.

Before I can talk myself out of it—or worse, overthink it entirely—I wrap my hand around the back of his neck and press my mouth to his. It's meant to be soft and sweet, just the briefest form of hello, but it doesn't take more than three seconds for me to crave more, and my tongue sweeps over the seam of his lips.

He parts for me, allowing my tongue to dive in deeper, claiming his mouth in a toe-curling kiss that damn near brings me to my knees.

Someone wolf-whistles, breaking my focus and reminding me that we're not alone, but Hayes is the one to pull away first.

"Get a room!" Holden calls out, and I lift my middle finger behind me, flipping him off while pressing another gentle kiss to Hayes' lips.

Pulling away takes pretty much every ounce of willpower I possess, but the smile on his face is worth the cost.

"That's some greeting," he whispers.

"I'm happy to see you. And in my jersey, no less," I murmur, barely loud enough for him to hear. I pull back and I wrap my arm around his shoulder. "How'd you manage to get your hands on that?"

A devious glint lingers in his gaze as I steer him toward where my car is parked outside the player's exit. "I…have my ways."

It takes me all of three seconds to realize Holden and Phoenix likely had something to do with it, but I don't mind. Had Hayes told me he wanted to wear my jersey to the game, I'd have happily given it to him myself.

Pressing a kiss to the side of his head, I mutter near his ear, "You can ask next time."

"That would take the fun out of it."

"Well, regardless, I don't think you've looked better in your life."

Hayes laughs, rolling his eyes as he playfully shoves me away from him once we're at my car. "That's such a jock thing."

"What is?"

"The sight of me in your jersey going straight to your dick," he surmises, leaning back against the driver's door. "Not that I don't look damn fine in it."

That he does, but what he fails to realize is that him in it does a helluva lot more to the organ in my chest than it does any other part of me.

But now that he mentions it…

"Well, I *am* a jock. Gotta make sure I fit the part." Stepping forward, my fingers pinch the collar of the jersey and a little smile forms before I add, "But if I was *really* trying to fit the part, I'd tell you I wanna fuck you while you're wearing it."

Hayes meets my gaze, lust and want and need blazing like the hottest blue flames within his eyes. Licking his lips, he leans forward and murmurs, "I find it hilarious that every time sex comes up, you think you're the one who'll be doing the fucking."

"And why's that?"

He smirks. "Guess you'll just have to fuck around and find out."

The filthy promise dripping from his words makes my blood heat with anticipation.

There is nothing I want more than to feel Hayes inside me. God, just the thought has my stomach swirling with anticipation, and for once in my life, there's no underlying nerves or anxiety about it. No question as to if this is the right person or time or anything else.

All I feel is desire.

"Virgin or not," I murmur, trailing my hand down the front of the jersey, "I've watched enough porn to know I can fuck you as a bottom. Just gotta be in the right position."

"And here I thought you needed me to teach you. But it sounds to me that you had it figured out all along."

Lust zings through me thanks to the pure sin and sex dripping from his voice, not to mention the dirty promises his gaze holds. It should be enough to drag him home and strip him down to nothing, maybe put those theories to the test.

Yet the only words that come out of my mouth are just the opposite.

"Want to hit the party at the Kappa Sig house with me tonight?"

"After the sexual tension from that conversation, going to a party was the last thing I thought you'd be asking me." Hayes frowns, smacking my hands away. "Uh, also, it's my night to pick the horror movie, remember? Or is that why you're trying to skip?"

Considering Hayes has been choosing the most disgusting, off-the-wall horror flicks on his nights, I don't think anyone would blame me if that's why. In reality…I kinda just want to hang out with my guy in public.

"We can still do that after the party." I wrap my arms over his shoulders, pinning him against my car. "C'mon, it could be fun."

His hands land on both of my hips, holding me against him. "So could jumping off a cliff attached to an elastic band, but you don't see me doing that on a Saturday evening," he points out.

"You came with me the last time I went to a party."

He arches a brow. "The one where you got stood up? Why in the ever-loving fuck would you wanna go for a repeat of that?"

"It wouldn't be a repeat, because the guy I'm seeing now isn't the type to just leave me hanging the way some random dude-bro off a dating app would," I rebut. Smirking, I wait for him to come up with some kind of argument for that. Because if I know Hayes as well as I think I do, he's got a smartass remark on the tip of his tongue he's waiting to unleash.

Only, it never comes.

Instead, Hayes isn't able to hide his grin from me referring to him as my boyfriend. But then the antisocial side of him still manages to roll his eyes just fine. "Fine," he grumbles. "But when we get back to the house, I'm ordering Thai and leaving you to starve."

"You wouldn't dare."

"You willing to bet on it?" he asks, cocking his head to the side. "Because I'm pretty sure we've got that head of lettuce in the fridge you mentioned wanting to eat instead."

I blanch just thinking about it.

"How 'bout a compromise?"

Hayes cants his head, evidently intrigued by my offer. "I'm listening."

I hold my hand up, ticking off the night's itinerary on my fingers.

"Go to the party for an hour—two max—then we go home, order *anything* but Thai, and watch your movie choice. Sound good?"

He tosses his head back and forth, making a show of thinking about it when I know damn well he's gonna say—

"I think I could—"

I don't let him finish, pressing my lips to his to seal the deal.

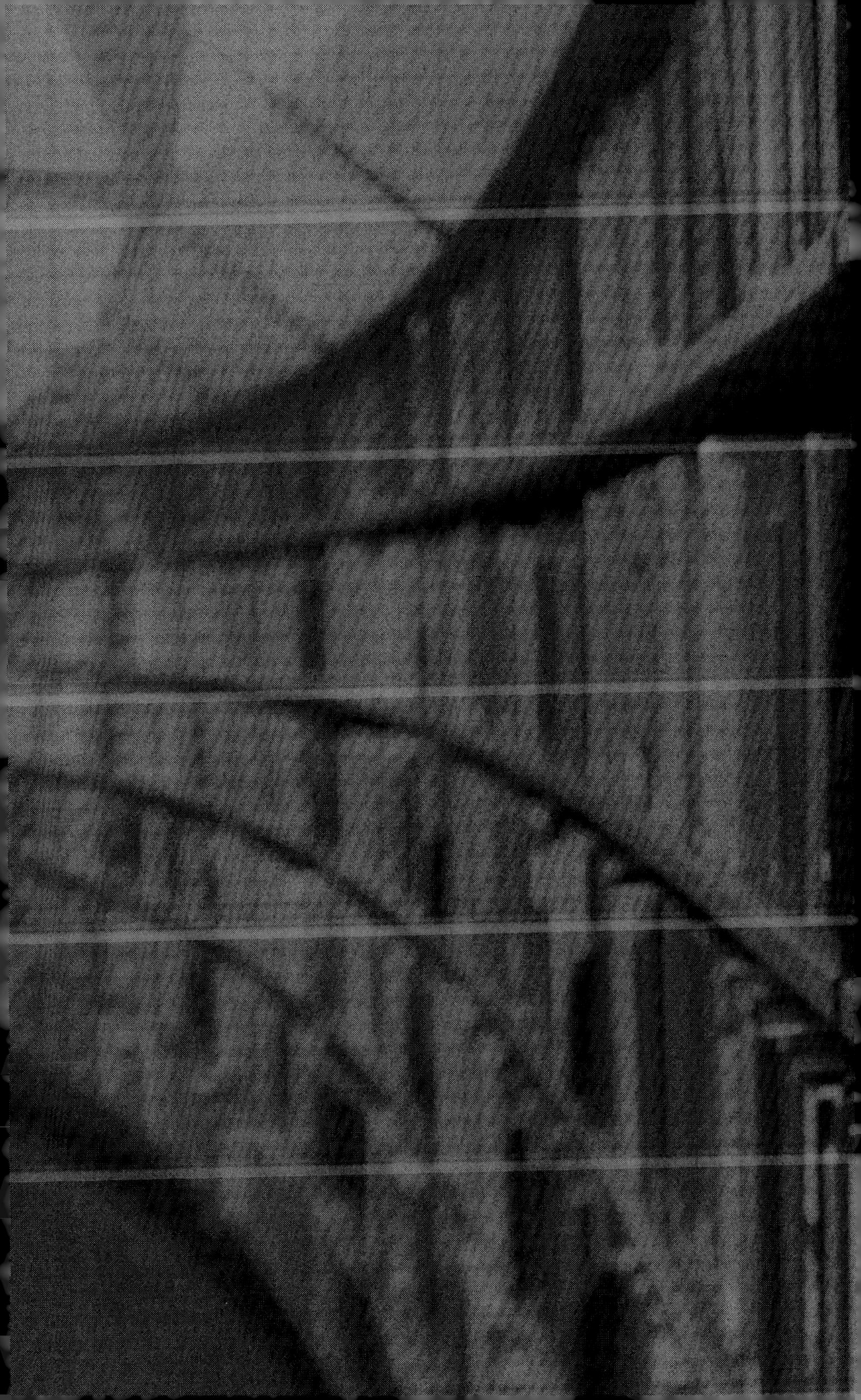

NINETEEN

Hayes

I'm out of bed long before Kason, already completely showered and ready to take on the day by eight in the morning, and feeling more chipper than ever. Not because of the fucking phenomenal session of sixty-nineing Kason and I had last night—though the sound of him choking on my cock will live rent-free in my head for the rest of my life—but because today is the best day of the fucking year.

Halloween.

It might be childish, but with my love for all things creepy and spooky that go bump in the night, it only makes sense for October thirty-first to be my favorite holiday.

Nothing—not a goddamn thing—will ruin this day for me.

And that includes Kason sleeping the damn day away when *we* have things to do.

When nine-thirty hits and he's still nowhere near awake, I sneak back into his room. He's peacefully sleeping, soft little snores coming from where he's now sprawled across the entire mattress since I snuck out.

I know I should let him sleep—after all, the game last night really took it out of him—but I'm too impatient to wait.

Crawling over his body, I press my lips to his neck, his jaw, his mouth, until he begins to stir beneath me.

"Good morning, sleepy head," I muse, smiling at the way he grumbles in grogginess.

"Mmm, go away," he groans, dragging his pillow over his head to stop my onslaught of affection. "It's too early to be awake right now. Even for sex."

"Sex wasn't what I was going for, and that's *definitely* not the spirit I'm looking for on the best day of the year, Kase. Let's try again." I grab the pillow and toss it on the floor. "Good morning, sleepy head."

His eyes peek open in something of a glare. "It would be a better morning if you left me the hell alone."

"Now you know how it feels to be woken up when you're trying to enjoy blissful slumber," I counter, my fingers playing with the wild strands of red-brown hair. "But I'm not letting you ruin my favorite holiday with your moodiness, and there's no chance in hell I'm letting you sleep it away, either."

"Five more minutes," he grumbles.

Not happening.

"Get up. We have things to do."

Kason chooses that moment to grab my hips and flip our positions, pinning me to the bed beneath him. His hands slide up my body until he shackles my wrists, dragging them up above my head.

I'm well aware he expects me to fight, try to wriggle out of his hold. But I have to admit, being helpless and at his mercy kind of has an appeal.

"You're absolutely insane," he whispers, his eyes wide with frustration and desire.

"No, I'm just feral for all things Halloweeen." Stretching up, I press a kiss to the corner of his mouth. "And I think it's the perfect occasion for me to take you out on a first date."

"You mean we're actually leaving the apartment? Going around *people?*" he teases while rolling his hips into mine. My dick thickens, his own erection grinding against it causing shivers to rush down my spine.

I know exactly what he's doing right now, trying to keep me here with the promise of sex. And fuck, if I'm not tempted to let him get away with it.

"Keep the sass up, and I'll change my mind. Maybe chain you to the bed and have my wicked way with you instead."

"That doesn't sound threatening at all, you know," he murmurs. Shifting his weight, he trails one hand down my ribs before sneaking beneath my shirt. "That actually sounds like way more fun."

The warmth of his skin trailing over my stomach has it tightening on reflex, and I'm already regretting playing this game with him. Because I just may well lose.

"Oh, so you're just using me for my body, I see."

He nods, zipping his head down to scrape his teeth over the pulse point in my throat before soothing it with his tongue. "Absolutely. No other reason at all. None whatsoever," he utters between kisses up my neck. "You're just a piece of ass to me, Lancaster."

"Well, that's too bad. You're not getting a damn thing from me if you make me miss out on celebrating my all-time favorite holiday."

Humming, he presses his lips to my jaw. "Does it have to be this minute?"

Harnessing every bit of strength and will and determination I have, I slide my fingers into the hair at the back of his head and pull, forcing his mouth away from me.

"Yes, so get your ass off me. We've got places to go and things to do."

He groans, his head landing in the crook of my neck when I release my hold. "But you hate people. Leaving the house requires peopling when we could just stay in bed all day. Then there's no people besides us."

He's doing his best to make a play at my weaknesses, but I'm not having his shit now. All temptation is gone. This is the one day of the year where my dislike for ninety-nine percent of the human population doesn't matter.

"I said *now*, Kason. Chop, chop."

To emphasize my point, I use his momentary distraction to slide out from under him, dragging the comforter off the bed with me.

Daggers are glared my way as I stare at his nearly naked form still on the bed. The muscular lines of his back, peppered with countless freckles. The way his boxer-briefs cling to his sculpted ass and thick, toned thighs.

He catches me staring and shakes his head. "You don't get to keep looking at me like that if you're making me get out of bed."

"You planning to stop me?" I taunt, crossing my arms. "You're gonna have to get out of bed to make that happen."

A sharp scoff leaves him as he finally, *finally* climbs out of bed, his feet landing on the floor with a soft thud. "Sometimes I really miss when you hated my guts, you know."

But hey, at least it gets him out of bed.

An hour later, we pull up outside the old movie theater on the outskirts of the city, the marquee sign glowing over the entry doors and box office.

"'Continuous horror marathon. All seats $5,'" Kason reads the text on the sign out the window, then turns to look at me. "This is your first date idea?"

"If you want to get technical, we've been on multiple dates already when I've taken you to the arcade or out to dinner," I remind him while shoving open my car door. He does the same, and I meet him on the sidewalk with an outstretched hand. "But yes, this is my perfect idea of a first date."

"You're absolutely ridiculous."

"And you love every minute of it," I rebut before I can stop myself from letting that pesky little L-word fall off my tongue.

To his credit, Kason either doesn't notice, or doesn't think anything of it. Instead, he stays in step beside me, his thumb rubbing against the back of mine as we enter the theater.

The line is short before we make it to the front of the concession line, where I order a couple of drinks, a bucket of popcorn, and two packs of Reese's Pieces for us before requesting our tickets for the Horror Marathon.

"Can we get extra butter, please?" Kason adds while the worker rings us up. The cashier nods and gives us the total, and I quickly hand over my card once I see Kason reaching for his wallet.

Frowning when he realizes I've beat him to the punch, he grabs the popcorn and his drink. "You can let me pay, you know."

The cashier's eyes quickly dart back and forth between us before she hands me back my card. "You're in theater three, which is about to start *Evil Dead*. Enjoy your movies."

"Thanks," I murmur, tucking my card away and grabbing my snacks. Turning my attention back to Kason as we head toward the theater, I circle back to his previous comment. "Who pays is of little to no consequence to me. You should know that by now. And two, I'm the one who asked you to go out, so why the hell would I let you pay in that case?"

Clearly ignoring my second point, he mumbles, "Says the one with money."

If there's one thing that has been made abundantly clear since Kason found out about the wealth I come from, it's that he doesn't give two shits about it. In fact, since finding out, he fights tooth and nail to pay for things as often as I do.

It's odd to have someone fighting for a bill when the people I used to spend time with—back when I was still sociable—always seem to expect me to be the one footing it. The only exception has always been Q.

And now, apparently Kason.

"I'll let you get the next round at the arcade. Deal?" I ask, doing my best to compromise.

He seems somewhat appeased by that plan, though I'm hopeful he'll forget by the next time we go and it won't matter. After all, I'm not really losing any money by being the one to pay there; it's just semantics so we can actually use the machines.

Besides, I have more money than I know what to do with between the trusts my family set up for me, and that's not including the still-overflowing college fund. Thanks to the academic scholarships I was awarded for attending Leighton, I've barely touched it.

Paying for dates is nothing. Honestly, it's the least I can do.

After finding theater three, Kason holds the door open, allowing me to enter first. It's already dark, and like the worker said, the opening credits of *Evil Dead* are playing on the screen. But more importantly, the place is relatively empty. There are maybe half a dozen people besides us scattered throughout the seats, and I'm pleased to find this is still another one of Chicago's best kept secrets.

Guiding Kason down the aisle, I turn into the last row of seats and settle us in two right below the projector window. It's the best spot in the theater, in my opinion, because most people go straight for the middle area, leaving the last few rows completely empty.

"There's no one here," Kason says as he immediately sets to dumping the Reese's Pieces in the tub of popcorn.

"There usually isn't," I tell him before grabbing a handful of heaven and popping it in my mouth. "I've never seen it full. Most people don't know about the annual horror-thon this place puts on, and if they do, they only come later in the day because of whatever other bullshit they deem as more important."

"You mean like work? School? Family?"

"Exactly. Bullshit," I say with a smirk.

He laughs softly and shakes his head. "You're not being a very good nerd if you're willing to skip school to spend the day at the movies."

"Sorry to disappoint you, but I'm only human. Even the nerdiest of us need a day off every once in a while."

That earns me a snort and another shake of the head before leaning in to speak in my ear. "Day off or not, you realize we could've done this exact thing at home, right?"

The heat from his breath coasts over my skin and sends shivers running down my spine, going straight to my balls, and part of me wonders how the hell I didn't notice the way my body reacts to him sooner.

Now, that's all I notice. Even when I shouldn't—like right now.

Turning my head, I let proximity work in my favor too, whispering. "Yeah, but where's the fun in that?"

From the flash of heat in his gaze, it definitely works.

"The fun is that we're in the comfort of our own home, can pause the TV for bathroom breaks, and get way cheaper snacks." Cocking his head slightly, he adds, "Not to mention privacy."

"You and I both know that the popcorn at the theater is twenty times better than any brand you can buy at the store," I mutter, grabbing another piece from his bucket and popping it in my mouth to drive the point home. "Besides, this is a tradition for me. I come here every year for their horror-thon."

A quick glance at Kason reveals him smiling at me. "You're adorable when you're being a complete nerd."

"Again, with the nerd comments." I grab a piece of popcorn, only to toss it at his head this time. "You should really be more careful before I start applying all the dumb jock stereotypes to you."

"See, the difference between us is that I'd wear that title like a badge of honor. Not fight you on it at every turn."

"Being excited about a horror-thon is probably the least nerdy thing about me. Or did you forget I memorized almost three hundred digits of pi for fun?"

He smirks before agreeing, "You're right, that's definitely nerdier." Then he takes a shot at me, tossing popcorn in return. But unlike him, I've been waiting for it and catch it in my mouth, which has his brows shooting up.

"Nice catch, nerd. I'm impressed."

"Thanks, jock," I counter immediately, grinning. "I happen to be pretty good with my mouth."

Kason rolls his tongue over his bottom lip, eyes getting dangerously heated when he utters, "Believe me, I'm well aware."

"Shhh," a disembodied person hisses from somewhere else in the theater.

I lean over toward him again, whispering directly into his ear. "I might be a nerd, but you're the one who is gonna get us kicked out of here."

"We wouldn't have to worry about that if we were doing this *at the apartment*. But someone here doesn't want to admit that."

He turns, clearly waiting for me to argue some more, but I'm too focused on his mouth. It's *right there,* and I force myself to not let my baser instincts kick in and devour his mouth mid conversation. Because with those delicious, pouty lips an inch from mine, I'm faced with the serious temptation to coax him into a movie theater hook-up rather than watching *Evil Dead* for the eight millionth time.

But as soon as the idea is in my head, my mind fixates on it, and the words fall from my mouth before I can think better of it.

"Maybe, but if we were at the apartment, you'd miss out on the chance to hook up in the back of a movie theater." Leaning forward even more and allowing my lips to brush against his when I speak, I add, "I wouldn't wanna be the one to deny you that rite of passage."

Kason's nostrils flare at the taunt, his eyes taking on a smoldering quality in the glow of the screen when I pull back and look into them. If I'm reading him correctly, he's not opposed to the idea.

"Are you serious?" he whispers, gaze searching my face.

Bingo.

"Why not?" A hellish smirk crosses my expression as my fingers skate up his forearm. "Who knows, maybe exhibitionism will be your kink."

There's a beat of silence before he murmurs, "Well, only one way to find out."

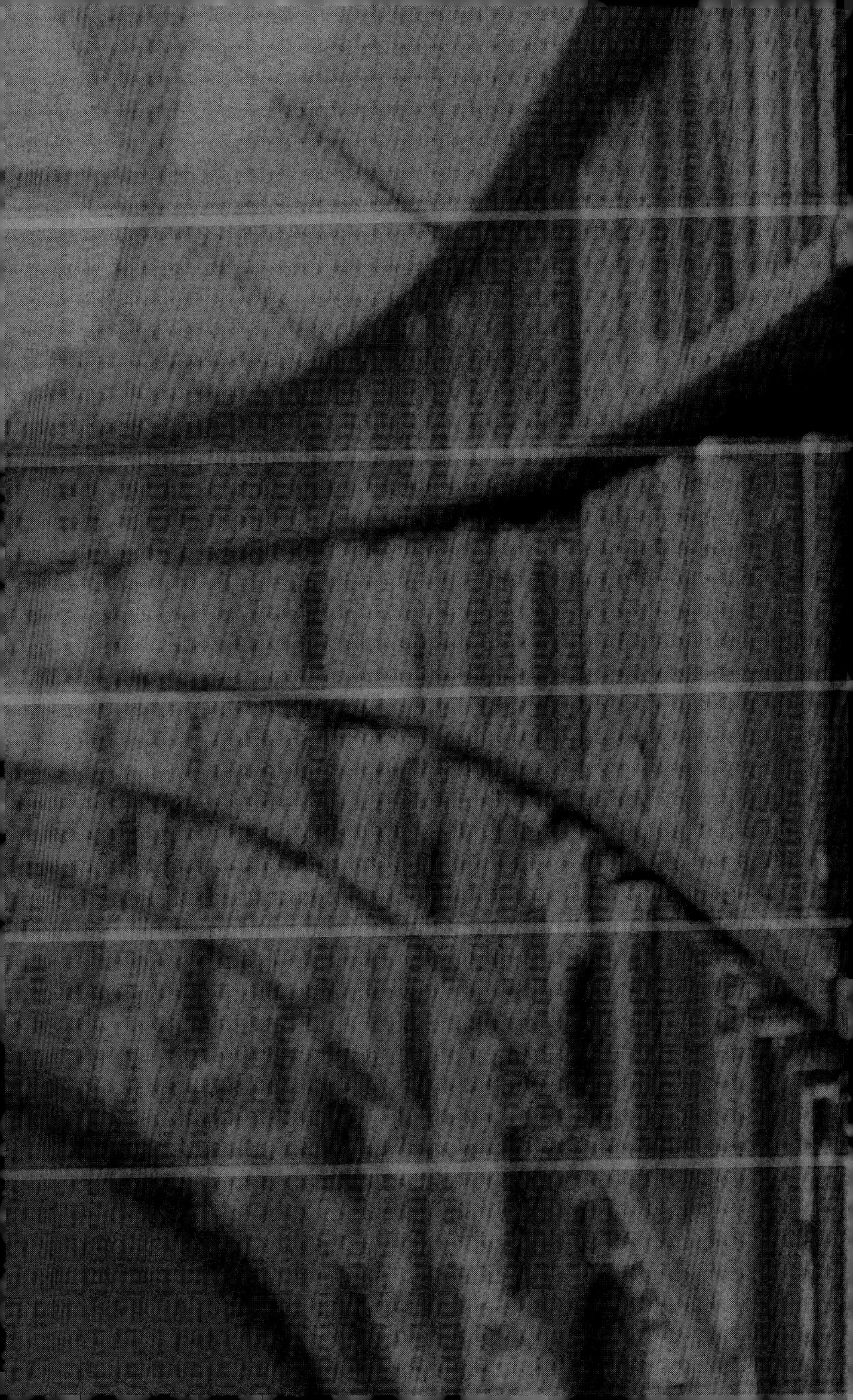

TWENTY

Hayes

I stare at Kason, not sure if I heard him correctly or if I somehow made that sentence up in my head. Because there's no way in hell the adorable, bumbling fool I'm sitting beside just made a pass at me without blushing redder than Rudolph's freaking nose.

There's just no way.

Yet, as his gaze slowly flicks from my eyes to my mouth and back again, it's obvious he did.

Sending up a thank you for this glitch in the *Matrix*, I take his lust-filled look as permission to close the remaining space between us, my mouth devouring his in an instant.

Kason's lips part the second my tongue brushes the seams, allowing mine to graze his in a coaxing taunt. His hand shifts, cradling the back of my head and adjusting the angle to deepen the kiss. A kiss I feel *everywhere*.

The amount of desire I'm feeling is consuming, drowning me in a tidal wave of lust I don't quite know how to navigate. Maybe because I've never felt it at this magnitude before.

My hand slips down his chest, skating over his taut stomach before stopping at his belt. With deft fingers, I quickly undo the buckle, flick open the button, and slide down the zipper of his jeans. To his credit, my movements don't even faze him, his tongue too focused on battling mine about whose mouth it belongs in.

But the second my hand slides into his underwear, wrapping my palm around his shaft, he falters.

A hand immediately wraps around my wrist, halting my movements.

Breaking our kiss, I look into his eyes while not moving an inch. "Do you want me to stop?"

It would suck, but if that's what he wants, I will. We can go back to watching the movie after I go to the bathroom and quickly relieve myself of the raging hard-on behind my zipper.

Kason's teeth sink into his lower lip for a second, worrying the flesh before he finally shakes his head and releases my wrist, giving me the go-ahead to continue.

Grinning, my free hand reels him back in, wanting to sink my own teeth into that perfect lip myself while stroking his already thickening cock.

I jack his length in long, torturously slow strokes, being as languid with him as I want and matching the pace of our kiss. He doesn't seem to be in a rush either, his free hand leisurely mapping up and down my thigh, squeezing it whenever I roll my fist around his crown.

I continue tormenting him like that, kissing him with bruising force, for what feels like hours. He's leaking everywhere at this point, precum coating my palm and his shaft. It twitches in my hold, clearly seeking release while he pants and moans softly against my mouth before I greedily drink them down.

He wants to come, I can tell. But something's stopping him from letting it happen.

"God, I wish we were at home. I want your mouth," he whispers when he breaks the kiss, finally needing air. "I wanna feel it wrapped around me while I come down your throat."

Shit.

My cock throbs in my pants at the filth in his words, having never heard it leave his lips like that before. Then again, I don't think I've ever seen him this turned on either.

Nipping at his lower lip, I soothe the bite with my tongue before replying, "That can be arranged, you know."

The offer has him pulling back to look me dead in the eye. I can tell he's trying to gauge my seriousness, his eyes tracing my features for any sort of joking mannerisms.

But he's not gonna find any. I'm more than happy to drop down and give him what he wants, right here.

"There's no way we won't get caught," he points out.

Quinton's track record from high school certainly would differ, but I keep that to myself. Instead, I just slide off the seat and aim a grin at him.

"Stay quiet, and we won't."

Shifting to kneel between his legs, I press them further open to accommodate my shoulders.

"*Hayes,*" he whispers, and though my name comes out as a warning, when my gaze collides with his, all I see is a plea. The question is if he's pleading for more…or for mercy.

Or maybe they're actually the same thing, because he makes more room for me between his thighs while he quickly slides his pants and underwear down further.

"You have to be quiet," I tell him again. "If you aren't, I'll have to stop."

My mouth takes him in a second later, a sharp hiss leaving his lips when my tongue teases his crown, playing with the slit at the head before rolling it around the head completely. His dick twitches when I take him deeper, the warm, musky skin sliding over the flat of my tongue with ease.

It doesn't take long for me to realize, I'm right. The idea that any one of these people could catch him with his cock in my mouth turns him on even more, the salty tang of his precum spreading over my tastebuds.

Kason does his best to keep silent, even has his eyes locked on the screen playing a movie he's seen a thousand times, despite never having a view like this down at his feet.

That simply won't do.

Ever so gently, I scrape my lower teeth along the underside of his shaft as I pull back, and it has him suppressing a gasp as best he can, covering it with a cough. His eyes flare when he looks down at me, and I smile around his length while I hold his gaze.

Now that I have his attention, I continue working him over like he's a sucker I just can't get enough of, licking and sucking until his hips start moving with me. Every tiny thrust he makes up in my mouth has me wanting more, and I grab his thighs to readjust so I can take him deeper. All the way to the hilt.

I stay like that until his cock is leaking precum like a faucet, using my tongue and throat to drive him wild with need, all the while never taking my eyes off him. Watching him watch me is a filthy fantasy I never knew I had, and I can't get enough of it.

But I'm greedy—fucking desperate—for more.

I want him to feel me everywhere. Make this a moment he'll never scrub from his memory.

Knowing he's gotta be damn close when his fingers squeeze my shoulder, I pull off him entirely, replacing my mouth with my palm. The sudden change of pace has him cursing under his breath and letting out a few rough pants.

"Why'd you stop? I was right there," he whispers, all needy and full of lust.

"I wanna try something," I murmur, stroking his length while waiting for an answer. "Do you trust me?"

His eyes are wild, brimming with need and desire as he nods.

Praise fucking Jesus.

His willingness to explore just might be the death of me.

"Scoot down a little," I utter, my lips tugging in a smirk. "So your ass hangs off the seat."

He does as I ask, a curiosity in his eyes as I push his pants the rest of the way to his ankles. A curiosity that only grows when I grab the discarded popcorn bucket.

Reaching into the bottom where all the remaining butter has pooled together in a nice, little puddle, I gather some on my middle and index fingers as best I can and bring the dripping liquid to his rim.

Kason watches what I'm doing with the butter intently, his Adam's apple bobbing. I can see the worry on his face, but I also see the burning flames of lust too.

"Is that safe?"

"I honestly have no idea," I whisper back. Logic says if we clean him up after, it should be okay, but the last thing I want is to pressure him. "We don't have to—"

"Fuck it, it's fine," he murmurs, green eyes blazing in the glow of the screen as he nods in confirmation. "Do it."

This guy.

He does something to me.

Something unexpected. Something confusing.

Something I can't get enough of.

I stare at him, half in shock, the other half in awe, while he nods again, giving me permission to…butter his asshole. The thought has me stifling a laugh as I lift my fingers to his crease, spreading the liquid over his rim.

"I can't believe I'm letting you do this," he mutters, his head leaning back against the wall behind him.

"Honestly, me neither. But I love seeing your kinky side." I swirl my fingertip around the tight ring of muscle another time before pressing in slightly. "Makes me wonder what else you'll let me do to you."

Kason hisses softly, his body fighting the intrusion.

"Relax. Let me in," I whisper, easing my finger back out while still stroking his cock with my other hand.

Wetting his lips, he nods, breathing sharply through his nose when I slowly press into him again. He doesn't fight it as bad the second time thanks to my thumb paying extra attention to the nerves beneath his crown.

It only takes a few more thrusts before I'm two knuckles deep, stretching him while he rocks his hips up into my waiting palm. Taking it as a sign to start working in a second finger, I play with his crown some more, letting him adjust to the widening intrusion.

"Good job, baby. That's perfect," I whisper, enamored by him. "You're doing so good."

God, forget horror movies. Watching him come undone is my new favorite form of entertainment, especially when it's because of me.

In no time, he's taking over the pace, matching me thrust for thrust. Both of my fingers are fully seated inside him now, buried to the hilt as he attempts to fuck himself on the digits, all while keeping as quiet as he can.

But when I curl them upward, applying the perfect amount of pressure to his prostate, a low moan slips past his lips.

My lips quiver, as I coax him back to silence. "We don't want everyone in here to know you're letting me finger-fuck your ass with popcorn butter, do we? You gotta be quiet."

Lifting his fist to his mouth, he bites down on his flesh to muffle the sound of his moans.

Grinning, I lean forward to take him in my mouth again, whispering, "Just tap my shoulder if it gets to be too much, okay?"

With another silent nod from him, my lips wrap around his crown with a gentle suck before taking him all the way to the back of my throat in a single go. Ready to truly bring out my A-game, I move over his cock in time with my fingers, swirling my tongue around the crown at the same time I brush over his prostate. Each thrust and suck has him getting closer and closer to the edge than he was before, and it doesn't take long for him to start rocking his hips with me. Back on my fingers, then up between my waiting lips.

We work in tandem, creating a rhythm that starts out smooth, but rapidly becomes more haphazard and frenzied. Kason's hands bury themselves in my hair, tugging and yanking the wavy strands as I continue tormenting him with my mouth and fingers.

"I'm gonna come, Hayes," he says with a whimper before biting down on his fist again. "I'm really fucking close."

Nodding, I take a deep breath and hollow my cheeks, allowing him to slide to the back of my throat. Kason's fingers have a painful grip on my skull now, and I'm pretty sure he's pulled out some hair too, but I don't care. The only thing on my mind is pushing him over the edge.

With my mouth, with my fingers.

With everything I have.

I swallow around him, the constricting sensation around his length and the perfect pressure to that little pleasure button causing him to finally find release. A choked moan leaves him, both his hands in my hair now as he holds me down on his cock and spills down the back of my throat.

"Holy shit," he whispers, panting heavily as I drink down his cum like it's my favorite movie slurpee—which now, it honestly might be.

I keep rubbing my fingers against his prostate, prolonging his orgasm as much as I can, enjoying every drop of salty tang that hits my tongue. Even after he's long since finished and I've pulled my fingers from his ass, I continue swirling my tongue over his skin in search of any remnants I might've missed.

It's only when I know he's been thoroughly licked and sucked clean that I release his now softening cock and look at him with lust-filled eyes.

"I think you missed a spot," he whispers, humor in his eyes.

I'm well aware he's making a joke, poking fun at how long I've taken to clean him up. But little does he realize, he's right.

I did miss a spot.

"Shoot, my bad. I'll get it right now," I tell him with a devious grin.

Grabbing his outer thighs, I pull his ass further off the theater seat and shift my body lower to the ground, making my best attempt at a good angle to get the one part of him that hasn't been cleaned up.

"Hayes, what are you—"

The question dies on his lips when my tongue swipes over his puckered rim, gathering the remnants of butter still lingering there.

"How many licks does it take to get butter off a booty hole?" I muse, lapping at his hole a few more times before he fists his fingers in my hair and yanks me away.

His eyes are a forest lit ablaze when my gaze meets his and he dryly mutters, "The world may never know."

Grinning, I move out from between his legs and slide back up into my seat.

"Someone's being a spoilsport," I whisper, tucking my straining erection up in my waistband. "I was just trying to clean you up."

"And you can," he mutters back, his head cocking to the side. "At home. In the shower. Privately."

I'll never be one to turn down a naked and sudsy Kason. Just the thought alone has my already swollen cock aching even more.

"Don't tempt me with a good time, Fuller. I'll make sure you pay up."

"It was more of a demand, actually." His gaze dances between my eyes and mouth. "You ready to get outta here? I feel like I owe you an orgasm."

Oh, thank fucking God. If I had to sit through the rest of this movie, I'd be in for a serious case of blue balls.

I smirk. "I could be convinced."

Kason becomes a man of action after that, righting himself while I gather our trash. Once we're sure both of us are decently presentable in daylight—or at least, we hope—we silently make our way out of the theater, dropping our trash along the way.

"Surprised you don't wanna take that home," Kason mutters when I toss the popcorn tub into the bin on our way out of the building.

"Why would I do that when we have some in the fridge I can just melt?"

He stops dead in his tracks on the sidewalk, staring at me completely dumbfounded, and I can't stop the chuckle that escapes me at his horror.

"I'm kidding, Kase. Calm down."

All he does is shake his head and sigh as we continue our way to the car. Of course, it's not until he's climbing into the passenger seat that I notice the butter stain on the ass of his jeans, but there's not a chance in hell I'm commenting on it.

I pull onto the street, the only thing on my mind as we drive back to the apartment is how long it'll take me to get Kason naked and in the shower once we're through the front door.

"There's only one thing I know for sure after that experience," Kason says, breaking through my fantasies as I turn toward campus.

"Dare I ask?"

I glance over just in time to catch a filthy grin tugging at his lips. "I'm never gonna be able to watch *Evil Dead* the same again."

TWENTY-ONE

Hayes

November

Ever since the theater, our weekends have quickly developed into all-day naked sessions once Kason gets home from his long-standing date with a stupid pigskin ball every Saturday. And I, for one, could not be happier about this change of pace.

More often than not, there's some kind of teaching on my part, and I'm pretty impressed with how quickly Kason is picking up on these little sex lessons. Hell, he didn't even flinch when I brought out a plug tonight, testing the waters to see just how much more work we have to go until he's ready to…*hide the salami,* as he so aptly put it.

Which, truthfully, isn't much.

As much as the sex-crazed horny part of me can't wait for that to come, I've also come to enjoy the moments where we're just existing together—naked or clothed. Though the moments like right now, post orgasm and curled up together in bed, happen to be my favorite.

That is, until Kason goes and ruins it with his garbling stomach.

"Jesus Christ, can you tell that thing to shut up? I'm trying to cuddle here."

He laughs, the vibration coursing from his body into where mine is laying half on top of him, lost in the sensation of his fingers dancing down my spine. "Depends, are you planning to let me out of bed at any point today, or am I gonna die from starvation? Because giving it food is the only way I know to make it stop."

"You eat more than anyone I know," I mumble indignantly.

"Because I burn a shit ton of calories every day at practice and in the gym." There's a brief pause when he presses a kiss to my hairline. "And now with you whenever you decide you can't keep your hands off me."

I lean back, looking him in the eye with a glare. "Uh, you're the one who started this. I was just trying to play *Apex* with Quinton when you so rudely interrupted me."

His eyes take on a playful gleam when he murmurs, "Yeah, but if I remember correctly, you definitely weren't objecting to the interruption."

The memory of my cock in his mouth from beneath my desk is one that's been brained into my frontal lobe—both for how fucking hot it was, but also because it was like trying to stuff a gorilla in a backpack for him to get under there in the first place.

"You can get up after I get five more minutes of cuddling," I concede, deciding that's the most I'm willing to compromise on the subject.

He chuckles, the sound rumbling beneath my ear. "We can cuddle on the couch when you aren't covered in your own cum, you know. There's no rule that post-sex cuddling can't be after we're cleaned up. Or after I get something to eat."

"But then you aren't naked anymore." My face burrows into his neck as my hands take on a mind of their own, roaming down the long, lean planes of his body. "And naked cuddles are so much better."

The vibrations from his laugh course through my body, and he squeezes me tightly against his chest in a warm embrace that completely juxtaposes the taunt he whispers in my ear.

"I knew you were just using me for my body."

I roll my eyes, despite him not being able to see it. "Obviously. We demisexuals are often known for only wanting to get some and get lost. I can't believe you'd expect anything different."

"Smartass," he mutters before pressing a kiss to the side of my throat.

It's on the tip of my tongue to say *but I'm* your *smartass,* but I manage to rein it back in. Despite the sentiment being true, something about that kind of declaration just feels a bit too big too soon.

We might be on solid ground, but what we have is still so new; delicate and fragile, like a piece of blown glass. There's no way I'm gonna risk saying something that'll shatter it.

Shoving the thought away, I allow my fingers to roam down his taut stomach, tracing the ridges and valleys his abs make, before following the V that leads to the Holy Grail of dicks.

I tease around it at first, not wanting him to catch on, before allowing my fingertip to lightly graze over the crown. Then I do it again up one side of it, from base to tip.

It's not until it starts thickening all over again from my stealthy ministrations that Kason finally notices.

"Stop that," he says, smacking my hand away from his dick. "I'm still sensitive, and there's no way we're going for another round on an empty stomach."

"I like tormenting you, though."

"Believe me, I'm well fucking aware of that. You've been doing it since the day I moved in here."

That gets my attention, and I rise up on my elbow over him. "Oh, no. If anyone was tormenting the other, it was you."

"Keep telling yourself that, babe." He glances over at the alarm clock on the nightstand before meeting my gaze again. "Oh, and look at that. Your five minutes are up. Time to eat."

Without waiting for a response, he slips his body out from beneath me, giving me a fan-fucking-tastic view of his sculpted back and ass that I've become thoroughly addicted to; the evidence clearly marked by a few teeth imprints on his left cheek.

Of course, my handiwork quickly disappears from view when he grabs the pair of sweats he was wearing from the floor and tugs them up to his hips.

"Commando?" I mutter, flopping to the mattress on my back and staring at the ceiling. "You're not being fair now."

"As opposed to you, the poster child for playing by the rules?" he counters. After running his fingers through his sex-mussed hair, he motions with his head toward the door. "You coming?"

"I could be, but someone's stomach is getting in the way." With a playful huff, I crawl out of bed regardless and grab a clean pair of sweats from my dresser. "Can I at least interest you in a shower before we feed your bottomless pit of a stomach? It seems I'm not the only one covered in my cum."

I motion toward Kason's left side, where dried, white streaks of my release stain his skin. He looks down, frowning when he notices before his gaze lifts to mine again.

"Can you keep your hands to yourself if I say yes?"

"Probably not," I admit honestly with a shrug. "But it would be saving water, and saving water saves the planet."

Kason's lips quirk, amused at my very reasonable proposal.

"Well, if it's for the good of the planet…"

My thoughts exactly.

An hour later, the two of us are nice and squeaky clean, thanks to a *very* thorough scrubbing down. We're both redressed—Kason, still sans underwear—and in the kitchen while he conjures up something for us to eat.

He's decided on a chicken stir-fry after scouring our cabinets and fridge, pulling out all the necessary ingredients and setting to work.

"What do you wanna do after dinner?" Kason asks from where he's dumping seasonings and sauces in a mixing bowl at the island, stirring them together.

I arch a brow from my spot on a stool across from him. "Uh, you promised me a date with the couch, a movie, and more cuddling, and I plan to cash in on that."

He laughs, his shoulders shaking as he drops the sliced up chicken breasts in the bowl next, coating them with the mixture of flavors he's already added.

"You laugh, but I'm being dead serious."

"I know you are, that's *why* I'm laughing." Dark green eyes find mine and he smiles in a way that has my stomach fluttering with those damn butterflies again. "I just never took you for such a snuggle-whore."

"I'm not one to show all my cards at once. Gotta keep you guessing somehow," I reason, watching him as he continues prepping the chicken. I let my eyes leisurely scrape from the food to him, noting the concentration with which he works. "And if we're being honest, I never took you for someone who'd know what they're doing in the kitchen. I guess we're both still keeping some cards close to the vest."

A snort leaves him. "It's not like it was some deep, dark secret."

"Neither is my cuddle obsession," I counter.

"Considering your distaste for ninety-nine percent of the human race, I'd beg to differ."

Okay, valid point.

With the chicken prepped and ready to go in the preheating oven, Kason moves to the sides, slicing mushrooms, broccoli, and various colors of peppers. I watch him work in silence for a while, filled with wonderment at how many different facets there are to him.

"How'd you learn to cook, anyway?" I find myself asking when he drops the veggies in a frying pan on the stove, the sound of sizzling filling the kitchen.

"Had to learn to fend for myself pretty early on." He drops the chicken in next, including all the different spices, before looking up at me while he stirs. "My dad wasn't exactly serving me home-cooked meals every night after mom left. And when the Mercer's started letting me spend time there, I'd already started to like cooking, so helping Phoe's mom in the kitchen wasn't a hardship. It actually became one of my favorite parts of the day."

It's weird to think about, but at the same time, I can picture a younger, ganglier version of Kason learning to cook beside the only mother figure he'd ever really had. And honestly, as wholesome as the thought is, it also makes my heart ache for him.

That he didn't have that with his actual mother. Or that he had to learn to take care of himself at all.

"I'm glad you had them."

He smiles a little, but it's a sad, somber kind. "Yeah, I am too. Who knows where I'd be without them."

"Well, I think you'd be well on your way to becoming Chef Fuller," I muse, leaning back against the back of the stool. "Kinda has a ring to it, actually. Maybe you could even have one of your own shows, like Gordon Ramsay."

He laughs, shaking his head. " I don't think I'm a big enough dick to be the next Gordon."

"Eh, we could be a duo. You do the cooking and I do the yelling. That's the perfect dream team, right there."

Amusement and something else—something a little daydreamy—lights up his eyes when he meets my gaze again, and he nods. "Yeah, maybe. I'll keep that in mind if football doesn't work out."

Kason goes back to watching the food, stirring the contents of the pan and adjusting the heat as needed, and I have to admit, he really does seem to know what he's doing. I think even my mother would be impressed, who, despite having a staff who cooked for us on the regular, always insisted on doing Christmas and Thanksgiving dinners herself.

Thoughts of the holidays have me taking a momentary pause, and I check my phone for the date, realizing that one of those very occasions is next week.

Hopping off my stool, I round the counter and cozy up beside him, watching what he's doing up close now.

"Speaking of cooking," I muse, my fingers trailing up his bare arm. "What are you doing for Thanksgiving break?"

He shrugs absently, eyes still fixed on the stove. "I think we will have practice at some point, so I was just planning to stay here. Hang out, play it lowkey. What about you? I'm assuming you're going home?"

Damn, I hadn't thought about his practice and game schedule. But I nod, answering, "Yeah, my mom usually has us do the whole big dinner even though it's just her, Dad, and my brother."

His eyes snap up to mine instantly and he turns to me. "In all the time we've been spending together, how am I just finding out you have a brother?"

I honestly hadn't realized that bit of information had been left out in all the endless conversations we've shared, discovering new things about each other. I guess this is just one more to add to that list of cards I've apparently kept in my hand.

"It wasn't intentional." I wrap my arms around his neck, playing with a few strands of hair at the back of his head by twisting them around my finger like those curlers my mother used to wear to bed. "Besides, you know I'm not good at sharing unless you ask to know something."

"Maybe, but you've gotten a lot better at it lately," he points out before smacking my hand away. "And stop that before it actually curls."

"You'd look cute with little *Annie* curls all over."

"And you'd look cute with my dick in your mouth for dessert, but that's not happening until you tell me about your brother," Kason counters as he steps out of my hold to take the food off the burner.

His eyes flick back to me, clearly waiting for me to divulge details about my only sibling. There's part of me that wants him to work for it a little more though.

Or maybe it's the part of me that loves seeing him get riled up a bit.

"Demanding little thing," I murmur before pressing a kiss to his shoulder. "I like this side of you."

"Call me *little* again, and I will drag you back to the bedroom and show you otherwise." He wraps his arms around my waist while we wait for the food to cool. "Now, tell me about your brother, please."

I don't know if I'm rubbing off on him with the quick wit or if Kason had this dirty mouth hidden beneath all his pent up sexual frustration. Either way, I don't really care, because I'm fucking loving every minute of it.

What he doesn't realize is that he is threatening me with a very, *very* good time, and there's a big freaking part of me that wants to poke the bear just to reap the consequences of my actions.

But I behave myself—barely—and think of the best way to describe my brother. "His name is Rhys. He's a few years older than me, and we usually only see him around the holidays. He's off in New York working for this big company Quinton's parents actually just partnered with last year; a holding company that deals with a lot of government funded projects." I shrug, not really sure what else to say. "I guess he's happy, though."

Kason nods, his face pensive in thought while he grabs plates and silverware from the cabinets, handing a set to me. He quickly dishes food onto both our plates and we slide onto the stools at the other side of the island.

We settle into silence as we eat for a little bit, but I can tell Kason's got something weighing on his mind, and it's to the point that I can't keep quiet anymore.

"You gonna tell me what's on your mind or you gonna make me guess?"

"Not that it's any of my concern," he starts, clearly treading carefully with his word choice, "but if he's the eldest, then why isn't he the one planning to take over the family business?"

I shrug, not sure why he'd worry about asking that.

"Because Rhys has no interest in it. He's always wanted to be part of the glitz and glam—the one percent of the one percent—and he wasn't going to achieve that by simply taking over Lancaster Financial Consulting. I think the only time my parents and him have truly ever fought is when he decided to take his job last year. I've never seen them that angry."

"And because of that, taking over the company falls to you," he supplies.

I nod. "If I don't, then who will, you know? LFC is our legacy. The last thing I want to see is something generations of my family have built be auctioned off to the highest bidder once my father wants to retire. Or worse, run into the ground or stripped for parts."

And honestly, I don't mind it. Unlike my best friend, I've never fought against taking over my family's legacy.

"Seems a little unfair to me is all." Kason frowns as he scoops some stir-fry from his plate and takes another bite. "You don't mind having your future just decided for you?"

Shaking my head, I spear a broccoli and pop it in my mouth. "I've always been good with numbers, money, things like that. I picked up on a lot from my dad, too. Meanwhile, Rhys was the charmer who could woo even the crabbiest of the rich and wealthy. So even when we were younger, it was what made sense. I think the only people his choice was really a shock to were my parents, because I saw it coming from a mile away."

"Not everyone is as observant as you," Kason reminds me, glancing over before taking another bite.

"Okay," I mutter, rolling my eyes. "But regardless, I'm actually looking forward to having that part of my life already lined up. It kinda takes all the guesswork out of it, you know? After this year, I know exactly where my career is heading, what the future holds, that kinda thing."

A long, drawn out sigh leaves him, and he nods.

"I can imagine that's gotta be some kind of weight off your shoulders." His eyes drop to his food, stirring it absently on his plate for a minute before stabbing a piece of chicken. "Sometimes I wish I had that kind of path too. I just don't know who I am without football. Besides the Mercers, it's the one thing that really saved me during those really tough years."

"You'll know soon enough, right?"

I catch his nod of confirmation before he replies. "Combine invites will go out before the bowl games are over. That's one step closer to my goal."

"Then why do you sound so down about it?" I inquire, a theory which he confirms when he shoots me a defeated look.

"It's just starting to feel like this massive waiting game, and in the end, I'll have wasted all this time only to not get drafted at all."

What?

I'm not sure where the hell that's coming from other than self-doubt, because it sure as hell isn't the way he's been playing this season.

"I understand the whole not-knowing part being a dark cloud of worry, but from what your stats have shown, you're gonna be one of the most sought after tight ends."

Smirking, he muses, "You've been keeping up on my stats, there, Hazey?"

"I wouldn't be a very good roommate if I wasn't."

"*Roommate,* huh?" he teases, his eyes glittering. "I dunno, that sounds more like boyfriend material to me."

The word has me pausing now, lowering my fork back to my plate as I map his face. "Is that what I am?"

"Do you want to be?" He cocks his head, that goofy little smile on his lips. "I mean, I thought it was kinda an unspoken thing, since we're not seeing other people, but if you don't want the label—"

"No, it's nothing like that," I immediately answer. "I just hadn't really thought about it in any specific term."

"Okay, then yeah, you're my boyfriend. Happy?"

I am, yeah. And there's a sliver of me—the logical, driven side—that hates how much. Because I'm well aware that the way my chest and stomach constantly swirl and tighten and flutter are far from fucking normal.

But apparently, I don't have it in me to care nor do a damn thing to stop it.

So instead, I lean into it.

"Well, then, yes. As a good boyfriend, I think it's my job to track your stats. And to tell you that your receiving yards for the last two years have been the highest in the conference, this year alone is the third highest in the country, and if you get forty-five more by the end of the regular season, you'll break the school record." I pause, cocking my head in his direction and begging him to discredit the facts. "So tell me again how you think you won't get drafted, because numbers don't lie, baby."

He stares at me, dumbfounded, his fork clattering to the countertop.

"What?" I frown before shoving another bite of food in my mouth.

"Nothing, it's just…sometimes I forget how stupidly smart you are," he murmurs before picking up his fork again.

"That's an oxymoron if I've ever heard one."

Kason blinks a couple times, his brows furrowing at the center. "And apparently I'm just a moron, because I have no fucking clue what that is."

"It's kinda like a paradox."

He shakes his head again. "Nope, not a clue."

"Jumbo shrimp. Old news. Pretty ugly. Two things that contradict each other but are still placed together."

"Oh, okay. Yeah, I didn't realize that's what those are called." He gives me a sheepish grin when he spears a piece of broccoli with his fork. "I kinda cheated off Phoenix in English all through high school. Just a little bit."

I laugh, not sure if I should be mortified or amused by that piece of information. "You were definitely the kid I hated back in those days. The jocks always used to fight about sitting near me in school, especially math class."

"Oh, I have no doubt about that," he says immediately, shaking his head. "Then again, there was a good period of time where I was the kid you hated these days too, remember?"

I do, but damn if it doesn't feel like a thousand years ago rather than a couple months.

Honestly, it's hard to believe there was ever a point where I didn't like Kason, didn't want him around, didn't see him for all the deep intricacies of who he is below the surface.

It's even harder to believe I could've missed out on him, all because of my stubborn, bull-headed nature. And knowing the amount of time I've already wasted makes it hard for me to rationalize wasting any more.

Setting my fork on the counter, I look over at him, a little nervous about the answer to my next question. "Do you wanna come for Thanksgiving dinner? To my parents' house, I mean?"

He pauses, a bite halfway to his mouth, and frowns. "Do you want me to come?"

"I always want you to come, baby," I murmur, my voice low and seductive as my lips lift in a filthy smirk. His cheeks bloom pink, like they often do when he leaves himself open for my dirty jokes, and I give him the small mercy of rerouting to the original question. "But yes, I'd also like you to accept my invitation. And if it'll make you more comfortable, you don't have to come as anything other than my roommate. Whatever you want."

"They won't mind?"

"Not at all." I turn on my stool to face him, one arm resting on the counter, the other on the back of my chair. "I can't tell you how many family holidays or vacations Quinton has crashed over the years, and they didn't care then." He still doesn't respond, clearly unconvinced when I add, "This is one dinner, Kase. I promise, they won't mind. I just don't want you to spend the holiday alone when I'll be twenty minutes down the road having some ridiculous feast my mom is inevitably preparing."

"Okay. Then I'll come," he whispers, that shy, sexy little smile tugging at his lips.

I let out a low, appreciative hum, unable to stop myself from teasing him on his word choice yet again.

"Hopefully in more ways than one."

TWENTY-TWO

Kason

The amount of tension and anxiety in my body as we stop at the gate outside Hayes' parents house could be cut with a knife, it's so thick, and the second the wrought iron doors shift open, giving way for us to pull through, it increases exponentially.

Hayes steers his car through the opening, and the second the house itself comes into view, my jaw might as well be on the ground.

"How much money did you say your family has?" I find myself asking while I gape at the massive home. I don't even know how to describe it other than that it looks like a ginormous version of those little cottages in Germany or Switzerland—with emphasis on the ginormous part.

Hayes glances my way from the driver's seat and smirks. "I don't think I did."

Oh, Jesus take the wheel.

The nerves only get worse when Hayes leads me through the front door, calling out to his parents that we've arrived before hauling me through the opulent foyer, then through the living room that's massive enough to hold half a football field.

I feel like I've just walked into a freaking fairytale, and now I'm just waiting for Cinderella to pop out of the damn broom closet to tell me I don't belong.

We round the corner to the kitchen—which looks like it belongs in a five-star restaurant rather than a home—where we find a middle-aged woman with Hayes' same dark curls and sapphire eyes who can only be his mother.

She may as well have stepped out of a magazine, dressed in an elegant knee length dress and heels, crimson painting her lips.

"Hayes, darling," she greets as soon as she sees us, a smile illuminating her face. "You're early. I thought you'd said you wouldn't be here 'til dinner."

"Hey, Mom," he murmurs, kissing her cheek as she wraps him in a hug. "Kason's Coach ended up giving them the day off. Figured I'd come help you get things ready."

"Oh, sweetheart, you didn't need to do that," she chides when she pulls back. Her glittering gaze flashes to me, and she smiles. "And you must be Kason."

Stepping forward, I hold out my hand, which she gingerly takes.

"It's a pleasure to meet you, Mrs. Lancaster. Thank you for allowing me to join you for your holiday dinner," I say with the most Southern charm I can muster.

Her smile is sugar sweet as I release her. "Of course. Any friend of Hayes' is welcome."

My eyes flash to Hayes, finding him waiting for me to make the next move. He's abiding by his promise to come as simply friends and roommates, but now that I'm here in freaking Martha Stewart's kitchen with his mother, I don't want to be anything other than his.

Giving him a discreet nod, I reach toward him. He meets me halfway, linking his fingers with mine.

"Actually," Hayes says, his attention flicking to his mother. "He's also my boyfriend."

To her credit, she doesn't so much as stumble at the information. In fact, I think her eyes take on the slightest sheen as she glances between the two of us, clapping her hands together.

"Even better." She smiles, all bright and cheerful. "We've got about an hour until dinner will be ready, so why don't you show Kason around, and I'll call when we're ready to eat?"

"Are you sure you don't need help?" I offer, doing my best to be polite. "We could set the table, and I'm pretty good in the kitch—"

"That's quite all right, dear. The table's set, and as for the food, I've got it covered."

With her dismissal, Hayes takes my hand and leads me around the family *estate* that has apparently been in his family for nearly as many generations as the family business—dating back to the late 1800s.

As hard as it is for me to imagine growing up in a place like this, I can see why Hayes is so guarded about it. It's easy to see how someone might be granted access to this level of financial security and do whatever they can to take advantage of it.

And while Hayes has mentioned that very thing being the case, it was hard to understand the scale and magnitude of why until now.

True to her word, Mrs. Lancaster sends one of their staff to find us nearly an hour later, well before we've seen all of the grounds, and escort us to the formal dining room where we're to have dinner.

Hayes' father and brother are already seated at the massive table that could easily seat a dozen or more people, both donning clothes I'd consider a bit fancy for a family dinner, though still consistent with the khakis and knit sweater Hayes is wearing.

Meanwhile, I'm in a plaid button down and the nicest pair of jeans I own, sticking out like a sore thumb in a house that likely costs more money than my father would make in his lifetime.

"Stop worrying," he whispers as we take a seat across from his brother and the empty chair, I'd assume, is for his mother.

Asking me to stop worrying right now is like asking the sun not to shine or birds not to sing, but I give him my best fake smile and pretend like I can anyway.

Mrs. Lancaster joins us a few moments later, followed by an entire wait staff who bring out all the Thanksgiving fixins imaginable. They serve us, which is by far the weirdest part of the night so far, and as the five of us dig into our food, that's when the real fun begins.

"So, Kason," Hayes' mother says across from me with a tempered smile. "Tell us a little about yourself."

Nerves eat at me as I offer her the most watered-down version of my life story imaginable.

"Well, I was born in Alabama. Raised there for part of my life until my dad moved us to Nashville when I was starting middle school. Then I lived there with him until college."

"Just your father?"

"Yep," I respond, the word coming out clipped and higher pitched than I'd like.

Hayes glances at me before looking at his mother. "His mom left when he was twelve. It was just him and his father after that."

"I'm sorry to hear that," his mother condoles, her attention flitting to her husband, then back to me. "It's a shame when parents don't think of their children over their own selfish interests."

Doing my best to ignore the insinuation in her tone, I muster up a smile as I continue cutting my turkey. "It's all right. If anything, it's made me more grateful for the people who treat me like family, despite not being blood." Lifting my gaze to her, I continue, "My best friend and his family would often let me spend time at his house. Kept me on the straight and narrow, made sure I focused on bettering my future instead of focusing on where I came from. If it wasn't for them, I don't know where I'd be." My eyes move to Hayes now, and I can feel them soften as I look at him. "Certainly not here with you."

He gives me a warm smile, and I do my best to harness the feeling it gives me, channeling it into enough confidence to get through this dinner unscathed. Telling myself, while they might be his family, at the end of the day, they're humans too.

None of them are perfect, no matter how much it might look so on the outside.

"Hayes told us you play football for Leighton, is that right?" Mrs. Lancaster asks, slicing through my calming efforts as easily as she does the sweet potatoes on her plate.

But she's asking about football. Something I can talk about all day.

Perfect.

"I do, yeah. I've been their starting tight end since I was a freshman."

"That must make keeping up with your academics challenging," she says almost immediately, and it has my stomach dropping.

Well, fuck.

I smile, though I'm feeling anything but happy about where this conversation is leading. "At times, it can be. But Leighton takes doing well in school very seriously, so they have a really great program for all their student athletes to make sure we stay on track with our course work."

"That's wonderful to hear," she bemuses as she slices her turkey. "Speaking of studies, what is it that you're majoring in?"

"Mom," Hayes interrupts rather sternly, and when I look over at him, his face absolutely matches his tone: stone cold, and not having any bullshit. It's a side of Hayes I haven't seen in quite a while.

"It's okay, Hayes," I murmur to let him know I'm fine. Yet from the way his jaw tics with tension, it must not be very convincing.

"No, it's not," he tells me softly before looking at his mother. "This is dinner, not an interrogation. Stop treating him like a criminal."

Mrs. Lancaster lets out a clipped laugh. "Oh, Hayes, darling. I know that. I'm just trying to get to know him. After all, he's dating my youngest child. Any decent parent would want to do the same."

Rhys, who has been quiet since we've sat down, lets out a snort and takes a swig of his drink, grabbing the attention of everyone at the table. When he notices, he holds up his hands in mock surrender.

"Oh, what? Am I supposed to act like you wouldn't do this with any person one of us would bring through the door?"

"Watch your tone, Rhys," Hayes' father grumbles from the head of the table, and truthfully, I think this is the first time I've heard him speak all evening too.

Up until now, I'd have thought the matriarch of the family was the one really in charge.

Then again, she *is* the one grilling me like a filet.

"No, it's okay." I say, smiling so hard it feels like my face might break.

"I really don't mind answering them."

Hayes glances over to me, and I do my best to offer him reassurance with my gaze. I know it's not much, but it seems to do the trick because he returns his attention to his mother when I go to speak.

"I'm earning a degree in sports management. Nothing fancy like Hayes, but I'm enjoying it."

"I see," she murmurs, nodding idly while cutting more of her food. "Is there a large market of jobs in the degree field?"

"Some," I confirm, though I leave out the part where it's a pretty difficult industry to get a foot in the door, or that I'd likely need a business degree on top of it to really get where I'd want to be. "It's not really my main goal, though. The NFL has always been plan A."

"Oh, really? I was under the impression that football was just for fun while you were still in school."

I'm not sure how she got that impression, and from the look on Hayes' face, neither is he.

"Kason is one of the best tight ends Leighton has ever seen. His stats have been the top of the conference the past two years, and he's one of the best in the country," Hayes chimes in, though I know that information is likely meaningless to them. It's clear they don't care for anything to do with athletics, but it doesn't stop him from tacking on, "There's a good chance of him being invited to the combine at the beginning of March and everything."

She looks rather impressed by that information, however briefly. "Is that some sort of contest?"

I roll my head back and forth, not really sure how to describe it to someone who has next to no knowledge of football. "Sort of. It's a process we go through after declaring eligibility for the draft. We're invited to attend the combine to perform various drills so a pro team can see what they're getting if they decide to sign us."

"Meaning there is no guarantee that a team even *does* sign you. Or even if you'll get an invite at all," Rhys explains before finishing off whatever dark liquor is in his glass. "There's always a catch when it comes to sports, Mom."

Hayes looks ready to bury his brother six feet under as he smiles and utters, "His chances are high," through gritted teeth.

The look in Rhys' green eyes tells me he's less than convinced, but surprisingly, chooses not to comment. Mr. Lancaster has remained silent through most of the conversation, clearly bored by the entire thing, his gaze fixated on his dinner.

Which leaves only Hayes' mother to continue pulling information from me.

"Say you do get drafted…" she starts, gently placing her fork back on the table and folding her hands in her lap. "From what I understand, there's no guarantee it'd be by the team in Chicago, or in a city anywhere near it. What would that mean for your relationship with Hayes?"

That…is a great fucking question. One I don't have an answer to, if I'm being honest. Neither of us have talked about that possibility; we've been too wrapped up in each other to think about the logistics of how this would look in the long term.

God only knows if Hayes even *wants* this to go past graduation.

I'd love nothing more, to be honest, but I'm also aware of how new this is, and more importantly, that it might be too soon to be asking these kinds of questions.

But unfortunately, from the expectant look on Mrs. Lancaster's face, it's not one we're getting out of answering.

Hayes stiffens beside me, and I don't take that as a good sign. In fact, I'm expecting anything other than what he actually says once he finds his composure.

"Plenty of people do the long-distance thing, Mom."

I can't help the way my heart fucking soars at that comment. This is a conversation we should be having privately, after all, and I can tell he's only feeding her the tidbits he can without talking to me first.

But damn, it feels good to know that we're somewhat on the same page.

Mrs. Lancaster, however, looks less than pleased by this information, pursing her lips again. "Of course, darling. Your father and I did long distance for almost a year when we were younger. However, it puts quite a lot of strain on a relationship, and that can cause priorities to start…shifting."

"And that's a bridge we'd cross if and when the time came." Hayes' hand lands on my thigh, squeezing it reassuringly under the table. "Besides, you know as well as I do, most of what I would be doing for LFC in the beginning can be taken care of remotely. There's really no need for me to be in the office day in and day out for work until I officially take over for Dad."

"So rather than go to the office, you'd just follow him around the country like some little groupie?" she asks, unable to hide her distaste of the idea.

Rhys snorts out a laugh. "They're actually called cleat chasers, Mom."

"Which I'm not one," Hayes snaps at his brother before turning his attention back to his mom. "And that's not at all what I'm saying. I was simply pointing out that distance doesn't *have* to be an issue."

"And to be clear, this is only if I were to get drafted," I add, doing my best to back Hayes up in this. "Who knows, maybe I get lucky and end up in Chicago or Indianapolis or somewhere else close by and it wouldn't matter."

Something about Mrs. Lancaster's tight expression tells me that's exactly the scenario she is hoping to avoid, but I try to shove down the insecurity as best I can.

"You actually making it to the NFL is when the real issues would arise, though," Rhys counters, pouring himself another glass of alcohol. "Injury, regular wear and tear on your body from taking those kinds of hits, they're all gonna add up, and it's a toss up if one of those will take you out of the game for good." He glances at his brother before adding, "You love your statistics, Hayes. Surely you were well aware that the average career length in the NFL is barely over three years."

"Well, that doesn't seem like much of a viable career path," Mrs. Lancaster says with a light chuckle. "It's a good thing you have a degree to fall back on, which would make much more sense to focus on for the remainder of your collegiate years."

"Or he could continue to pursue a career in the NFL, because it's his choice what to do with his life," Hayes offers, the bite in his tone unmistakable.

His mother doesn't seem to care or notice, though. Her eyes remain set on me, her head canting to the side ever so slightly while she replies to her son.

"Of course, dear, and it's Kason's prerogative to do as he wishes. But prioritizing his future's longevity by choosing a more sustainable career path is simply something he should think about. Especially if he were to consider what would be more befitting as a partner." Her lips lift ever so slightly before she adds, "Wouldn't you agree, Kason?"

It takes me a second to find my voice, and once I do, the only thing I can say is, "Duly noted, ma'am," and let it be.

And because small mercies do exist, the rest of dinner is filled with idle chit-chat between Rhys, Hayes, and their mother, where she takes her turn to weaponize their life choices against them too—though that is more reserved for Rhys than Hayes. Honestly, I'm just glad to see I'm not the only one on the receiving end of her tactful, yet effective, verbal smackdowns.

After all, it's still lingering in my mind even as Hayes and I wish his family a happy holiday and exit their home.

"Was that as bad as I thought it was?" I ask as we descend the steps toward his car. "Because as good as it might have started, by the end, I felt like I was thrown to the wolves and eaten alive."

Hayes purses his lips before glaring back at the house. "It wasn't bad, but it wasn't good either."

Fantastic.

Blowing out a long sigh, I shake my head. "I'm sorry. I really wanted to make a good impression on them. I—"

"Baby, don't worry about it," he says immediately.

Taking a step toward me, he closes the distance between us and cups the back of my head. His eyes are close to a navy color in the evening light as they silently search mine.

"Lancasters are notoriously hard to impress. Trust me, I'm one of them. And you won me over, right?"

I concede to his point, but not without muttering, "It took a while."

"Yeah, but you wore me down," he reminds me, turning my face toward his when I try to look away. "It might take time, but it'll happen eventually. Okay?"

Taking in a deep breath, I nod, though the last thing I want is to think about any future encounters with his mother. From the way his expression softens, Hayes seems to pick up on it too.

"C'mon. Let's go home," he murmurs, brushing a kiss to my jaw. "As repayment for a terrible *'meet the parents'* moment, you can choose what we do for the rest of the night."

"How 'bout the rest of the weekend?" I barter, the mood already starting to lighten.

His soft laugh coasts over my skin. "Depends. What are your terms?"

"Well, considering your mother's deep concern about me taking school seriously, I think it's about time we had a new lesson."

My eyes flick to his, gauging his reaction, only to find them searing with a heat capable of melting Antarctica in an instant.

"I think I can be convinced."

TWENTY-THREE

Kason

We're back to the apartment within twenty minutes, but it's the most tortuous drive of my life. Even worse than the one *to* his parents, and it's all thanks to Hayes' less-than-ideal hand placement on my upper thigh the entire way there.

If anyone would've told me I'd be horny after the way tonight's events went, I would've laughed in their faces and told them to kindly fuck off. But here I am, wanting nothing more than to rip my boyfriend's clothes off and feel him sink inside me for the first time.

If I'm being honest, I've wanted this for weeks now; Hayes has been the one making sure we take things slow. I know it's because he doesn't want me to regret anything, even if he hasn't expressed it aloud. But this is one thing I'm certain I won't.

The only person I can picture as my first is Hayes.

"You're sure about this?" he asks, dropping his keys on the counter. The sound echoes through the otherwise silent apartment like a gunshot, and it has my heart hammering in my chest.

But not out of fear. Out of anticipation.

Nodding, I step closer and wrap my hand around the back of his neck. I don't kiss him, though. Instead, I just tilt his chin up the tiniest fraction, forcing his sapphire gaze to collide with mine.

"I want you, Hayes. More than anyone or anything else."

His eyes remain locked with mine, as assessing and analytical as ever, and I can see the questions in them, running rampant in his brilliant mind. And it's ironic, because there was a time when I swore I'd never get a read on the guy—or would read him wrong entirely.

Now I can read his expressions as easily as I could my favorite novel.

Right now, it's all lust and worry.

"And how exactly do you want me?" he finally asks, breaking the unbearable silence.

"Inside me, for one," I murmur, leaning in and brushing my nose against his. "As for the location, I think a bed would suffice. And when it comes to the position…well, I'll leave that to the more experienced of us to decide."

I don't let him overthink it after that, crashing my mouth to his. We stumble down the hallway, blindly searching for a door leading to a bed, not caring who it belongs to. Our hands grip at each other's clothing, peeling and stripping the fabric free until we're left in only our underwear.

Hayes' tongue rolls against mine, teasing and taunting when we fall onto the mattress.

I love the way he takes control. How he'll allow me to have the lead, set the pace, but then flip things on a dime. It might be the sexiest thing

I've ever experienced.

My anticipation is at an all-time high when Hayes breaks away from me to grab the lube from his nightstand. His eyes stay locked on mine, gauging my features as he pops open the bottle and applies copious amounts to his fingers. Watching him multiplies the butterflies swarming in my stomach, heightening the thrill rushing through me as goosebumps pepper my skin.

Continuing to hold my gaze, he settles between my thighs and brushes his cool, lubricated finger down my crease. My nerve-endings are on high alert, desire setting my blood to a boil as he skillfully massages my rim before breaching the tight ring of muscle and sinking a long digit into me.

A tortured moan slips free, my ass bearing down as he slowly thrusts it in and out. He wastes no time, leaning in and carving a path down from my neck with his mouth, skating over my chest and stomach, until he finally reaches my dick. His free hand wraps around the base, and as he slowly slips a second finger inside me, he damn near swallows my length whole.

The dual sensation fills me with a burning lust that I've quickly grown addicted to.

"Oh, shit," I mutter, arching into his touch as his talented tongue lavishes my cock with attention. His fingers slowly pump in and out of me, swiping over my prostate on the down thrust.

I look down in time to catch him smiling around my dick, and Jesus Christ, the sight is far sexier than it should be. No one should look that good with a cock in their mouth.

My heart slams against my ribs, my pulse beating uncontrollably in my throat as desire barrels through me, curling my toes. Anchoring my hands in his hair, I guide him up and down my length while working magic with the fingers inside me.

No more than a couple minutes with his mouth and hands on me, and

I'm already a leaking, needy mess. A lit fuse, ready to explode.

But I only want that to happen with him seated fully inside me.

"More, Hayes. Please," I pant, not above begging him.

My head slams back against the pillow, arching and thrusting and moving with his touch, seeking more of whatever he's willing to give.

He starts rolling his tongue around the head, giving the bundle of nerves under the crown all his attention while his fingers hone in on my prostate. Pressure on both of those spots has stars lighting up behind my eyelids, and it takes everything in my power to not come on the spot.

"Fuck. I need you inside me. Now." I make an attempt to pull him off my length, using my hold on his hair to do so, but he barely gives an inch.

My eyes fly open to find him looking up at me, a devilish taunt in his eyes before his mouth releases me.

"Someone needs to learn patience," he murmurs, his lips trailing back up my stomach, taking detours over my pecs, nipples, collar bone. Anywhere he can bite or suck or lick, he does, and it's fucking torture while he still plays with my ass.

"Please, don't make me beg you."

Grinning, he rises up between my thighs, pulling his fingers free from my body. "Don't worry, baby. That's a lesson for another day."

Goddamn.

There's no doubt in my mind, the filthy promises that fall from Hayes Lancaster's lips will be the death of me.

Thankfully, he takes mercy on me, spreading me wider before methodically adding more lube to my crease. His gaze lifts to mine when he finishes, assessing my features.

"You're still okay going bare?"

I nod, another zing of anticipation going through me. We've both been tested and cleared, and since this thing between us is exclusive, I don't wanna feel a damn thing but him the first time he's inside. Or anytime after, for that matter.

Permission granted, he douses his length with the liquid, spreading it down his shaft before settling between my thighs again. I feel him at my crease seconds later, the cool lube swiping up and down over my rim as he rubs his crown against it.

His eyes are equal parts worry and lust, like they seem to be every time we tackle a new step, and he wets his lower lip.

"Tell me if you need me to stop or if it's too much, okay?"

And just like I do every time, I nod in assurance, still finding it a little ironic that he's more nervous about all my firsts than I am.

Then again, it just shows he actually cares, even if he doesn't say it in that many words.

Pressing his hips forward, I brace myself for the burn I've grown accustomed to. It's slight at first, paired with the pressure of his cock stretching past my rim, and I breathe through my nose while my body adjusts.

"Good?" he asks, his voice coming out a little strained.

I nod, my jaw clenching in effort. He takes that as permission to continue, drawing his hips back ever so slightly and pressing in deeper. The burn intensifies as he slides further into me, more discomfort than pain that eases again when he pulls back a second time.

It's not until the third thrust, when his hips land flush against my ass that the bite of pain hits. I feel fuller than I thought possible—like I might burst at the seams. And it's the strangest kind of pleasure I've ever experienced, stealing all the oxygen from my lungs.

"Holyfuckingchristonacracker," I hiss, my fingertips digging into his waist hard enough, it'll likely bruise.

Hayes stays completely still, apart from raining kiss after kiss across my jaw and throat, allowing my body time to adjust from his intrusion. Slipping one hand between us, he wraps his palm around my cock and starts stroking it ever so slowly.

"Breathe, baby," he coaxes before brushing a kiss on my lips. "Breathe and try to relax for me. Focus on my hand."

I follow his request, drawing in a large gasp of air and fixate on the way his hand feels jacking my length. And it works. It doesn't take long for the burning to subside, replaced with pleasure as pre-cum leaks from my tip that he's quick to gather and spread down my shaft.

"That's it, Kase. That's perfect." He whispers his praise before stealing a kiss. "I'm gonna start moving now. Just tell me if it's too much."

Nodding, I brace myself for the burning to return, yet it never does. It remains in the background as he slowly pulls back and thrusts in again, and after a couple minutes, it's gone entirely.

All that's left is mind-numbing pleasure, and I quickly lose myself in it. In the way his hand torments my cock, his thumb rolling over the bundle of nerves below the head. Or the steady pistoning of his hips as he impales me with his dick.

It's torture. It's bliss.

It's like nothing I've ever experienced.

"Don't stop," I pant, my head thrown back against the mattress while he drives into me with long, measured thrusts that have sharp pangs of lust zipping through me like lightning.

Pressing a quick kiss to my jaw, he murmurs, "Wouldn't dream of it."

True to his word, Hayes makes no sign of letting up, and it doesn't take long for me to start moving with him. With every thrust, I meet him halfway, our bodies colliding together while we chase a high like no other.

In fact, I can feel myself right there already, teetering on the edge of climax when Hayes lights me up from the inside out, the head of his cock swiping over my prostate.

"Fuck, Hayes. Keep doing that," I plead, my hands tracing down his back until I reach the tight globes of his ass. "I'm so fucking close."

Hayes' hips piston forward at a relentless pace now, and after adjusting the angle, he nails my prostate with every thrust now. Every cell in my body is on fire, craving the release he's promising.

"Jack yourself. Show me how you touch yourself when you're alone. When you're thinking of me."

Mother of fucking God.

Palming my cock, I start stroking my shaft in long, quick succession, rolling my fist over the head before dropping back down the base. I match the rhythm Hayes has set, moving quicker when he does as his lips land on mine.

His tongue spears into my mouth, rolling against mine while he fucks me clean into the mattress, no part of this slow or gentle now.

And it's fucking heaven.

The combined sensations cause my release to hit me out of nowhere, cum spilling from my dick onto my hands and abs while he drives into me. The orgasm causes my ass to bear down on his length, squeezing and pulsing around him, and the groan slipping from his lips tells me I'm dragging him toward climax too.

"Fuck, baby. You're like a vise," he rasps, his forehead pressing against mine as he continues thrusting into me with reckless abandon. "You feel so good. I'm right there with you."

From the pulsing vein in his throat and the strained look on his face, he's barely holding it together, every piece of him begging to shatter right along with me. And God, how I want it.

I wanna see him lose control, watch as he falls apart.

And I wanna be the reason for it.

Releasing my cock, I anchor my hand on his hip, the other curling around his neck. My fingers weave through the hair at the base of his skull, and I drag his lips to mine. I tease the seam with my tongue before slipping between them, diving in for more.

The hand on his hip coaxes him to move faster, harder. Whatever it is he needs to find release.

I'm hypersensitive, every thrust and swipe over my prostate creating the most delicious sensation in my lower stomach. It builds and builds, tightening all over again while he pounds into me, all finesse and rhythm gone.

"I—" I gasp, "Fuck, Hayes."

The same sensation as earlier—being shoved off a cliff into oblivion—slams into me again, causing stars to light up behind my eyelids. The only difference is, this time, nothing spills from my cock.

What the—

I don't have time to think about what just happened, because Hayes' climax slams into him at the same time, his hips colliding with my ass in quick, rapid thrusts while he hisses out a string of expletives. The feel of his cum filling my ass is foreign, as is the sensation of it leaking out from his continued movements, but it's not unwelcome. In fact, it's the opposite.

And as Hayes' thrusts finally cease and he collapses over me, it's like some sort of missing piece just snaps into place.

I feel whole in a way I never have before.

Wrapping my arms around his sweat-slickened lower back, I draw in as much air as my lungs can hold while waiting for my heartbeat to slow to normal. I can feel the rapid beat of his too, pounding like a racehorse against my chest as he buries his face into the crook of my neck while we come down from our orgasm high.

"Holy shit," Hayes murmurs, the words coming out muffled.

He can say that again. I might as well be reduced to mush beneath him; boneless and made of gelatin, which is why I have no fucking clue how he manages to prop himself up on an elbow to look down at me.

"You just had a prostate orgasm, didn't you?"

I chuckle softly. "You ask that like I know what you're talking about."

He grins, and the sight of it has my stomach flipping. "You came a second time, just without the cum."

"Then I guess, yeah."

But it's not the orgasms that have my head all in a daydream. It's the feeling I got afterward.

"I've never felt anything like that before," I whisper, my eyes locked on the ceiling.

"I'm almost a little jealous," he says with a laugh before pressing a kiss to my shoulder, then the side of my throat. "The beauty of the prostate."

I hum, a smile tugging at my lips. "Mmm, not exactly what I meant, but I definitely agree."

"Wait, what did you mean then?"

My head rolls back and forth on the pillow as I shake it, unsure of how to describe whatever it was that I just felt.

"It was like…I don't know. Something just clicked inside me. Kinda like a puzzle piece or a lock snapping into place."

Hayes pulls back, just barely enough to lock gazes with me. It's guarded, of that, I'm certain, but there's something else in it I can't quite put my finger on.

Something softer. More intimate, almost.

"Is that not normal?" I whisper, vulnerability hitting me square in the chest. The kind I haven't felt since the night we decided to really give this thing a go.

He slowly shakes his head, eyes never once leaving mine. "No, baby. That's not normal."

My heart sinks ever so slightly, but I swallow down my disappointment and force out my next questions.

"So you didn't feel it?"

There's a beat before he clears his throat.

"No, I felt it, too."

TWENTY-FOUR

Hayes

December

I'm lounging on my bed, staring at my ceiling while I wait for Kason to get back from his last final for the semester, my mind on the way my last two finals went earlier today.

A good portion of the tests were fine, but there was a chunk during each where I felt myself stumbling through, thinking about a billion other things than the paper in front of me, and that never happens. Or it didn't, until today.

What's worse is, as soon as I walked out of that building, I couldn't help but wonder if my parents hit the nail on the head about Kason being a distraction in more than just the literal sense.

Physically, yeah, he's been taking up a lot of my free time, making a huge dent in the amount I'd normally spend studying, but I'd made sure to compensate for that.

But I haven't been prepared for all the space he'd take up mentally.

Because the moments where my mind refused to focus, it was thinking about the two of us in bed this morning, curled into each other while he slept. Or the way I stripped him bare again last night and watched him ride me for the first time.

He's consuming my time, my thoughts, my life.

And the strangest part is, I don't care the way I know I should, and definitely not the way my parents want me to.

The sound of my phone dinging pulls my mind out of daydreaming, and I check it to find a text from Q.

Q: I know you've got finals, but are you alive over there? I haven't heard from you in almost two weeks.

Guilt slams into me immediately.

I hadn't been ignoring his texts or gaming requests, I've just been busy with school and class work and consumed by Kason.

Fuck, I haven't even told him *anything* about Kason and me.

Me: Alive? Yes, but barely. You got a minute to talk?

It doesn't take more than ten seconds before a FaceTime notification from Quinton pops up on my screen. Accepting the call, I find my best friend lounging on a couch, ice pack wrapped around his left shoulder.

"Hey, man. What's up?" he asks while adjusting the black rims on his face.

First things first: I need to rip the bandaid off about Kason, but I don't exactly want an audience for it, which is why I hesitate before questioning, "Are you alone right now?"

A tiny smirk curls the corner of his lips, popping a dimple. "Oakley's in the shower, so I have a few minutes of solitude. Why?"

Once again, I hesitate, not sure where to start with the events of the past two months.

Just fucking say it.

"I slept with Kason," I finally blurt out.

He can't hide his surprise, brows shooting upward in an instant. "No shit."

I nod, before adding. "Since October."

I'm not sure how I expected him to react, but it definitely wasn't his jaw dropping open and him shouting, "You've been holding out on me, you fucker!" loud enough to wake the dead.

"Calm down, you overly dramatic nympho," I hiss, not wanting him to draw Oakley's attention. "I didn't think you wanted the dirty details of my sex life."

Snorting, he mutters, "You should know me far better than that."

He does have a point. Q's been around for the few relationships I've been in, and he knows I'm not the type to just sleep with someone on a whim. It's one of the many ways my best friend and I are total opposites: He's a manwhore—albeit reformed, now. Meanwhile, I'm the equivalent of a monk in a cock cage thanks to my need to emotionally connect with someone before ever sleeping with them, and that's not even taking into account my distaste for people.

The same distaste I had for Kason that Quinton knows all about. It's why the question in his eyes is loud and clear well before it finally leaves his mouth. "How the hell did it happen? I mean, I thought you hated him." He pauses, his eyes widening animatedly before he adds, "Wait, are you hate fucking? Can you do that when you're demi? Hate is as deep of an emotion as any—"

"Oh, my God," I cut in, chuckling at his barrage of questions. "We aren't having hate-sex, so you can cool it. We're…in a relationship."

The fact that he looks disappointed in that answer has me laughing even more.

"Okay, so if it's not hate-sex, where the hell did that come from?"

I shrug. "Left fucking field, apparently."

"Look, I know you're basically a genius," he starts, arching a brow, "but that's the wrong sport, Hayes."

"Oh, fuck off," I mutter, laughing some more. "Leave it to you to bullshit with me when I'm telling you semi-earth-altering news."

He lets out a hum, face contorting in disagreement. "Earth-altering isn't exactly the way *I'd* describe it, but—"

"I'm hanging up now."

Quinton chuckles, both dimples in full view now. "Dramatic as always. But I take it this little call is for more than just to tell me your dry spell is over. So what's up?"

"I dunno, I just…" A stupid smile crosses my face, and I shake my head. "I dunno. Anyway, how's it—"

"Oh, my God," he cuts in, sitting up through the phone screen. "You really like him."

"Obviously I like him if I'm in a relationship with him."

He rolls his eyes, evidently annoyed by my smart-assery. "Don't bullshit me, Hayes. I've known you too long for you to get away with it."

He's right.

I'm in really fucking deep, being dragged under by emotions I don't fully understand yet. In the few relationships I've been in, I've never felt this. The want to keep going forward. Looking toward the future, and feeling excited for what it might hold, despite it being unknown.

And I can't help the smile that crosses my face all over again.

"I do, yeah. A lot."

"Damn, that's wild considering you were ready to murder him the moment he moved in." He shakes his head, clearly still trying to process the information. "What changed?"

Everything.

Okay, maybe that's actually being dramatic, but it's partly true. The second I let my guard down enough to actually get to know him—allow parts of myself to be vulnerable with him and receive those pieces of him in return—something clicked.

Just like Kason said the night after he met my parents, and it's stayed that way every moment since.

Rolling my tongue over my lip, I try to find the best way to describe it, only to come up with something that barely scratches the surface.

"He's…exactly like I expected, but at the same time, he's entirely different."

"That'll do it." A grin splits Q's face before he glances over the screen—probably in the direction Oakley's in. "Trust me, I know the feeling well."

Sighing, I mutter, "It wasn't supposed to happen, though."

"The sex, or…"

"None of it." Sitting up, I shift back against my headboard and prop my phone on my knee. "This year was supposed to be easy. I'd go to my classes, make the grades, get the degree—"

"Then get in at your dad's firm, I know," he finishes for me, still smirking. "That's been your life plan since we were kids. At this point, I know it better than my social security number."

I snort out a laugh, despite the helpless feeling of it all. "That's not my fault if you can't remember a simple nine-digit number."

"I was being facetious, you dick, but feel free to continue with your quarter-life crisis."

"It's not a *crisis*," I rebut, though there's a good part of my brain that would beg to differ. "It's more that nowhere in all that planning did a relationship fit into it. Let alone with an NFL prospect who could very well be living on the other side of the country by this time next year."

"And you think Oakley was part of any future I saw for myself?" Quinton lets out a sharp laugh. "Love was the last goddamn thing on my mind when things between us started. All I cared about was hockey and winning and fuck everything else. But when he showed me the parts of him I didn't know existed, there was no way to prevent my heart from being stolen." His eyes flash off the screen again before coming back to mine. "You don't get to choose who you fall in love with. It just happens, and no amount of planning is gonna stop it."

Hell must've froze over if I'm even debating taking real, mature, adult advice from Quinton de Haas…and it's actually making sense.

"Slow down, there, Q. It's a little soon to be mentioning the L-word."

"What's that saying about protesting too much?" he immediately counters, smirking.

"But at least the two of you wanted the same thing," I reply, ignoring his comment. "You ended up in the same place, get to see each other every day, live together…"

The thing is, I've pictured things between Kason and me for the long haul. Maybe not in extreme detail as to *how* it would work—which is uncharacteristic in itself—but enough to feel like this could really go somewhere.

And yet…

"If he gets drafted, that's basically all out the window," I whisper, defeated.

"You seem to forget Oakley and I still had a damn good chance of being on opposite sides of the country when we entered the NHL draft. We had no idea where either of us would be going, but we were committed to doing it together, no matter what."

I roll my eyes. "Yet it all worked out in the end."

"It did, yeah. But that's only because we were willing to risk it all, even if the odds were stacked against us. And I'm glad we did." A daydreamy expression crosses his features, and one of those dopey, love-drunk smiles pulls at his lips. "You should've seen his face when he realized we'd actually be able to live together, let alone play together again. I've never seen him happier. And to be the reason he smiles that way? It's fucking powerful." His attention moves back to me now, his gaze imploring and earnest when he adds, "You just gotta be open to changes in the plan."

I let out a frustrated sigh, wishing like hell it was as simple as he's making it sound.

Kason's come to mean a great deal to me, and even though this is still really new—and also kind of insane—I wanna see where it can go. But now, I'm starting to question if it's even worth trying, and I hate it.

Before Thanksgiving, none of this shit had even entered the equation for me. I was in a blissful little sex bubble with Kason where the only thing that existed was the two of us getting to really know each other. Now, my family has popped it with an ice-cold shard of reality.

He studies me, icy blue eyes analyzing my every feature before he asks, "What aren't you saying?"

Damn him for knowing me so well.

Sighing, I mutter, "I took him to meet my family for Thanksgiving."

A low whistle leaves him, and he shakes his head with a chuckle. "Damn, you do mean business with this one."

Yeah, I kinda do.

"Don't start planning a bachelor party just yet, because it didn't exactly go well."

He snorts and shakes his head. "I find that hard to believe. Your parents are the ones I wish I would've had."

"Yeah, well, they're the reason I'm all in my head and worried about what it means if he gets drafted thanks to treating dinner like a goddamn interrogation. Asking him a shit-ton of invasive questions about what his plans are for the future and how I would fit into it, if he has any backup—" I cut myself off when I notice his eyebrows inching toward his forehead while he attempts to hide a smile. "What's that look for?"

He holds up his free hand in surrender. "Nothing, it's just…those seem like pretty standard questions to me."

"It was the way they were asking them more than anything. Like they expected us to have answers when this whole fucking thing is so new. It's only been a couple months." I blow out a sigh and run my fingers through my hair. "I'm not saying this is forever; I don't fucking know that yet. I doubt Kason does either. But I hope it could be, and I don't want to sit here and think about the possibility of it ending before we really have a chance to make it start."

"That's valid, it is. But your parents are realists, and though I wasn't there to see it, I'm willing to bet they were just trying to look out for you. I've been around them long enough to know they only have your best interests at heart, even if it didn't feel like it at the time."

Narrowing my eyes, I ask, "Why does it feel like you're on their side?"

He shakes his head immediately. "I'm not. I'm *always* on yours."

"*But?*"

He tosses his head from side to side, visibly looking for the best way to voice his thoughts. "I just think they might be forcing you to look at things a little more realistically, before either of you end up getting hurt. And that can be a tough pill to swallow when you're trapped in the love bubble."

Again, with that fucking word.

But I ignore it, instead focusing on the real topic at hand. "Telling

Kason he'd be better suited giving up on his dreams for the NFL has nothing to do with me, though. Or harping on him about having a viable plan for when things inevitably don't work out the way he wants." My jaw tics, and I look away from the screen briefly. "Realists or not, there's no fucking reason for them to shit on his dreams like that, especially when they just met him."

Q's frowning when my gaze returns to my phone, a quizzical look on his face. "That sounds more like my parents than yours. They were always so supportive of me trying to play in the NHL."

I'd be lying if that thought hasn't crossed my mind a time or fifty since we left their house after dinner that night. My mom and dad were one of Q's biggest cheerleaders; they'd come to games with me. They were literally his second family.

Which begs the question, *why?*

Why is Kason any different than Quinton in their eyes? Why are they holding him to a completely different set of standards?

Because the only answer I can think of isn't a good one.

But it's also the most obvious.

"I don't know, Q. It felt like they were treating him as just…less than. Because he grew up poor in the South with shitty parents who didn't treat him well when he had no control over the cards he was dealt." I adjust my shoulders, trying to push down my building annoyance. "If anything, he's using all that negativity he came from and trying to build something new and better for himself, yet they're treating him like he's some kid from the wrong side of the tracks that's distracting me from everything I've worked toward."

I'm breathing a little heavily when I finally stop speaking, feeling just as frustrated and worked up by their treatment of him now as I was when it happened.

Quinton must realize it too, because he gives me a sympathetic smile. "Take your parents out of the equation for now, okay? Their opinion on your life doesn't matter at the end of the day, only that you do what's best for you."

"Except I don't know what that is."

Or maybe the real issue is that, right now, it's feeling a lot like what I want and what's best for me are mutually exclusive.

"You'll figure it out, man. You don't have to have all the answers today or tomorrow or next week like you think you do. So just take it a day at a time."

I nod, knowing he's right but not having a single clue how to practice what he's preaching. Because my thoughts are still spinning, and I feel no closer to figuring out what the hell to do now than I was before he called. The only thing I do know is that hope feels too far out of reach, and yet it's pretty much the only thing I'm clinging to at this point.

Defeat and frustration have me rolling my head back and forth against my headboard, wishing for some kind of distraction from my own thoughts.

"I just want to get away from it, you know? Chicago, my parents, this looming unknown we have hanging over us now," I mutter with a sigh. "I want to enjoy what's left of college and my time with him without fucking worrying about what comes next."

"So do it," Q says automatically. "Is Leighton in the playoffs?"

I nod, pulling up Kason's schedule I've long since put in my phone. "Their bowl game is the week before Christmas."

A devious grin crosses his face—one I've seen plenty of times over the years—and I know he's already got a plan cooking up in his brain.

"Then you better get that credit card out, because I have the perfect solution."

TWENTY-FIVE

Hayes

Two delays and an extra hour sitting on the tarmac to de-ice our plane in Chicago later, Kason and I land in Newark, and there's no doubt in my mind that the two of us are damn near bursting with excitement about finally being off the goddamn plane.

Even in first class, sitting around watching them spray the plane down so we don't plummet to our deaths isn't my idea of a good time.

"Jesus Christ," Kason mutters as we make our way through the terminal. "I thought O'Hare was busy when we got there at fucking four in the morning, but this place is a nuthouse."

"It's what we get for traveling the day after Christmas."

"This was your idea," he reminds me. "I was ready to bundle up on the couch with you and an endless movie marathon until next semester when you decided to plan an impromptu trip to the Big Apple."

He makes a fair point, but we both needed to get out of Chicago.

And more importantly, I needed to get out of my damn head.

"Q was harping on me to visit, and we needed to leave the apartment before our dicks fell off from overuse. This was two birds, one stone."

"Mhmm. Sure," he murmurs with a smirk. "If you wanted me to meet your family and your best friend all in the span of a month, you just had to say that, Hazey. You just better be careful or I might start thinking you actually like me."

I roll my eyes, both at his dramatics and that ridiculous nickname that's started to grow on me. "Oh, shut up. You know I like you plenty."

"And yet you didn't take me up on my offer to join the Mile High Club on our way here."

I turn and look at him, my eyes widened in alarm and I whisper, "You're a six-three monster of a human, and the bathrooms are barely big enough to fit you by yourself. There's absolutely no way I'd be able to fuck you in there."

"That wouldn't have happened if we would've taken the private jet," he teases in a sing-songy tone.

Snorting, I shake my head as I step onto the escalator heading to baggage claim, and more importantly, where Quinton and Oakley are supposed to be waiting for us.

"I should've just kept my mouth closed about that."

"Probably. But it's great information for whenever I feel like ribbing you about the hardships of being a one-percenter." His fingers link with mine as baggage claim and all the people waiting for their loved ones come into view. "You said they'd be waiting at baggage, right?"

I nod, my eyes scanning the crowd until they fall on my best friend and his boyfriend. Of course, the second they do, I wish they hadn't.

Kason must see him too, because he clears his throat and mutters, "Does that say—"

"Sure fucking does," I reply, the words coming out clipped as I read the massive sign Q is holding for the entirety of the airport to see.

Congratulations on your penile implant surgery, Hayes!

"Oh, my God," Kason laughs from behind me. "I *knew* your dick couldn't naturally be that big."

And now I'm wishing I would have agreed to Kason's movie and sex marathon back in Chicago.

Shaking my head as we step off the escalator, we head toward my idiot best friend, who is grinning from ear to ear.

"You look rather pleased with yourself," I note, glancing between him and his ridiculous sign.

"What? This?" Q asks, shaking the posterboard he's still holding. "I wanted to make your entrance a grand one."

"For the record, I told him this was overkill," Oakley tells me while reaching for one of my bags. "It's some shit Holden would've pulled."

I meet Oakley's gaze on the hand off. "I have no doubt you did. Just like I'm sure he told you to shove it and did it anyway."

"Nail on the head, as always." Oakley smirks, nodding to me before adding, "Glad to see you, Hayes."

I nod too, a tight smile on my face as I mutter, "Likewise."

I'm about to formally introduce the two of them to Kason when Q makes a buzzing sound with his lips and glances between me and his boyfriend. "We're not having any of that shit this week," Quinton gripes. "Everything is fine, it's all water under the bridge, and I'm happy. But I'd be a lot fucking happier if my best friend and boyfriend would do a little more than tolerate each other's existence."

Oakley and I stare at each other briefly, eyes wide as we wait to see if ragey-Quinton is gonna make an appearance.

He doesn't, thank God, and instead turns to Kason. "I hope you know what you've signed up for with this one, football star," Q warns, smacking him on the back of the shoulder before motioning toward me. "He holds grudges like no other."

"A mild exaggeration," I mutter before linking my fingers with Kason's as we all head to their car in short-term parking. "Is it too late to take you up on the whole movie and sex marathon thing back in Chicago?"

Kason chuckles, his eyes glittering with amusement. "Absolutely not. Drama is kind of fun to watch when it's not mine."

"Hey, I heard that," Q calls from where he and Oakley are a few paces ahead of us. He glances over his shoulder to look at Kason with a menacing glare. "I also hear you're attempting to steal my best friend, so you better watch it. Otherwise you can sleep in the garage next to my bike."

Kason's eyes widen comically when he looks at me, the words *help me* etched in his features so prominently, they might as well be tattooed on his forehead.

"Aw, c'mon, babe," Oakley chides. His flashing to us as we stop behind their Navigator, popping the hatch to load up our bags. "He could at least sleep in the car."

That makes Kason laugh, glancing into the opening of the luxury vehicle. "This thing is about the size of my bedroom growing up, so you wouldn't see me complain."

After tossing our bags in the back, the four of us load into the vehicle; Oakley driving, Quinton in the passenger seat, and Kason and me in back.

"I thought you lived in Jersey?" I ask when I catch Oakley heading for the tunnel to Manhattan.

Q glances at me from the passenger seat and shakes his head. "We got a place up between Greenwich and SoHo about a month after Oakley got traded. It made more sense since he wouldn't have to commute to Philly like we originally thought."

I frown. "And you didn't think to tell me that?"

"What? And let you be the only one keeping secrets in this friendship? I think not."

"Oh my God, it's like there's two of you now," Kason whispers, a little grin on his face as he looks between Quinton and me.

"I've always called him my brother from another mother," my best friend supplies, clearly eavesdropping.

I scoff. "You have never called me that in your life."

"In my head, I have," he rebuts, turning to look at the two of us in the back seat. "And trust me when I tell you, I'm the one who is a lot more fun. And better looking."

Kason's gaze moves to me before holding out his hand, which I take instinctively. His palm is as warm as his eyes, and he gives me a smile that does something stupid to the neurons firing in my brain.

"Sorry, Quinton. I think we'll have to agree to disagree on that one."

"It's not too late to just take them back to the airport," Q says, looking at Oakley now. "There's not a chance in hell I wanna ring in the new year with this spoilsport."

My lips curl into a devilish grin, my attention still focused on Kason as I say, "Funny. I've called him that once before too."

"Huh. Isn't that something," Quinton murmurs while Kason shoots me a warning look, telling me he knows *exactly* where my mind is right now.

Oakley, on the other hand, has no idea what's happening other than that his boyfriend is being a little bit of a dick. And from the frown on his face, he's not amused.

"We're not taking the guests *you* invited back to the airport ten minutes after they land."

Q slumps back in the passenger seat, glaring over at Oakley, who keeps glancing between him and the road with one of those looks that's some mixture of confusion and *are you fucking high right now?*

A look that only intensifies when Quinton snaps, "Quit looking at me like that, or I'll butter your asshole."

I catch Oakley's eyes widen comically in the rearview mirror. "You'll do *what?* What does that even mean?"

Biting my lip, I do my best to keep from smiling, but the second my best friend turns to look at me with a massive, shit-eating grin on his face, I'm done for, and we both burst into hysterics.

Stomach-cramping, breath-gasping laughter that makes no sign of stopping.

"Am I the only one who's lost here?" Oakley asks slowly, eyes darting between the road and the three of us.

"Who knows what's going on with these two," Kason answers before Q or I can. But the death glare he's aiming at me says this conversation is far, *far* from over, once we're somewhere private.

Quinton surprisingly drops it, though not before I catch him fighting against another round of laughter that would surely have Oakley thinking we've lost our minds—and have Kason ready to strangle me before we even make it to the city.

Of course, from the way he's staring at me, gaze full of hunger and promise, I'm not entirely sure if strangling is the thing on his mind.

I give him an innocent look before whispering, "What?"

"You're *so* getting payback for telling him about that," he threatens before leaning over and brushing a whisper of a kiss over my lips. One that's soft and far too fleeting for my liking.

"I have no idea what you're talking about," I say, though I know my ridiculous grin would beg to differ. "But don't worry, you can have whatever you want after knocking Q's ego down a peg."

"Good to know. I'll make a habit of it the whole time we're here, then."

Arching a brow, I murmur, "Do that, and we won't be leaving the bedroom."

"I have no problem wracking up some IOUs." A seductive grin on his lips, he softly adds, "As long as you pay them back. With interest."

Thanks to our delays this morning, Quinton and Oakley don't have much time to do anything other than drop us at their condo before heading to the rink, meaning Kason and I are on our own when it comes to entertaining ourselves this afternoon.

Of course, that means I have to pry Kason away from the massive windows showcasing the Manhattan skyline long enough for us to actually *leave* their condo.

"Anything you wanna do in the city today?" I ask, stepping up behind him. My arms wrap around his waist, and I press my lips to the spot between his shoulder blades, then the side of his neck. "We could go ice skating in Central Park, or hit one of the bajillion art museums. Maybe a Broadway show? We could be super touristy and do the Empire State Building or the Statue of Liberty?"

Kason's eyes brighten with amusement as he wraps his arms around my shoulders. "Look at you, wanting to go out in public. Who are you, and what have you done with my boyfriend?"

Fuck.

Just when I think I'm getting used to him using that word, the stumbling my heart does proves otherwise.

"You've never been to the city, and I'm not gonna let my anti-social side ruin your first time here," I reason, arching a brow. "That's all, so don't read into it too much."

"Sure. Heaven forbid you admit that you want me to be *happy* or something. The world might end," he teases, my favorite, sexy smirk appearing. "I'm honestly down for whatever. But considering I'm the clumsiest person ever on ice skates, that's probably a no."

"Don't let Q hear you say that, otherwise that'll be the first thing he chooses to do when they get back," I warn with a laugh.

"Speaking of, shouldn't we wait for the two of them to get back before we go do things?"

I frown, my brows crashing together. "Why? They're not gonna be back for hours. With traffic, we'd be missing half a day if we did that."

He frowns right back, cocking his head in confusion at *my* confusion. "Because we're staying with them and Quinton is your best friend?"

I'm not sure I'm following his point.

"Yeah, but they don't care. They live here and they both have work, so there's no reason we can't go do things without them." I pause, noticing his frown hasn't softened at all. "Why do you still look so confused?"

Shaking his head, he murmurs, "I guess I just find your relationship with him kinda different."

"Because we don't have to do everything with each other?" I ask. When he nods, I shrug. "We have our own lives, our own interests, live in two different states, and we're still thick as thieves. There's nothing wrong with loving someone from a distance just as much as you do up close."

I can't help my smile while he waffles with the idea before letting out a sharp laugh. "It's just wild to me. Like, for the longest time, before all the shit that happened with Phoe, I thought those were just like unicorn friendships."

"And by that, you mean healthy ones?"

"Exactly," he replies with another laugh. "It's just funny to see other best friends function like normal people after being tied to Phoenix's hip for so long, that's all. But I dunno, it's also kind of refreshing, I guess?"

"Refreshing," I echo, my brows shooting up.

"That might not be the right word. Again, I only passed English because of Phoenix, remember?" he adds, grinning. "It's more that I'm glad to see it with my own eyes."

"Keep working on things with your therapist, and it can be you and Phoenix too, you know."

From the eye roll I get, he knows I'm right, he just doesn't want to admit it. Further proven when he reroutes the subject entirely.

"Since we're on the topic of best friends and messy relationships, are you gonna tell me what the deal is with you and Oakley?"

My lips pull up in a wry grin, and I shake my head. "Well, let's see. In addition to having a general dislike for people and definitely not trusting them, like Q warned earlier, I also have a tendency to hold a grudge."

"So what you're telling me is now that I'm on your good side, I better stay on it," he supplies.

Arching a brow, I counter with, "Who said you were on it in the first place?"

He leans in, his lips a hair's breadth from mine, and whispers, "Well, if having your mouth wrapped around my cock until I come is what it's like to be on your bad side, then I can't wait to be on the good."

The Kason standing in front of me is a far cry from the nervous, bumbling fool he was when we first met. Sure, he has his moments where I make him flush to high heaven, but the snarky filth that leaves his mouth these days leads me to think this change is due to me being a very bad influence.

And, God, I fucking love it.

"Okay, you made your point," I murmur, playing with the hair at the back of his head. "With Oakley, though…I just saw how badly he hurt Q. It's hard to see someone you care about be completely decimated by another person who claims to love them. And though forgiveness isn't necessarily mine to give, it seems like I'm the one refusing to hand it over."

"Because you're a good best friend," he whispers before pressing a kiss to my lips; soft and sweet and gentle. "But Quinton is his own person, perfectly capable of protecting his heart and making his choices. Maybe that should be reason enough to let sleeping dogs lie."

And now I'm the one who doesn't want to admit he *has a point.*

"Look at you, taking your turn to play therapist," I muse with a laugh.

He snorts and shakes his head, his gaze full of humor that matches mine. "I've been seeing mine for so long, God knows I should be able to retain some of what I've learned."

I can't help the pervy little thoughts that sneak in, and I whisper, "Well, I happen to know you're an *excellent* student, so I can't say I'm surprised."

Lust fills his eyes instantly, that sinful grin appearing again, and from the way his hands start trailing toward my waistband, I know exactly where his mind has headed.

Too bad for him, I'm not having it.

"Nuh uh, Fuller. Don't look at me like that," I chide, making an attempt to step away. A failed one, because he just reels me right back in.

He takes a page from my playbook earlier, blinking at me with innocent doe eyes and asks, "Like what?"

"We're not spending the entire day in bed."

This time, I do manage to sneak out of his hold, bolting away from him toward the front door. I grab my jacket and hat from where they're still draped over the entry table and quickly shove them on, knowing we need to get out of this condo if we have any chance of seeing *anything* today.

Meanwhile, Kason is just staring at me from where I left him.

I give him a *c'mon* look, arching a brow. "Sex can wait. We've only got five days in the city that never sleeps. Now, grab your coat and tell me what you wanna do first."

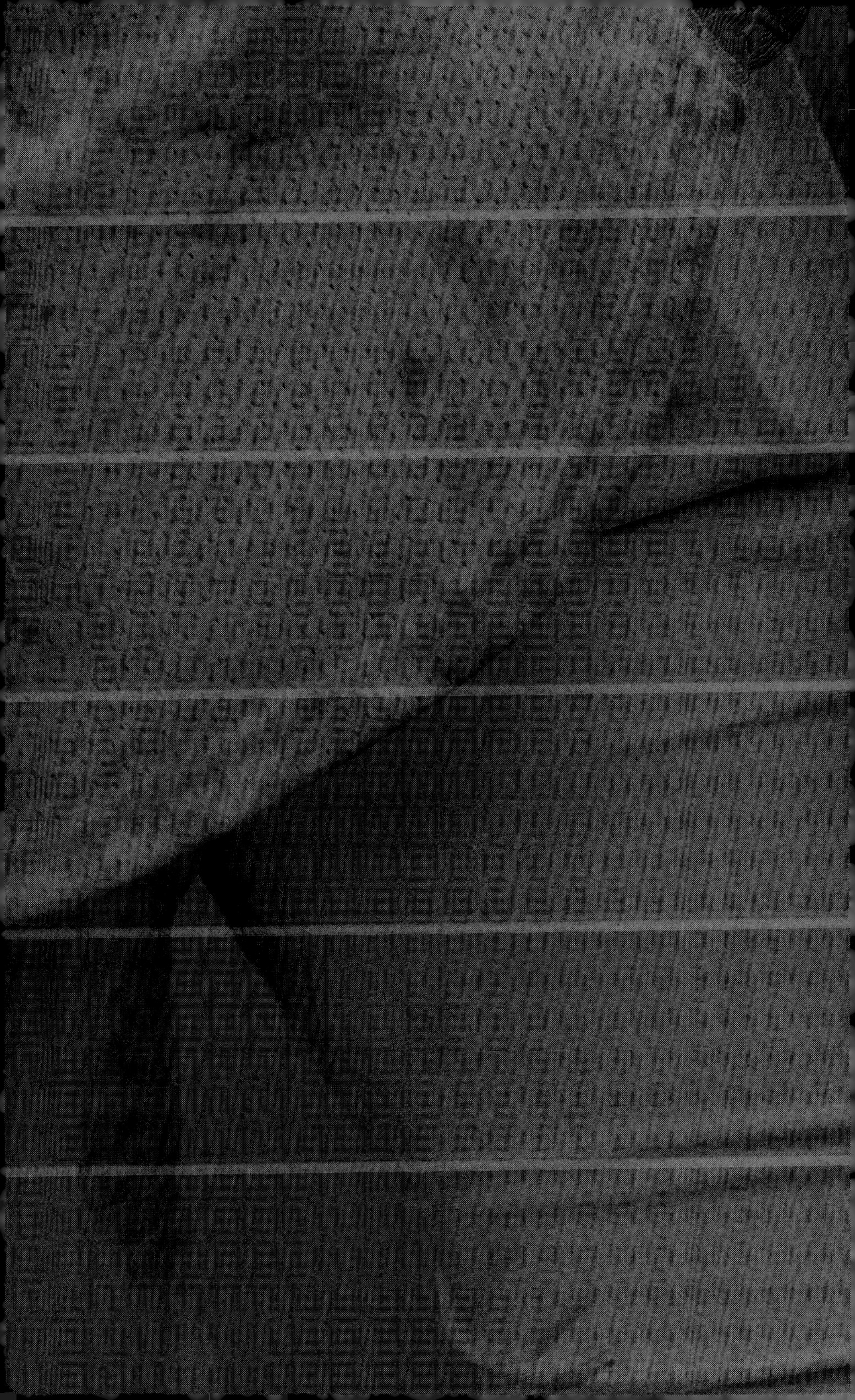

TWENTY-SIX
Kason

The first two days we spend in New York City are loaded with sight-seeing most of the big attractions: Times Square, the Empire State Building, a couple art museums, and Hayes somehow snagged the four of us last-minute tickets to a Broadway show.

I know it has to be wearing on Hayes, though, to be going out and doing so much. After all, this city is bustling with residents and tourists alike—especially with New Year's Eve only days away—and I'm even starting to feel peopled out.

Which is why I'm tempted to keep him in bed all day, just like he is right now, curled into my side while he runs his fingers up and down my chest. Well, that is, until he slips free from my hold and crawls out of bed.

"Where do you think you're going?"

"To shower?" He says it like a question, arching a brow before tacking on, "Is that okay?"

Not particularly, but the thought of him naked, wet, and soapy also has some allure.

"Someone is feeling feisty this morning, I see." I muse, sitting up against the headboard. "Am I being greeted with dickish Hayes today, or the sweet, cuddly one?"

A laugh leaves him, that filthy glimmer I love taking over his eyes.

"Fuck around and find out," he says, his smile devious as he heads to the bathroom down the hall.

Fucker.

Drawn to wherever he is, I climb out of bed and grab a set of clean clothes before following him down the hall. Sneaking into the bathroom, I find he's already turned on the shower, steam filling the air.

His toned back and perfect ass cheeks face me, and when he glances over his shoulder, I find a smirk pulling at his lips. Then, as if I'm not even there, he steps all the way into the tub and closes himself in behind the curtain.

"You mind? I'm trying to take a shower here."

Oh, hell no.

"Then why'd you leave the door unlocked?" I ask, immediately dropping my clothes to the counter and shoving my underwear to the floor. Sliding the curtain open enough to step in behind him, I murmur, "It's almost like you wanted me to come in and join you."

He smirks from beneath the spray as he pushes wet hair off his forehead. "Oh, really? Then with that same logic, you wanted me to join you that morning when I walked in the bathroom and caught you fiddling the flute?"

He says it as a joke, all teasing and ribbing as he steps out of the way for me to get under the water. But little does he know, his assessment is pretty fucking accurate.

Desire and lust rush through me at warp speed at the mere memory, my dick thickening between my legs as I wet my hair.

"Trust me, I would've rather had your mouth wrapped around me than my hand," I rasp, unable to keep the lust out of my voice. "It was everything my fantasies were about that morning."

My dick is giving a full salute at this point, aching to be touched, and it only gets worse when his lips brush soft kisses over my overheated skin. Starting between my shoulder blades, he moves up my spine to the back of my neck, and I might as well be on fire now.

"You wanted me on my knees for you? Sucking you until you came down my throat?" he whispers against my skin. "That's some filthy things to wanna do to your roommate, baby."

His mouth carves a path up the side of my throat now, and the closer he gets to my mouth, the tighter his body seals against mine. His hard cock presses against my crease, slipping and sliding between my ass cheeks as he reaches around, wraps his palm around my shaft and gives me a long, slow stroke.

"I know. I couldn't help it."

His thumb plays with the sensitive spot beneath the crown before rolling his palm over the head on the down stroke, and paired with the way his mouth is terrorizing my throat, that's all it takes to have me primed and ready to go.

"How 'bout I do you one better?" he asks with a taunting lilt.

"Depends. Aren't we gonna have to be quiet?"

He laughs, his breath coasting over my skin. "I listened to those two have sex more times than I can count. They could use a little payback."

"So it *is* dickish Hayes today," I muse, glancing over my shoulder to meet his gaze. "Good to know."

He smiles, wicked and fierce, before wrapping his hand around the front of my throat. Using his hold as leverage, he turns my head and angles it to meet his waiting lips. His mouth is warm against mine as he gives me a kiss so insistent and demanding, it has my toes curling where I stand.

Sliding his tongue against the seam of my lips, he seeks entry that I'm more than happy to give. Our tongues twist and tangle, mating together in an erotic dance I've become addicted to. It takes everything in my power to stay upright while he pillages my mouth, stealing my oxygen, my thoughts, whatever he wants.

I've fallen prisoner to his touch, and I have no desire to escape it.

"Fuck, baby," he murmurs, nipping at my lips. "I want inside you. Right fucking now."

He wouldn't have to say anything for me to know that. It's obvious from the way he's rocking and sliding between my ass cheeks; rutting into me at a haphazard pace that's driving me crazy.

Because I want more. More of all of this. Of everything he's doing to me. The blistering kisses and his scorching touch…it's absolute perfection.

But fuck, it's not nearly enough.

"Believe me, I'd love nothing more. But there's just one problem." I gasp, the sound quickly turning to a moan when he pinches the head of my dick, then rubs the sensitive nerve underneath.

"What problem?"

Fucking God, his touch has deduced me to two brain cells, and it takes all my willpower to rub them together and speak a coherent sentence.

"We don't have lube," I pant, my balls now seizing with desire. "And there's no fucking way we're using body wash."

His response is immediate. "Oh, so butter is fine, but you draw the line at body wash?"

"I'm serious."

Hayes lets out a chuckle, the heat of his breath coasting over my already sizzling skin. "I know, baby. I'm not a complete animal. I was going to suggest conditioner."

I can't help the laughter that bubbles up, and I clamp my hand over my mouth to keep quiet. He, on the other hand, doesn't seem to care about noise, because he jumps out of the shower and starts making a racket in the bathroom, slamming cabinets and drawers like he owns the place.

"What are you *doing?*" I hiss, peeking my head out just in time to see him coming back with— "Where did you find lube?"

"Under the sink." Hayes steps back under the spray and pops the cap open, squeezing some on his fingers. "You forget I lived with Quinton for three years? There's probably a bottle of lube hidden in every room in this place."

"Small mercies," I murmur with a grin.

"Exactly. Now, turn around and bend over."

Immediately following his command, I spin and step out from beneath the water, pressing my palms to the shower wall. A low chuckle leaves him at my enthusiasm, but damn, I can't help it. I'm addicted to the feel of him inside me; owning me, claiming me.

Every time we've been together, it's better than the last, and I can only assume it's because it's as fun as it is sensual. We can laugh and smile and not take ourselves too seriously.

The lack of awkwardness or judgment makes it easy not to worry.

And I can't get enough.

"Someone's eager," he murmurs, his lube-covered fingers sliding up my crease and swirling around my rim. "It'd be funny if it wasn't so fucking sexy to see how much you want my dick inside you."

"Then why don't you quit talking and make it happen?" I ask, glancing at him over my shoulder.

He smirks at my sass at the same time he presses two fingers past the tight ring of muscle, causing me to gasp. I spread my feet further apart and bend at the waist, allowing the digits to sink in even deeper. The stretch is delicious, and it only takes a few thrusts for me to start pushing back into his hand.

But before I can even get him to swipe over my prostate, he pulls from my body, and I let out a frustrated groan.

"Hayes," I hiss, my forehead dropping to the tile.

A soft chuckle comes from behind. "Your next lesson is gonna be in patience."

"Fine, but we can save that for next time," I snap, glaring over my shoulder.

That's when I find him spreading lube up and down his length, slowly stroking his cock while he stares at me bent over in front of him.

Oh.

He smirks, eyes full of sinful promises when our gazes collide. "Are you done with the snark, or do I need to fuck it out of you?"

I can't do much more than blink and stare at him, more turned on than a vibrator in a sorority house. Because, while I might be getting used to freaking amazing sex, there's no part of me that will ever remain composed when shit like that leaves his mouth.

"Thought so," he murmurs before stepping up behind me.

My stomach tightens with anticipation as his head nudges against my hole, swiping over my rim before he finally presses forward ever so slightly. He crowns me, sliding past the rim before sinking in to the hilt, his pelvis flush against my ass.

I release a breath, my head dropping down as my body stretches to accommodate him, jacking my cock to help the process. He rains soft kisses over my shoulder when he slowly starts to move, testing the waters, and it draws a soft groan from his lips.

"You feel so good, baby. I could make a home inside your ass."

I'd fucking let him.

Having him inside of me is nothing short of euphoric, and over the past weeks, I've become insatiable.

A glutton for him. An addict in need of a constant fix.

For his body, his praise, his time, his mind.

Him.

His hips collide with my ass cheeks, the only noise in the room now is that of water pouring over skin meeting skin, tangled with our rough breathing. I've been so turned on since stepping foot in the bathroom, I know it won't take long for him to send me over the edge.

My hand shuttles over my dick as he picks up his pace, and I can feel release building and building inside me like two magnets ready to snap together at a moment's notice.

"You've never looked better than you do right now. Bent in half, my cock buried inside you," he whispers with a sensual roll of his hips, pegging my prostate. "I think you were made to take me like this."

The filthy praise causes me to clench around him, bearing down on his length. The head of his cock continues stimulating that button, lighting me up like Times Square from the inside out. Desire knots on itself, building tension inside me, and I know my orgasm is *right* there as more foul words fall from his decadent lips.

"I can't wait to fill you with my cum, baby. I love watching it spill from your ass when I pull out, knowing I'm the only one who's claimed you."

Oh, my fucking God.

My hand moves faster over my dick, wanting these sinful promises to come to life.

Needing him to make good on them.

He's riding my ass like it's the last thing he'll ever do, and every single movement shoves me closer and closer to the edge of the oblivion I crave. I press back into him too, responding to his thrusts in kind, chasing the pleasure his body so freely gives mine.

"I'm right there. Fuck, Hayes," I pant, my forehead colliding with the cool wall of the shower. I'm heading into freefall, the lust coiling in my stomach until it's wound so tight, there's no other option but for it to snap.

"Come, baby. I'm right behind you."

I stroke harder and faster at his command, chasing my release until cum jets from my cock, spilling over my hand and to the shower floor. Working myself through the orgasm, I feel my ass clench and pulse around his length, and it sends him into a downward spiral of his own.

His teeth sink into the skin between my shoulder and neck, the bite of pain causing my ass to clench around him, drawing out his orgasm until his movements cease completely.

"Fuck," he whispers, panting and gasping.

Resting his forehead between my shoulder blades, we both catch our breath, his fingers skating up and down my ribs before he wraps his arms around my stomach. He clings to me, not a single molecule of air between our bodies while we both come down from the high.

"I feel flimsy like Jell-O," I tell him with a laugh as he finally pulls out of me. I turn in his arms, my back pressing into the cool shower wall, only to find a little grin on his lips.

"Does that mean I wore you out too much to leave the condo today?"

Snorting, I shake my head. "Not to burst your bubble, but it's the heat of the shower."

"Well, good," he murmurs, his eyes dancing with glee. "Because I have a surprise for you."

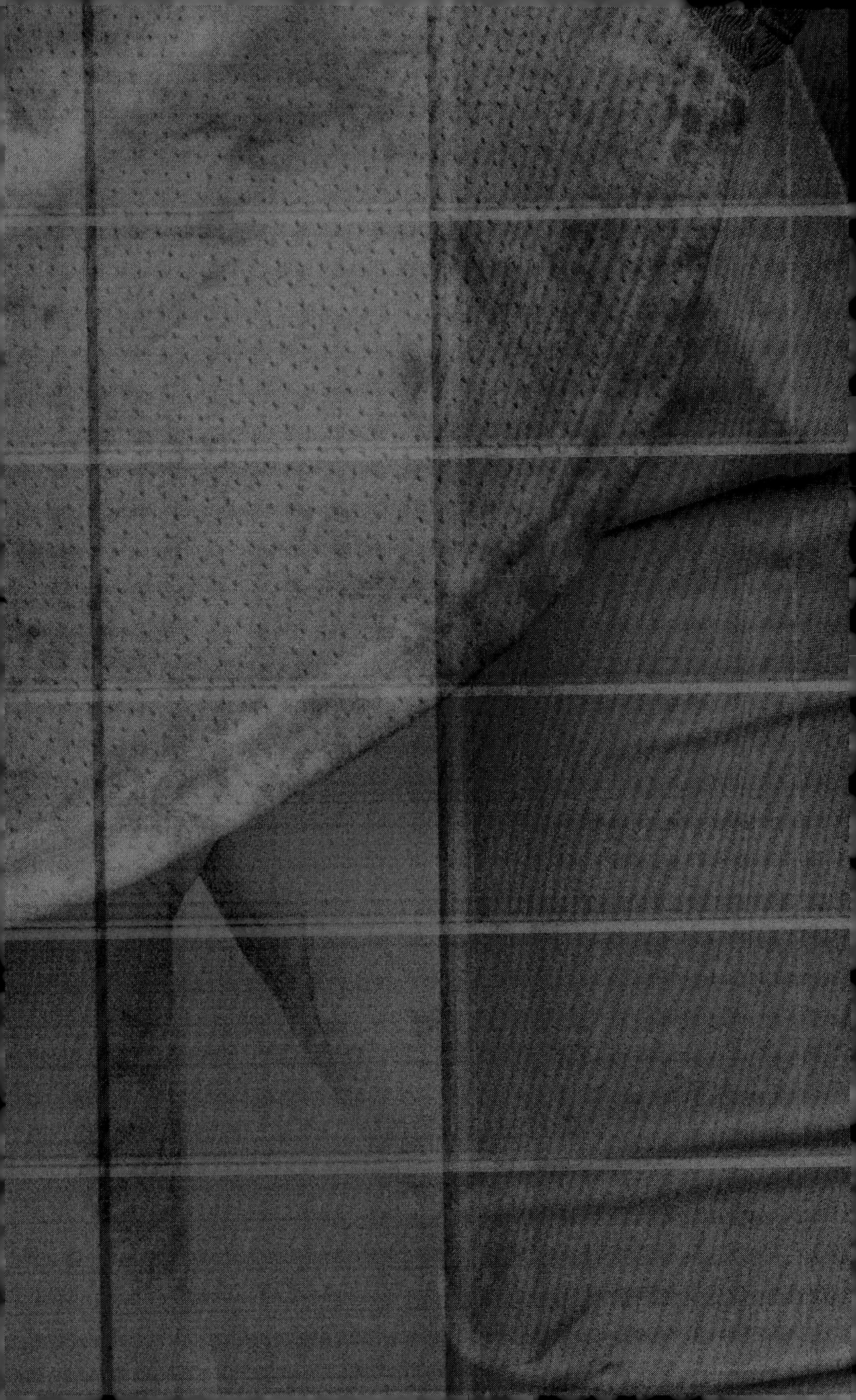

TWENTY-SEVEN
Kason

"Are you gonna tell me what the hell is going on yet?" I ask as Hayes pulls me blindly from the cab out onto what seems to be a sidewalk. The cool, winter air hits me like a shard of ice, and I bundle into my jacket a little deeper.

"No," he says, linking his fingers with mine. "I thought I taught you patience with all those sex lessons we had. Apparently we need a refresher course."

"Unless you're planning to fuck me outside in the dead of winter for God knows who to see, I don't think we're talking about the same kind of patience," I remind him, doing my best to keep up with his pace. Which is a lot harder than it seems when Hayes has tugged my beanie down over my eyes in a makeshift blindfold.

"I'm pretty sure the same basic principles apply to any situation—sexual or otherwise," he reminds me.

We continue down the sidewalk, hand in hand, and I give up on getting any answers. Instead, I do my best to enjoy what my other senses can tell me about where we are. The snow crunches beneath our feet as cars pass and horns honk, alerting me that we're still near a bustling street, but they quickly start to fade the further we walk. The only thing I can smell is brisk winter air and fresh snow, which came down in heaps while we slept last night.

And as for touch, the only thing I can really focus on is the warmth of his hand in mine, even through the fabric of our gloves.

Hayes stops suddenly and releases my hand before taking a few more steps by himself. The anticipation is damn near killing me, but thankfully, he puts me out of my misery by telling me the words I want to hear.

"Okay, you can open your eyes."

Pushing my hat back up, I blink as my sight is restored, the bright, snow-covered scene coming into view, complete with a horse-drawn sleigh waiting along a wooded path. I glance from the sleigh to Hayes, finding his eyes shining with a devious glimmer.

All I can do is stare at him. At this man who is nothing like I thought him to be.

Who never fails to amaze me.

Who makes my heart skip a beat whenever he smiles at me the way he is right now.

"A sleigh ride?" I find myself asking.

Hayes nods, glancing over his shoulder at my surprise. "He's ours for the next hour."

"You two ready?" the driver—a middle-aged man in a top hat—asks.

Nodding, I follow Hayes up the steps of the sleigh, my heart stumbling and stuttering the entire time. We settle in beside each other, dragging a blanket over our laps as the driver offers us hot chocolate before we're on our way, slowly riding through what I have to assume is Central Park.

"Are you surprised?"

In more ways than one.

"Uh, yeah. Who knew you were such a closet romantic?" I say with a laugh, shaking my head.

"It's Christmastime in New York. It wouldn't be complete without a sleigh ride through Central Park." He grins before knocking his shoulder into mine. "Well, and ice skating at the Rockefeller, but *someone* said no to embarrassing himself in public. So I guess this will have to do."

"Considering I embarrass myself enough on my own, I don't think we need to add ice skates to the equation."

"True," he murmurs before leaning over and pressing a kiss to my jaw. "But I hope you like it regardless."

A comfortable silence blankets us like the snow does the Earth, the only sound coming from the horse's occasional huffs and the bells jingling on the sleigh as we're led down countless paths of New York's most iconic park.

Everything about this moment is magical, and though it's hard for me to pick a favorite I've shared with Hayes, I think this might be my new one. Or maybe it's tied with the moments where we share soft glances and lingering touches, when we're talking about anything or nothing at all.

It's the closeness I crave. The vulnerability that he freely shows me when we're like this.

It's a side of him I didn't know existed, one entirely different from the one I met during our unfortunate run-in at the coffee shop back in April.

This one lets me see through some of the cracks in his armor, allows me to capture more of who he is, piece by piece, and I've been addicted to it since the very first time he gave me the tiniest glimpse.

Now, I feel like I've memorized every morsel of information he's given me, absorbing them the same way I would a playbook. And with each nugget I learn, I'm beginning to realize *this* is the very thing that's been missing from my life.

Not sex, but *intimacy*.

"You look quite pensive," he muses, his thumb running over the back of mine beneath the blanket. "Something on your mind?"

Truthfully, my head is full of so many thoughts, I don't even know where to begin.

"You're not like I expected you to be."

His lips quiver. "Dare I ask what you mean by that?"

"I guess what I actually mean is, I'm glad I get to see this side of you."

"You mean the side of me that isn't a complete dick?" he asks, his tone playful and teasing.

"Well, I wasn't gonna say it like *that*."

The half-grin turns into a face splitting one, but it's the sound of his laugh that has my stomach doing gymnastics. "I hope you know I'm just messing with you. Though, I wouldn't be offended if you thought that. You would've been right. But for whatever it's worth, I'm sorry I was so standoffish in the beginning."

"Yeah, you wanna tell me what was up with that? Because I honestly thought you hated me," I recount, arching a brow.

Hayes grins sheepishly, a little pink tinting his cheekbones. Then again, it could just be the light bouncing off the snow. "I mean, not in so many words. But in case you haven't noticed this about me, I don't really like people."

"Really? I had no idea," I say, sarcasm lacing my tone. "That might be the most shocking thing I've learned about you in the past few months."

"Okay, smartass." He gives me a playful nudge with his shoulder. "I mean, I just kinda tolerate the existence of people. There are very *few* I can actually stand being around for long lengths of time, who I'm willing to share my space with, and Q was the only one I ever had to do that with."

"And I was some stranger coming in and fucking with your vibe."

When I glance over, he nods, teeth sinking into the side of his cheek. "Pretty much, yeah."

It's crazy to sit here and think about where this all started; the rocky and tumultuous beginning of what we are now. Moments that could have ended us before we ever began, full of awkwardness and tension. Days where we would inevitably end up in a weird, uncomfortable place whenever a disagreement would arise or mistakes would be made.

But that's not how it is anymore.

We can talk about the hard shit. The things that aren't so pretty, and share the deepest secrets and most out-there dreams. And even as we continue exploring each other—both naked and otherwise—there's no pressure, no insecurities, no shame; only guidance and laughter and fun.

He makes me feel safe. In every way possible.

And to see him finally start showing me I do the same for him? It means more than getting drafted ever could.

"I'm glad you gave me a chance," I whisper, my hand tightening in his.

"I am too." His cobalt eyes take on a softness around the edges, almost like sorrow. "Though it doesn't excuse it, I have a hard time trusting people's intentions. I've been fucked over by enough people in the past who've only seen me as a bunch of dollar signs or a way to get to my parents. But you've done the opposite at every turn."

"Because that's not what I see when I look at you."

His jaw tics, glancing away briefly before his attention returns to me. "I'm so sorry for making you feel like I didn't want you here. That I didn't treat you the way you deserved."

It's impossible to miss his word choice or the way it echoes the conversation we had about my life growing up or the abuse from my father. There's a heaviness to them, a weight of more than just one meaning that's reinforced in the way he looks at me.

Like he'd move mountains to change the past or take away the pain.

Like he'll stop at nothing to make sure it never happens again.

Swallowing roughly, I whisper the only thing I can think of. "Thank you."

"You're welcome." A soft, remorseful smile lifts his lips at the corner. "Are we done with the heavy shit now? Because I'd really like to kiss you."

I barely have time to nod before his fingers wrap around the back of my neck and he pulls me in. The first brush of his lips is soft; sweet and gentle enough to have those damn butterflies swarming in my stomach with a vengeance.

And if I didn't already know I'm falling in love with him, I sure do now.

Quinton and Oakley meet us somewhere in Greenwich Village after they're done with practice, texting us the address to this queer-owned rooftop restaurant for an early dinner, which is closed in sort of like a greenhouse for the winter. Of course, with it being an early dinner, we also get a fucking stunning view of the sunset going down over the Manhattan skyline that I can't seem to keep my eyes off of.

Oakley, on the other hand, doesn't seem too thrilled about his boyfriend's choice in dinner venues.

"I can't believe I let you talk me into coming back here," Oakley mutters, taking another swig from his drink—his second of the night.

"Did you not like the food or something the last time?" I ask, frowning.

"No, he's afraid of heights," Quinton supplies, grinning when he looks at his boyfriend. "But don't worry, baby. I'll make it up to you later."

I glance over the edge of the building, noting that we're not even *that* high up. It's not like we're having dinner on top of the Empire State Building or something, but I choose not to comment on it.

Hayes, on the other hand?

"And now *I* think I'm gonna hurl, and it's definitely not from the heights," Hayes mutters before sipping on his own drink.

I shoot him a look, hopefully reminding him to play nice with his best friend's guy. From the way he smirks and rolls his lips inward, he definitely gets the message.

Quinton, on the other hand, ignores him entirely, instead focusing his attention on me. "So I hear you're planning to make yourself eligible for the Draft now that the season is over."

"Yeah. I mean, that's the goal, assuming the combine goes well."

"And securing that invite was the next step to making that goal a reality," Hayes reminds me now, aiming a gentle smile in my direction.

My heart stumbles in my chest at the sight of it.

"Well, shit. That's definitely the right direction," Oakley says, looking a little calmer than he was earlier.

I nod. "It's just waiting and training now, which I think is the hardest part. But I just keep telling myself it'll be worth it. And from the looks of it, I'm right. The two of you seem to be loving the pro-athlete life."

"It definitely has its perks." Oakley agrees before shooting a look at Quinton. "Do you happen to have someone representing you already?"

Wincing, I shake my head. "I haven't made it that far, unfortunately."

"Well, if you're looking, we can definitely refer you to Louis," Quinton chimes in. "He's a pain in the ass, but he's good at his job."

"*You're* the pain in the ass, babe," Oakley says, arching a brow. "You're the loose cannon he's constantly worrying about, which is why he's always harping on you."

Quinton literally shrugs Oakley's comment off. "I've yet to get in a fight since I signed with him."

"Yet, being the operative word," Hayes says, grinning at his best friend.

He shoots me a wink after, but I'm too occupied by Quinton's offer to flirt back.

"I'd absolutely be open to meeting with him if he's looking to take on any new clients."

"Louis is never *not* looking for new clients, no matter what he tries telling you at first," Oakley replies with a laugh. "We'll put the two of you in touch."

"I'd really appreciate that," I tell them, a little bit of hope rising in my chest.

Louis Spaulding is something of a legend when it comes to professional athletics, and having him in my corner would make things a helluva lot easier, should things go the way I'm hoping. Not to mention the amount of queer athletes he already represents outside of Quinton and Oakley.

The rest of dinner goes by rather quickly, though I think that's more for Oakley's benefit than anything. Both Hayes and I noticed he was looking a little green by the time the waiter came with the dessert menu, and we quickly asked for the check.

And I have to admit, it was nice to watch Hayes lose the battle on paying to Quinton.

Once we get Oakley back to solid ground—his words, not mine—the four of us walk back to Quinton and Oakley's condo a few blocks away. And boy is Oakley a man on a mission to get home, leaving the three of us behind while he damn near power-walks down the street.

But what surprises me is when Hayes presses his lips to my cheek before calling for Oakley to wait up for him.

"Look at those two, making nice," Quinton muses from beside me, his eyes locked on where Oakley and Hayes are chatting ahead of us. "Sometimes all it takes is a little nudge in the right direction."

"Nudge?" I echo skeptically. "I'd call it more of a violent shove, but that's just me."

He laughs, knocking his shoulder with mine. "I'm sure you keep Hayes on his toes with that quick wit."

"Who do you think I learned it from?"

The comment has Quinton's eyes lighting up, and before I know it, he's calling out to Oakley and Hayes in front of us.

"I have someone who can corroborate my claims about you corrupting me, Hayes. Better watch your back!"

To his credit, my boyfriend doesn't so much as glance backward at his best friend's outburst, simply choosing to flip him the bird while he and Oakley continue talking.

"You know, I've been wondering how someone like Hayes and someone like you became friends." I glance at Quinton to find him arching a brow at me. "I mean, you have to admit, it doesn't make sense when you look at it on paper."

Quinton laughs, his eyes glittering with the same sort of energy I've often found in Holden's. "Well, it helps that we grew up together. Kinda forged a friendship because our families run in the same circles, despite them being entirely different types of people."

I tilt my head, frowning. "You both come from buckets of money. How would that make your families different types of people?"

"Let's just say Hayes and I had the same opportunities afforded to us by our family wealth, but we had very different upbringings. His parents have only looked out for his and Rhys' best interests, even if it was a bit… overbearing." He gives me an apologetic smile, and it takes all of three seconds for me to realize Hayes must've told him about Thanksgiving.

"And your parents?" I ask, curiosity getting the best of me to pry on such a personal matter.

Quinton doesn't seem to mind, though, shrugging as he puts his hands in his coat pockets.

"They're overbearing in a different way, because they only cared about themselves, their money, or the way I made them look to the public. Other than that, I may as well have not existed." His eyes slide from where our guys are walking ahead of us, landing back on me. "And while they might not have physically laid a hand on me, their words still did plenty of damage over the years. A lot of shit I had to work through in my own time and my own way, you know?"

I'm a little shocked by hearing the resemblance Quinton's upbringing holds to mine. Never in a million years would I have guessed it, either. But it also adds another layer of insight as to why Hayes seemed to understand my trauma so easily, if not take it in stride.

He's seen it before. Cared about someone who's gone through neglect and abuse, all at the hands of people who are supposed to be programmed to love us unconditionally.

The parallels are uncanny.

"Yeah," I find myself whispering. "Though I came from a completely different upbringing, I understand the circumstances."

"I thought you might," he says with a sigh. "But through it all, I've learned one thing: It's not always about blood. It's the family you choose that matters." He motions toward Hayes and Oakley with his chin. "Those two are more my family than my parents ever were. As long as I've got them, I'm good."

Nodding, my mind immediately goes to Phoenix and his family. And, before I can stop it, it lands on Hayes too, making my heart stumble all over again.

"I definitely know the feeling."

The two of us walk in silence for about half a block, watching the snow start to fall as we round the corner toward the condo. Our partners are already standing outside the door waiting for us, and I can feel Hayes' eyes locked on me as we approach.

Quinton's icy gaze flashes to me too, and he smirks knowingly.

"You don't need my stamp of approval, but you've got it regardless. It's obvious how good you are for him."

I can't stop myself from smiling when I whisper back, "Not as good as he is for me."

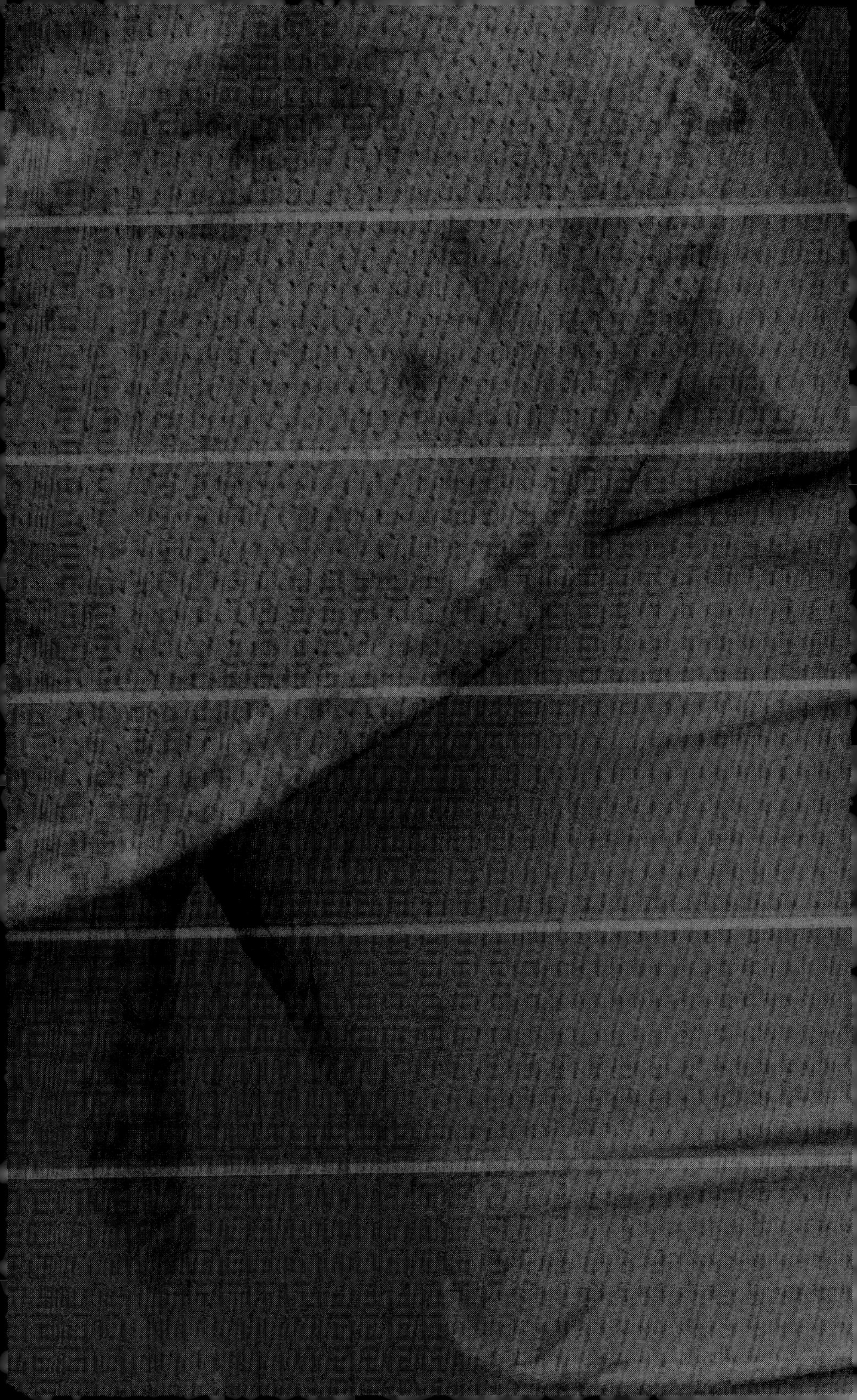

TWENTY-EIGHT

Kason

January

Break comes to an unfortunate end far sooner than either Hayes or I would like, and we're already a week deep in the new semester when Hayes mentions a party he needs to attend at his parents' house the following weekend. It's an off-handed comment more than anything, and while the way things went at Thanksgiving makes me less than thrilled about spending more time around his parents, I offer to go anyway.

If I want this for the long haul, it has to happen.

Of course, now that I'm outside their home wearing a freaking suit and bow tie, I'm starting to rethink my decision.

The anxiety coursing through me is higher now than it was the first time I came here. Maybe because this go 'round, I know what waits behind those doors, and it's far more terrifying than not knowing.

A valet opens the passenger door for me, and I'm struck with another wave of nerves as I climb from the car. Hayes does the same, handing off his keys to the attendant before joining me on the passenger side.

I straighten my suit jacket, running my hand over the fabric to ensure no wrinkles or pleats or whatever the fuck else is out of place. God knows I already feel that way enough, I don't need to look the part too. Yet, despite donning the nicest suit I own and making myself as presentable as humanly possible, I still feel inferior beside Hayes, and I know with absolute certainty the feeling will only be worse once we set foot inside the lion's den.

Because tonight, it won't just be the Lancasters present. All their friends and colleagues will be there too, including Quinton's parents, if I had to guess. The who's who of Chicago's upper class and high society, all boozing and schmoozing their evening away.

And then there's me.

A counterfeit. A misguided dreamer.

An unwelcome outsider.

Hayes must feel the emotions rippling off me like a cologne, because he reaches over and takes my hand, squeezing it in his. The smallest touch gives me enough reassurance to know, no matter what waits on the other side of those doors, at least I have him by my side.

And that's enough.

"Are you ready?"

The honest answer is no, but I plaster on a smile anyway and give him a watered down version of the truth. "Ready as I'll ever be."

Hayes leads me through the front door of his parents' estate, and unlike Thanksgiving's quiet gathering, the entire place is bustling with people, chatter, music, and dancing, everyone dressed to the nines in tuxes and floor-length gowns.

"*Holy shit,*" I mutter, more to myself than anything.

As we travel further inside, my gaze travels around the sunken living room that has been completely transformed—all the furniture removed, leaving the marble floor bare. Cocktail tables with elegant floral arrangements are scattered around the outskirts, creating a circular opening for people to gather and talk or dance in the center.

And it's almost as if...

"Your living room doubles as a *ballroom*?"

A low chuckle comes from Hayes. "Only sometimes."

Lord have fucking mercy.

I blink a couple times, still stunned by the severe contrast to the home I'd previously seen, before looking at Hayes again. He's watching me with laser-like focus, arching a brow when our eyes find each other.

"Good?"

"Yep," I say, though I'm pretty sure my voice went up an octave halfway through the word. Clearing my throat, I add, "Your parents really know how to throw a party."

"It's obscene," he mutters, shaking his head. His analytical blue gaze travels around the opulently decorated room before returning to me. "Their anniversary is just another stupid excuse for them to flex their pocketbooks to anyone who comes."

"I think they succeeded."

He laughs and leads me down the steps toward the pop-up bar at the other side, his hand at the small of my back, guiding me the whole way. And while I know it's only in my head, I feel like everyone in the room is staring at us.

At *me.*

The one thing here that isn't like the others.

"Stop fidgeting. You look perfect," Hayes murmurs from behind me, his lips brushing the shell of my ear. "And your ass looks good enough to eat."

I can feel the heat creeping up my neck until it reaches my cheeks, tinting the skin a deep shade of pink. "Of all the moments you could choose to whisper filthy things in my ear, you had to do it when your parents are in the same room?"

Granted, I don't know *where* in this room, but I know they're here somewhere.

"I had to make this night a little fun for us," he whispers with a laugh, nuzzling the side of my throat. "We don't have to stay long. I just need to make an appearance, see my parents, play the doting son. Maybe ninety-minutes, max?"

I turn to face him. "It's fine, Hayes. We'll stay as long as you want."

He smirks a little. "If it were up to me, I wouldn't be here at all. Love my parents and the family business, but there's no part of me that enjoys *this* part of being a Lancaster."

"I'm sure it was incredibly difficult to grow up with a silver spoon in your mouth," I say dryly, lacing my tone with sarcasm. "How ever did you survive it?"

A dark chuckle leaves him and he presses his lips to mine.

"You're so paying for that later," he whispers against my mouth before pulling away.

God, I can't wait.

Ever since I saw him in that tux, I've been fantasizing about ripping it off him once the night was over. Stripping him out of it, piece by piece, until there was nothing but bare, naked skin greeting me.

That filthy promise only ups the ante on the anticipation.

"I'm looking forward to it."

True to his word, Hayes finds his parents pretty soon after we get our drinks—a great forethought on his part to take the edge off. And while neither of them look thrilled to see me, it doesn't feel any more uncomfortable than it did last time. Whether or not that's progress, it's too soon to tell.

Regardless, getting his obligations out of the way early gives us freedom to enjoy the rest of the time we're here, and with a drink in me, I'm feeling a little animated.

"Dance with me."

His brows arch, equally playful and curious. "Do you know how?"

"Only one way to find out," I coerce with a wink.

Wrapping my fingers around his wrist, I drag him to the center of the room and spin him into my arms. We settle into the rhythm of the classical music playing, and though I haven't done this in *years,* it's no different than riding a bike after a few moments.

"You planning on telling me how you learned to waltz, there, Fuller?" Hayes murmurs, a little grin on his lips that almost has me missing a step.

"That'd be thanks to Mal. She taught me when we were kids. Pestered me night and day until I agreed to let her. Guess it's one thing that really stuck from my childhood."

He grins, his sapphire eyes brimming with amusement. "I guess I'm not the only one full of surprises."

"Gotta keep you on your toes somehow."

"Any more hidden talents I should know about?" he asks, sex and innuendo dripping from the words.

"Now, why would I tell you?" Cocking my head, I aim an equally filthy smirk at him. "That'd just spoil the surprise."

Even though the song ends and another begins, neither of us make a move to leave the dancefloor. Instead, we stay right where we are, in each other's arms. And even though I'm in an opulent home that's far outside the realms of reality, surrounded by a group of people who I'll never fit in with, I've never felt more at home.

Because I'm with him.

Hayes shifts to wrap his hands over my shoulders, allowing them to hang loosely near the nape of my neck. We move into more of a sway than a dance, the two of us rocking gently to the classical music like we're the only ones in the room.

And for the first time, I truly feel at peace.

Like I *belong* here.

Our gazes stay locked together as we move, and more than anything, I wish I could read his mind. See what thoughts lurk past their ocean depths.

Know if he happens to feel the same way.

He wets his lips, drawing my attention to them briefly, before whispering, "Thank you for coming with me to this."

A gentle half-smile tugs at my mouth. "Of course."

"No, seriously." His tone is earnest with eyes to match as they gaze into mine. "After what happened at Thanksgiving, I wouldn't blame you for never setting foot within a mile of this place. It means a lot to me that you're here."

There's something in his expression I can't quite get a read on, but it's the softest and most vulnerable I've ever seen him. Almost like he's finally removed that last piece of armor from around his heart.

Maybe because he's used to people wanting him for his money or the connection to his family, and he never considered it could have the opposite effect.

"There's not much in this world I wouldn't do for you, Hayes." The words come out in a gruff whisper, and I smile. "Including taking on your extremely intimidating parents who literally hate my guts."

He winces. "They don't hate you—"

"They don't like me, either, and you know it," I counter. I'm not looking to spend the night arguing with him, though, so I quickly tack on. "But they're just gonna have to get over it, because I'm not going anywhere anytime soon."

I might as well have hung the moon and all the stars from the way he smiles at me, and it's all the confirmation I needed to know coming tonight was the right call.

"I'd do the same for you, you know." His fingers lace together, twining through the hair at my nape. "I know you said things with your father will likely never change, but with your mother. My family has connections. Private investigators who can—"

"No," I whisper immediately, shaking my head. "I don't want to taint this with people I've left in my past, especially the ones who've left me. I've accepted they have no place in my future."

He smiles gently, nodding in concession. "The offer stands, if you ever want to take it."

I know I won't, but the gesture is more than enough to have my heart crawling in my throat. The fact of the matter is, neither of my parents deserve to know the person I've become. Because I'm not that same cowering boy I was a decade ago, just searching for a way to be enough for them. To be worthy of their love, because I don't need it anymore.

Because now, as Hayes and I move slowly together with the music…I have his.

And I swear I can see him thinking the same thoughts currently running through my mind; three little words sitting on the tip of my tongue like a naughty secret, pleading to spill from my lips.

One monumental sentence, just waiting to be spoken into existence.

Yet no matter how much I might feel them, I can't quite bring myself to say them, so I rein them in and lock them down. Box them up and push them to the back of my mind.

Except it's impossible for them to be entirely out of sight when he's still right here, in my arms, staring at me like he's doing everything in his power not to say them too.

"Do you mind if I step out for some air?" I whisper as the song comes to an end. "I think I'm still a little overwhelmed by all this."

The half-truth tastes bitter on my tongue, only growing worse when he nods and presses a kiss to my jaw.

"Of course, baby. I'll be here when you get back."

TWENTY-NINE

Kason

The cool, winter air hits me as I step onto the terrace off the living room, and it's exactly what I needed to release some of the tension knotted in my back and shoulders.

My fingers wrap around the railing overlooking the yard at the back of the expansive estate, the sculpted gardens covered in snow only serving as another reminder that I don't belong here. That I'm nothing more than Cinderella at the ball, waiting for the clock to strike midnight.

The only difference is my Prince Charming is inside, knows exactly who I am down to the marrow of my bones, and I can't seem to find the courage to face him. To tell him that, while catching feelings was never part of the plan, it happened anyway.

That there's no doubt in my mind about him.

It's the questions lingering in the background that have me stumbling;

the ones put there the first night I came to this house by the woman who—

"Kason. I thought I might find you out here."

All the tension I just released is back in spades as my boyfriend's mother steps out closer to where I'm resting against the railing.

"Mrs. Lancaster. Sorry, I didn't see you." A tight smile pulls at my lips as she approaches. "I was just grabbing some air and thought I was alone."

"Oh, you were. I followed you out here." She wraps her shawl around her a little tighter and pastes on a smile. "Do you have a minute, dear? There's something I wish to discuss."

My hackles rise instantly, not knowing what to expect, only that it can't be good. "What can I do for you, ma'am?"

One of her tempered laughs leaves her, and she waves her hand. "Oh, you Southern boys with your *ma'ams* and *sirs*. It's almost endearing."

The slight is just that—ever so fucking slight. Pair it with her prim and proper demeanor, and it'd be easy to miss. Hell, maybe even take it as a compliment.

I don't, though.

Decoding the hidden messages in her words is simple after our first meeting, and I'm tired of playing nice to someone who only views me as inferior.

The gloves are off now.

"Almost as endearing as this *small* gathering you've thrown together."

Mrs. Lancaster's lips purse tightly, a soft little *hmph* sounding from her. There's a brief pause where we take turns sizing each other up, her sapphire gaze colliding with mine, before she finally speaks.

"After you and Hayes visited for Thanksgiving, his father and I had a rather lengthy discussion about your *involvement* with our son. I'm afraid to admit, the two of us are rather concerned about his lack of direction since the two of you started seeing each other."

"Lack of direction," I echo, nowhere near close to picking up whatever she's trying to put down. "Hayes is the most focused, driven person I know. To say he's lacking direction is laughable."

"Is it, though?" she challenges, one manicured brow rising. "You heard it yourself, he's been a bit more lax in his studies, distracted by this new relationship you've embarked on. Then, of course, there's his clear disregard for what this relationship would mean for his future that's all the more troubling."

I click my tongue, equally amused and appalled by her assessment of the situation.

"I hadn't realized enjoying college and not spending every second locked in the library with his nose stuck in a book was considered problematic."

"It is when his head is being turned away from the things that matter, and by someone who has nothing to offer him in the long term, no less." She blinks at me, the seemingly picture-perfect mother, who is nothing more than a viper waiting to strike. "You know as well as I do, the path you're looking to take doesn't align with the one Hayes is destined for."

"Plans can change. Even the best-laid ones, as I'm sure you've heard."

Another faint *hmph* leaves her. "We think it's best it end here. Before either of you have too much to lose."

I almost laugh, but then I remember the audacity this woman has, and all I can do is stare at her while I attempt to process her request. Fuck, who am I kidding? Coming from her, it was a demand, no matter how much she tries to dress it up.

"You think I should break up with him."

She nods, giving me a smile that I only find malice in. "Yes, dear. I think that's what would be most beneficial to both of you."

This time, I really do laugh, unable to stop myself as I shake my head. "Thank you for your input into *our* relationship, and pardon my language, but there's not a chance in fucking hell I'd ever end things with Hayes. He's one of the best things to ever happen to me."

"I have no doubt about that. After all, my son is one in a million."

It's the closest thing to a compliment I've heard her pay, and even if it is a dig toward me as well, I find myself in agreement.

Hayes is one in infinity.

"Then why wouldn't you want him to be happy?"

"I do, dear. That's *why* I'm doing this. Staying with you? Following you across the country while you chase a ball around a field for a couple years? It would only hold him back from reaching his true potential." Her expression tightens before she adds, "And then there's the little matter of your upbringing to consider."

I saw this coming from a mile away, but it doesn't stop the comment from slicing through my stomach like a rusty blade.

Scoffing, I run my thumb across my lower lip. "Which is more the issue for you, ma'am? The drunk of a father or the absentee mother?"

"Neither, actually. While you may be a product of your environment, you didn't choose your parents, nor the life they raised you in. Which is why it makes all the sense that you'd seek something better from an outside source."

The floor drops out from beneath me.

This fucking—

"You have no fucking clue what you're talking about," I snap, my fingers clamping on the railing like a vice. "And quite frankly, it's an insult to—"

"You were roommates with Phoenix Mercer last year, weren't you?" she cuts in, ignoring my outburst. "Spent a lot of time with him and his family throughout your high school years?"

How the fuck does she know that?

Frowning, I ask, "What does my relationship with the Mercers have to do with Hayes?"

"Simply observing your habit of cozying up to people with wealth and status," she bemuses.

My temper flares at her insinuations, and it's taking everything to keep it in check now. Every piece of love I have for her son to not completely lose my shit on her.

"I don't give a shit about their money or yours. It doesn't mean anything to me," I say slowly.

"Yes, well. That's easy to say when you have none, dear. But that can all change in the blink of an eye."

My molars grind together so hard, I'm shocked they have yet to crack.

"You might as well speak plainly, Mrs. Lancaster. After all, we Southern boys do need things dumbed down for us."

"My husband and I are prepared to offer you a deal in exchange for ending this *relationship* with our son. Twenty-thousand dollars cash, plus the buy out of your lease."

It's not her obvious distaste for Hayes and me being together that catches my attention, nor the lump sum of money she's offering. Those are par for the course, at this point.

It's the lease part that has my heart crawling into my throat.

"You want me to move out of the apartment too?"

A short, tempered laugh leaves her. "You really think we'd allow you two to continue living together? Please, we weren't born yesterday."

I gape at her, wondering where the fuck she lost the plot to think I'd ever take her money, let alone kick me out of where I live.

"Maybe not, but you're sure as hell out of your mind. No amount of money on this planet is worth more to me than Hayes."

Her lips press together, forming a thin, red line. "Oh, dear. I had a feeling you might not see things our way."

"Then why offer it at all?" I snarl.

"Because I was hoping to save our son from having to make the decision instead."

Shards of ice slice through my veins while my brain tries and fails to play catch up. "What the hell are you talking about?"

She studies me the same way a predator would their prey, searching for the perfect attack pattern to go in for the kill.

And my fucking God, she's found it.

"New deal. Take the money, move out, end things with our son. If you don't, we will be forced to put the choice in his hands instead." Her eyes gleam with venom as she utters, "His future, his inheritance, his trust funds…or you."

To drive her point home, she opens the clutch she's holding, producing the check in question, and holds it out to me.

I can only stare at it, floored—absolutely baffled—by this turn of events, and it takes me a minute to find my voice, let alone form a coherent response.

"You'd threaten to disown and cut off your own son because you don't approve of the person he's dating?"

"Approval has nothing to do with it," she says, tone clipped and perturbed. "The chance of my boys choosing someone up to my standards is already slim. But when one is clearly bringing home a piece of gold-digging trailer trash? Well, I always like to see that it's put out."

"Unfortunately, this *trailer trash* isn't fucking interested," I snap, glaring at the check she's still offering.

She clicks her tongue, nodding. "You're loyal, I'll give you that. The real question is, do you truly believe that my son would be willing to choose you in return?" Folding the check in half, she reaches out and tucks it in the breast pocket of my suit. "Take the week to think about it. We'll be awaiting your answer."

And with that final comment, she spins on her heel and rejoins the party, leaving me staring after her in shock.

My mind is spinning at a thousand miles an hour, unable to focus on anything other than...*Hayes*. What I'm supposed to say to him, how I can even bring up this ultimatum his mother's dropped on us like a guillotine.

And there's a big part of me wondering if I should say anything at all.

I have to talk to him. There has to be some way around this.

The next thing I know, I'm bursting through the terrace doors leading back to the party, finding it in the same state I'd left it. People dance and eat and mingle, enjoying their evening without a care in the world.

Meanwhile, it feels like mine is falling apart.

It doesn't take long, spotting Hayes across the room speaking to some finely dressed man and his equally glamorous wife. He notices me as I'm about halfway across the room, a smile lighting up his face while I approach.

The same smile he's been giving me all night. The one I continuously get lost in every time it's aimed my way. And it's at that moment I realize I can't do this.

Not here. Not now.

Rather than continuing in his direction, I make a beeline for the front door. An escape is what I really need right now, some space and time to process. Gain some clarity on the ultimatum just thrown into my lap without warning.

Fingers wrap around my wrist, halting me in my tracks just before I reach the exit, and I turn to find Hayes looking at me in confusion.

"Baby, what's going on? Where are you going?"

I don't want to lie, but there's no chance I can tell him what just happened without breaking down—or worse, blowing up. So I settle for another half-truth, hoping it isn't as transparent as I currently feel.

"I don't think the hor d'oeuvres are settling right with me. I'm just gonna grab an Uber home."

Hayes shakes his head, a piece of dark hair flopping onto his forehead before he brushes it back. "Okay, I'll go with you. Just give me like ten minutes to say a few goodbyes—"

"No, no. You stay. I'll wait up for you back at the apartment," I tell him, forcing a smile.

"Are you sure?"

My jaw strains with effort as I nod. "Yeah. Yeah, I'll see you at home."

I don't wait for a response, simply pressing my lips to his for the briefest kiss, and heading for the exit, loosening my tie as I order an Uber and go to wait outside.

I hold it together the entire ride back to the apartment, fixing my gaze out the window at the city lights passing by. Even manage to keep the emotions at bay while I climb the stairs and unlock the door. But the second I'm in the apartment alone, the dam breaks, and all the pent-up feelings spill out.

The check in the breast pocket of my jacket burns through the fabric, and I quickly yank the damn thing off, throwing it over the back of the couch like it's on fire.

But the pain won't relent, won't ease, just won't fucking stop.

Because the check isn't the problem, It isn't the source.

It's my heart.

And it's cracking in my chest at this impossible decision.

THIRTY

Hayes

It's nearly one in the morning when I finally make it back to the apartment. Thanks to everyone's inability to say their goodbyes quickly, I was stuck at my parents' party for longer than I thought, when the only thing I wanted was to get home to Kason. It's late enough now that I fully expect him to be passed out, even if he did say he'd wait up for me. Which would be understandable, though unfortunate, considering how much I'd wanted to rip that suit off him after we got home this evening.

My assumptions seem correct too, because the apartment is dark, save for the light left on above the stove in the kitchen, as I drop my keys on the counter. Not a peep comes from down the hall where our bedrooms are either.

The door to my room creaks open as I enter, and I immediately find Kason's motionless silhouette in my bed beneath the covers.

My heart ratchets a little at the sight, pounding against my ribs hard enough, I swear they might crack. Shatter at the seams with every beat, and it only confirms everything thought in my mind back at my parents.

That Quinton was right.

I love him.

The word doesn't even startle me when I think it, which in itself is astounding. With the rocky way things began between us, there was a point I thought I'd never be able to tolerate his presence. Now, here I am, head over heels for him.

Slowly peeling my jacket off, I fold it over my desk chair and strip out of my remaining clothes. My eyes never leave him as I do, unable to look away from the person calling to me like a moth to a flame.

Left in only my underwear, I climb onto the mattress and slip beneath the sheets beside him. Craving the strong warmth of his body, I shift until my chest is flush against his back, the heat of his skin on mine grounding me. A soft sigh leaves him when I drape my arm over his waist, and I feel his body relax into mine.

I've never felt more at home than right here, like this.

"Hey, baby," I murmur, pressing a gentle kiss to his shoulder, then the side of his neck. "I missed you the rest of the night."

In his slumber, Kason lets out another soft moan, his subconscious arching his neck for my lips to have better access.

Skating my fingertips over his obliques, I'm met with the elastic waistband of his boxer-briefs. I slide my finger beneath it, just barely, and follow it around to the spot below his belly button.

My lips trail over his shoulders, peppering over the countless freckles I've become obsessed with while I slip my hand under his waistband. His cock is half-hard, even in his sleep, and it only takes a few strokes to bring it completely to life.

"Mmm," Kason mumbles, arching his hips into my touch.

I'm not sure if he's still asleep, awake, or in some in-between state at this point, but I continue kissing any part of his body within reach, murmuring against his skin, "It was unfair, how good you looked tonight in that suit. I'm a little disappointed I didn't get to strip you out of it myself."

One of his hands reaches back, sliding along my thigh until he reaches my ass. He grabs and squeezes it through my underwear before urging me to rock forward into him, and I smile against his skin.

"I wish I would've listened to my instincts telling me to take you upstairs and have my way with you," I whisper, rolling my hips in time with my strokes. "The thought of bending you over the end of my bed and fucking you while everyone else was downstairs almost had me coming undone."

Kason's arching into my touch now, his dick sliding through my fist with enough force to know he's definitely awake. His breathing is coming out in soft pants, lust-filled tension lining his back and shoulders.

"Hayes." He whispers my name on a sigh before turning in my arms and taking my mouth in a deep, slow kiss.

I roll over top of him, settling between his thighs as I start to move my body against his. The ridge of his cock is thick and hard against mine, and I can feel the heat through the fabric of our underwear.

Every part of me is ready to bury myself inside him, but I don't want to rush this.

I don't want to lose this feeling.

So I take my time, breaking free from his mouth to kiss down his body, taking detours every chance I get; tracing his abs with my tongue, brushing my lips across his sternum, taking his nipples in my teeth. But it's when I reach the spot over his heart—the thing I so desperately want to hold in the palm of my hands—I stop.

My body trembles as I press kiss after kiss to his left pec, right where his heart is, unable to stop myself.

I've never been so consumed before. So desperate and full of need for someone else.

It's unraveling me at the seams.

"Want you so much, baby," I whisper against his skin, and it's not lost on me that the words aren't just meant for him as a whole, but also the organ beating in his chest.

The thing I want more than anything else in this world.

"Then have me," he utters back, filling the darkened room with the words.

Always.

The word is as instinctual as breathing, and it spurs me into action, stripping him of his underwear before ridding myself of my own. The lube from my nightstand is in my palm a few seconds later, popping the cap and coating my fingers with it. Nudging his knees apart, I slide them up his crease, spreading the lube around his rim before slowly dipping inside. He's tight and warm and fucking perfect as I slowly work him open, my eyes fixated on his face while he watches me.

And the entire time, all I can think is…

I love you.

My fingers tremble inside him, and I quickly pull them free. Emotions clog my throat as I grab the lube again, rolling to my back and dousing my cock with the cool liquid.

Soft pants spill from Kason's lips while he watches me stroke myself from root to tip, his nostrils flaring with lust and desire. And it's almost like he crawls inside my brain, knowing exactly what I'm wanting when he slowly climbs over top of me, his thighs bracketing mine.

"Ride me, baby," I whisper, lining myself up with his hole, the head pressed against the tight ring of muscle. "Fuck yourself on my cock while I watch."

His teeth sink into his lower lip as he lowers himself with a smooth drop of his hips, my crown breaching his rim drawing gasps from us both. Two midnight forests stare down at me as he adjusts to my cock's sudden intrusion, neither of us breathing, let alone moving, once I'm fully seated inside him.

My chest tightens, my stomach twisting itself into knots of love and lust while he shifts his pelvis, lifting up before impaling himself on my length again, testing the waters.

It's torture and bliss all wrapped into one, watching him use my body for his pleasure.

"That's it, baby. Ride me, just like that. I got you."

The praise falls from me without thought, and my hand reaches for him, wrapping around his shaft and giving him a leisurely stroke. I roll my fist over the head of his cock, playing with that sensitive spot below the head, and a long, low moan leaves him.

"Fuck, Hayes," he moans, and my God, there will never be a day in this lifetime where I don't love the sound of my name on his lips.

His jaw tics with effort as he starts moving faster, fucking himself on my cock at a pace that I match with my hand. The free one anchors on his hip, using it to guide him up and down on my length.

It's not long before I'm taking over completely, both hands locked on his waist while my hips snap up into him from below. His body weight drops forward when I do, his mouth inches from mine now, and the new angle has me swiping over his prostate with every thrust, drawing breathy moans from him.

Both of us pant and gasp for air, his fingers weaving through my hair and anchoring there while we move together, synchronized down to the molecular level.

"You're so perfect, baby," I whisper, my gaze lifting to his.

"Kiss me," he pleads, fingers tightening to the point of pain. "Kiss me, Hayes. Please, just kiss me and—"

I steal the words off his lips, swallowing them whole at the sound of his voice cracking like a sheet of glass.

Our movements are quick and brutal after that, both of us chasing the high that comes from the fall. Kason's ass clamps around me, and from the ragged pants he makes against my lips, he's right there, teetering on the edge.

All he needs is to let go.

"Come, baby," I rasp, driving into him like a madman. "Come for me."

Kason's cock twitches in his palm, and I watch in rapture as his release spills onto my torso. It coats my stomach and chest in white hot liquid, branding me with his essence.

Claiming me as much as I claim him.

"That's it, baby. Fucking perfect," I rasp, my hand moving up to the back of his neck.

The other moves too, gripping his waist, and I flip our positions. His back hits the mattress while my cock remains buried to the hilt, and I take over where he left off. My pace is rough and relentless, my hips pistoning in and out without any rhythm or reason. The only thing I'm thinking of is release.

Of falling off the cliff, tangled in each other.

My forehead drops to his shoulder, pressing a kiss to the pulse that might as well be my own, and I whisper against his skin.

"You're so tight, baby. So perfect. So fucking mine."

His fingers slide into my hair, holding me against him before uttering one, heart-stopping word.

"Always."

And that's all it takes.

I lose myself inside him, shattering into a thousand pieces when my orgasm slams into me like a wrecking ball. His continued clenching around my length draws out my climax, keeping me in freefall until every last drop of cum leaves my body, filling his instead.

My forehead drops to his, our ragged breaths tangling between our lips before I steal another kiss.

And I'm gone.

Decimated beyond repair, and I've never felt more alive.

I pull from his body and roll off to the side, dragging him into me and wrapping my arms around him.

The emotions in his eyes at this distance are undeniable as I stare into them. They're swirling there like a storm, circling around his pupils as they trail over me, and it has words spilling free from me.

Ones I don't mean to say during our post-orgasm high, but I can't stop regardless.

Ones that will undoubtedly change everything.

"Tonight, when you took me out on the dance floor?" I murmur, my fingers skating over his jaw. "That's when I knew I was completely gone. If I hadn't realized I'd fallen in love with you before, I knew it then. Felt myself slipping past the point of no return every time you smiled at me."

His jaw works beneath my touch, his gaze flicking between my eyes before pressing his lips to mine in a kiss that steals my breath as easily as he stole my heart.

There are some things in life that don't need to be said in order to know they're true, which is why I don't care that he hasn't said it back. When he pulls back and I look into his eyes, I know he feels it just as deeply as I do.

I might not know where the future will lead us, but of that, I'm certain.

He shifts, tucking his face into the crook of my neck, his forehead pressed against my throat. The soft strands of his auburn hair brush against my cheek, and I nuzzle into them while trailing my fingertips down the length of his spine. I map the valley between the muscles on either side, committing them to memory as I, once again, find myself giving him the secret my heart has known for a while.

"I love you, Kason."

His body starts shaking against mine, a vibration that'd barely be noticeable if we weren't plastered together at every inch.

It's not until it becomes almost violent and little warm droplets fall to my skin that I realize something is very, *very* wrong.

THIRTY-ONE

Hayes

Shifting onto my elbow, I stare down at Kason, who still has his face buried in my shoulder. His silent tears coat my skin like rainfall, and I stare in abject horror as he falls apart before my eyes.

"Kase, what's wrong?" I whisper, trying to sit up better. He doesn't let me, though, tightening the arm slung over my waist like a vice.

Fear hits me like a punch to the gut, and I force the knot in my throat to loosen enough to speak.

"Is it what I said? Because, baby, you don't have to—"

He shakes his head a few times, and the vibrations of his body slowly start to subside. But he still doesn't respond; just keeps pressing his skin into mine like it's the gravity keeping him anchored to Earth.

My fingers scrape against his skull, running through his hair as I press kiss after kiss to the side of his head, my heart cracking at the pain he's so clearly in.

"Talk to me, baby. Please. I'm right here."

A choked sob leaves him, and he sucks in a breath before muttering, "I don't know how to say this."

"Don't worry about that," I whisper, shaking my head. "Just say it. I'm not going anywhere."

He finally peels himself away enough for me to look down at him, only to wish I hadn't. His expression, a mixture of pain and confusion, has my stomach roiling with worry. I don't think I've ever seen a person more torn as the words leave his lips.

"Your parents are trying to blackmail me, Hayes."

I'm not sure what I was expecting him to say, but it certainly wasn't anything close to that. The mere idea of what he's saying being the truth… fuck, it rips the rug right out from under me.

And as much as I don't want to believe it, he has no reason to lie to me. Not about this.

"Blackmail?" I echo, the word barely coming out more than a whisper.

Kason winces, shaking his head. "Well, I'm not sure if it's more blackmail or extortion or bribery—"

"What are you talking about, Kase?" I cut in, searching his face. "When did this happen?"

"Your mother found me outside tonight at the party. She and your father offered me," he pauses, letting out a sharp, watery laugh. "Well, a lot of money—"

My hackles rise instantly. "How much did they offer you?"

Gone is his confusion, leaving only pain building to agony. I can see it in his eyes, he doesn't want to answer. Just like I'm sure he can see it in mine that I need him to.

"Twenty-thousand dollars plus buying out my portion of the lease."

And now it's my turn to vibrate, but not with fear or worry. With rage.

Over the past few months, I've gotten to really know Kason. See the guy he really is—not just the football star everyone else seems to see. His damage, his truths, his fears and dreams have all been laid bare before me. There's no ulterior motive with him, no desire to hurt anyone if he can help it.

So I know it has to kill him to dismantle the image I've had of my parents for my entire life with that single sentence.

And I fucking hate her for it.

"What did you tell her?" I ask, my voice a deadly whisper.

"I said no, of course." He finally pulls away, staring up at me with warm, green eyes that I've come to know as my favorite color. "Hayes, I'm not interested in their money or yours. The fact that you have as much as you do makes me feel…*inferior*."

Shaking my head, I cup the side of his face. "It's just money, baby. It doesn't mean anything to me."

"Well, your parents don't seem to share that sentiment," he utters in abject defeat.

But I'm not fucking having it.

"Then it's a good thing it's not their fucking decision, isn't it?" I tell him, my voice low and calm, though I feel anything but.

Kason worries his lower lip with his teeth, and though this conversation should be resolved, a heavy sense of foreboding sits on my chest. Because none of his anxiety has lessened. If anything, it's only ratcheted up another twenty levels.

"There's something else, isn't there?" I whisper, my thumb tracing over his cheekbone. When he nods solemnly, it's like a vice tightens around my lungs. "Tell me."

"She said if I didn't accept the offer, then they'd bring the option to you. Threaten to cut you off, tank your future, the whole shebang."

My stomach drops, and I swear the entire world tilts on its axis.

That they'd stoop so low, go to these lengths…it's proof that I barely know the people who've raised me.

"They didn't say a word to me this evening. Even after you'd left."

"No, they wouldn't have yet. They gave me a chance to reconsider their offer now that I know the stakes." He clears his throat before he adds, "They want my answer by the end of the week."

I drop down from my elbow onto my back and stare up at the ceiling, willing myself to wake up from whatever bad dream this is. Because that's what it has to be, right? Some ridiculous nightmare that my subconscious is cooking up from stress and worry.

There's no way this is reality.

And yet…

"This is insane," I mutter, shoving my fingers through my hair. "Why would they do this?"

"I think the reason is obvious." Kason's voice cracks, and I glance over at him to see him shaking his head. "They don't think I'm good enough or worthy of you or driven enough. All the above, probably. And hell, maybe—"

"Maybe they're full of shit? Yeah, that's exactly it," I cut in. Rolling to my side, I cup the side of his face and brush away the remnants of his tears. "Please tell me you don't believe a damn word of what you just said."

His gaze falls to my chest, and all he does is shake his head.

And the sight damn near cracks my heart in two.

"Kason. Baby. I want *you*. I *love* you. Please tell me you believe that."

"I do," he whispers, his voice cracking like shards of glass. "But I also believe they'll follow through on their threats."

The unfortunate thing is he's probably right. I don't comment on that, though. Don't confirm the threat is anything but empty.

But I can't lie to him either.

Instead, I tell him the most honest thing I can.

"I don't want to lose you."

"And I don't want to watch you lose everything you've worked for. Every plan you've ever made for yourself." He shakes his head, a sad watery laugh leaving him. "You can't just give up everything for me."

"Then we'll come up with a new plan," I tell him, pressing my forehead to his. "We can pretend to end things. You move out—hell, *I'll* move out, even. We play things cool for a while. Sneak around, see each other when we can between classes and everything. Then when things blow over—"

"That's not gonna work, and you know it," he whispers.

His hand sliding down to find mine, our fingers interlocking. The warmth of his palm against mine grounds me, and my eyes fall closed.

"Then let them cut me off," I mutter, my forehead rolling against his as I shake my head. "I have trusts they can't touch. Everything that's left in my college fund is all mine too. And look at Quinton, you know? He's been able to make it work, and I don't think he's been happier in his life after being free from the shackles his parents had on him."

His hand tightens around mine ever so slightly. "What's your fallback, though? Because he has a professional hockey career. You don't have one of those."

"I have two degrees," I counter. "That's more than enough to get me a job. Sure, it might not be my family's company, and maybe it'll be a lot harder to make happen, but it will all work out."

"But that's the thing. It won't be everything you've worked your ass off to get." His hand rubs across my jaw, the touch featherlight, almost like a ghost. "It won't be what you *deserve*. And you deserve everything, Hayes."

I remain silent, unable to do anything other than wrack my brain for some other option. Because there has to be one. There's no way there isn't another solution, and if we look hard enough—

"Look at me," he whispers, shattering my train of thought. "Please."

Pulling back, I force myself to meet his gaze, and it's a knife to the gut, seeing the agony in them. The sorrow and pain that he doesn't deserve, that I'd do anything to take away…yet I'm the reason behind it.

My throat constricts, and I shake my head.

Physically rejecting the thoughts I can see in his eyes. Read in them, clear as day.

"You want to end this, don't you?"

"That's the last fucking thing I want. But I think it's the only real option we have." His eyes are filled with more unshed tears, his voice cracking when he mutters, "I'm not gonna let you throw away your entire future for me."

"So instead, we have to throw away ours?"

My chest aches as I look at him, at this perfect, amazing guy who is everything I never knew I needed.

How do I tell him that the future I want has him threaded and woven into the fabric now? How can I fight him on something he seems so dead-set on?

He shakes his head, a sad smile creeping over his lips. "We don't know what'll happen after this. But I have to believe, if we're supposed to work, then we will. It doesn't matter if it takes six weeks, ten months, two years; it'll happen. But for now, it's just not the right time."

Not the right time.

The sentiment feels ridiculous considering where we were only a few weeks ago. Laughing and sight-seeing and stacking more building blocks of a relationship unlike any other I've had.

And now we're here. To this.

To goodbye.

Brushing my fingertips over his tear-stained cheek, I find myself filled with regret. For the time we wasted, and more importantly, for the time we're about to lose.

"The day you moved in, I started counting down to graduation," I tell him, the words barely audible. "I spent every morning checking off the remaining days I had to deal with you in my presence, my space, my life. But now…I want all those days back."

I want all the ones still to come.

"I know," he whispers, it coming out raw and grated. "I know."

My forehead comes to rest against his again, and I force myself to keep it together. To rein in the hurt and the anger and the pain, even if it's just for right now. Because it's possible this is the only time we have left.

"How do we say goodbye?" I ask, my voice crumbling beneath the weight of the question. Of the emotion it drags to the surface.

"I wish I knew."

I wish we didn't have to.

I lean in at the thought and press my lips to his mouth, his jaw, his face; peppering them over his skin, kissing away all the tears before taking his mouth again. Then I kiss him like it's the last thing I'll ever do—because it very well might be.

Because the ache in my chest is so severe, it feels like I might die on the spot.

Like I might cease to exist.

Kason is the first to pull away, his jaw straining with effort as three words that shatter my heart leave his lips.

"I should go."

My body immediately rejects the idea, panic hitting me square in the chest. The thought of him walking out this door and not coming back…I just can't. Not now, not ever.

"Kason."

He shakes his head, the tears flowing freely at this point from both of us, as he shifts to the edge of the mattress. I watch, helpless, as he grabs his boxers from the floor, and before I can stop myself, my hand is on his wrist to stop him.

"Stay," I whisper, not caring if I have to beg, plead, or lose all form of self-respect. I can't let him leave. Not yet. "Please, baby. For just one more night."

If I thought he looked decimated before, it's got nothing on his expression when he hears my plea. The way my voice shatters right along with my heart.

And though we know it'll do neither of us any good, he concedes anyway. Drops his boxers back to the ground and crawls right back in beside me, chest to chest.

"Okay," he murmurs, his forehead pressing against mine. "One more night."

We curl into each other, our limbs tangled in a mess of cum, sweat, and sheets, but we don't dare move to clean up or redress. The second we do, the bubble bursts and reality will set back in.

A reality neither of us are ready to face.

His breathing evens out before mine, the hand that was tracing lines over my shoulder falling to the side.

I'm grateful he's the one to succumb first, because it gives me a chance to memorize every inch of him. Each strand of hair laying out of place, all the freckles dotting his nose, the way his eyelashes brush over his cheekbones when he sleeps, every rise and fall of his chest as he slumbers.

I take all these little pieces of him for myself, gathering them one by one in my mind. There's no doubt I'll have to box them up eventually, put them under lock and key in order to move on from the one thing I want to keep forever.

So I collect as many of them as I can, fighting a losing battle with sleep until unconsciousness eventually pulls me under. And when I wake in the morning, I don't have it in me to look to the other side of my bed.

Because I know it's empty.

Just like the cavity that once held my heart.

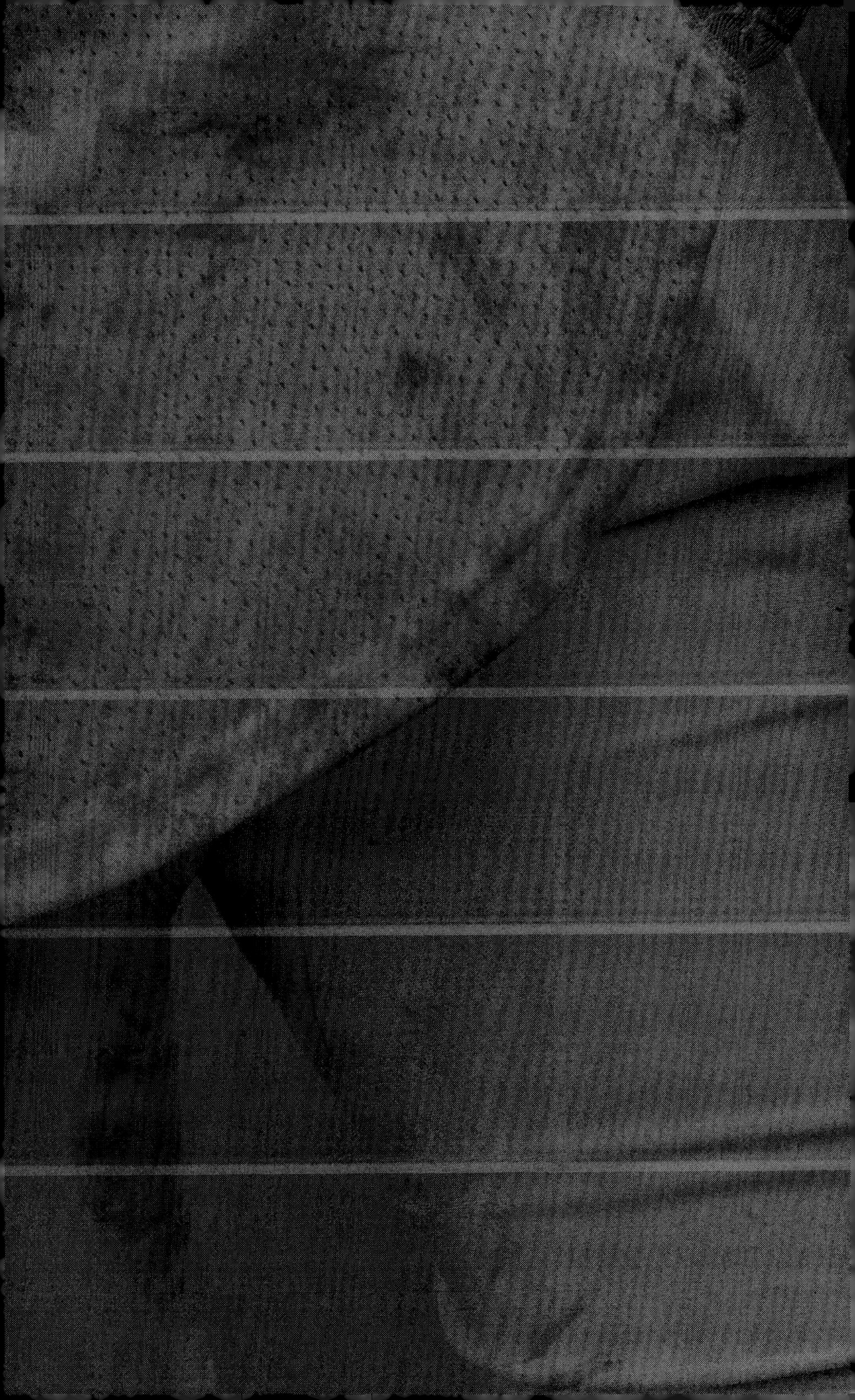

THIRTY-TWO

Kason

One Week Later — February

A hand shakes me on the shoulder, stirring me from sleep in the chair I'd been occupying on the fifth floor of the campus library. I startle a little, my eyes bursting open as I lift my head to find Holden leaning over me.

"Hey, sorry to scare you," he says, taking a step back. "I called your name and when you didn't respond, I noticed you were asleep."

Huh. I didn't realize I'd dozed off, my textbook sliding out of my grip and to the floor at my feet. Then again, I haven't been sleeping much, if at all, the past week I've spent living on Mal and Ivy's couch.

I doubt I'd be sleeping much regardless if I was in the world's comfiest bed, though. After that last night with Hayes, sleeping alone is pretty much impossible.

When I don't respond to him right away, Holden waves his hand in front of my face. "Kase? You good?"

Blinking rapidly, I shake my head to clear the fogginess of sleep. "Shit, sorry, Hold."

Holden stares down at me with a frown, clear concern lining his features. He motions with a thumb over his shoulder toward the set of stairs leading down to the main lobby.

"They're about to close up. Unless you're planning to stay the night."

As much as I don't want to sleep here, no part of me wants to go to Mal's.

Or anywhere else for that matter.

The only thing I really want—what I've wanted since the moment I moved out—is to go to the apartment and pound on the door until Hayes opens it. And then I want to kiss him like my life depends on it, like it's the only thing keeping me grounded to Earth, before dragging him to his bed and showing him all the ways I've been missing him the past seven days.

But I can't. And it's killing me.

"Paging Kason Fuller. You still waking up in there?" Holden says, pulling my attention back to him.

"Sorry." I shake my head, as if it would be enough to clear my rampant thoughts. "I guess I am."

Rising from my seat, I shoulder my bag and head for the stairs, Holden by my side.

"You wanna walk out to my car with me? Or better yet, you want a ride home so I know you won't pass out on a bench on your way there."

"I, uh…" I pause to clear my throat as we exit the building, moving down the lamplit path to the parking lot. "I drove, actually. No worries about me spending the evening on a park bench for tonight."

"You didn't just walk from home?" he asks, motioning toward the direction of the apartment I'd shared with Hayes. "Isn't it only like two blocks from here?"

Home is such a funny word. Especially considering I'm pretty much homeless for the time being. And hearing it right now is like a knife to the gut, slicing deep enough, it might as well disembowel me.

I want to lie. Make up some excuse as to why I'd drive here. After all, the issues with my love life, or life in general, aren't for Holden to worry about. Or anyone else, for that matter.

Yet I find the truth spilling from my lips anyway.

"I'm actually staying with Mal and her girlfriend." When his confusion deepens—I'm assuming about who Mal is—I add, "She's an old friend from Alabama, and one of the Leighton cheerleaders?"

"No, I know who Mal is." Holden is every kind of confused now, his brows crashing together and shaking his head a few times. "But I need you to back up. You and Hayes aren't living together anymore?"

God, just the sound of his name has my heart squeezing uncomfortably. "We were until last week, yeah. But then things got…complicated, and I had to move out."

"In the middle of a lease?"

"My portion was bought out," I murmur, my voice cracking and crumbling on the words.

I hadn't accepted the check Hayes' parents offered, nor the money to buy out the rest of the lease. When I finally had the courage to find the damn thing where it was left in the breast pocket of my suit, I'd ripped the damn thing to shreds and sent it right back where it came from.

The money to buy out my half of the lease, on the other hand, was a lot simpler for them to take care of by sending a check straight to the management company of our apartment complex.

Holden frowns. "Damn. I didn't realize the two of you had a falling out. You were really good together, from what I could tell."

A low hum slips out without my permission, muttering a simple, "Yeah," in response.

Awkward silence fills the air between us as we stop next to Holden's Jeep, and I need an escape route from Hayes being the topic of conversation.

Confiding in Holden would be too hard, I think. Not because he isn't worthy of it, but because the entire time, I'd be wishing I was talking to Phoenix instead. Wondering what *he* would say.

"I gotta get going, but it was good to see you," I tell him, before thumbing over my shoulder toward my car.

Holden must read my discomfort, because he doesn't push me for anything more. He just offers an understanding nod before telling me, "Don't be a stranger, okay?"

I nod. "I'll try my best."

"I'm serious, Kase." His gaze softens as he cocks his head. "Even if we're officially no longer teammates, I'm always in your corner."

Emotions cause my throat to tighten at his unexpected declaration, and all I can do is nod in thanks while I attempt to clear the baseball currently sitting on my trachea.

A pained smile crosses my face, and I know I'm barely keeping it together now.

"Thanks, Hold," I rasp, unable to keep the gravel out of my voice, even when I try to lighten the mood. "And thanks for not letting me get locked in the library overnight."

He waves me off before grabbing the door handle on his Jeep. "Don't mention it. You'd do the same for me."

Nodding, I leave him at his car and head toward my own near the other side of the lot.

My long shadow cast by the light from the lampposts is my only companion now, and I try to shove down the emotion clogging my throat and threatening to spill from my eyes.

It was only a few months. I shouldn't be this destroyed by losing someone after that short of time. Yet in the span of this week, I've never felt more alone.

Not when my mom left.

Not all those years being bullied or beaten.

Not after everything that happened with Phoenix.

This tops it all, and I don't know how I'm gonna survive it.

A couple tears coat my lashes, and I blink them away before they fall completely as I unlock my car and yank open the door. I climb inside haphazardly, tossing my backpack and phone in the passenger seat, and debating whether or not going to Mal's in this state is a good idea.

She'll want me to talk through it, get my feelings out in the open, and force me to stop wallowing on something that isn't going to change. And I know I probably should do those things. My therapist would likely agree, if I actually called her to reschedule the appointment I'd canceled earlier this week.

I just can't.

Not right now. Not with any of it.

Deciding that a drive to clear my head might be best before going to Mal's, I turn my key in the ignition and my car roars to life. I'm about to throw it in reverse when movement out of my peripheral pulls my attention out my driver's side window, only to find Holden right there, scaring the absolute shit out of me.

Apparently I can't handle jump scares in horror movies or real life.

Rolling down my window, I ask, "Are you trying to give me a heart attack tonight?"

"Well, if you would have answered your phone, I wouldn't have needed to scare you."

Frowning, I check my phone to see a missed call from him. "Sorry, it was still on silent from being in the library."

"Mhmm," Holden murmurs dubiously, crossing his arms. "If you didn't want to talk to me, you could've just said that."

I scoff at his dramatic antics, equally annoyed and humored by them in my current state. "You gonna tell me why you called, or are you planning to leave me in suspense?"

He ignores my snark, unsurprisingly, before shocking me into silence.

"I wanted to ask you to come stay at the house with us."

Offering me a place to live was the last thing I'm expecting to come out of his mouth, and I can't help but gape at him.

"You gonna say yes, or just sit there and look at my pretty face?" he asks, matching my sarcasm from earlier with a smile while I struggle to form a response.

"I...Hold—"

He holds up a hand to stop me. "Before you argue or ask if I'm kidding, yes, I'm being a hundred percent serious."

There's not a doubt in my mind that it's a genuine offer. I just don't think I can take him up on it. Not without at least knowing that I wouldn't be walking into a lion's den at that townhouse.

Wetting my lips, I address my concerns as tactfully as I can. "Do you really think that's a good idea? I mean, did you talk to Phoe?" I hate the way the question comes out, all insecure and helpless. And it only gets worse when I keep talking, and in turn, make more of an ass of myself. "Because we're supposed to be taking this break to *stop* depending on each other. Me moving in with you kinda defeats that purpose."

"I just called him. He was the one who told me to ask you," Holden tells me immediately.

It does little to assuage my concerns, though.

Sighing, I slump back against the seat and shake my head. "I don't know, Hold."

"You wouldn't be putting us out, if that's what you're worried about. I don't even use my room ninety-nine percent of the time." Holden pauses before he adds, "And come to think of it, that other one percent is only when I *really* piss him off and he forces me to sleep alone."

I snort, having a hard time believing him. "That's only one percent?"

"These are made-up statistics, okay? No need to be a stickler."

My tongue rolls along the inside of my cheek, taking a moment to seriously debate this.

Mal was right about one thing at the beginning of the term: I do not love sharing one bathroom with two girls. But there's part of me that's hesitant to even entertain this. I've made so much progress this year, and the last thing I want to do is impede it by slipping into old habits.

But God, sleeping in a bed again sounds fucking heavenly.

"Do you actually mean it or is this a pity offer you're hoping I don't accept?" I ask hesitantly, hating myself for how helpless this entire situation makes me feel.

His whiskey eyes soften around the edges, and he leans down, crossing his arms on the opening of my window. "Here's the thing, Kase. People generally don't offer things unless they mean it. There's always exceptions, and yeah, things still might be rocky between you and Nix. But we're still your friends, and we'll still look out for you."

"I just don't want you or him or anyone else to feel like they need to play white knight. I can take care of myself. Stand on my own feet."

"You can still do that while accepting help."

He cocks his head to the side, waiting for me to disagree.

But the thing is, I can't.

Sighing, I hold up my hands in surrender. "Okay, fine. I'll stay with you guys."

"Don't make it sound like such a chore," Holden jibes with a laugh. "Look, I know it's getting late, but we'll get your shit moved in tonight if you want. Just text me the address to Mal's place and Nix and I will meet you over there to help you load up."

I hesitate, not wanting to be more of a pain than I already will be by moving into the house. Doing it at this time of night would be pushing the envelope.

"You really don't have to. I can grab my stuff tomorrow after class when it's not so late."

"And spend another night on a couch that's likely six inches too short for you? Okay." He rolls his eyes before demanding, "Let. Us. Help. You."

I wince under his stare that's likely an equal match for a disapproving parent. "Fine, you win. I'll let Mal know you're coming over to help. Make sure she and Ivy aren't asleep or busy or anything."

Holden waggles his eyebrows suggestively, echoing, "'Busy or anything.' What's that mean?"

"Glad to see that being in a serious, committed relationship hasn't pulled your mind outta the gutter."

"It was born there, and more importantly, it's never leaving," he says, stepping back from my driver's side door to head back to his Jeep. I watch as he goes, gratitude filling my chest when he pauses and turns back to me. "And Kase? While you're staying with us, would you do me a favor and make up with my boyfriend already? He's kinda insufferable without you."

"I'm telling him you said that!" I call back, knowing there's nothing I'd love more than getting my best friend back.

Well, almost nothing.

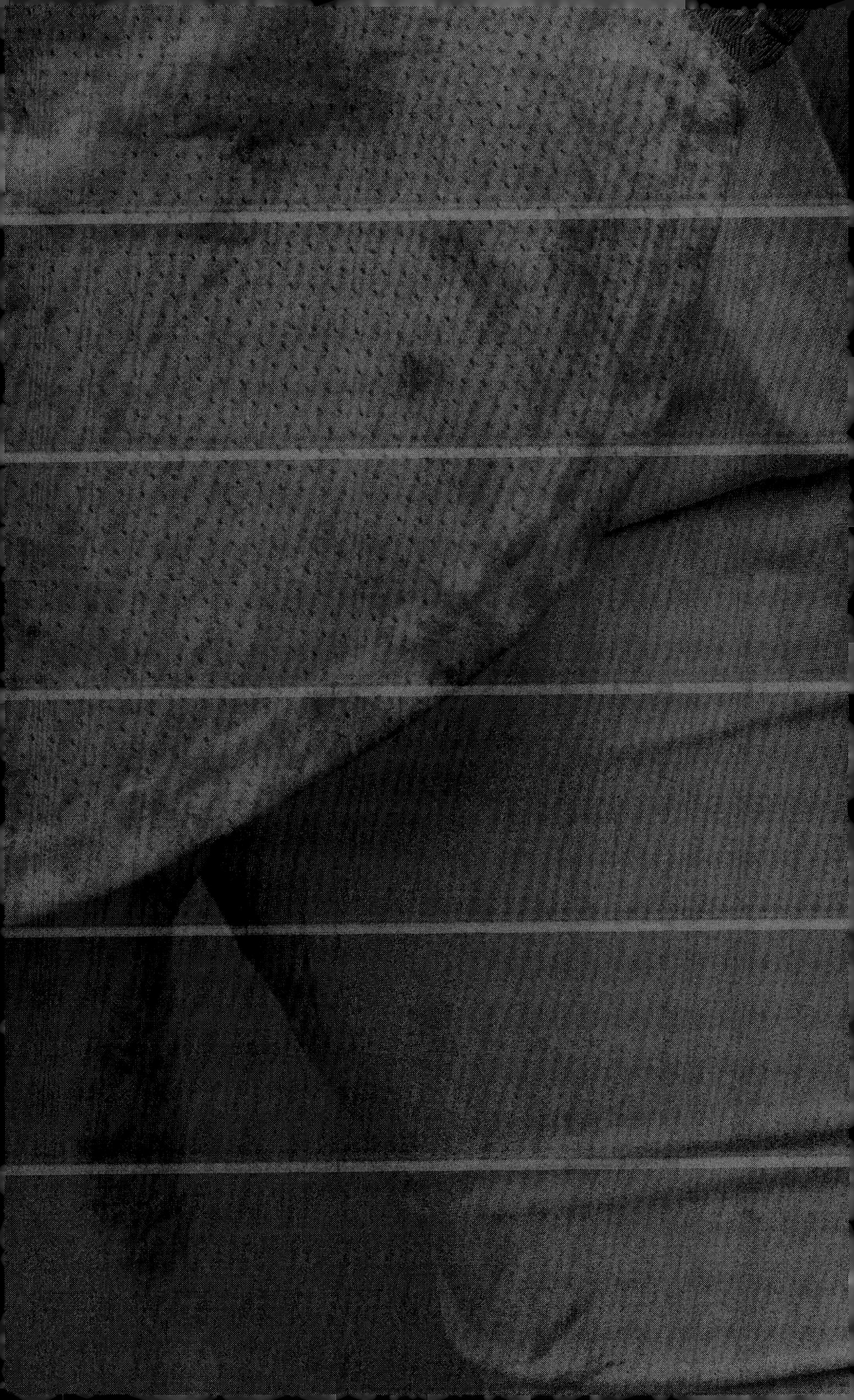

THIRTY-THREE

Kason

T heo and, I'm assuming, Camden are sprawled out on the living room couch when Phoenix, Holden and I enter the townhouse just over an hour later, boxes of my belongings in tow. Both of them sit up when they see me, Theo grinning and Camden looking a bit confused.

"Well, look what the cat dragged in," Theo says as he jumps up from the sofa. "Long time no see, Kaseykins."

I grimace at the pet name, shaking my head vehemently. "Please do not ever call me that again."

Theo's nose wrinkles up and he nods in agreement. "Yeah, it felt wrong as soon as I said it."

"Uh, hi. Someone wanna tell me what's happening here?" Camden questions, still looking as confused as he did when I walked in.

My stomach drops clear out of my ass, and I glance between the four of them. "Did y'all know I was coming?"

"He's just messing with you," Theo tells me, clapping me on the back. He motions to where Phoe and Holden are stacking a couple of boxes by a door I'm assuming leads to the basement. "You think these two yay-hoos are inviting someone to live here without running it by the rest of us first?"

Fair point.

But apparently not fair enough for Camden, because it's clear he has no clue what's happening.

"I don't remember agreeing to this," Camden murmurs, pursing his lips in thought.

"Cam, it was in the group chat," Phoenix tells him, crossing his arms.

Camden scoffs. "No, it wasn't."

"You literally gave the message a thumb-up emoji," Holden adds with a laugh.

Camden frowns and pulls out his phone, only for it to deepen a few seconds later when he must find the message. Letting out a sigh, he drops his phone to his lap. "God, this is what I get for opening texts when I'm half asleep."

"Yep, pretty much." This comes from Theo. "And now you don't get a vote. Sorry, pal. This isn't a democracy anymore."

Camden's frown deepens, and he opens his mouth to say something, but Theo quickly holds up a hand to cut him off at the knees. "Don't you dare ask what a democracy is. You're a history major, for fuck's sake. How are you even passing your classes?"

Without missing a beat, Camden smirks and comes back with, "Wouldn't you like to know."

"We all know you sleep with the girl who takes your tests for you, Cam. You're not as sly as you think you are." This comes from Holden, who shoots me a wink.

"Welcome to the chaos," Theo says, grinning wide. "Too late to back out now."

It really is chaos, but to be honest, I'm already loving every second of it.

"I'm just thankful you're letting me add to it for a while."

"Nah, man. We're happy to have you." Theo's arm around my shoulder lifts, pointing toward Phoe and Holden. "Though, you're the unfortunate soul who has to stay in the room across from these two exhibitionists."

"Exhibitionists," I echo, my eyes falling to my best friend. "Really?"

Theo nods, his nose wrinkling up in disgust. "Really, really. So unless you're into watching, I'd definitely make your presence known before coming down the stairs."

"Don't listen to a fucking word he says," Phoenix tells me before giving Theo a sly look. "Theo is just crabby because he's not getting any."

Theo studies him briefly before he scoffs. "You know nothing about my sex life, Mercer. And all I'm doing is warning our friend Kason that he should maybe shield his eyes from the sectional in the rec room whenever he goes down the stairs. Unless he's looking to get an eyeful—"

"That was *one time*," Holden shouts on his way back out to the car for the rest of the boxes.

"Yeah, you really need to get over that," confirms Phoenix, following his boyfriend out the door.

"I'll get over it when I'm able to scrub the memory of it from my brain," Theo calls after them. "God knows I can't live, laugh, love with it in its current condition."

"Lobotomies are still legal, you know," Camden offers from where he's sitting on the couch. "Live, laugh, lobotomy."

Theo glares at him, muttering, "You're so lucky there isn't a bowl of popcorn out here right now."

Fuck.

My chest squeezes, and I do my best to shove down memories the word *popcorn* invokes. But as they barrel through my mind, I shove them to the side and force myself to focus on the present.

On this group of guys who are picking me up when I'm at my lowest—and I couldn't be more grateful for it.

"I really do appreciate y'all for letting me stay here for the rest of the term. Sleeping on a tiny couch was already getting old," I tell Cam and Theo with a dry chuckle.

"Please, you're doing us the favor by cutting the rent down," Theo says as Phoe and Holden return with the rest of the boxes. Waving his hand at them again, he gripes. "Besides, these two fuck-heads don't need two separate bedrooms when they never use one of them."

"Hey, I use my closet," Holden gripes from where he's setting one of my boxes by the stairs.

"Better tell Phoenix to make some room in his, because Kason's about to be taking yours," Theo tells him, a big grin on his face.

"You're enjoying this," I note, watching the glee on Theo's face.

"Oh, absolutely. And now that you're here, I have an extra brain to combat the idiocy that happens around here."

With that, Theo gives a pointed look in Camden's direction, who is watching, wide-eyed, as this all unfolds.

As if on cue, Camden asks, "Am I the only one who's lost as to *why* we're getting another roommate?" He holds up his hands when I glance at him, quickly adding, "Not that I mind! I just think I missed a chapter or two."

"A chapter or two?" Holden echoes with a laugh. "Try the whole fucking book, Cam."

A knock on my bedroom door the following week pulls my attention up from my laptop, only to find Phoenix leaning against the door jam.

"Hey. You busy?"

Truth be told, I've been scouring my streaming services for a horror movie to watch, only to realize they've all been tainted with memories I'd rather not think about right now.

So in other words, nope. Not busy at all.

Shrugging, I close the screen of my computer and set it beside me. "Nothing that can't wait."

Taking that as permission to enter, he steps into my room, closes the door behind him, and drops to the end of my bed.

"I just wanted to see how you were," he says slowly, gaze searching my face. "Are you settling in okay?"

Putting on the best smile I can muster, I wave him off. "Oh, yeah. Makes it easier that I hadn't unpacked while I was living on Mal's couch all last week."

There's a beat of silence where he just stares at me, his eyes soft and glossy at the edges, and it takes every piece of strength I have left not to break on the spot at the sight.

"You know you could've called me. Told me what was going on," he murmurs in a gruff whisper. "We would've gotten you in here last week if that were the case."

I shake my head immediately and clear the emotions clogging my throat. "I can't just lean on you all the time, Phoe. That's what this whole break was about in the first place."

"Leaning on a friend to help you during a heartbreak isn't the same thing as all the toxic shit that was happening before," he argues, though it comes out more pleading than anything. "Just because you need help every once in a while doesn't mean you're dependent on me. There's actually such a thing as hyper-independence, and that's not healthy either."

My therapist mentioned that at one point, telling me that it can be a direct reaction after breaking out of a codependent cycle like ours. I thought I was doing a good job to keep that from happening, making sure I still allowed myself to accept help when it was offered.

But seeing as how difficult it was to accept his and Holden's last week, I guess that isn't the case.

"I'm still working on it, clearly. I just don't want to go back to how it was before. The toxic part, at least."

"Yeah, I get that. I don't either. But that doesn't mean I don't care about your happiness or want to see you get everything you deserve. We just…"

"Need to find balance," I finish for him with a somber smile.

"Exactly," he murmurs. His eyes lock with mine for a moment, and I swear, I know the question in his head before it ever leaves his lips. "Do you wanna talk about what happened with Hayes?"

I don't, but I know I need to get some of it off my chest before I implode.

Dropping my focus to my bedding, I pick at the stitching and do my best to recount my run-ins with Hayes' mother in a condensed version. "Basically his parents don't think we're a good fit, but not because of anything I've actually done or said. At least, not on purpose?" Blowing out a sigh, I shake my head and say words that taste acidic on my tongue. "They see me as some poor kid who only wants to use him for his money or distract him from his true potential. They even offered me twenty-grand to break things off with him."

"Okay," he says slowly, attempting to piece together how we've ended up here. "I'm assuming you told them to shove it where the sun don't shine?"

"Absolutely, I didn't even bat an eye at the check. But then they threatened to cut *him* off instead. Including from their family business that he's planned his entire life around taking over."

"*Shit,*" Phoe mutters, shaking his head. "So that's why you left."

"I told him first, but yeah. And then I ripped the check to shreds and sent it back to them."

His jaw drops, eyes widening in shock. "You didn't."

"Of course I fucking did. I don't give a shit about his money, or yours, or anyone else's for that matter. I went without it for a good chunk of my life, and there's no reason I couldn't continue that way. The only thing I wanted was him, but I couldn't just let him leave it all behind for me." My throat catches when I look up at him, my voice full of gravel when I whisper, "I couldn't be the reason someone missed out on their dreams all over again."

It takes him a second to realize I'm not just talking about Hayes.

After all, the reason my best friend is here is because of me, and the fucked up, codependent web we were tangled in.

Shaking his head, he utters, "I hope you know I've long since moved past choosing Leighton instead of Foltyn. And honestly, it's not to say that I wouldn't have ended up here in the end anyway from missing your sorry ass too much from the other side of the country."

I snort, not believing that for a second. "You and I both know that isn't true."

"We don't, actually. My therapist tells me I have a little bit of a hero complex, always needing to be needed. To do the saving." His lips quirk when he notices my surprise about the therapist comment. "You aren't the only one who's been working on yourself, you know. And it doesn't take a genius to see how much you've grown, even from a distance. So I'm thinking maybe it's time we both give ourselves, and each other, a bit more credit."

"I think you're right," I whisper in agreement.

"Does that mean this break is over? Because I'd really like my best friend back."

My lips twitch into a bittersweet smile as I nod, hating that the person who helped me grow enough to get my best friend back is now the one I'm missing instead.

"As long as you don't make me sit through your favorite *Friends* reruns to celebrate."

He chuckles. "I wouldn't dare. That form of torture is reserved for Holden now."

"Oh, thank God. If that's all it took to get me out of watching that damn sitcom, I would've told you to get a boyfriend years ago."

"See," he says, grinning. "If anything, I should be thanking you. If I never came here, I'd never have met Holden, and then you'd be stuck watching *Friends* with me for the rest of our codependent lives."

Shooting him a playful grimace, I tease, "Well, in that case, you're welcome."

We both laugh, and I have to admit, this feels good between us. Like things are the same, but different. A fresh page at the beginning of a new chapter we both desperately needed. But despite the mood lightening, I still feel like there's a darkness lingering over me, but I know it has nothing to do with Phoenix.

Not directly, at least.

My eyes lift to his, only to find him staring at me intently. "I want you to know…I get it now. What it means for you to be with Holden. Why you felt like you couldn't give up what the two of you have."

"I tried to. For you, and for our friendship." There's a beat of silence where he gives me a helpless little shrug. "He's in my veins, though. I can't help the way I feel about him."

I nod, understanding his point all too well.

"Just so you know, I stand by what I said last spring. I want you to be happy, and now that I know what it feels like to find that with someone else, I'd never want to be the thing standing in the way of it."

"And circling back to Hayes," he hedges tentatively, raising a brow. "Dare I ask how you're doing with all this?"

I smile, and I know without even looking in the mirror, it's likely the most desolate one he's ever seen.

"I feel like a piece of me dies inside every day I don't hear from him."

A sadness contorts his face, and I wouldn't have to be his best friend to know he's remembering the time he and Holden spent apart last year. The time *I'd* kept them apart.

"I wish I could say it gets easier," he whispers with a shrug. "In reality, I think you just get used to it. Living with the pain."

My eyes trail over his features, noting how he appears the same on the outside, but it's almost like I can see the change in him too. Almost like he's lighter. Less worried and burdened, constantly playing the hero.

"You really have grown," I tell him, arching a brow. "The old version of you would've already grabbed your keys and went over there to give him a piece of your mind. And possibly your fist."

"Yeah, well, it's obvious you wouldn't let me if I tried. Which is how I know you have too."

He's definitely got a point.

"Look at us, being healthy and shit."

He chuckles, shaking his head. "And on the topic of health, I'm gonna lecture you for half a second and remind you not to let the grief eat you alive." Aiming a knowing look at me, he continues, "Call your therapist. Talk to me or to Hold or someone on the team or to the freakin' barista at the coffee shop. Just don't bottle it up, okay? We're all here for you."

I suck in a dramatic breath through my teeth, needing the air in the room to lighten back up again. "I don't know, you already let me move in here. Talking shit out with you on top of that? I think it's a bit too codependent for my taste."

"Shut the fuck up, you dick." He laughs, shoving me hard enough, I have to catch myself from falling off the bed. "For real, though. I'm glad you're here. I wouldn't want you to be anywhere else while you're going through all this."

"Me either, Phoe."

He goes to rise off my bed, but I don't let him get far before grabbing his wrist and pulling him into a hug. As my arms wrap around his shoulders, it feels like a piece of my soul has finally been returned, but I can't help noticing the other missing piece I feel just as deeply.

"Get some rest," Phoenix says when he releases me. "You've got some big training days coming up."

"Will do. Thanks, Dad," I mutter, rolling my eyes.

He points at me as menacing as he can while a giant grin is on his face. "Call me that again and I'll give you a curfew too."

"Oh, the terror."

Laughter fills my room as he stands and heads for the door, and I can tell both of us are feeling pretty good about this new place we're in. Good enough for me to pull out some taunts and jabs for old time's sake.

"Hey, on a side note, can you and Hold keep it down a little bit at night? The walls in this place are thin as hell, and my lonely, heartbroken ass really can't handle listening to a happy couple rail each other for hours on end."

My best friend throws his head back in laughter. "It's not us, man. We know how to keep a lid on it."

"You're telling me I'm hearing one of the others from two floors away?"

"To be fair, it could just be one floor," Phoe counters, brow arched.

I blanch before my face contorts in a grimace. "You're telling me they're doing it on the couch where we all hang out? Or in the kitchen where we *cook?*"

My best friend shrugs, holding up his hands. "All I'm saying is Theo might've been quick to call me out for my semi-public sexcapades, but he should be thankful I haven't returned the favor."

"Jesus Christ. This place might as well be a fucking brothel," I mutter, shaking my head.

"Believe me, Kase, you don't know the half of it."

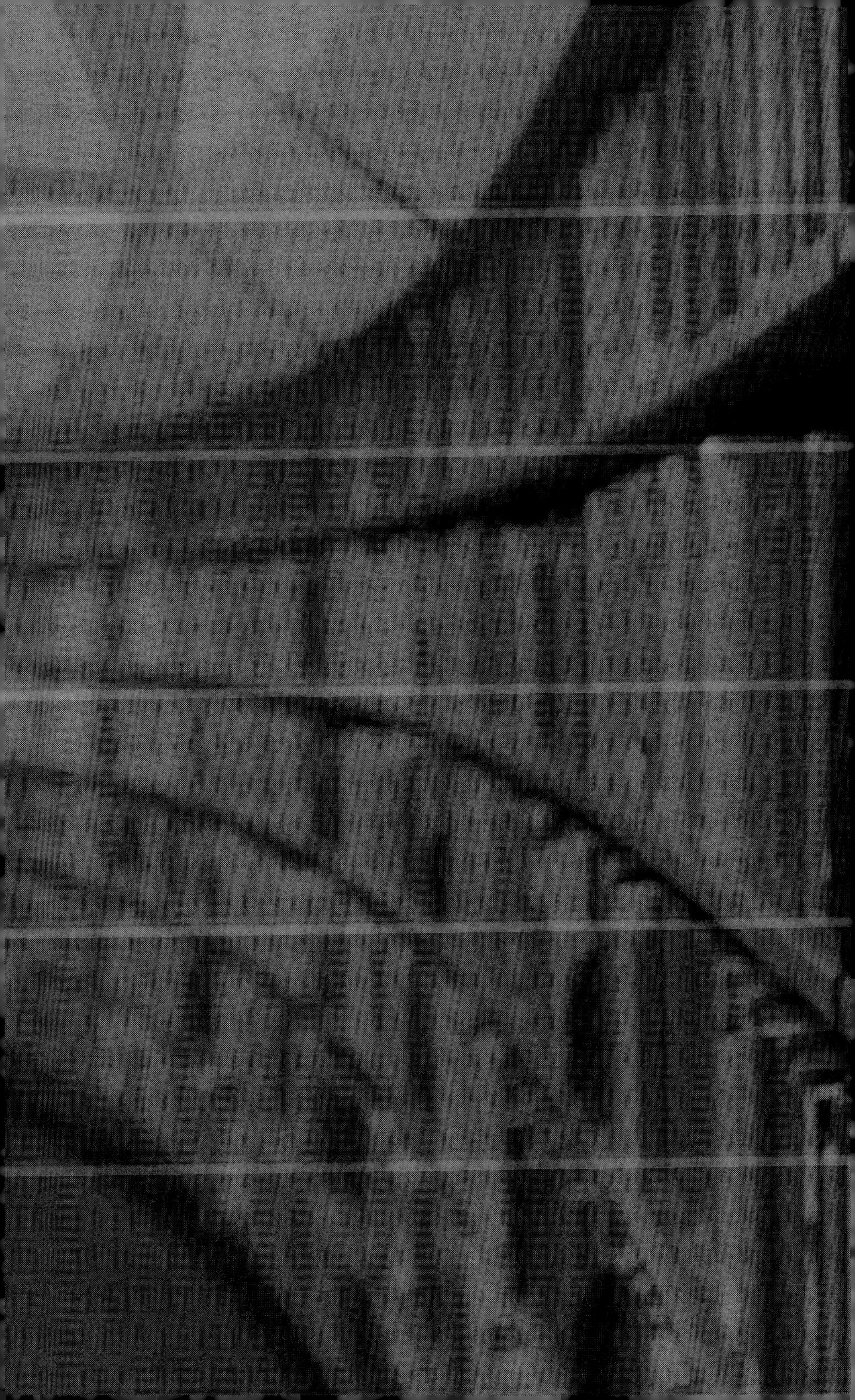

THIRTY-FOUR

Hayes

March

It's been just over a month since Kason moved out, and I'm coping no better now than I was the first morning I woke up alone to find him, and his stuff, gone. Which merely translates to shutting down emotionally on all levels, refusing to feel a goddamn thing other than empty inside.

It's not my best strategy, I'll admit, but it seems to be the only way from losing it completely. So I'm pushing through the pain, shoving the heartbreak down, boxing up the haunting memories and locking them away.

School work has been the best distraction of all, throwing myself back into my studies, but now that I've managed to finish all the reading for *all* my classes through the rest of the term, I'm not left with much else to keep my mind occupied.

So now it just wanders. At all hours, but only to one place.

Kason.

And it fucking hurts, a constant, aching weight on my chest that never seems to subside. The kind that only grows the more I try not to think about it, making its presence known at any given moment, and often, the most inopportune. Like when I realize I haven't eaten in nearly a day, only to find fucking Reese's Pieces in the closest vending machine to my next class.

Moments like that, I flip my brain into autopilot. Try to numb the ache as best I can, all while knowing the only way for it to truly stop hurting is to let it out.

I *need* to get it out.

Which is why on the third day in a row that I've refused to even leave the apartment, let alone my bed, I find myself typing out a text to Quinton.

Me: You got a minute?

Q: About thirty, actually. What's up?

Taking it as free rein to call, I hit the FaceTime button instead of texting back, only for Quinton's face to appear on the screen moments later, clearly in the car and looking over at Oakley in the driver's seat.

"Where are you going?"

"Practice. You're on speaker too, by the way, and interrupting our jam session, so this better be—" Whatever ribbing comment he has on his tongue falls short when he finally looks at his screen and sees me. "What's going on?"

My jaw tics, and the words leave my lips in a gruff whisper. "My mom and dad tried to pay off Kason to break up with me."

Q blinks a couple times, processing my statement that no doubt seems as far-fetched as aliens riding unicorns. After all, I can hardly believe it myself.

But then he lets out a sharp laugh and shakes his head. "What in the ever-loving fuck is wrong with our parents?"

"Your guess is as good as mine." I mutter, rubbing my forehead. "It's some shit I'd expect from yours, not mine. No offense."

Snorting, he replies, "None taken. I know this apple falls far, *far* from their trees."

"How the fuck do you manage to make everything sound perverted?" asks Oakley's disembodied voice from the driver's side of the car.

Quinton smirks, looking at his boyfriend. "God given talent, obviously. One of the many things I excel at more than you." Returning his attention to me, he quickly reverts to the subject at hand. "So obviously from the state of your facial hair, Kason didn't exactly tell them to fuck off and eat shit when they made this offer."

"No, he did," I mutter, my head falling back against my headboard. "That's when they threatened to cut me off instead."

"Holy shit," Oakley mutters and at the same time Quinton shouts, "Why is it you never tell me anything anymore!"

"I wasn't trying to keep it from you. I've just been…a wreck, for lack of a better term." I hold my phone out, letting him see the disaster that is my bedroom, then me, still in a spot I haven't moved from since Friday afternoon.

"Yeah, I've been there," Q mutters, frowning. "But hey, living without the money gets easier. It just takes some adjusting."

"That's the thing. I'm not."

His brows clash together behind his glasses. "They were bluffing?"

I shake my head, emotion crawling into my throat. "He went and played the fucking martyr and left. Moved out a day or two later while I was in class, blocked my number…" The memories flood my mind, and I choke on them when I whisper, "I have no idea where he is. I haven't heard from him since."

Quinton curses under his breath, a little bit of fury lighting up his eyes.

"So he took the original offer to keep you from losing everything."

"Minus the money."

I don't have proof of it, of course, but I have the sneaking suspicion Kason didn't. If I've learned anything about him in our time together, it's that the money would never be motivation.

Saving me was the only thing he was worried about.

"You seem certain," my best friend notes, eyes narrowing.

"As certain as the way I feel about him."

He rolls his tongue over his teeth, glancing at Oakley as he does, then back to me. "Then what are you gonna do?"

"What is there to do?" I ask, but it comes out with more bite than necessary thanks to my agitation. "I don't know where he is. Other than going lowkey stalker on his ass like Oakley by showing up on his doorstep and banging down the door in hopes he'll hear me out, I don't have many options."

I hear Oakley's sharp cough. "I was going for a romantic gesture, not stalking."

"Who says stalking isn't romantic?" Q asks, eyeing his boyfriend before blowing him a kiss.

I blanch, both annoyed and disgusted by their perfect little love life. "And on that note, I'm gonna go back to wallowing in misery all by myself."

"No, you're gonna go to him and plead your case. And you'd better hope whoever his new roommates are, they won't be nearly as protective as you were when Oakley did the same thing." Q's lips pull up in a bittersweet smile, but when he looks over at his boyfriend, it quickly turns to a frown. "Why do you look like you know something?"

"I don't look like anything," Oakley responds, but his boyfriend isn't buying it.

"Spill. Now."

I hear a long-winded sigh leave Oakley before he indignantly mutters, "I know where he is, okay?"

And now Quinton looks like he wants to castrate Oakley, rather than kiss him. "You're keeping secrets too?"

"Holden made me swear!"

"That rule doesn't apply to your boyfriend! Everyone fucking knows that!" he screeches before looking back to me through the phone screen. "Back me up on this, Hayes."

"I'm not getting involved. Not until Oakley tells me where my guy is," I inform the both of them, holding up my free hand. "So yeah, I'd suggest you spill the fucking tea, Oakley."

There's a beat of silence before Oakley mutters, "I'm so fucking toast for this."

After the world's quickest shower—not even taking the time to shave whatever dead animal has grown on my face—I throw my car into park outside the townhouse that Oakley gave me the address to. Shoving open my driver's door, I storm toward the place where Kason has apparently been living with Holden, Phoenix, and a few others.

I'm well aware I could've texted Holden or Phoenix, given them a heads up that I was coming here to see him. It probably would've been the smart thing to do, considering the circumstances. But the last thing I wanted was one of them trying to talk me out of it. Or worse, telling Kason so he could disappear before I got here.

I've done enough waiting, enough aching, enough fucking pining.

I just need to see him. To put this shit in the past.

To fight harder for us.

But all the fight inside me dies the second a tall, dark-haired guy covered in tattoos slips out the front door. One that's familiar enough to have my stomach roiling at the sight of him.

"Madden?"

He halts in his tracks, brows crashing together. "Hayes, right?"

"Yeah," I say slowly, stopping beside him. "Do you live here?"

Madden glances back at the townhouse he'd just left, then back to me. I swear to God, if he says no, I might actually—

"No, I was just…visiting someone."

My heart drops into the pit of my stomach, and I don't know if I want to scream, cry, or vomit on the spot. All I know it that there's a good fucking chance that I'm too late.

Please, don't let me be too late.

"Listen, I gotta get going," he says, frowning while glancing back at the house. "But it was nice to see you again."

"Yeah. You too," I manage, though I'm feeling the exact fucking opposite.

A plethora of emotions wage a war inside me as I stand here, watching him jog to a car parked down the street and climbing inside.

Sadness, panic, anxiety, fear…numb.

But then I get fucking pissed.

Storming up the sidewalk, my fist lands on the door with three hard knocks, and then I wait. My stomach is knotted and coiled like a viper ready to strike when the door finally opens.

"Seriously? I said *sneak*—" The brown-haired guy answering the door pauses and frowns. "Oh. Sorry, you're not who I thought you were."

I blink at him and try to shake off the weirdest way anyone has ever answered the door. "Is Kason here?"

His dark brows shoot up over sage green eyes, and he crosses his arms.

"Maybe. Who the hell are you?"

"I'm Kason's—" I cut myself off, not knowing how to describe myself. Because saying I'm his ex *anything* doesn't sit right.

Thankfully, I'm saved from having to figure it out, because Phoenix appears behind the wannabe bouncer's shoulder, popping his head in the opening.

"What's going…Hayes?" He frowns when he notices me before asking, "What are you doing here?"

"Looking for Kason, apparently," the other dude says.

Phoenix's eyes dart to him, then back to me. "Kason's not here."

For the briefest, *briefest* moment, I feel relief. But then I remember all the mornings Q left the house with a girl still in his bed, only for her to sneak out later, and I'm hit with that same, panicked anxiety all over again.

"Do you know when he'll be back? I can wait if—"

"He won't be back 'til Monday," Phoenix says, cutting me off. "He's down in Indianapolis for the Combine."

Son of a fuck-knuckle.

I suck in a deep breath as I build up the courage to ask the question—or maybe to hear an answer I might not want to hear.

"The guy who just left," I start, hating the obvious insecurity in my voice. "Is he…Was he here for Kason?"

Phoenix looks confused as he glances over my shoulder to where Madden just was. "What guy are you talking about?"

"Dark haired, lots of tattoos. His name is Madden."

Phoenix looks like that cat that just ate the canary when he glances at the blowhard beside him. "That's a question for you to answer, Theo."

Theo the Bouncing Blowhard. Got it.

Theo's wearing a pained expression now as he glances at Phoenix, giving him one of those *don't talk about Fight Club* looks. "Madden's my step brother. He was just here to deal with…parent stuff."

Phoenix hums, clearly enjoying whatever the hell is happening. "Parent stuff. At barely eight in the morning. Sounds logical."

"I'm gonna let you two talk," Theo says slowly before backing out of the doorway.

Phoenix moves out of the way for his roommate to head back inside, a shit-eating grin on his lips as he takes Theo's place in the doorway.

Leaning against the doorframe, he shoots me a wry smirk. "You don't know this yet, but I just won a hundred bucks because of you."

"Yeah, that's great and all, Phoe, but I really need to talk to Kason."

His expression immediately takes on a more guarded look, and it makes me wonder what Kason told him about how things ended. Or maybe it was my unintentional use of Kason's nickname for him that's clearly become part of my vernacular.

"Like I said, he's not here. He's down in Indy. And not to sound like a dick, because I do like you, but if he hasn't talked to you, it's probably for a reason."

"Which is only because he thinks we don't have another option," I try reasoning, that helpless feeling inside me growing exponentially. "He's had to have told you what happened. You're his best friend."

"He did, yeah."

"Then what would you do here? Would you fight for the person you want to be with?"

Something about his expression tells me he'd be exactly where I am right now, even if he won't admit it.

"The question is, do you even know what you're fighting for?"

"I'm fighting for him. For a future together. For—"

"But what does that future look like?" he insists, his head tilting to the side. "You're a planner, Hayes. I knew that about you the moment I met you. So tell me, what's the plan? Have you spoken to your parents? Decided what you'll do if he gets drafted? If he doesn't? And then there's the big one—if he's worth giving up everything you thought your life would look like? 'Cause from what he's told me, no matter what path he takes, that's *your* reality if you choose to be with him. Are you really ready to face that?"

The truth is, no.

I haven't thought about the variables, the possible outcomes, the ways to make them work. I've been too busy living in self-pity to truly think about what choosing him entails.

But the thing is, spending the rest of my life without him doesn't even feel like a choice.

"Look, I'm not gonna tell you what to do. If you wanna get in your car now and drive down to Indianapolis and make some grand love declaration, then I'm not gonna stop you. Hell, you can hitch a ride with Holden on the way down. But what I will say is…think about it before you do something rash."

He pauses, I'm sure to wait for me to argue or something. But when I remain silent, he continues, soft and sincere.

"From what I can tell, he's finally gotten into a good headspace to perform today, despite the turmoil he's been going through since he moved out. And you going down there? There's a good chance that, even if it all goes well, it will have him distracted or fuck with his emotions on the one weekend that his career could be riding on. He deserves to be focused on his future and achieving his dreams, same as you."

"But he *is* my future," I snap, unable to hide the defeat from my voice. "I'd figure you, if anyone, would understand that."

Phoenix holds his hands up. "You don't need to convince me, I've seen the two of you together. Which is why I'm not suggesting you don't fight for him. I hope you do, because he's one of my favorite people, and I want nothing more than to see him happy." His patient gaze stays locked on me, and the sincerity in them has my heart squeezing uncomfortably. "All I'm trying to do is encourage you to think about the variables before either of you make promises or decisions you'll regret, and it'll lead to both of you hurting all over again."

I don't know what to do, what to say, or think or feel. The logic in me knows this isn't the right time, but the stupid organ in my chest doesn't want to believe that's true.

I sink down to the step I'm standing on, dejected and miserable, and stare out at the street, wondering where the hell I go from here.

The sound of the door falling closed behind me has me thinking Phoenix went back inside, having enough of…whatever this is. But a few seconds later, he's sitting on the step and staring at the street with me.

"Look, I know first-hand how fucking much this sucks and how helpless you feel right now. I get it, and I wouldn't wish it on my worst enemy. But we both know how hard he's worked to be where he is right now, how much it means for him to even have this opportunity at all. And he's earned this chance to see his dream through. Or at least to know if that's the path he's gonna be taking."

I know he's right. Kason deserves a fair catch.

A shot to get everything he wants, no interference from me.

My eyes move to Phoenix, who is studying me with deep brown eyes, waiting for me to say something—anything.

But the only thing that manages to come out is, "I'd follow him anywhere."

"That may be true. But being with him while his dreams come true shouldn't be at the expense of yours. Not if you don't want to risk giving them up."

As soon as he says it, I know I don't want to give them up.

I'm not ready to walk away from the legacy I've prepared my entire life to inherit, the company that my family has built over generations. On the best-laid plan that was a guaranteed, fulfilling, and successful future.

And even if all that wasn't what I truly wanted, am I really willing to risk it all on something—someone—that isn't a guarantee?

Because, as deeply as I feel about him, that's what the stakes are.

My heart says yes. Immediately and without question.

But my head…

I press the heels of my hands against my eye sockets, damn near ready to claw them out of my skull at this point.

"I wish I knew what to do," I finally murmur, the epitome of dejection.

Phoenix lays his hand on my shoulder in a touch that I'm sure is meant to be comforting, though I find anything but comfort in it. If anything, all it makes me want to do is break down and fucking cry.

"I hope you figure it out, Hayes. I really do. What the two of you had was special, and that doesn't come around everyday." When my gaze lifts, I find him offering me a sympathetic smile. "You became everything he ever wanted and all the things he didn't know he needed."

"He's the same for me," I whisper, feeling the depth of that truth.

We sit in silence for God knows how long after that, staring out at the street as cars pass by, beginning their day. I know I should let him get to his too, and that's the only reason I find myself rising from the concrete steps.

"You said Holden's going down to watch him at the combine?"

Phoenix nods solemnly as he stands too, following my cue. "He and some of the guys from the team, yeah. I would be too, but we've got away games this weekend."

Nodding, I produce a five-dollar bill from my wallet before silently handing it over to Phoenix.

"Can you give this to Holden for me?"

He takes it, frowning as he tucks it in the pocket of his sweats. "What's it for?"

"I think you already know."

THIRTY-FIVE

Kason

Stress and anxiety have my heart pounding in my chest as I look around the stadium in Indianapolis hosting the Combine, sizing up my competition and taking in the experience all at once.

Players from some of the best college football programs are here: Alabama, Ohio State, Clemson, the list goes on. Some I grew up playing against, some who have decimated us on the field just this year, and as I look at them all, I've never been more intimidated. Not even standing off with Hayes' mother compares, and this is the moment I've been preparing for since the day I put on my first set of pads.

Being the only one from Leighton doesn't help matters, because most of these guys are here with at least one of their teammates, if not more.

I'm doing this all on my own.

Shoving down the nerves as best as I can, I keep stretching on the sidelines while I wait to be called for the forty-yard dash. Nothing short of willing my body to release some of the tension clinging to it like a parasite is gonna get me through today when I know my entire future is riding on my performance in these drills.

I belong here. I've earned this spot. I—

"Hey, Fuller! Get your ass over here!"

The sound of my name drags my attention behind me. Confused, I turn to find Holden, Luca, Harrison and Noah walking along the sidelines of the field.

I try to look not as confused as I'm feeling while I jog their way. After all, I'm more than happy to see them, but still not sure what they're doing here.

Or more importantly—

"How the hell did you get down here?" I ask, pulling up short of the four of them.

"Holden sweet talked his way down here," Harrison replies with an eye roll. "I swear, some people must think he's got gold shoved up his ass, they want him to reconsider not declaring so bad."

"Bold of you to assume I don't have a few gold nuggets stashed up there," Holden counters, which makes Harrison's nose wrinkle up in disgust at the visual.

"You and Phoenix have some weird fucking foreplay if that's the case."

Holden just shrugs. "Yeah, you're right. We use a twenty-four-carat plug for that instead."

And there are some things I just don't want to know about my best friend's sex life—jokingly or not.

"I can't believe you guys actually drove down to Indy for this," I remark, doing my best to change the subject to *anything* else.

"Well, duh," Noah says, a ridiculous grin on his face. "We have to show support for the only one on the team dumb enough to try going pro this year."

Holden socks Noah in the shoulder and gives him a dirty look. "Just because you're too much of a chickenshit to be rejected."

Noah grumbles something under his breath I can't quite make out, though I think I catch the phrase *should've stayed home* in there somewhere.

"What he means to say is we thought you could use some moral support." Holden bites his lower lip before adding, "Phoenix wanted to be here too, but—"

"He's got games this weekend, I know. That's why I'm surprised you're here."

"They're over in Michigan this weekend, and there's not a chance in hell I was driving up there just to freeze my ass off." He holds his hands up in resignation. "I love him, but I also have limits."

"Right," I say dryly, knowing damn well that Holden would do just about anything for Phoenix. That much has become obvious in the past few weeks I've been living at the house with them.

"Well, he also wanted you to have someone here to cheer you on," Holden states, his signature smirk on his lips. "He was the one who insisted we come, actually, since it was only a couple hours drive."

"He asked us to give him a play-by-play of how the entire day goes. All the stats and times you put up, videos of whenever we can sneak them," Noah relays before shaking his head. "If he wasn't gonna be on the field for a good chunk of the day for their double header, I'd bet he would ask us to FaceTime him so he could watch."

Luca glances over at Noah, muttering, "Yeah, and we'd much rather have him here than you, considering how fucking obnoxious you were the entire ride here."

Holden and I share a look—one we often give each other when it comes to these two—before Holden gives them a tight smile.

"Can you guys grab us some seats, please? Somewhere down in the front?"

Noah and Luca share a disgruntled look before Noah heads back the way they came, Luca following a few paces behind.

Harrison looks some mixture of unamused and annoyed before asking, "You're really gonna make me go babysit them, aren't you?"

"Unless you're wanting to bail one of them out of jail for killing the other," Holden retorts with a shrug.

"Who's to say I wouldn't just help bury the body?" Harrison replies, and for the briefest second, I think he's considering letting the two of them head off on their own. But then Luca calls for him to hurry his ass up, and he relents, jogging over to catch up.

"How're you feeling?" Holden finally asks now that the others are gone, his tone becoming far more serious than I've ever heard it.

I blow out a long breath. "Nervous."

"Honestly, I'd be worried if you weren't." He offers me an encouraging smile. "Just don't get in your head about it. You're gonna kill it out there and make the rest of us look like slackers."

"I'd just be confirming what they already know," I shoot back immediately.

A sharp laugh leaves him as he throws his head back. "Cocky. I like it. Keep that energy up, and you'll be a first-round pick. Guaranteed."

I nod, trying to harness the side of me that knows this is exactly where I'm supposed to be. And I'll admit, having him—and the other guys too—here for support means more than I thought it would. Apparently, I was in more need of a pep-talk than I realized.

"Speaking of first-round picks, I'm still surprised you decided not to declare." I arch a brow his way. "You know, considering you likely would've been the bone all the dogs were fightin' over."

He waves me off. "Maybe, but I think I have a way better offer waiting for me."

Phoenix told me about their plan to move back to Nashville after graduation—Holden working as an intern for his Dad's label, and him working at some fancy marketing firm—and nothing makes more sense in my head. More than either of them making a go for the pros.

If I've learned anything through my time living across the hall from the two of them, it's that they're everything each other needs, and even if it hurt me in the beginning, I'm so fucking glad Phoenix didn't allow me to stand in the way. Seeing the happiness they have together is completely worth it.

Happiness I get to be part of again.

"You know, you're right," I confirm, nodding. "You'll have a lot more fun wining and dining musical talent than having to maintain top-tier athletic form. I'm not lying, part of me is a tiny bit jealous you can get fat and happy now."

"One, gyms still exist outside of athletic training, and two, you've been wanting to go pro for as long as I've known you, so I'm not buying your 'jealousy' for a damn minute."

I laugh, despite his accurate assessment of the situation. Though, my desire to go pro has only ever been because I didn't think I had another option. I've never been the smartest kid like Hayes, and I've never had such defined hobbies or drive for a career the way Holden and Phoenix do.

Football is the only thing that made sense for me, and after seeing Ciaráin Grady get drafted to New England a few years back, I have less worry about being ousted by the League because I'm openly gay.

Now, it's as simple as proving I'm good enough to be out there with the best of the best, playing the sport I fell in love with the first time I ever watched it.

"For all the shit I'm giving you, I know Nashville will be a good fit for you, Hold. It's the right choice. There's no doubt in my mind."

"Same goes to you about being here." Holden's whiskey eyes lift to mine, and he smiles. "And thanks, Kase."

We share that brief moment, gratitude and optimism building inside me before I glance back toward where I was originally standing.

"I probably should get back to stretching and warming up, but I really do appreciate y'all showing up. It means a lot."

"Wouldn't have it any other way, man. Seriously. You'll always be our teammate, even when you're off making millions in the big leagues." His head slants to the side and he grins. "Just remember who made you look good all through college when you're handing out those comp tickets for your home games."

"Even if I'm drafted to a team on the other side of the country?"

"Especially then. I'll need some sort of getaway from the Mercer clan every once in a while, once Nix and I are sharing a zip code with them."

Laughing, I shake my head, because if there's anyone who loves the Mercers as much as me, it's Holden. But I can play along with his game.

"I'll be sure to keep that in mind."

"Holding you to that," he says, pointing at me with a smirk.

He starts backing away to follow after the rest of the guys, but he stops short.

"Oh, shit, before I forget," Holden says, producing two blue Gatorades from God knows where. "These are for you. Should help you kick some ass."

Grinning, I grab them from him, tucking one under my arm and cracking open the other. "Phoe must've thought I needed extra luck today if he had you bring two, huh?"

Holden's lips lift in a little smirk, like he knows something I don't. Then again, who knows with him. He's always got some wacky scheme or smirk up his sleeve, which he more than proved with his little stunt using Phoenix's baseball glove.

I pause with the drink halfway to my mouth, meeting his expectant stare, and…

"Did you just pull these out of your pants?"

He bursts into laughter, shaking his head before he grabs the strap of his drawstring backpack. "Had them in here, you fucking weirdo. I know better than to fuck with the mojo like that."

Thank God for small mercies.

"Okay, well now that I don't have to worry about contamination," I tell him, taking a swig of the sports drink.

Holden rolls his eyes. "Yeah, yeah. Now get going and kick some ass, will ya? Make those stats your bitch. We'll see you after."

I nod in agreement before heading back to where I was stretching, only to make it five feet before Holden calls out to me again.

"Oh, and Kase?"

When I turn to look at him, cocking my head in questioning, he nods toward the drinks he'd just given to me.

"You should know, only one of those is from Nix."

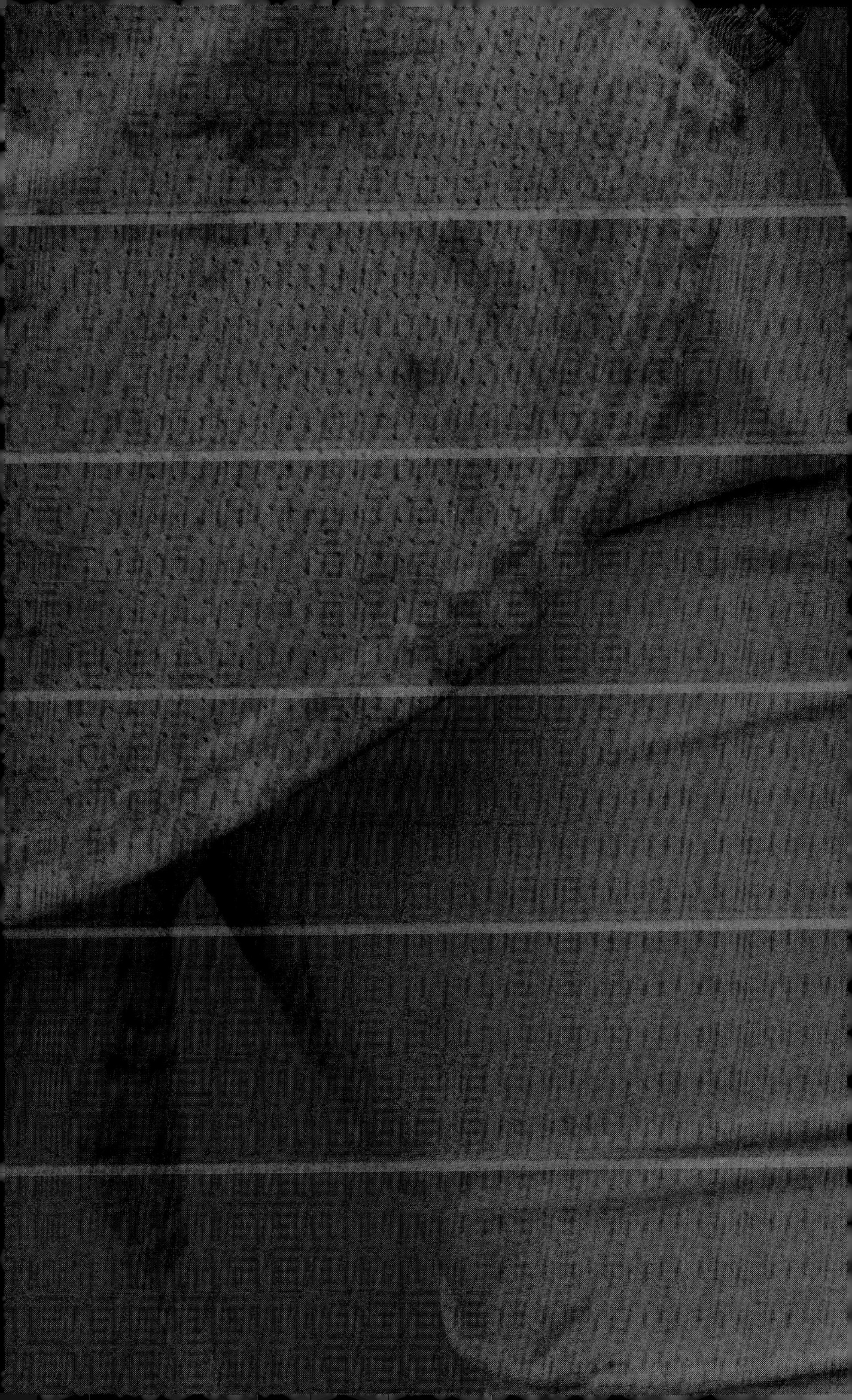

THIRTY-SIX

Kason

April

Every year on the last weekend of April, the football team throws a Leighton Draft Day party to celebrate anyone who declared themselves eligible. A good chunk of the team shows up to whatever locale is hosting said festivities in support for the guys who are waiting to hear if they are destined to enter the National Football League.

Basically, it's an excuse for three entire days of fucking insanity and partying, but regardless, I've attended them every year myself, knowing one day, I'd want all mine to do the same for me.

And boy, they didn't disappoint.

When I got home from class this afternoon, the house was already filled to the brim with people, all waiting to see if the commissioner will call my name later this evening. Both the TV in the rec room downstairs and the one in the living room are casting the event, and someone—I'm betting Holden or Phoenix—got me a cake with my face on it for the occasion.

Because this year, I'm the only one from Leighton who declared for the draft.

Yesterday was a bust, seeing as they only announce the first round, but I knew there wasn't a chance in hell that I'd be going that early. Today is reserved for rounds two and three, though, and I'm feeling equally giddy and nervous.

"Regretting not declaring?" I ask Holden, who has been nursing the same beer for what might be a record amount of time.

Holden shrugs. "My love for football isn't strong enough to carry me through to the pros. I'd have fun for a while, sure, but I know damn well I wouldn't be happy long term."

"You say that now, but I'm willing to bet you'll be singing a different tune come fall when you aren't suiting up and taking the field for the first time in your life."

His brow arches. "Care to put your money where your mouth is?"

Snorting, I shake my head. "Absolutely not. I'm not about kicking a man while he's down." When he frowns, not following my train of thought, I smirk. "What? You think Phoe didn't tell me all about the little bet you lost about Theo—"

"Shut up, shut up! Oklahoma City is about to pick!" Noah shouts, waving at everyone in the room to stop talking. "I can't fucking hear over all you hooligans."

"You're not the one who *needs* to hear," Luca, who is lounging on the other side of the sectional, points out.

Thank the dear Lord someone had enough sense to separate the two of them, though it would probably be better if one of them was upstairs. Putting as much space as physically possible between the two of them is for the welfare of humanity.

And yet the two of them somehow managed to end up in the same city again next year.

"With the 61st pick in this year's NFL Draft, the Oklahoma City Twisters select…Marcus Desmond. Tight End, Auburn."

Holden's eyes flash to me immediately. "Hey, that's the first tight end all night, so things are about to get moving now."

I know he's right. Marcus Desmond, the senior tight end from Auburn who was just selected, absolutely annihilated the competition at the combine, myself included. And logically, with my stats coming in right behind his for almost every drill, I should be the one to go next.

Fingers fucking crossed.

But rather than keep the optimism alive, I mutter, "I'm gonna grab a drink."

Glancing over at Holden, I see he's still got well over half a beer, and he waves me off as I'm about to ask if he wants something different. With that, I head up and grab a beer from the fridge, needing something in my hands to keep myself from fidgeting; and maybe to take the edge off a little bit.

"There you are! I've been looking for you everywhere!"

I glance up from the fridge to find Phoenix walking into the kitchen. He reaches over the door, grabbing a beer for himself too, before I let it fall closed.

"I can't imagine why it took you so long. It's not like there's anyone here," I muse, motioning toward the plethora of people in the living room, which may or may not be more chaotic than those downstairs.

"I know, right? I can't believe no one showed." There's a playful smirk on his lips when he pops the cap on his bottle. "Guess you aren't as cool as you thought you were, Fuller."

A soft snort slips out, and I can't help shaking my head. "Thanks for this, man. Seriously."

"The football team throws the party, not me."

I roll my eyes. "As much as the team would love to take credit—and they probably will—I know better. You played a big hand in this."

From the little shrug he gives, I know I've hit the nail on the head. And it only solidifies how good it feels to have my best friend back, especially on a night like this.

His eyes lock with mine, and he cocks his head. "Real talk, you okay?"

"Oh, yeah. I'm good."

"You forget I've known you longer than just about anyone? I know when you're lying." Arching a brow, he asks, "Is it just nerves?"

Tossing my head back and forth, I do my best to figure out how to answer that. Nervous isn't the right word exactly.

"I'm just ready to know, you know? I'll be fine either way, but it's not knowing which direction my life is about to take that's got my stomach in knots."

"Well, the good thing is, there's still time. It's only the second round, and you know as well as I do, tight ends usually don't go in the first couple. The fact that Marcus went already is wild to me."

I nod, though I don't have much more to say about it. And since he's Phoenix and can't help himself when it comes to cheering me up, he offers me a wry smile.

"C'mon, let's head downstairs. New England is picking next, right? We've gotta see if you're gonna be a Boston man."

As it turns out, I'm not meant to be a Boston man.

Or New York. Or Philadelphia. Or Denver, Cleveland, or Chicago, either. And as picks keep happening and we near the halfway point of the third round, my hope has long since dwindled into nothing but a sad pile of dogshit at my feet.

The guys must be picking up on my mood too, the party down here taking a more sober turn despite the copious amount of alcohol present—and the ones who are looking to still party move themselves upstairs instead.

Unfortunately, Noah and Luca aren't two of them.

"You good? Need anything?" Luca asks, dropping back onto the couch after grabbing himself another drink.

"I just asked him that like five minutes ago," Noah tells him, a look of annoyance on his face. "He said no."

I shake my head anyway before looking at Luca, who is currently shooting Noah a death glare. "I'm good, thanks man."

Luca shrugs with indifference before turning to converse with Holden, who seems to be the only one as sober as me, surprisingly. Of course, pretty much everyone else has been drinking since well before I got here, so it's not hard to beat.

I decided early on, if things go the way I want, I'll want to remember the moment and celebrate afterward. Which means limiting my alcohol intake. And if it doesn't go that way...well, there's always the option to drown my sorrows into oblivion as well.

Even Phoe has loosened up a bit more than usual, tossing back a few drinks since this whole thing started.

Then again, he may be just as nervous about this as I am.

"I'm not gonna ask if you're good, because I can read your face better than a children's book, but is there anything I can do?"

I release a long-winded sigh. "Not unless you can speed up time between these rounds."

Phoenix frowns and shakes his head. "Yeah, unfortunately, that particular infinity stone is on loan at the moment."

That earns him a laugh. I'm about to ask him when he started moonlighting as Dr. Strange when it sounds like a herd of elephants with monkeys on their backs starts stampeding around upstairs. There's jumping and running and hooting and hollering above us that shakes the entire house, causing those of us remaining in the basement to look at each other like deer in headlights.

"Jesus Chrsit, what the hell?" I mutter, glancing toward the stairs leading up to the living room. "Are they trying to get the cops called?"

Phoenix shrugs from his seat on the other side of the sectional, clearly unperturbed by the noise at this point. "I'm pretty sure Cam mentioned something about a beer pong tournament—"

"Nashville is picking!" Noah yells, breaking up our conversation in time to watch the commissioner reappear on the flatscreen.

"With the 77th pick in this year's NFL Draft, the Nashville Nighthawks select… Kason Fuller. Tight End, Leighton University."

The basement erupts in cheers and shouts, all the guys jumping and bouncing around like *they* were the ones just…holy shit.

Drafted.

"Now we know why they were so excited. The TV up there has been like ten seconds faster than this one all night," Holden says, jumping over the back of the couch and into my lap like I'm fucking Santa Claus. He holds out an invisible mic to my lips before asking, "You just got fucking drafted to the Nashville Nighthawks, Kason Fuller. How do you feel?"

Honestly, I don't know yet.

Most of me is in shock. Stunned silent while the television plays some of my highlights from this season. But the part of me that's caught up to reality is ready to do one thing.

"Like it's time to party!" I shout.

Everyone joins in with my cheers, raising their bottles or Solo cups to the air. Some of the guys that were watching in the living room rush down here, another stampede happening as they storm down the stairs to join the rest of us.

That's when the pandemonium really begins.

I'm met with hugs and pats on the back and the occasional ass slap, mostly from Holden, as the night continues, everyone partying like their lives depend on it. I get texts galore from people who couldn't be here tonight, like my coach here at Leighton, Mal and Ivy, and Phoenix's parents. It's only when one comes through from Louis Spaulding—who'd agreed to represent me a few months back—saying he'd call me tomorrow so we can iron out some details—does this sink in as reality.

I'm going back to Nashville and competing at the professional level for a team I grew up watching.

But even among all the celebration, I can't help feeling like there's something missing from this moment. Or rather, some*one*. And I hate it, almost as much as I hate myself for swiping open my phone and hovering over his name.

We haven't spoken since the night before I moved out, and I know it's likely for the best that we make a clean break. Dragging it out or trying to be friends would only make things more painful in the end.

But God, I want to share this with him. More than anyone else.

"So, Nashville, huh?"

Glancing up, I find Phoenix holding out another beer for me, and I gladly accept.

"Looks like it to me. You think that city is big enough for the two of us?" When his brows crash together with worried confusion, I add, "I'm talking about me and Holden, obviously."

Gone is the panic, and my best friend bursts into laughter. "I don't think *anyone* is ready for Holden. Especially my father." He shakes his head, still chuckling. "Lord knows what he was thinking when he offered him that internship."

"Probably about how happy it would make you," I point out.

A small smile forms on his face and he nods. "And speaking of happy, I hope you know how fucking happy I am for you, Kase. You deserve this more than—"

Theo comes barreling into the conversation, startling both Phoe and I with his theatrics.

"Where's the fire?" I ask with a laugh,

"It's at the door waiting for you," he says with a pant as he looks at me.

Frowning, I make my way up to the main level, wondering who the hell would be coming this late. Of course, there are plenty of guys on the team who aren't here—and Mal and Ivy could definitely be stopping by, now that I think about it—so those are always options.

Part of me is expecting it to be Louis or someone from the Nighthawks just showing up here, though I'm not exactly sure if that's how this sort of thing works.

Regardless, as I pull the front door open, I can't really believe my eyes.

Because the last person I expected it to be is the person standing in front of me.

"Hayes."

THIRTY-SEVEN

Hayes

The sound of my name on Kason's lips has my heart squeezing in my chest painfully, but not nearly as much as the way his eyes immediately take on a sorrow-filled gleam in the porch light.

Fuck, maybe this is a bad idea.

But it's too little, too late now, so I steel myself for yet another rejection by his hand and ask for the reason I'm here in the first place.

"Can I come in? To talk?"

Under normal circumstances, I'd offer to take a walk instead, but it's been a downpour for the last few hours and making no signs of letting up. The other option is having it out right here, but the last thing I wanna do is have this conversation on his doorstep in the pouring rain where anyone could interrupt.

I will if I have to, though. I'm already soaked as it is.

"I…" Kason glances behind him, where I can hear ruckus through the door and walls of the house from here. "It's kinda loud in there, but we can if you want."

My gaze flicks from him to the front window, where I can make out quite a few guys hooting and hollering and generally having a good time.

"There's gotta be somewhere more quiet, right? Your room, or something?" I inquire, doing my best to keep the tiniest spark of hope alive despite the gutting sadness in his eyes. Yet, for whatever reason, he nods in agreement and opens the door behind him, ushering me inside.

I think the only time I've seen this many athletes in one place, it was at one of the football games earlier this year. Except it's not just football players; I notice plenty of Quinton's old teammates, and also Phoenix, who told me he's on the baseball team. And it's pandemonium as they're all drinking and buzzing around while the Draft plays on the television.

Kason quietly leads me down the stairs, only for us to be greeted with the sight of even more people in a second living/rec room. ESPN is playing on an even bigger flatscreen down here, but it's not enough to stop all eyes from falling to us when we come into view.

I quickly recognize one of them as Phoenix, glad to see at least one friendly face. He gives me a small nod, and I think it's meant to be a hint of encouragement, as Kason leads me through the door to his bedroom. With a quick flip of the lightswitch, his room is illuminated, and I glance around, noting the familiarity of it. Besides different colored walls and a few different pieces of furniture, it's nearly identical to his room back at the apartment.

The fact doesn't sit right with me.

"Do you wanna sit?" Kason asks as he shuts the door behind us, flicking the lock in place.

Acting on his offer, I perch myself on the edge of his bed, leaving plenty of space for him to sit beside me if he wishes. He grabs his desk chair instead, and I try to ignore the little piece of me that dies inside because of it.

"So this is where you've been living," I observe, hating myself for choosing awkward small talk to break the ice.

No, dumbass. He just has a second set of all his belongings to keep here too.

"Yeah," Kason says slowly, lacing and unlacing his fingers with the same nervous energy I'm feeling. I guess I can at least be grateful I'm not alone in that.

Though I have no right to know, I still find myself asking, "Is that going okay?"

He nods, and I'm glad it is while simultaneously wishing it wasn't. And I don't think I've ever felt more selfish than I do right now for the thought.

"Things have a way of working out," he murmurs, his eyes locked on his interlocked hands. "Phoenix and I were able to mend fences, start rebuilding a healthy friendship that isn't so codependent."

"I'm glad to hear it." There's an awkward pause before I find myself filling it with another stupid question. "I'd assume that's part of the reason for the really mixed crowd out there?"

Kason rocks his head back and forth briefly, "Sorta, but the athletics here are pretty tight knit. It doesn't matter if we play different sports, we still do our best to show up for each other when we can."

"I'm glad you had them in your corner tonight."

Really, Hayes? What else are you glad for? That he didn't slam the door in your face when he saw you?

"Me too."

An uncomfortable silence blankets the room, not at all unlike the way things were in the beginning of our sordid tale, and I hate it almost as much as I do the abysmal distance between us right now.

The only thing I can do is stare at him, longing for the moments I never expected to crave.

"What is it you wanted to talk about?" he finally asks, the first to break the unbearable silence.

I open my lips to speak, but now that I'm sitting here in front of him, I really have no clue what to say. Where to start, or how to do this. All I know is that my life has lost all its direction the moment I woke up alone in that bed, then again when I came home to his room being entirely empty a couple days later.

I haven't known sleep, peace, fucking happiness since he left.

There's no plausible way for me to survive the rest of my life this way: missing the piece I didn't realize made me feel whole.

"I wanna talk about us."

Wincing, he slowly shakes his head. "Don't, Hayes…"

I do anyway, because if I'm gonna fight for us, I have to be willing to show him my hand. Every goddamn card in it, and let the chips fall where they may.

"No, baby. I was a fucking idiot when I let you walk away."

A frown tugs at his lips. "You didn't let me do anything. We looked down every avenue for another option, and we agreed this was the best one."

"Us not being together isn't an option for me."

"You think I like this? Sitting here across from you, wanting nothing more than to kiss you and hold you and love you, but knowing I can't? Because I don't." Tears well in his eyes, and his voice breaks, cracking over the words as he speaks. "This option wasn't the one either of us liked, but we both agreed this was the one we had to take."

"Maybe we agreed to it, and maybe it was the best option at the time. But it's not what I want, Kase."

"What other choice do we have? Hayes, your family's company and your entire future is here…and I'm heading back to Nashville." … "The Nighthawks drafted me."

My lips lift in a small smile when I whisper, "I know, I was watching."

"So you know that this wouldn't work," he reasons, his tone equally harsh and broken.

"It would. Because I want to come with you."

He blinks, frowning. "What?"

Rising from his bed, I walk to where he's seated in his desk chair and crouch in front of him. It's the closest we've been since the day he left—within arms reach—and I don't have the fight in me to keep from touching him.

So I don't even try.

I set my hands on his thighs, feeling his warmth through the denim as it seeps into the cold, lonely marrow of my bones.

And then I finally lay down all my cards.

"I said I wanna come with you. Consequences be damned."

He blinks at me, his eyes screaming *yes* while his mouth asks, "Are you insane?"

"It feels like it, but no, I'm not. For the first time in my entire life, I don't really have a plan. I have no idea what comes next. But one thing has never been more clear. The only future I want has you in it."

"Hayes, no. I can't let you give up everything—"

"I'm not sacrificing a damn thing. Not one fucking bit. The only way that'd be true is if I had to go on living the rest of my life with the *what ifs* of choosing you, and I'm not willing to do that." Squeezing his thighs in my palms, I whisper, "I love you, Kason. There's nothing I want more than you.

To see you accomplish your dreams, and be at your side while you do it. So I'll go wherever you go, if you'll let me."

"But what about your parents?"

"I called my mother about a month ago, told her that I knew what happened at the party. As you can likely imagine, it didn't go all that well." My lips twitch into a sardonic smile. "She seems to still hold onto this ideal that I imagine no one could actually meet, and I told her who I love isn't her decision to make."

"So they don't know about you wanting to go with me."

I shake my head. "Every time she's tried calling me since, I've ignored. I haven't had anything else to say to her until now."

"And now?"

A small smile tugs at my lips, and I pull my phone from my back pocket and search for my mother's contact. After hitting the dial button, I switch it to speaker and set it on top of his thigh, waiting for the source of all this pain and misery to pick up on the other end.

My mother's proper, sugary tone comes from the speaker a few moments later, sending ice through my veins.

"Hayes, darling. What a surprise."

A sardonic laugh slips out before I can stop it. "Considering you've been attempting to get me to return your calls for over a month now, it shouldn't be. So why don't we cut the crap, Mom?"

"I see," she says, her tone now clipped. "And I take it you still haven't seen reason?"

"I'm more firm in my choice than ever," I tell her, my eyes locked on Kason's. "Kason was drafted to Nashville, and whether you like it or not, I'm going with him."

"You're making a mistake, dear. I'm just trying to look out for your best interest."

Yeah, she said that last time.

"If that were truly the case, you wouldn't have treated Kason as if he were some meaningless fling or a gold-digger after the family fortune—neither of which are remotely true."

"I will not apologize for protecting my child," she retorts matter-of-factly. "Especially when they've been subjected to being used in the past."

It's a low blow, to bring up all the times I've been hurt in the past, but at this point, I should come to expect it from her. She's more than shown me her true colors by now.

"No, you're not protecting me. You're protecting yourself," I snarl, my fingers gripping Kason's desk chair. "You're protecting the image you and Dad have built for this family. One of wealth and high class and status. But the thing is, those things aren't what's important to me. Kason is."

She scoffs, and I can almost see her eyes rolling in my head. "You're twenty-two, for God's sake. You're barely an adult. You don't know what's important to you."

"How quickly you seem to forget you were my age when you met Dad," I shoot back immediately.

"It was a different time, and *very* different circumstances."

Yeah, because you both were part of wealthy, upper-class society, and Kason isn't.

I somehow manage to stop that from falling off my tongue, choosing a different route instead. One straight and to the point, where there's no mistaking or misconstruing my meaning.

"I'm not gonna keep going round and round with you on this, Mom. You either accept him, or you lose me. That's the real ultimatum here. Because there is no doubt in my mind that he is what I want. More than the future I've got mapped out, more than your money…" Wetting my lips,

I let out a sardonic laugh. "There *is* no choice. It will always be Kason."

"Hayes Richard, I will not be threatened—"

"You can let me know what you decide at graduation next week," I say, cutting her off.

And with that, I end the conversation and the call all at once. Flipping my phone to silent, I shove it back into my pocket and lift my gaze to Kason's.

He swallows roughly, his throat bobbing with effort, and I'd give anything to know what he's thinking. To take a peek at what's beneath that head of soft, auburn hair and—

"Your middle name is Richard?"

My brows arch, not sure I heard him correctly. Because there's no way *that's* the piece of information that his brain decided to fixate on.

"Let me get this straight. I just, for all intents and purposes, told my mother to go kick rocks, and you're wanting to confirm my middle name?"

A tiny, wry grin pulls at his lips. "I think the rest of me is in shock you actually just did that."

Part of me can't believe it either, but despite that, I've never felt more free in my life. Even with all the unknowns looming on the horizon, there's one certainty: We'll tackle them together.

That is, if he'll have me.

"I can," I murmur, resting my hands on his thighs again. "Because I love you. And if you can take them on for me, I sure as fuck can do the same for you."

"Are you really sure about this?"

My response is as easy as breathing, falling free without a second thought about them being the truth. "There's not a doubt in my mind. Not when it comes to you."

Kason rolls his lips inward, and I wait, patiently and silently, for him to speak. For the feelings so clear and evident in his eyes to finally be spoken.

For us to finally know that we were wrong about this being the wrong time.

"Say something," I whisper, my fingers curling around his thighs. "Tell me to come with you to Nashville or tell me to go to hell, but please, tell me what you want. You can have whatever it is, baby. Just say the word and it's yours."

He shakes his head. "I already have everything I want, as long as you come with me."

It takes a second for me to process what he's said, to trust that I actually heard him right. But when I do, I'm in his lap damn near instantly, my thighs bracketing his hips, and finally pressing my mouth to his.

My chest tightens in the best way possible as it brushes his, losing myself in a kiss that decimates all others. His hand curls into my hair and my hand cups his jaw, and with every brush of our lips, it feels like I'm drowning in emotions. They drag me under, wave after wave slamming into me at once until I'm consumed by more love than I ever knew existed.

Maybe because, before him, it didn't.

Kason breaks away first, and it's almost like he's crawled inside my head to pluck out my thoughts when he smiles at me.

"I love you so fucking much, Hayes. I'm sorry I didn't tell you before. It felt too selfish to say it and leave. But, I do. I love you." His emerald eyes dark and pleading as they stare straight into my soul, his words barely more than a whisper. "And if I'm certain of anything, it's that I'm a better person for having been loved by you."

In all my life, I've never needed to hear those words from another human. But now that I know how they sound falling off his lips, there's no way I can go another day without hearing it.

"I love you too," I murmur, the words infused with emotion.

My heart crawls into my throat as I stare at him. At this amazing, talented, and hardworking man who continues to teach and inspire me just as much as I do him. Who has only ever wanted from me is my time. My attention. My love.

And if I have it my way, he'll never have to want those things again, because they'll already be his. *I* will be his.

Always.

Playing with the hair at the back of his neck, I murmur, "Do you wanna go home and celebrate, Mr. Football Star?"

Kason smiles before leaning in, pressing his lips to mine again in a long, slow kiss.

He breaks away far sooner than either of us would like and rests his forehead against mine, breathing in each other's air.

"Is that a no?" I ask, all breathless.

"No, it's not a no," he whispers softly, his fingers dancing over my lower back.

I frown, leaning back. "Then is it a yes?"

My favorite smile appears when he shakes his head.

"It's an…I think I could be convinced."

EPILOGUE

Hayes

Three Months Later — July

"Hayes?" Kason's disembodied voice calls. "Where are you? This place is a maze!"

I roll my eyes, because a three-bedroom condo in the heart of Nashville can only be so big, even if this is our first day actually in it.

"I'm in the master!" I call back, my gaze still locked out the floor-to-ceiling windows on one wall of our bedroom.

Kason's footfalls echo through the nearly-empty condo as he approaches, becoming louder and louder until they stop directly behind me.

"There you are," he murmurs, wrapping his arms around my waist. A kiss lands on my temple before he rests his chin on my shoulder. "Getting used to the view?"

"Eh, I've seen better."

Kason chuckles, nuzzling his nose against the side of my neck. "So have I, and all of them include you naked."

A smirk tugs at my lips, and I turn in his arms. "Getting pervy on me already? At least let us get a bed in here first."

"I don't know, I've seen plenty of flat surfaces around here. The island in the kitchen, the counter in the bathroom. That shower is just begging for us to use it." His eyes light up when he glances behind me. "Or you could pin me to the glass right here?"

All of the above sounds fantastic, but we've only got another ninety minutes until we need to return the moving truck.

"In good time, you nympho. We've got work to do."

"And yet I seem to be the one moving all the boxes."

"I was taking a break." To drive the point home, I slip free from his hold and head out of the master and down the hall. "And now I'm getting back to work."

Kason's right on my trail, grabbing my wrist and pulling me into him as I enter the kitchen.

"More like taking in the view," he muses, his tone light and teasing. "I just can't believe we live here."

Cocking my head, I ask, "In this condo or this city?"

His lips purse for a second before he shrugs. "I dunno. Both, I guess?"

I'll be the first to admit, the condo will take some getting used to…for him. Comparatively, it's a much smaller version of where Quinton grew up, but I'm well aware it's a far cry from the upbringing Kason had.

And as for the city part…

"How are you feeling about it? About being back here?"

He frowns for the briefest moment, but it's more of a puzzled kind rather than upset. "I thought I'd feel some type of way about it, but honestly? It feels like a fresh start. Even if this city carries a lot of shitty memories from over the years, now I get to experience it with you."

I smile, feeling the same way, only for the past to come sneaking in again when I remember one of the people responsible for all those shitty memories he has.

One who is very intent on speaking to their son as of late.

"I saw your dad called again."

"Yeah," he murmurs, the word coming out clipped. "I have nothing to say to him, though. There's no point. I got all the closure I needed the last time I was in that house."

He's said that many times, but regardless, his father seems hell bent on getting in touch with him. Ever since Kason was drafted back to Nashville, he's been reaching out a couple times a week.

The cynic in me thinks it's likely for money, but I can't lie and say there isn't part of me that hopes it would be for better reasons. Like rebuilding a relationship with his son, despite Kason's well-deserved rejection of the idea.

It's not my place to pry or push for him to mend fences with either of his parents, even if I want that for him. Everyone deals with their shit in their own way, and he respects me enough to give me that courtesy too.

The least I can do is return the favor.

As if reading my damn mind, like he seems to do a lot lately, he shoots me an inquisitive look. "Have you heard from your parents at all?"

Blowing out a breath, I mutter, "Not since graduation."

They showed up like nothing happened, even embraced Kason and congratulated him on both being drafted and his degree. To his credit, he was much more polite during the entire interaction than I would've been if the roles were reversed.

Hell, he was nicer than I was, and they were my fucking parents.

But the second Kason was pulled away by Noah so they could get a team graduation photo, I let the two of them have it. In front of everyone who was there, ending my outburst with something along the lines of, "*If this is what it means to be a Lancaster, then I no longer wish to be one.*"

After that, they handed me a graduation card, went on their way, and I haven't heard from them since.

I'd be lying if I said it doesn't sting a little, but there was only one way this could end, and it was with me and Kason together. So the way I'm choosing to view it is that I was the one to cut them off, not the other way around.

As the saying goes, that's what helps me sleep at night.

"Did you ever open that card from them?" he asks suddenly.

Pausing, I wrack my brain before ultimately shaking my head. "Nah, I'm pretty sure I never took it out of the glovebox when we left graduation."

Kason produces it from behind his back, offering it to me.

"Yeah, I know."

I take it from him, looking at the envelope with my name written on it in my mother's neat cursive. Questions swirl in my mind as I stare at it, then move my gaze back to my boyfriend.

"Why do you have it?"

"I got a text this morning, from your mother of all people. She mentioned it." A frown pulls at his lips before he mutters. "I'm not really sure how she got my number, to be honest."

I give him one of those *you don't wanna know* looks while shoving my finger under the envelope flap. "She might've married into the family, but she's a Lancaster through and through."

Tearing it open, I tug the card out and flip it open, shifting the check out of the way to read the note written inside.

Hayes—

Enclosed is the money we offered Kason. When he returned it ripped to shreds, your father and I were floored at him throwing away that kind of money, considering he came from none.

He saw more value in you than we did, and for that, we can never apologize to you enough. Nor can we expect his clemency for how unfairly he's been treated at our hand. With time, however, we hope to earn forgiveness from you both, along with a place in this new life you intend to create together.

Please consider this an olive branch, and use this money, along with the additional sum, to follow whatever path you choose.

—Mom and Dad

My eyes flick to the check, noting the dollar amount is…my entire inheritance.

What the fuck?

Looking to Kason with a frown, I ask, "What did her text say?"

Swiping over his screen, he pulls up a text thread and passes me his phone. I absently hand him the check and card in exchange, my eyes already fixated on the text thread.

Mrs. L: Kason, dear. Can you please check with Hayes about depositing his graduation gift? The ninety days are nearly up before it becomes void. Otherwise we can wire the money directly. Thank you.

What. The. Actual. Fuck.

I set his phone on the counter, more confused than anything when I look at Kason, who is still reading the card.

"Holy shit, that's a lot of zeros for a graduation gift," he mumbles, his eyes staring at the check in his hand. When they lift to meet mine, they're damn near bugging out of his skull.

"It's my entire inheritance."

Saying they were cutting me off if I chose to be with Kason must've been a bluff after all.

"Are you gonna use it?" he asks as he drops both the check and card to the counter, swapping them for his phone. "I mean, I won't judge you if you do. That's a lot of money."

I don't know what I want to do with it. It feels dirty and tainted now, like accepting it would be acting like all is forgiven when, in reality, it's anything but.

"What do you think?"

He arches a brow. "It's not my choice, babe. I will say, it's not like we need it. With my salary alone, you wouldn't have to work at all if you don't want to."

Snorting, I shake my head. "I'm definitely not cut out to be a househusband. I'd go stir-crazy, especially considering we don't have any plants or pets for me to take care of."

His gaze takes on an amused gleam as he steps into my space, pinning me to the counter with his hips.

"Trying to lock me down already, Hazey?" he teases.

"Hate to break it to you, baby, but you're stuck with me until one of us inevitably kicks the bucket at the ripe old age of ninety-eight."

One hand moves up to cup the back of my head, his eyes dancing playfully between mine. "It's a bit soon to know that, don't you think? I mean, we *just* moved in together, and you're the one who's always talking about taking things slow."

"Funny," I mutter dryly. "Too bad you signed that contract with the Nighthawks, because you're gonna miss your calling as a comedian."

"We'll circle back to that when I retire." His thumb brushes over my jaw in a painstakingly light touch, like he's holding a precious piece of china. "But when it comes to bringing any living things into this house besides us, that's your choice too. I just don't want you to be lonely when you're here by yourself."

The sentiment is meant to be sweet, loving, caring—

"Did you forget who you're talking to?" I ask, my brows crashing together. "I'm gonna be living it up when you're gone. Dancing around this place naked, ordering Thai every night, having a grand ole' time."

Amusement twitches on his lips. "And not missing me one fucking bit, huh?"

Sighing in concession, I murmur. "Okay, maybe I'll miss you just a little. And I'll be sure to show you how much every time you get back from an away trip."

He hums, all dirty thoughts and sinful grins, before stealing a soft kiss.

"If you take the money, you could just come on the road with me instead," he counters against my lips. "Then you don't have to miss me at all."

I'll admit, there's an appeal to the idea, but it wouldn't be sustainable. I need my alone time as much as he needs his space to grow with the team and become a big shot NFL superstar. And though I don't need to, I *want* to work.

My mind searches for ideas of what to do with it, other than just letting it sit in my bank account doing absolutely nothing. There's the most obvious solution, of course, which is investments. Planning for a future retirement, maybe a family, who knows. And yeah, a good portion will go to that too, but with that amount...

"Tell me what to do," I groan, letting my forehead fall to his chest.

He chuckles and presses a kiss to the side of my head while wrapping his arms around me in a hug. "I don't care what we do with it. If you wanna rip this one up and send it back to them for good measure like I did, I'm fine with that too. We don't need it."

That's not helpful at fucking all.

A long sigh slips out, and I roll my forehead against his chest with indecision.

"You could use the money to start your own company," Kason says, resting his chin on my shoulder. "I know your plans were to take over Lancaster Financial, so it's not exactly the same thing, but—"

"No, you're onto something," I say, cutting him off.

Stepping out of his embrace, I pull my phone from my pocket and tap into the email app before typing out a message. I don't make it more than a few lines, stating my intent and requesting a meeting at their earliest convenience, then add both my mother and father's business emails.

Before I can overthink it, or talk myself out of it, I hit send and let my phone clatter to the kitchen counter.

Kason's eyes flick between me and it, confusion written all over his handsome face.

"Wanna tell me what just happened?"

"I sent an email to my parents," I breathe.

His eyes widen almost comically, and he takes a step toward me. "What'd you say?"

"That I've received their olive branch, for one. And that I want to branch off from LFC. Make this a secondary location here in Nashville. One run by me." I shift my attention, gaze colliding with his. "Do you think that's stupid?"

Kason's brows furrow, and he shakes his head. "I don't know a damn thing about investing or anything like that, so it's hard for me to say. But your name carries weight in that world, babe, and if your gut is telling you to do it, then I'm all for it. As long as you're happy."

Besides having Kason to come home to every night—at least when the team is in town—I can't think of much else that would.

"I think it's worth a shot," I tell him honestly. "And who knows, it might be a moot point if my parents say no."

"Then you just start your own firm. Build it from the ground up," he counters. His brow hikes up and a little smirk forms. "In case you've forgotten, we happen to know someone else whose name holds a lot of power in Music City."

I frown, not entirely following his line of thinking. But then the lightbulb goes off, and my eyes widen.

"Phoenix's dad is a label head," I whisper, wondering how I didn't see it sooner. "He's got contacts for some of the biggest names in music."

He nods, smiling. "I'm sure it wouldn't happen overnight. You'd likely have to build a reputation for yourself, but once you're more established, I'm sure you could get client referrals from him. Even if they aren't from his label."

It's brilliant. And even if my parents do somehow agree to this slightly insane idea, it would still be a good idea to branch into music. Most of the clients who employ LFC are old money families or the up-and-comers in the tech industry.

Music—and entertainment in general—is an entirely untapped market for us.

Ideas are already running rampant in my head when my phone buzzes on the counter, dragging me from my daydreams. Quickly grabbing it, I check the screen to find a new email notification.

My stomach clenches as I open it, finding a meeting invite waiting in my inbox.

"What is—"

"She wants to hear what I have to say," I whisper, more shocked than anything as I stare at the screen. "They want to set a meeting for next week."

A mixture of relief and excitement courses through me, and I'm already making a mental checklist of the things I'll need to do, starting with depositing my inheritance and working up a business plan to bring them.

I can't help the grin spreading over my face as my attention moves to Kason…only to find his lips pressed in a line while he frowns at me.

Oh, shit.

"What's that look for?" I ask slowly.

Worry floods me that maybe I've jumped the gun on this. That it's actually a terrible idea and will only end up screwing with this relationship we fought so hard to see through.

"Hayes, I love you. You know that," he starts, his tone low and gentle. "But if we're gonna be living together until the ripe old age of ninety-eight, I'm really gonna need you to stop interrupting me when I talk. Because you do it constantly."

Relief spreads through my body, and I start laughing, loud and free and with more happiness than I could've ever imagined.

"You know I love you too," I tell him, a playful lilt in my tone. "But I told you the day you asked for a fair catch, that was my hard limit. It's not my fault you weren't listening."

THE END

Acknowledgments

This book is entirely different from anything I've written to date, and it's both exciting and nerve wracking. Many of you readers know, there are always pieces of me in every character I write, but this one felt a little more personal than most.

While my own demisexuality is a new discovery to me, I knew early on that Hayes would also be on the ace spectrum. But as demisexuality is so broad in itself, with no singular lived experience to define it, I was constantly stressed that I would be writing it "wrong." After all, my knowledge and my own lived experience with it was so limited in the beginning, as I was still figuring things out for myself. But as writing this book went on, it became a way for me to claim this part of myself as well; learn things about where *I* fall as a demi person. I can only hope that Hayes and I did the beauty and diversity within the asexual spectrum justice while explaining it within these pages.

With that said, the first people I have to thank are Taylor and Liz, for their sensitivity reading on this novel. I appreciate you both making sure Hayes' demi experience is both realistic and relatable, even if it doesn't directly align with your own.

To Becca, for getting my ass in gear to finish this book on time. Your encouragement not only makes me more efficient, but your friendship keeps my brain grounded in the story and not in my self-doubt.

To Emily, I loved nothing more than to surprise the masses with this *stunning* yellow cover.

To my alphas/betas, Emily, Holly, Jackie, Montana, and Abby, and anyone else I might be missing: Thank you for making sure this book wasn't a freaking mess like I thought it was. And let's be real, it was a mess for a while: just like sweet baby Kason.

To my editor, Amanda. I don't have the words to describe how grateful I am for you turning this around so quickly. Things got chaotic there at the end, but you're a rockstar and I'm forever in your debt.

To my Enclave and my Legacies. Thank you for supporting me, promoting me, and being my core readership—some of you since my very first book.

And to anyone I may have missed (because there's always someone), and to my readers. Thank you for continuing to come back for more, and for trusting me on whatever journey I may take you on.

I love you all to the ends of the Earth.

—CE Ricci

About the Author

CE Ricci is an international best-selling author who enjoys plenty of things in her free time, but writing about herself in the third person isn't one of them. She believes home isn't a place, but a feeling, and it's one she gets when she's chilling lakeside or on hiking trails with her dogs, camera in hand. She's addicted to all things photography, plants, peaks, puppies, and paperbacks, though not necessarily in that order. Music is her love language, and traveling the country (and world) is the way she chooses to find most of her inspiration for whatever epic love story she will tell next!

CE Ricci is represented by Two Daisy Media.
For all subsidiary rights, please contact:
Savannah Greenwell — info@twodaisy.com

Made in the USA
Middletown, DE
14 May 2025

75489152R00247